To Ghita Reuben Olit

*Whenever I came back from school ("Don't slam the door!"),
she was home.*

*Whenever I asked her how to spell a word ("anthropomor-
phothiest"), she knew.*

*Whenever I wanted her opinion on a speech from a book or a
play ("The quality of mercy is not strained"), she was ready
with a thought.*

*Whenever I needed her, she was always there.
And she still is.*

*Imparting knowledge. Dispensing wisdom.
And telling me not to slam the door.*

Mom, this book is for you.

ACKNOWLEDGMENTS

Many parts of this books were inspired by the artwork in the possession of the Delaware Art Museum. Dr. Mary F. Holahan, registrar, and Harriet B. Memeger, librarian, were incredibly generous in making works of art and archives accessible to me, and in making me feel welcome at their truly wonderful museum.

I was given invaluable insights into how museums work, how paintings are created, and about the chemistry of art conservation by Dr. Selma Holo, director of the Museum Studies Program at the University of Southern California, Ed McCormack, artist, and Richard Wolbers of the Winterthur Conservation Labs.

I am grateful to Ed Fanuzzi for teaching me about surveillance systems; Norma Varga for picking the music; Thomas Chastain for telling me stories about his hometown in Georgia; and Jacqueline Kyle Kall for pointing me in the right direction on City Island.

And, as always, I send a bouquet of thanks to my husband, Charlie King, who is still teaching everything I know about how to investigate a fire.

SPENT MATCHES

1

He was the only person he'd ever known who actually wrote with a quill pen. The feather was about eighteen inches long, and red. The color red he'd heard described as cerise. Or perhaps vermilion. It was a shade of red that he was sure had once glistened (softly) on the lips (slightly parted) of women (damsels) who lived in King Arthur's court. The same red as was on Sir Galahad's shield in the painting by Watts in *The Knights of the Round Table* book that his father had given him for Christmas all those years ago. Or maybe he'd just imagined that particular shade of red.

But the quill itself was real. Some meticulous work with a soldering iron on a calligraphy pen he'd recruited from his last job at Peter Fleming Paints, and . . . voilà! He dipped the nib of the quill into an antique ink bottle—well, maybe it wasn't really an antique. But it contained black ink. Ink so black that it perfectly captured the evil glint at the centers of treacherous Sir Mordred's eyes.

He hunched over the white vellum on his desk and touched the pen to the paper.

"Cam. Cam, darling! Can you hear me? Drat you, Cam. Are you even in the house?"

He lifted the quill pen away from the paper and blew on the nib. Then, seeing the feather flutter, he blew again, all up and down the length of the quill, playing the ruffles of the feather with his breath as if it were a harmonica.

"Cam, I know you're there, but someone, and who that someone *is* shall remain nameless, but *someone* left the window ajar in the kitchen, and I distinctly feel a . . . "

He put a small cork stopper in the ink bottle, laid the pen neatly alongside the blank sheet of drawing paper, and reached for an old leather-bound volume of Tennyson's *The Idylls of the King*. The cover was gold embossed, and the edges of the paper were frayed.

Aloud, he read:

A lusty youth, but poor, who often saw
The splendor sparkling from aloft, and thought,
"An' I could climb and lay my hand upon it,
Then were I wealthier than a leash of Kings."

He looked out the window of the attic room he had made into what he called his Ivory Tower. There was a narrow bed—a cot, really, along the north wall. He'd had a solid, sturdy, real bed with a box spring and a mattress downstairs in what she still called "his room." But when he told her that he wanted to move it upstairs to his Ivory Tower, she said, "Ha! See how long you persist with this Ivory Tower folderol while you're sleeping on that old cot from the garage!" Then, as though it were an epithet for all of the most contemptible concepts encompassed by the English language, she ended her tirade by spitting out the word "Dreamer!"

That had been ten years before, when he was thirteen years old. He still slept on that same relentlessly narrow and unyielding cot. He was still up in his Ivory Tower.

And he was still dreaming.

The voice from below reached out at him again.

"Cam. Are you staying home today? What *are* your plans today, Cam? And what did the people at the employment agency say when you rang them up? I can't seem to find today's paper, and you know I simply can't function without my television guide. Cam, where . . ."

His eyes reverted to the open book on his desk. In a strong, deep voice, rehearsed in front of his medicine cabinet mirror, he recited:

But ever when he reach'd a hand to climb,
One that had loved him from his childhood caught
And stay'd him, "Climb not lest thou break thy neck,
I charge thee by my love."

A fog horn blew loud, low and froggy from a ship making its way into Long Island Sound. He looked out the window over his desk. Thick, bright haze covered everything beyond the cyclone fence that separated his yard from the house next door. Of the road, the three houses and the larger and higher cyclone fence that closed off the beach from the dead-end street on which he lived, he saw nothing. Morning fog on City Island. In another half hour, the sun would burn it away.

"Enie meanie minee mo, catch a Camden by his . . . Wonder of wonders, Cam, darling. I found the newspaper I was looking for. It was under the tan jacket I wore when I played Stella in *Streetcar*. And what was that old thing doing out, you may ask? Ha ha. And well you *might* ask! But there's no arts section in this newspaper, my fine-feathered friend. So, you shall have to look elsewhere to find out about your precious exhibit in that precious museum where you're wasting away your . . . "

The foghorn sounded a second time. A gravelly moan that seemed to come from deep inside the chest of a ship too big, too old, and too lumbering to make its way over yet another wave.

He lowered his head again to read from the book of poetry; this time his voice was less confident, less theatrical and low, as though oppressed by the weight of too many words:

. . . and so the boy,
Sweet mother, neither clomb nor brake his neck,
But brake his very heart in pining for it,
And past away.

The foghorn howled a third sorrowful time. He closed the book of poetry. From downstairs—she was probably on the sofa in front of the television set, she always was—again came that all-pervading throaty voice, like a dank and crawly wind that insinuates itself into the tight places between your collar and your shirt sleeves and then strikes you right at your heart.

"Cam . . . Cam . . . "

No answer.

"You've been talking to yourself again, Cam. Haven't you? Spiteful boy. Because I know you really *are* upstairs."

No movement. No whisper of a sound.

"You're cross with me now, Cam. Aren't you? And you know I can't bear it when you're cross with me."

Continued silence.

"Cam. Cam, darling." In that carefully cultivated voice, that brittlely enunciating voice that broke words into syllables and syllables into affectations with a slight but distinct British accent.

"It's because of the arts section, isn't it, Cam? That's why you're so angry . . . because you think I stole your precious paper. But I didn't steal it, Cam. I was just kidding. And here's the article you wanted. Right here, it says that an exhibition of Pre-Raphaelite paintings will be opening this month at the Zigfield Art Museum. Did you hear? Is it all right now, Cam? Son . . . are we still friends?"

He took one last look out the window. His room faced the western shore of City Island, a tiny body of land off the lower tip of the Bronx, surrounded completely by the waters of Long Island Sound. His mother had a house on City Island, and he lived in that house, cut off from the rest of New York City, in a room that he called his Ivory Tower.

He looked down at his watch. Five minutes after seven. If he hurried, he could still make the express bus for the thirteen-mile trip to midtown Manhattan.

He pushed his chair away from his desk, stood up, and said in a voice too soft for her to hear, "Coming, Mater."

2

When a writer for the financial section of the *New York Times* dubbed Wegman Zigfield "Fast-food King," the forty-eight-year-old business-man was already a multimillionaire. Twelve years later, at age sixty, he made two simultaneous purchases. The first catapulted the owners of a vast collection of nineteenth-century British art into a fortune, and the second angered one landmark preservation committee, and made one religious organization very happy indeed.

The first purchase saved the Lord Harrington-Beckwith estate over three-hundred thousand dollars in sales commissions, because instead of waiting for the estate's art collection to come up for auction, Zigfield bought it in its entirety directly from the heirs.

The purchase of the Harrington-Beckwith Collection (for an amount said to exceed the total of all the uncollected traffic fines, plus interest, in both America and England from 1915 to the present) precipitated the second purchase, which is the one that got the landmark people "mad" and the Catholic church glad.

During the previous two years, attendance at the house of worship known to some as Our Lady of Perpetual Frowns had been steadily declining, and it was an open secret that the only thing preventing the church from putting a FOR SALE sign in the rectory window was the fear that once they had done so, the landmark people would begin costly litigation to prevent the sale to any buyer who might propose reconstruction, demolition, or renovation of the property.

Having heard of the church's dilemma from his wife's hairdresser (whose brother-in-law's father had been the janitor at Our Lady for over fifteen years), Mr. Zigfield immediately arranged a luncheon with Cardinal Connoley. Lunch evolved into a discreet tour of Our Lady's church and rectory, a deposit check being drawn on the spot against the Wegman Zigfield Enterprises account, and a complete sales transaction, including transfer of deed from the Catholic Archdiocese to the newly incorporated Zigfield Art Museum, all within a period of thirty-five days.

By the time the landmark preservation people heard about the sale, Mr. Zigfield had already hired architects and rewired, restored, replaced, and replastered over fifty percent of the space that would house what, over the next twenty years, would come to be called (by admirers) the Wegman Zigfield Collection, and (by detractors), Zigfield's Folly.

Wegman Zigfield's wife's hairdresser's brother-in-law's father, Luis Cabrerra, had been with the church/museum for thirty-five years. After Luis's triple bypass operation, Mr. Zigfield promoted him to a position that required him to perambulate from gallery to gallery at his own discretion, making note of all that was or was not amiss, and reporting any relevant observations to Mr. Zigfield personally.

Although officially untitled, Luis Cabrerra called himself the museum's "security director." As such, it was his unofficial function to open the Zigfield Art Museum in the morning before the staff started to drift in, and reset the fire and intrusion alarms in the small security room to the left of the lobby.

On the Friday morning of the fire, Luis Cabrerra, wearing a uniform resembling that of a musical comedy Ruritanian army general, arrived at the museum at 7:00 a.m. The smoke alarm in the Parlor Gallery was activated exactly two minutes and thirty-five seconds later.

Luis's instinctive response to the alarm was to run up the wide rectory staircase, forgetting about his heart condition, and fumbling with his keys as he ran. He shielded his nose with one hand, unlocked and flung open the gallery's huge oak doors with the other, and was stunned to find that there was *nothing* on fire inside.

Absolutely nothing.

But all of Sarkin Zahedi's paintings had completely disappeared.

The Sarkin Zahedi exhibition, which had been hung the previous Friday in the Parlor Gallery, was reduced to empty rectangles suspended on sooty walls over neat piles of debris that had accumulated on the floor. Dirty black streaks extended from the bottom of each frame, marking the metamorphosis of the painting from wall . . . to flame . . . to ash . . . to floor.

Luis returned to the security room and called the fire department as a backup to the transmission of the museum's silent, automatic alarm. And he made a mental note to ask someone why smoke or toxic fumes had not seeped under the doors of the Parlor Gallery and set off additional alarms in the Hall of Marquetry or the library, the first being located directly across the corridor from the Parlor Gallery, and the second immediately next door.

He consulted the museum log sheet to see if anyone had entered or left the building prior to the fire, and then he called Wegman Zigfield at his estate in Riverdale.

Despite his age, the catastrophic news, and the rude awakening, Wegman Zigfield was instantly in command.

"Do you know who Max Bramble is?" he barked at Luis Cabrerra.

"Yes, Mr. Zigfield. He is the museum's attorney. I have his office number, and his home telephone number."

"Good. Call him at home. Tell him what happened. Then tell him to go directly to the museum. I'll get there myself in a little over an hour."

3

Webster's Dictionary defines *fire* as "the phenomenon of combustion manifested in light, flame, and heat." Earlier in the dictionary, *combustion* is described as "a chemical process (as in oxidation) accompanied by the evolution of light and heat." Both definitions are technically accurate, but tepid, dry, boring. Neither conveys the awesome, compelling, terrifying, hypnotizing, and devastating *magic* of fire.

> *Behold, the bush burned with fire,*
> *and the bush was not consumed.*

Through fire and *in* flames, the Bible says that God first spoke to Moses, and gave him and all mankind the Ten Commandments, thereby proving that, although "poems are made by fools like me," only God can set fire to but *not* burn a tree.

The rest of us have no such pyrotechnic capabilities.

When we set fire to a piece of paper, a leaf, a cellophane wrapper, a cardboard box, a diary, a love letter, a log, it burns, it carbonizes, it turns black, it is chemically altered, and its essence—that which it once was— permanently disappears.

When *our* bushes burn, all we have left after the fire is a memory, ashes, and a stump.

In the real world, if not in the world of mythology, three criteria are necessary if we want to warm our hands or hearts over open flames.

We must have a combustible fuel. Such as a bush.

We must have an oxidant. Such as the air surrounding the bush on Mount Sinai.

We must have an ignition source.

For Moses and *his* burning bush, the ignition source was God. For us, it would have to be a carelessly discarded cigarette, a butane lighter, a bolt of lightning in an electrical storm, static electricity . . . a match.

We must have all three components for a fire to occur. And we must have all three of them present at once.

A dry bush in an airtight box will not burn, because there is no oxygen.

If we cut a window in the box to let the air in, but we take out the bush, no matter how many lighted matches we throw through the window, we still wouldn't get a fire, because without our bush, we don't have fuel. Nor, if we have our bush in place, along with copious amounts of oxygen, would we get a fire, unless we also had a lighted match or a bolt of lightning.

Fuel.

Oxygen.

Ignition source.

Without all three, we cannot have fire. With all three, we cannot help *but* have fire.

4

The first thing people noticed about Wegman Zigfield was his height. He was only five feet, three inches tall. The second was his style. He had been on one or another Best Dressed List for the past forty years. In his column on attire for *Today's Man*, Robin Cowling described Wegman Zigfield as "a perfectly appointed room, for there is nothing human about the way he looks. Have cottons been invented yet that fold without retaining a crease? Have shoes been manufactured yet that keep an eternal shine? Has there yet been a collar that rejects a perspiration ring? Or a silk tie to which soup or marinara sauce will not cling? No. No. A thousand times no. Except for Wegman Zigfield, on whom no dust settles, no lint accumulates, no mud spatters, and where wrinkles fear to tread. Beneath his perfect upholstery, a heart no doubt beats. A brilliant mind certainly stirs. A soul undoubtedly strives and achieves. But that which clothes the body is as serenely untouched by the vicissitudes of fate as the masterpieces on display behind the roped-off areas in his museum."

At eighty years of age, Wegman Zigfield moved like a boxer. Graceful. Fast. Deliberate. First here. Then there. Arm bent at elbow. Finger jutting at smudge on wall. Arm down. Turn. Bend. Pick up pamphlet. Fold. Jam in pocket. Jab up button at elevator. Exit elevator. Rapid one, two, three of feet. Hand on doorknob. Open door. Shut door. Raise receiver on telephone. Bark into mouthpiece. First here. Then there. Now you see him. Now you don't.

"Hello, Joy. Is Max Bramble here yet?"

"Yes, sir. He arrived at nine o'clock. First he asked to speak to Luis. Then he went up to the Parlor Gallery. He's been there for over an hour."

"I'm going up."

"He isn't alone, sir. A gentleman came with him."

"Who?"

"A Mr. Wylie Nolan. He's a fire investigator."

"Appropriate."

"And, Mr. Zigfield, there's quite a crowd here that want to get into the Parlor Gallery."

"Such as . . . "

"Someone from our insurance company. Someone claiming to represent Mr. Zahedi, who says that he's also an insurance investigator. Mr. Zahedi is here himself, and he's behaving rather emotionally, since all of his paintings were burned up. Fromer is here, of course, but I'm afraid your son is making something of a commotion. And Mr. Zahedi is . . . "

"An idiot."

"I beg your pardon?"

"Never mind. Where's Jiri?"

"Mr. Hozda is in his office. He said that he prefers not to return to the scene of the tea cup until the tempest has passed."

"Ha, ha! If Jiri isn't there, then who's keeping the wolves at bay?"

"Mr. Bramble is, sir. He and Mr. Nolan have locked themselves inside the Parlor Gallery, and they won't let anyone else in. There are rumors that Mr. Nolan menaced several people with a weapon. But I believe your son started that rumor. Only Mr. Bramble has prevented Fromer from calling the police. Actually, it's getting pretty loud out there, Mr. Zigfield."

"I bet it is."

"And there's one other thing, sir."

"What?"

"Georgiana Weeks is here. She's the guest curator for the Pre-Raphaelite exhibition. I know that you were expecting her, but under the circumstances . . . "

"Never mind circumstances. Let her in. Get her coffee. Fuss over her. Get Jiri out of his damn office, and tell him that I asked him nicely to take care of her until I've assessed the damage to the museum. Have him bring her to lunch or take her to Paris or marry the damn woman. Just don't bother me with her until I beat off the jackals."

"All right, Mr. Zigfield."

"And Joy?"

"Yes, sir?"

"You're a good girl."

"Thank you, Mr. Zigfield."

"But you know what you can do for me?"

"What, Mr. Zigfield?"

And his voice boomed. "Get some spine!"

5

The room in the museum where the fire had started and ended was known as the Parlor Gallery, because it had served as a parlor for resident monsignors throughout the long heyday of Our Lady of Perpetual Frowns. On the north wall of the gallery, ornately carved sliding wood doors led to a library. Each door was three and a half feet wide by eight feet high. The Parlor Gallery itself measured twenty-two feet by eighteen feet. It had a twelve-foot ceiling, and skylights that ran along each of the room's four walls. There were three stained glass casement windows beneath the skylights on the Fifth Avenue side.

Because of these windows and the doors leading to the library, as well as the massive wood entrance doors from the corridor, there was less space for hanging pictures than might have been supposed.

The main sources of illumination were the skylights and the artificial ceiling lights. The diffuse glow coming from the stained glass windows contributed more to the room's aesthetic than to its illumination.

Sarkin Zahedi—A Retrospective, was the name of the Parlor Gallery's current exhibition. Despite the ambitious implications of the title, the show consisted of only five paintings, instead of the ten paintings the artist had originally wanted installed. Each painting was six feet wide by five feet high and displayed the artistic trademarks characteristic of Sarkin Zahedi's work of twenty years before: thick gobs of oil paint; colors limited to browns, grays, and blacks; and clumps of fabric, straw, cotton balls, cellophane, and tissue paper attached randomly to the canvas like prehistoric insects with their feet stuck in the muck.

Wylie Nolan fingered flakes of char beneath a picture frame labeled *Process*. There were similar black clusters under the other four frames in the gallery. Each frame bore a different bronze plaque. The titles of the pictures were: *Germination, Creation, Destruction*, and *Chaos*. Wylie rubbed his thumb and forefinger over the powdery residue of *Process*.

Wylie Nolan was long and lean, and there was a lackadaisical gauntness about his face that suggested shoot-outs, showdowns, and gunfights at high noon. He had big ears that stuck out from his head, and dark, marble blue eyes that had the sharp, hard, almost beautiful glint of a man who's tried to stare down the sun a few too many times without blinking. As he hunkered down in his worn jeans and battered jacket, he looked more like a trapper or hunter puzzling out the clues at a campsite, than a New York City–based private arson investigator studying the remnants of a fire.

As soon as Max Bramble had hung up on Luis Cabrarra that morning, he'd called the museum's insurer to get Wylie Nolan assigned to the case.

Wylie stood up and slapped his hands against each other like dusty chalk erasers.

"What time is it, Max? I forgot my watch."

Max was leaning toward a frame labeled *Creation*.

"This is going to end up in litigation, Wylie. You know it is. I know it is. It always does." He made a notation on his legal pad. "The artist's insurance company is going to reimburse him for the loss of his paintings. Then they'll turn around and subrogate against the museum. They'll say that *somehow*, unspecified as to how, we were responsible for the fire. Which we probably were. Names, dates, titles. I need them all in case I have to prepare a defense."

Max made one last jab with his pencil and stared at a bronze plaque.

"Sarkin Zahedi? What kind of a name is that?"

"What time is it, Max?" Wylie asked again.

"Ten-thirty. Why?"

"The marshal who did this fire will be back in his office at eleven-thirty, and I want to touch base with him."

"Why?"

"To ask him how he called it."

"How do *you* call it?"

Wylie Nolan shook his head. "It's one of the weirdest damn fires I've ever seen. If I didn't know any better, I'd say the room committed suicide."

"How so?"

"Take a look around," Wylie instructed. "The area is practically spotless. The windows are clean. There's no apparent smoke damage. No soot. No forced entry. No footprints. No burn patterns. No residue of flammable liquid. No unexplained smells. And no connecting fires from one painting to the other. All we've got left to tell us the story of what happened here are barely burned, empty frames and a little bit of char."

Max Bramble looked around himself. He saw a large room with highly polished parquet floors. Other than the fire damage to and directly under the five large frames on the walls, the room was immaculate.

"I don't get it." Max said. "Who or what could have done this?"

"I have a theory," Wylie said.

"What?"

"A ghost did it."

"A ghost?"

"Yes. One with an incendiary device. A ghost who held the flame from this device against the canvas of the first painting and waited for it to ignite. Then he went on to the next canvas, and the next and the next, until they were all gone. A ghost who then put his incendiary device back in the invisible pocket of his invisible suit, and dematerialized through the walls." Wylie Nolan shook his head. "Weird fire."

He walked to a pew in the center of the gallery where he had put his camera bag and the bruised black leather suitcase he called his "arson kit." The pew faced the stained glass windows overlooking Fifth Avenue, instead of the paintings, which may or may not have reflected the museum director's opinion of the artist's work.

Inside the arson kit was Wylie's fire investigation equipment: a dry paint brush for sweeping away ash; a large kitchen spoon to scoop up ash; a folding shovel for digging through debris; a dentist's mirror for looking into inaccessible corners; a tape measure; a magnet; a flashlight; a small crowbar; a hammer; a screwdriver; a tin of bandages; a roll of paper towels; and a folded black tobacco pouch.

Wylie flipped open the pouch and started to fill the bowl of his pipe.

"These are the facts as we know them," he said as he dug a disposable lighter out of his shirt pocket and held the flame over the tobacco. He sucked in one, two, three times. "Take notes."

Max took out his pencil.

"At seven o'clock this morning, whoever-he-is arrived. What's his name?"

"Luis Cabrerra."

"Luis unlocks the door and looks around. Everything's fine. He goes to the security room beside the entrance doors to reset the fire and intrusion alarms. While he's doing that, at . . . When, Max?"

Max flipped through his notes and read, "Seven-oh-two and thirty-five seconds."

"At two minutes after seven, a smoke alarm is activated. Luis checks the alarm control panel to see where it's coming from. The panel light is on for the Parlor Gallery. Luis also makes a mental note that the lights on his security panel indicate the heat detector in the Parlor Gallery has *not* been activated. Are we in agreement so far on the facts?"

"So far."

"Luis crosses the hall."

"Narthex."

"Gesundheit."

"No, Wylie. 'Narthex' is what they call the vestibule leading into the sanctuary of these old churches. This used to be a Catholic church."

"How do you know that?"

"Before Mr. Zigfield hired the architects and interior designers, or even bought this place, he consulted me on liability. That's when I learned all these things that I didn't want to know about churches."

"Narthex."

"Right."

"Hall."

"Right."

"Okay. So, Luis goes past the entrance doors, this time to the right side of the hallway-slash-vestibule-slash-narthex, where there's a door leading to the old rectory, which is now a museum. He crosses the rectory hallway to the staircase leading to the galleries, etcetera, on the upper floors. He runs up the stairs to the fourth floor, runs down the hall-slash-vestibule-slash-narthex . . . "

"No, Wylie. Only the corridor leading into the sanctuary is called a narthex."

"Gesundheit."

"All of the other halls are just halls."

"He unlocks the doors to the Parlor Gallery . . . "

"Go on."

"That's the point."

"What's the point?"

"I can't go on."

"What do you mean?"

"I mean that if the ghost—the one with the unspecified ignition device—didn't do it, then I don't know who or what did start this fire."

Max smiled recklessly. "You're joking, Wylie. Right?"

Wylie's eyes glinted. He grinned back. "I'm joking, Max. Wrong."

"But I always tell my clients that you're a genius. That if you'd been alive at the time of the Chicago fire, you would have arrested Mrs. O'Leary's cow. That you can figure out where any fire started."

"I don't have a problem with *where* these fires, plural, started, Max. I just haven't figured out yet *why* they started. Or *how*."

"But . . . but . . . at least you can tell me if it's arson or not. I mean, that much should be obvious. It is arson, Wylie, isn't it?"

"I don't know. Is it?"

"You don't know? Jeez, if *you* don't know how the fire started, what am *I* going to tell Mr. Zigfield? Damn, I feel lousy."

"I'm the genius," Wylie said contemptuously. "How do you think *I* feel? Ghosts!" He puffed one last time on his pipe and then tucked it into his shirt pocket.

27

Max stared at the pocket.

"Wylie, you're going to set your shirt on fire."

Wylie looked at the small spiral of smoke rising out of his shirt pocket, removed his pipe and laid it on the lid of his suitcase. He reached for his camera bag.

Wylie raised his camera, aimed at the stained glass windows, and took a picture. On the north side of the gallery, the large doors leading from the adjacent library soundlessly slid open. The camera flashed once; Wylie swiveled to photograph the sliding doors. Through the glare of the camera's flash, a dapper, perfectly groomed, small old man emerged.

Wylie lowered his lens.

"Well, hello," he said.

The imperious old man's piercing light blue eyes looked at Wylie with the meticulous precision of a document copier.

He neither smiled nor moved.

Wylie said, "Am I missing something here? Should I be kissing your ring?"

Max whispered, "For God's sake, Wylie. That's Mr. Zigfield. *The* Mister Zigfield. Try and behave."

Wylie winked at the attorney, strode across the room, and thrust out a strong, hard hand.

"Wylie Nolan. I'm your insurance company's fire expert."

"Wegman Zigfield. I own the museum." He also extended his hand. "And I'm not wearing a ring."

Wylie laughed.

Wegman Zigfield's light blue eyes glinted for a second.

"Gentlemen," he said. "Can we get down to business?"

Wylie took a fresh roll of film out of his camera bag and popped it into his shirt pocket. One side of his denim jacket fell open, exposing a scarred leather holster clipped onto his belt.

Wegman Zigfield pointed an accusatory forefinger. "Exactly what is that?"

Wylie looked down. "This? This is my cannon."

Max shook his head and murmured, "Wylie . . . Wylie . . . "

Wegman Zigfield snapped, "I've been advised by my secretary that you menaced several insurance people, as well as my son, with that instrument of destruction."

"Who's your son?"

"Fromer Zigfield."

"Scruffy, unshaved, wire-rim glasses, watery eyes, and a weak jaw?"

"An apt, though uncharitable, description."

"Well, no, Wegman. I don't particularly remember menacing him with my famous six-minute draw. Has anyone else out there made a similar accusation?"

"The artist in whose shambles of an exhibition we are now standing. Sarkin Zahedi."

"Did I shoot him . . . according to your sources?"

"No."

"Who else out there is whining about me?"

"Assorted claims representatives, lawyers, and insurance adjusters."

Wylie nodded as he calmly cracked open the cylinder of his revolver and ejected five bullets onto his palm.

"This is a Smith and Wesson thirty-eight. It's a revolver. It's called that because of this little cylinder here that goes around. I took this revolver with me when I left the fire department. They didn't want me to, but there wasn't much they could do to stop me. I don't know if Max here told you, but I learned how to do what I do when I was a fire marshal for the City of New York. A Smith and Wesson thirty-eight holds five rounds of ammunition. Now, let me see. One, two, three, four, five. Nope. It doesn't look like I shot anybody this morning."

Wylie reloaded his gun, snapped the cylinder shut, reholstered it, and said, "Sorry, Wegman." Then he spun around and took a photograph of the door that led from the Parlor Gallery to the corridor . . . the door through which he and Max Bramble had entered, and behind which could still be heard the angry drone of the artist, insurance investigator, and other interested parties who were gathered outside. Wylie ignored them as he led Max and Wegman Zigfield across the room.

"Come over here. The both of you. I want to show you something." Wylie indicated the doors through which Mr. Zigfield had just entered.

"These lead to the library. Right, Wegman?"

The museum director nodded.

"Forgetting the windows for a minute then, there are two ways of getting into this gallery. One, this one, is from the library. And the second is from the hall."

"That is correct."

"Other than you, Wegman, who could get in through these library doors?"

"Nobody. The library doors are always locked."

"Who has the key?"

"I do."

"Who else?"

"Luis has one key, and there's a master key in the security room."

"Are any of those keys missing?"

"No. I had Luis check on my way in."

"How about the keys to this gallery. Who has them?"

"I do. So does Luis. There's the master key, of course. And . . . "

"And what?"

"I'm not sure, but Jiri may also have a set of keys to all of galleries."

"Who is Jiri?"

"Jiri Hodza. He's my curator and the associate director of my museum."

"I'd like to speak to him later."

"I'll arrange it."

"I need someone to write what each room or gallery is used for on a blueprint or schematic of this wing of the museum. Storage. Office. Bathroom. Permanent collection. Library. That sort of thing."

"Done. What else?"

"I want the installation manual on your fire and intrusion alarm system, and a list of what doors are keyed, and how. I want to know what records are kept of entry and exit to secured areas of the museum, where they're kept, and I want access to them."

"Luis will give all of that to you."

"I need a list of your employees, their job descriptions, when they work, their home phone numbers and addresses. And it wouldn't hurt if you sent them a memo asking them to cooperate with me."

"Done."

"I want a tour of the museum. Everything from loading dock to storage facilities to galleries. I want to see how the artwork is received, what security precautions are taken, and so on."

"I'll ask Jiri Hozda to walk you through."

"I want the picture frames in this room sent to my office. But leave them exactly where they are until Ali Baba's forty thieves have finished their investigations. It shouldn't take them more than an hour, at most. And before we remove the frames, I want those jokers to state explicitly that there's nothing else they want to remove from the fire scene, and that they are giving you their permission to dispose of the debris. Then and only then, send me the frames."

"Why all the rigamarole?" Max asked.

"Because if any of those fire divas think *I* want the frames, then *they'll* want the frames, and whenever they get their hands on the evidence, nine times out of ten, it disappears. We don't want that to happen here; that's why I want the frames delivered to my office. Today."

"Luis will order a van. You'll have them this afternoon."

"Good. And one last thing, Wegman. I want you to give me whatever paperwork you have on this exhibit. Newsclips, catalogues, contracts. And photographs of what the paintings looked like before the fires. Can you do that?"

"I can."

"How about biographical information on the artist?"

"In my son's files. Sarkin Zahedi is Fromer's protégé, God help us. I'll have Joy, my secretary, put together a package of everything you've requested."

"Thank you, Wegman."

"One more thing, Mr. Nolan. As an art collector and the director of this museum, I feel that I may have some insights into the mind of the art criminal of which you may not be possessed."

"You have a theory, Wegman?"

"Not precisely a theory, Mr. Nolan. Merely an observation. When I stepped into this room less than fifteen minutes ago, and observed the pictureless frames on the walls, my instinctive response was to assume that someone had slit out the paintings with a razor for the purpose of stealing them. I realize that there is ash residue present. I perceive, also, that the frames are tinged with soot. And yet . . . "

"Go on."

"Art theft is a lucrative business."

"But what about the fire, Mr. Zigfield?" Max Bramble asked. "How do you account for that?"

Wegman Zigfield shifted his gaze to Wylie Nolan.

"How do we account for that, Mr. Nolan? Can you tell us anything at all about this fire?"

"Not yet."

"And what about the doors, Wylie?" Max asked. "How to get into and out of the gallery? What was or wasn't locked at the time of the fire? What was that all about?"

Wylie walked to the doors leading to the hall; he pointed his camera at the lock and snapped.

"Look at this." Wylie ran his finger over the area of the lock. "There aren't any scratch marks or dents here, so it's fair to assume that the lock wasn't tampered with. And here, around the doorjambs and the hinges. We can see that the doors weren't jimmied. This tells us that there was no forcible entry into the gallery prior to the fire. The same can be said of the doors to the library. And I checked with your security man Luis. He said his log shows that nobody entered the museum from the time he set the alarms at seven o'clock yesterday until the time he got here this morning; which means that if both sets of doors to this Parlor Gallery were locked at the time of the fire, and nobody could have gotten inside the museum prior to the fire in order to set the fire, what we have here is a problem."

"More than just a problem," Max added. "It's a mystery."

Wegman Zigfield snorted. "Are either of you familiar with detective novels? Whodunits? Books of that sort?"

"I am," Max volunteered.

"And you?" Mr. Zigfield looked at Wylie Nolan.

Wylie nodded.

Wegman Zigfield went on, "There is one particular kind of a detective novel—a sub, subgenre, so to speak, of which I am *not* particularly fond."

"What is it?" Max asked.

"Locked room mysteries. The kind in which a murder is committed inside a room. Nobody could have gotten into the room to commit the crime. Nobody could have gotten out of the room after the crime was committed. And yet inside the room is a body." Wegman Zigfield's glittery blue eyes narrowed. "I do not like locked room mysteries, Mr. Nolan."

Wylie pivoted away from the owner of the museum.

"One, two, three, four, five," he counted, pointing at a different empty frame for each digit.

"Five bodies," he said.

Then he pointed at the doors leading to the library and the doors leading to the corridor.

"Locked doors," he said.

He pointed to the windows.

"Locked windows," he said.

And finally he pointed at Wegman Zigfield, and grinning around his teeth like a Cheshire cat, he added, "Outta luck."

6

"Marshal's office."

"This is Wylie Nolan. Who am I talking to?"

"Fire Marshal Virgil Madison."

"Do I know you, Virgil?"

"No, sir. But I know you."

"Sorry, Virgil. I don't remember when . . . ."

"Oh, you never met me, Mr. Nolan."

"Wylie. Then how . . . "

"You're a legend around this place, Wylie."

"I think I'll play it safe and *not* ask what kind of a legend. Is Gus Grogan there?"

"He was supposed to be here an hour ago, but we got a fire at a social club on East 125th Street with a possible six DOA's. He's out on that."

"Well, Virgil, since Gus can't help me, how's my credit with you?"

"What do you want?"

"Whatever you've got on the fire that took place at seven-oh-two this morning at the Zigfield Art Museum. That's Z-I-G-F-I-E-L-D. Location is Fifth Avenue and East Seventy-ninth Street."

"Give me a second. I'll check."

"Thanks, buddy."

"OK. Nothing in the file, but I found a preliminary report on Grogan's desk."

"Good. What did Gus write down for the cause of the fire, Virgil?"

"Let me see . . . Jeez, his handwriting stinks."

"He must have gone to a Catholic school."

"OK. For origin of fire, he has five pointings . . . What the hell is five pointings? No. That's not what it says. I got it. Five paintings. And for cause, he's got 'undetermined.' "

"Is that all, Virgil?"

"It's all I can decipher. Want me to have Gus call you when he gets in?"

"Just tell him I'm working on it, and if I get anything I think he'd be interested in, he'll be the first to know."

"This is a bullshit fire, Wylie. It isn't going anywhere. But off the record, what do you think happened?"

"Off the record, Virgil, it beats the hell out of me."

7

The woman was startling. Whether she was tall, short, legitimate, phony, intelligent, bold, brash, brazen, or beautiful was incidental to the overall impression she made when she first entered a room.

Joy Miller, executive secretary to Wegman Zigfield, looked up. Her fingers dropped motionless to her typewriter, and she stared openly, impolitely . . . unconsciously absorbing the woman's effect.

Joy noticed her hair first, a wild, electric orange-red, the color of cellophane on fire. And then she noticed the woman's eyes. Luminescent. Imperative. Bright green. The color of street lights signaling traffic to go . . . go . . . go.

And the woman walked briskly, if you could call what she did walk. Because it seemed to Joy much more than just the motion required to get from point A to point B. It was a swirl or a whirl or a gallivant, if there was such a thing.

The red-haired woman stopped abruptly opposite Joy Miller's desk. She extended a slim, perfectly manicured hand.

"Hello, I'm Georgiana Weeks."

She both drew out and punched up her words as she spoke, her accent quicker than southern, less twangy than Texan.

"You were expecting me."

Joy blinked, and then shook off her languor. She blinked again, and gave Georgiana Weeks's outstretched hand a salutary jerk of fingers.

"I'm Joy Miller. Mr. Zigfield's secretary. Dr. Weeks. Of course. The Pre-Raphaelite exhibition. We were expecting you. Won't you sit down? Mr. Zigfield asked me to convey his personal apologies that he won't be able to meet with you this morning, but he's . . . "

The door to Joy's office swung open again. A man with steady brown eyes and thick, silver-streaked brown hair strode in. The ends of his mustache twirled rakishly upward, and there was a debonair sweep to his beard that suggested a kinship to pirates and buccaneers.

"Jiri!" Joy Miller stood up and reached out eagerly.

Jiri caught her extended hands and made a fist around both of them; he lifted them gallantly to his lips, and then he released them—as though setting two sparrows or butterflies free.

"My dear," he said. "Why such a flurry of excitement?"

His voice was deep with a soft European accent that impressed itself on the words he spoke as subtly as embossed letterhead on expensive paper.

"Jiri, Mr. Zigfield said I was supposed to find you, and I've been calling and calling, but you weren't . . . "

"Now, now, little Joy. How can my small diversionary expedition to obtain coffee and doughnuts have created such a flurry of activity that you are forgetting to introduce me to our beautiful and distinguished guest, whom I understand, from your frantic messages, is to be my responsibility for the remainder of the day? For shame!"

He frowned in mock disappointment, turned and declined his head toward the woman standing beside him. The effect, rather than a nod, assumed the intimate elegance of a bow.

"My name is Jiri Hozda. I am associate director of this treasure house of art to which I welcome you, and I have been eagerly awaiting both you and your exhibition since Mr. Zigfield's negotiations with you first began." He punctuated his words with slight lifts and drops of his eyebrows. "And alas, I cannot restrain myself from asking you, Georgiana . . . if I may call you that?"

"Sure. Go ahead."

"I cannot restrain myself from inquiring if you can possibly have failed to notice that your mere presence here, in accompaniment with the paintings that you are bringing, puts one rather at a loss for words."

"I can guarantee you, Dr. Hozda, that I did *not* notice you were at a loss for words."

Jiri's eyebrow arched. "Perhaps 'loss for words' is putting it too strongly."

"Perhaps."

"Surely, though, the resemblance has been pointed out to you before?"

"Resemblance?"

"Not in feature. Yours are more delicate. The lines of your bones more finely chiseled. But in . . . indeed . . . in almost all other aspects. The vibrant copper of your hair. The rare, electric illumination of your eyes. Your eyes themselves, a shade of green both bright and translucent, as if it had been stolen from the wings of butterflies. And your skin— pure ivory with but the barest tinge of coral."

"I sound like a shopping list for body parts."

"But, it's perfectly obvious, Georgiana, that you could *be* a Pre-Raphaelite painting yourself. Surely you have seen confirmation of this in your own mirror?"

"Surely, I have not."

"Not even your beautiful Pre-Raphaelite hair?"

"My hair and I were both born in Oklahoma. Not England."

"Your hands. Exquisitely formed. Long, delicate fingers."

Georgiana held up her hands and turned them this way and that.

"Not bad. But I'd have more respect for them if they could do something useful. Like spin gold out of straw."

Jiri shook his head.

"You are laughing at the rapturous enthusiasm of a full-blooded American male," he said as he placed a large white paper bag on Joy's desk and began to remove from it pastries wrapped in small sheets of waxed paper.

Georgiana looked at Joy Miller.

"Is he always like this?"

But before Joy could answer, the telephone rang.

"It's me, Joy," Wegman Zigfield said. "Is Jiri there?"

Jiri whispered, "Ten minutes ago, I left for Paris."

"He's right here, Mr. Zigfield."

"Put him on the phone."

Jiri took the receiver.

"Hello, Wegman. You are, if I might say, a spoilsport."

"Glad to hear it. Why?"

"I was about to invite our lovely Dr. Weeks on a tour of the museum. This phone call, however, I perceive to be a harbinger of absolutely no good."

"Nonsense, Jiri. Your plans fit right in perfectly with mine. Two of my people are on their way to your office. Max Bramble, our lawyer. You know Max. And Wylie Nolan. Nolan's the insurance company's fire expert. He wants to be shown around the premises, too. So why don't you take Max and Nolan along with you. Now, let me talk to Georgiana."

Jiri handed her the telephone.

"Welcome," Wegman Zigfield said. "I'm sorry I wasn't able to greet you in person, but we had a little problem in one of our galleries. I'll tell you about it when I see you."

"Will this 'little problem' that you aren't talking about affect my timetable? Because the Pre-Raphaelite paintings are scheduled to get here on Tuesday."

"I don't foresee a conflict."

"Good. But as far as the tour of the museum goes, I have to make a few phone calls, so could I put it off for a while and borrow a desk and phone instead?"

Jiri said, "If you will permit." He took the telephone from Georgiana. "Wegman, our lovely guest may, of course, use my office until hers is available."

"Fine, Jiri. I'll send Max and the fire expert over to you now. They want to know everything about the museum and the Sarkin Zahedi exhibition. Show them. Tell them. Give him what we have, and if we don't have it, get it."

8

A museum is unlike any other building, because its sole purpose is to acquire, display, and protect items that are considered to be of infinite beauty and unparalleled value.

A private home that has been turned into a museum is not a museum, because the visitor's focus is divided, whether intentionally or not, between the architectural detail, the interior design, *and* the art. In even such an exquisite setting as the Frick Museum, with its Rembrandts, Whistlers, and Tintorettos, our focus inevitably is drawn away from the gorgeous Titian to the left of the mantel in the living room, and toward the sofas . . . the armchairs, the lamps . . . the divan, and the fantasy of entertaining (intellectuals, royalty, stars of the stage) in such a room, *if* such a room in such an edifice had been our own.

What is a museum?

Poetically, a museum might be described as the open palm on which the exotic Flame of India ruby is displayed . . . the support against which the portrait of a peasant girl leans as she listens to the whispered instructions of her saints . . . the windowed wall through which sunlight streams as it highlights the muscular statue of God's first man.

A museum is a jewel box.

Man's highest creations are the jewels.

But jewel boxes are locked things. They are fortified containers hidden behind pictures in bedrooms, tucked into reinforced steel cabinets accessible only to fingers that know secret combinations. They are encased in vaults called safety deposit boxes or buried in backyards.

Jewel boxes are dark, secretive places.

They hide. They exclude. They covet.

And yet, a museum is a jewel box.

But one whose purpose is the opposite of what all other treasure chests and hidden boxes are intended to do.

For a museum is a jewel box on a grand scale. A jewel box in which the paintings and sculpture, instead of being hidden, are exhibited openly, flagrantly, indeed . . . proudly, in rooms where they are easily accessible and attractively displayed.

The jewel box that is a museum throws its doors open and proclaims (on banners, in newspaper ads, through articles, brochures, and books), "Come to me. Stand nose to nose with my Renoirs, my van Goghs, my Rubenses and my Caravaggios.

"Enter, but don't stay.

"Admire, but don't linger too long.

"Look, but don't touch.

"And, when you leave (and you *must* leave), all that you may take with you are inspirations and exaltations.

"You may not take anything else.

"You may *not* take anything else.

"You may not tamper with the works of art.

"You may not go into unauthorized areas.

"You may not smoke; you may not eat; you may not drink; you may not take photographs; you may not set fires.

"You are the citizens whom we make welcome. But we do not know you. You are somebody. But you are also anybody. Your motives may be pure. But they may also be horrendous."

How then do the directors of museums perform the neat trick of being both accessible and inaccessible at the same time? How do they make sure that visitors do not go berserk within their hallowed halls? That they do not run amok and desecrate or rend or plunder or vandalize or burn or destroy?

How?

Security.

What then, exactly, *is* security?

9

Jiri Hozda's fingers moved with staccato precision over the keypad next to an immense steel door in the basement of the Zigfield Art Museum.

"So, you can't get in without a personal code?" Wylie asked.

"Exactly." Jiri pressed a final digit. "And my entry time is automatically recorded on a printout in the security room. When I leave and reset the code, my departure time is also recorded. And all of the printouts are saved."

"That's it?"

"No, my friend." Jiri extracted a metal key from a crush of keys on a large chrome ring. "One is also obliged to use more conventional methods of entry." He turned the key in the lock, and slid the heavy door open along a stiff, metal track.

Jiri flicked on the overhead lights and Max Bramble peered into the cavernous opening.

"What's this room used for?"

Jiri clicked on more lights, revealing an immense rectangular space. Giant sliding panels fitted into horizontal grooves that crossed the room like deep ridges in corduroy.

Hundred of paintings—large, small, ornately or plainly framed, recognizable from art books and postcards, or obscure canvases, rarely if ever seen—hung from top to bottom on these dozens of sliding walls.

Max stepped around a panel facing the back of the room. For a moment, he was hidden from the view of the other two men. A few seconds later he came out, an awed expression on his face.

"Do you know what I just saw in there? A painting by John Sloan. Another one by Reginald Marsh, and two Bierstadts. What are they all doing in here? Why aren't they out on exhibit somewhere?"

"They will be soon, my friend," Jiri Hozda answered

"Are the frames broken? Is the canvas torn? Is the paint cracking? Is something wrong with these paintings?"

"None of those symptoms, Max. They are here because they are between exhibitions, or because they are waiting to be sent out to another museum on loan. All of the paintings in this area are in fairly good condition, but even if a problem should develop, we would be ill-equipped to repair it. We are a comparatively small museum, and we don't do any conservation work ourselves."

"Conservation means what?" Wylie interjected. "Cleaning paintings? Fixing what's broken? Torn?"

"That and more."

"Do you need some sort of chemicals to do this cleaning and repairing work?"

"Indeed, one does."

"So, what kinds of chemicals do you store on the premises?"

"We do not store any."

"None? What exactly are we talking about here? Which chemicals do art conservators use?"

"Turpentine," Jiri answered. "Mineral oil. Paint thinner. Linseed oil."

Wylie nodded. "And those are all combustible. What do you use the linseed oil for?"

"As I said, my friend, we do not use it here at the Zigfield Art Museum. An artist or an art conservator, however, would use linseed oil to speed up the process of drying."

"Drying what?"

"Oil paint."

"What else would be here if you did your own art conservation?"

"That would depend on what type of restoration or art preservation was being done, but as a rule, an art conservator might have tubes of oil paint, walnut oil, poppy oil, beeswax, and gum arabic. If we repaired our own frames, we would also have a supply of glues, varnishes, and oily rags. We'd have stains of varying . . . "

"Excuse me, but what's that?" Wylie's eyes drifted to a small box mounted to the left of the entry door. Jiri followed Wylie's glance.

"Aha!" he said warmly. "It appears that you have found our thermostat."

"Is this room temperature controlled?"

"Yes, my friend. The approved temperature range for the storage of artworks is between 68 and 72 degrees Fahrenheit, with a relative humidity of 55 to 58 percent."

"What about the rest of the museum? Not just the storage areas. Are the galleries climate controlled, too?"

"Indeed they are."

"Meaning what?"

"Meaning that wherever artwork is present, air conditioners always hum a merry tune."

"So the air conditioners were on last night? Before the fire?"

"Blowing like Gabriel at the gates of heaven."

"And this morning . . . at the time of the fire?"

"I can but assume that such was the case."

Wylie's glance shifted across the ceiling. "And what's that?"

"That is a mechanism which detects motion. To the right of it is a heat detector."

"So, if there were an intruder?"

"His movements would be detected."

"How about in the galleries?"

"There are no motion detectors in the galleries themselves. However in the corridors outside the galleries, there are motion detectors that are turned on whenever the museum is closed, and at night."

"But down here in the basement?"

"Down here, we have both."

"And if there were a fire . . . " Wylie began.

"Both the heat and motion sensors would transmit that information to the fire and security annunciator in the security room. From there, an alarm would go automatically to the fire department."

Wylie continued to scrutinize the ceiling.

"No sprinklers?" he asked.

Just then, Max stuck his head out from behind a panel at the far end of the room.

His voice was electric. "A Howard Pyle, an N. C. Wyeth, and two Alma Tademas. I died and went to heaven."

"I know, my friend. I have often felt that way myself. However . . . " Jiri jiggled his keys significantly.

"Sorry," Max said; he emerged smiling.

Jiri Hozda led the two men out and slid the door of the storage room shut; he again keyed in his personal security code.

"Follow me," he said.

The rest of Jiri's tour of the basement area included the art preparator's and photographer's rooms, where none of the artwork was stored, and which were secured with just conventional keys.

Jiri pointed out that more sophisticated precautions were needed for the rooms used to store works of art on paper, and for the temporary storage of paintings on their way to and from exhibitions. Entry to both was achieved by keypads, conventional keys, and through sliding fire doors. There were also motion and heat detectors, and the rooms were temperature controlled.

"You never answered my question about sprinklers," Wylie said as Jiri unlocked a heavy door marked EXIT, and preceded the other two men through it.

Jiri relocked the door behind them, and led them up a steep stairwell.

"We do not have sprinklers in the museum."

"Where are we going now?" Max asked.

"Back to the security room on the ground floor. The printouts and other material that Wylie requested will have been collected by now."

Jiri stopped at the top of the stairs. "Before we continue, however, I will explain how the artworks arrive at and are shipped from the museum."

He pointed toward three enormous overhead doors approximately thirty feet away.

"This is our loading dock area. When the crates containing the art shipments are delivered, they are left here undisturbed to acclimatize for twenty-four hours. And it is from here that they are sent to the appropriate gallery or storage room to be unpacked. All packing material is retained in a climate-controlled environment, and the very same packing material that came with the artwork is then used to repack it for shipment after the exhibition."

Max pointed to a huge box made out of boards so excruciatingly clean they seemed to emit the smells of pine needles and sawdust.

"Is that one of the crates the paintings come in?"

"Yes. One of the smaller ones."

"Smaller. Hell," Max said. "If I put it on the corner of Third Avenue and East Seventy-ninth Street, I could sell it to a family of four as a condominium!"

Jiri smiled. "Indeed, the crates are well constructed. A highly specialized fine arts shipper builds, packs, and unpacks them. This shipper is an expert in protecting the contents from temperature changes, moisture, and shock; also, the crates are insulated with special absorbancy materials to protect the contents from vibrations. Few newborn babies are carried in their mother's wombs as carefully as artworks are transported from one museum to another. Now come."

Jiri led them through a door labeled FIRE EXIT ONLY and down another long corridor.

Wylie asked. "Where are we now? I'm all turned around."

"We came up the back staircase from the basement, and we are walking around the north side of the sanctuary." They continued for another ten or twelve feet and then stopped. "This is the door to the security room. You were here before, but this time we approached from the north side of the narthex. The narthex is through these double doors. Now do you know where you are?"

"No," Wylie said. "But I stopped caring."

Jiri unlocked the door to the security room. A large panel box was mounted on the back wall opposite the entryway. Two rows of lights and numbers ran down the front of the box.

"This is the fire and security annunciator I mentioned earlier. If an alarm is activated, one of these lights goes on." Jiri pointed to a large laminated floor plan adjacent to the annunciator box. "And this decodes the light and number for the security director, so that he can tell in which room that heat or smoke detector has gone off."

Jiri took a loose-leaf binder from a shelf and handed it to Wylie Nolan. With a sweep of his hand, he indicated another dozen books and binders.

"Sprinklers," he said.

"What about them?"

"To sprinkle or not to sprinkle? That is the question."

Wylie put the binder back on the shelf.

"Are you telling me that there's no industry standard?"

"Not exactly. Historically, The Smithsonian Institute in Washington, D.C., has set the standard for museum security. For a long time, they resisted the idea of sprinklers, because they feared water damage more than they did fire. But of late, they seem to be rethinking their position."

"How about you? Are you rethinking your position?"

"Do you mean am I for or against sprinklers?"

"Right."

Jiri shrugged. "I'm ambivalent. Do I prefer my masterpieces to be incinerated or irreparably damaged by water? That is not the kind of a question I like being asked."

Max smiled and interjected happily, "Are you still beating your wife?"

Both men looked at him.

" 'Do you want your paintings to be destroyed by fire or water?' is the same kind of a question. The hidden premise is that one disaster or the other has to occur. But is that true?"

Jiri shook his head. "Indeed, my friend, one prays that his collection will be protected forever from such a calamity. And, as well as he is able, he provides the very best security that is available."

He lifted several manila folders off a desk.

"These are for you, Wylie." He read off the folders one by one and gave them to Wylie Nolan.

"Blueprint of museum with rooms labeled appropriately; printout of keypad activity; printout of alarm system activity; security system installation manual; and climate control printout and operations manual." He handed over the last folder. "That's it. The rest of the material you want is upstairs in Joy's office. Joy Miller is Mr. Zigfield's secretary, Wylie. I don't believe you've had the pleasure of meeting her yet."

"I haven't."

"Then come." Jiri once again led the two men out of a room. "I will take you to the final stop in our tour of the museum."

10

Wylie and Joy Miller stood on either side of Joy's desk, Max having gone off to White Plains to take a deposition and Jiri having left the two of them to go through the material in Joy's office.

Wylie grinned at Joy Miller.

"Alone at last."

Joy blushed. "I have everything you asked for, Mr. Nolan. But I thought it would be easier to explain if we went through the material together."

A discerning eye would have described Joy Miller's figure as slender, lithe, and lovely. One less perceptive, though, might only have noticed that she stood with her shoulders hunched modestly forward, the way a schoolgirl stands when she is embarrassed about her developing breasts.

As it was, everything about Joy suggested that awkward stage of in between.

In between girl and woman.

In between confident and self-doubting.

In between unequivocal, undaunted romanticism, and the unwavering conviction that adventures only happen to somebody else.

The top of Joy Miller's head stood five feet, three inches above perfectly shaped toes shod in shoes with heels that were not quite high enough to be stylish, nor quite low enough to be dowdy. Her hair was a lank, dark blonde. Her eyes were the straightforward shade of light blue that's on Willow plates. She wore no mascara on her long, dark lashes. Her face was small and narrow, every delicate feature somewhere between pretty and plain, waiting only for the animation of self-confidence to transform her from a mope into an eye-riveting beauty.

"Would you like a cup of coffee, Mr. Nolan?" Joy asked shyly.

"Yes, ma'am. I thought you'd never ask."

"You can call me Joy. I'll brew you a fresh pot, if you don't mind waiting."

"I never mind waiting for a cup of coffee."

"Mr. Nolan, do you mind if I ask you a question?"

"Ask away."

"Do you carry a weapon? I know Fromer, Mr. Zigfield's son, said that you had a gun, but he's very excitable and you can't always believe what Fromer says."

"Well, Fromer hit a homer this time. He must have seen my holster when I picked up my camera bag on my way into the Parlor Gallery."

"Do you . . . are you . . . "

"Am I carrying my gun now?"

Joy nodded.

"Yes. I am. But God help us all if I have to use it. It's been so long since I fired off a round, the dust in the barrel would probably explode."

"Then why do you still carry it around?"

"Well, it's like this. When I was a New York City fire marshal, I was expected to arrest the bad guys who started fires. And I was a New York City fire marshal for such a long time, that my gun wore a rut right here in my gut. One day, after I went private, though, I decided to leave my gun at home, just to see what would happen; and what do you know but a breeze started up between the bottom of my trouser leg and my belt buckle. And that breeze gusted and eddied in the middle of that empty space where my gun was supposed to be, and it was so bad, I got goosebumps on my bones. So, instead of taking the risk of that happening again and my coming down with a pneumonia, I wear my gun all the time. Just to fill up the rut in my gut."

A smile tugged at the edges of Joy Miller's lips.

"You're lying, aren't you?"

"Of course I am. I wear my gun out of habit, and hope I'll never have to use it, because if I did I'd probably shoot myself in the foot."

"I don't believe *that* for one minute!"

The coffee percolator went into a violent gurgle for fifteen seconds, and then stopped. Joy filled two cups.

"I guess I'd better show you what I have, Mr. Nolan."

"Mr. Nolan is the guy who submits the bill to the insurance company. I'm Wylie."

Joy sat and indicated the stack of folders on the coffee table.

"I've separated the material you requested into four categories, and I color-coded the folders."

She handed a green folder to Wylie as he sat down across from her.

"This contains information about each of our employees."

Wylie hefted it on his palm.

"Not very heavy, is it?"

"We aren't a very big museum. Including myself and Mr. Zigfield, there's just Jiri Hozda, who's both our associate director and our curator. Felix Saint-Clare used to be our registrar, but Felix's mother had a stroke a few weeks ago, and he took a leave of absence. While he's been gone, Jiri and I have been handling his responsibilities, but Felix just told us he isn't coming back, so we'll have to hire a new registrar. The others here are Luis Cabrerra, our security director. And we also have a full-time guard, a full-time preparator, and . . . "

"What's that?"

"A preparator is also called an exhibition technician or an installation technician."

"OK. I get it."

"Bill Toomis is our guard, and Mikos Piatigorsky is our preparator. Mikos called in sick this morning, but he'll be doing the actual installation of the Pre-Raphaelite paintings next week, and it was he who did the installation for the opening of Mr. Zahedi's retrospective on October seventh."

"Anyone else?"

"Yes, but they're all part-timers. We have a press relations lady,

Phoebe Cullen Gill. And two part-time volunteers run the gift shop, Eleanor Overheiser and . . . and . . . Camden Kimcannon."

"Why did you hesitate just now?"

"Did I?"

"Yes. When you said the last name. Kimcannon."

Joy Miller's face turned dark pink.

"Oh," Wylie said. "I get it. Is that all of them?"

"That's the whole list. Not a very big staff, but as I said, we aren't a very big museum. In this folder are our employees' names, job descriptions, résumés, job applications, and current addresses and home telephone numbers. Tomorrow is Saturday, so all of them will be in, except for Mikos, if he's still sick, and Mrs. Overheiser and Phoebe Cullen Gill."

"Who is Overheiser again?"

"She's our alternate at the gift shop. Her husband died last year, and she's been volunteering to keep busy. If you like, I can ask her to come in tomorrow."

"You're closed Mondays, aren't you?"

"Yes. Most museums are."

"Is Overheiser coming in on Tuesday?"

"Yes."

"How about the others?"

"Everybody should be in on Tuesday, because we're getting ready for the Pre-Raphaelite opening."

"How about this Phoebe Pickle Dill? Who is she?"

"Phoebe Cullen Gill." Joy smiled delightedly. "She's the part-time public relations lady, and I'm sure she'll be here on Tuesday. Why? Do you prefer to talk to them then?"

"I prefer. Next in your pile." Wylie pointed to the orange folder.

"This is what I pulled out of our insurance file. There are special fine arts brokers for artists and art galleries, and museum insurance can be confusing."

"It's a thick file."

"I know. But even this is just a small part of the paperwork involved in insuring a museum. I left out everything I didn't think was pertinent.

53

What you have here are only the insurance policies for the museum structure—the building itself—and for the actual works of art."

Joy flipped open the orange folder and plucked out a piece of paper. "I also put this in the insurance file."

"What is it?"

"It's a signed release from Sarkin Zahedi."

Wylie read silently for a moment, and then mumbled, ". . . Blah, blah and 'We know that this does not meet the professional standards for exposure to light' . . . blah, blah, and so on. What does it mean?"

"It means that natural light, like the light from the sun, emits ultraviolet rays. Windows or skylights in a museum usually have filters to reduce the most dangerous rays, which prevent them from damaging or fading a painting or other work of art. The skylights in the Parlor Gallery aren't fitted with those filters, though, and this release protects us from liability in the event Mr. Zahedi claims that his works were damaged by the sun."

Wylie tapped the release. "Why would he sign something like this?"

Joy compressed her lips tightly.

"Out with it," Wylie insisted.

Joy shrugged. "Maybe because his retrospective was so short, he knew that his paintings weren't at risk. They'd only be up from November fourth through November twenty-fifth. Maybe he just didn't want to make any more waves."

"Make any *more* waves? Do I detect some internal friction concerning the Zahedi exhibit that you're keeping from me?"

Again, Joy Miller made a rigid line of her lips.

Then she laid her hand on the stack of tan folders and looked Wylie dead in the eye. "These are our files on Sarkin Zahedi. *Decision* magazine recently did a six-page cover story on what they call his 'rediscovered masterpieces.' In recent years, Sarkin Zahedi's paintings haven't been selling. Last December, though, he announced that ten paintings he'd done more than twenty years ago had been discovered in an abandoned SoHo loft. Since they were representative of the canvases that Mr. Zahedi did when he was at his peak of fame, their discovery has caused a considerable commotion in the art world. His work is back in demand, new and old, and he's a celebrity again." Joy tapped the top tan folder. "It's all in here. Plus photographs of Zahedi and some of his early paintings. Plus eight-by-ten color pictures of the five paintings that made up the retrospective. Plus newsclips, press releases, catalogues, and so on."

Joy moved her hand to the fat blue folder, last in line on the coffee table.

"And this is the Double-ADF paperwork."

"Double-ADF, Joy?"

"American Art Development Fund: Double-ADF. They subsidized the Sarkin Zahedi retrospective."

"You mean as in government subsidy?"

"Exactly."

"But I thought that the Zigfield Art Museum was privately owned."

Joy nodded somberly. "It is."

"I don't get it."

"It's complicated."

"Use words of one syllable."

Joy Miller sighed.

"Okay, Wylie, but it goes back a few years to when I started working for Mr. Zigfield, just before Jiri Hozda came here. At that time, it was Fromer Zigfield who held the position of associate director of this museum. Fromer is Mr. Wegman Zigfield—the founder's—son."

"So far, this isn't too complex for me. Go on."

"Mrs. Zigfield, Wegman's wife, is suffering from Alzheimer's disease. Fromer has always been considered, by both husband and wife, to be something of a . . . a . . . "

"Loser?"

". . . and after Mrs. Zigfield was diagnosed with Alzheimer's disease but before it had changed her personality or interfered with her ability to function, she asked Mr. Zigfield to give Fromer one more chance, and bring him into the museum as his associate director. I actually heard Mrs. Zigfield laugh about it. She said, 'The good thing about this Alzheimer business, Wegman, is that when Fromer does whatever disastrous thing we both know he's going to do, I won't be around—men-

tally, at least—to know it. But you, my dear . . . it won't be easy for you.'
And it hasn't been."

"Is Mrs. Zigfield alive?"

"Yes. And Mr. Zigfield still loves her very much."

"What happened with Fromer?"

"Just what we expected. Mr. Zigfield hates all abstract art. He hates
abstract expressionism. He hates assemblage. It's the policy of the museum to exhibit only representational art, either classic or contemporary,
and Jiri Hozda was hired because he has an international reputation for
discovering . . . "

"Woah. You're getting away from me, Joy. We aren't talking about
Jiri Hozda now, we're talking about Fromer Zigfield."

"Sorry. Fromer is an ardent admirer of Sarkin Zahedi's work. Mr.
Zahedi is also Fromer's closest friend. At least, this year's closest friend.
He changes them regularly."

"Go on."

"When Fromer decided to do the retrospective, Mr. Zigfield was not
happy. In fact, he forbade Fromer from bringing Mr. Zahedi's work into
the museum."

"The plot thickens."

"So, behind his father's back, Fromer applied to the American Art
Development Fund for a grant. And even though he can't do anything
else well, Fromer is very good at getting government money."

"When did Wegman find out about all this?"

"After Fromer had sent out press releases to the media, and the
AADF money had already been spent on catalogues and posters for the
retrospective."

"Wegman must have loved that."

"The way Fromer planned it, we had to put on the retrospective.
Cancelling would have involved both the museum as an institution and
Mr. Zigfield as an individual in expensive litigation. And Mr. Bramble
advised us that if Mr. Zahedi sued, we would probably lose the case."

"So your boss was not a happy camper."

"I've never seen him so angry."

"What did he say, Joy? What did he do?"

"Well, first Mr. Zigfield cut down the number of the paintings in the exhibition from ten to five."

"Could he do that? Legally?"

"Yes. Mr. Zahedi's contract didn't specify which paintings were to be displayed, or how many."

"Then what?"

"He moved the retrospective from the Hall of Marquetry, which is considerably larger and has much better light, to the Parlor Gallery, which has stained glass windows, restricted wall space, and skylights."

"Which is why Zahedi had to sign the release?"

"Exactly."

"What else?"

"Mr. Zigfield fired Fromer, and hired Jiri Hozda, which he'd wanted to do for a long time anyway. Jiri is the perfect associate director for the Zigfield Art Museum. He's not only a brilliant scholar, but because of his experiences in Czechoslovakia, he's even more outspoken in his opposition to government subsidized art than Mr. Zigfield, and Jiri . . . "

"Never mind Jiri. What happened then?"

"Then Sarkin Zahedi's exhibition opened."

"And?"

"And this morning, it seemed as if . . . well, it looks very much like . . . I mean, all of Sarkin Zahedi's paintings seem to have disappeared."

11

The *New York Times* article about the forthcoming Pre-Raphaelite exhibition threw its guest curator, Georgiana Weeks, a bone for her "impeccable professional credentials," allowing that Dr. Weeks studied art history at Northwestern University, and then went on for her masters and doctorate degrees under Dr. Selma Holo at the University of Southern California's Museum Studies Program.

"Dr. Weeks is a curator in every technical sense of the word," the article stated. "However, in the scheme, scale, scope, and presentation of her work, she appears to be more impresario than curator, and her description of the exhibition scheduled to open on December ninth at the Zigfield Art Museum is more suggestive of the revival of a Broadway musical than of a scholarly display of respected works of art."

The article briefly discussed some of Georgiana Weeks's more controversial exhibitions.

"Dr. Weeks appears to know her art," it went on. "What she does not know is how to detach the elevated aesthetic from the rank association of pedestrian allure."

Which, translated into English, meant that she put on shows people liked to go to.

When interviewed about the success of her exhibition on American western art from Charles Russell and Frederick Remington to the present, she responded to the charge that her work brought art down to the level of the masses (yes, there was music from the Sons of the Pioneers and a cowboy did do rope tricks on opening night) by stating, "I prefer to think that I'm bringing people up to art. Look at it this way: If I put on a show and some mailroom clerk or stockbroker sees a picture of a campfire in front of a blazing western sunset, and this guy, who only came in because he wanted to see a cowboy twirl a lasso, *liked* what he saw, and comes back next time to look at the Greek statues, or goes to a library and takes out a book on Albert Bierstadt, or buys a set of watercolors and decides to tinker with paint himself, then none of the artwork in the museum has been lowered, cheapened, or diminished in any way. The only thing that's changed is the mailroom clerk, who has been uplifted and improved by what he's seen, because what he has seen is beautiful."

The exhibition that Georgiana Weeks was bringing to the Zigfield Art Museum was called *Artists, Lovers, Poets, and Friends: The Pre-Raphaelites—A Passionate Grouping*.

Georgiana's decision to put on the exhibition had not evolved in any way out of her undergraduate or graduate studies. Nineteenth-century British Pre-Raphaelites were neither taught nor respected when she went to school.

She didn't even know who they were until she went on a weekend excursion to the Brandywine Valley; she was browsing aimlessly through the Delaware Art Museum (she calls it "art grazing") when she wandered into an area that contained the Samuel Bancroft Collection.

Which was when she saw them for the first time.

Proud, long-necked women who flaunted exuberant masses of golden, copper, chestnut, or raven black hair. Luxuriant hair so glorious, it seemed to be stating a principle, or standing up for some noble and heroic cause, instead of just surrounding faces that were either sensuous, intense, or sad. But strong. Always strong.

The first painting Georgiana noticed was called *Mnemosyne*, by Dante Gabriel Rossetti. It depicted a huge, gray-eyed goddess with bare shoulders, draped in a flowing green gown. According to the caption under the painting, the model for *Mnemosyne* was Jane Morris, mistress to Dante Gabriel Rossetti and wife of William Morris.

A label to the left of the painting stated that William Morris was the founder of a textile firm for which Dante Gabriel Rossetti (among others) had created patterns, and that all of the walls behind the art currently on display were covered with Morris wallpaper.

Georgiana looked again at Rossetti's painting of his mistress, and then at the lush, red poppy wallpaper that had been produced by the mistress's husband; she nodded, although she wasn't quite sure at what, and went on to look at the next painting.

It was a parable of a woman and a child.

THE PRIORESS'S TALE
by *Edward Burne-Jones*

The woman was wearing blue. Her head was surrounded by a pale ring of light as she gently placed a piece of grain into the mouth of a young boy. The faces of both boy and woman were of an unearthly beauty.

The label beneath the painting said:

THE ORIGINAL CONCEPTION FOR *The Prioress's Tale* WAS RENDERED IN OIL BY BURNE-JONES ON A CABINET GIVEN IN 1860 TO WILLIAM AND JANE MORRIS. BURNE-JONES, ALONG WITH ROSSETTI, FREQUENTLY CONTRIBUTED DESIGNS TO WILLIAM MORRIS'S FIRM.

Georgiana Weeks stared at the painting. In style and color, it was subtler than those of Rossetti, but it was vibrant and hypnotizing in that same unapologetically passionate way.

She returned to *Mnemosyne* and reread the inscription. Yes, she had gotten it right. Jane Morris was Rossetti's model and mistress. She was also William Morris's wife. And the original for *The Prioress's Tale* had been given by Burne-Jones to Morris. The same Morris for whom both Burne-Jones and Rossetti had produced designs.

Connections, Georgiana Weeks thought.

Interesting.

She entered a room papered in trellised green wallpaper on which bluebirds, leafed vines, and red flowers wove in and out.

The first picture she saw was called:

CALAIS
by John Ruskin

It was a small pen-and-ink of boats in a harbor on what appeared to be a stormy day.

Ruskin, according to the caption, was both art critic and author. His book *Modern Painters* had strongly influenced the Pre-Raphaelites to be "true to nature," and he was their ardent advocate and friend.

Among those whom he defended against vitriolic criticism was John Everett Millais. When Charles Dickens described Millais's Madonna in *Christ in the House of His Parents* as "so horrible in her ugliness . . . she would stand out from the rest of the company as a monster in the vilest cabaret in France," Ruskin angrily protested, "It is reserved for England to insult the strength of her noblest children . . . and to leave to those whom she should have cherished and aided, no hope but in resolution, no refuge but in disdain."

In a small oil painting immediately to the right of Ruskin's drawing Georgiana observed a pretty woman wearing Highland dress and sewing the white badge of the Jacobites to her lover's cocked hat.

THE WHITE COCKADE
by Sir John Everett Millais

The model, according the painting's label, was Effie Millais. Effie, the artist's wife, had previously been married to John Ruskin (Millais's champion), and had met and fallen in love with Millais during a trip to Scotland, when he was painting Ruskin's portrait.

Georgiana stared at the label.

Then her eyes shifted to a small, elaborately framed picture on the same wall. It was an ink-on-paper of a handsome man with fine, aquiline features, bent compassionately over a recumbent female form.

STUDY FOR LAUNCELOT AND THE LADY OF SHALOTT
by Dante Gabriel Rossetti

Rossetti and Millais, the caption explained, had been commissioned to illustrate Alfred, Lord Tennyson's book *Poems*. And the model for Rossetti's Launcelot was none other than fellow Pre-Raphaelite, Edward Burne-Jones.

Georgiana shook her head and muttered lowly.

"Artists, models, friends, protégés, wives, mistresses, ex-wives, poets, painters . . . what next?"

She turned a corner and came upon a painting of robed figures in a courtyard. Three monks gathered beneath a window out of which a fourth man waved. The picture had an overall crisp, pale green cast. The title of the painting was *The Pilgrim Folk*; the artist, Maria Spartali Stillman.

"OK," Georgiana said as she moved toward a drawing of a beautiful woman holding a partially-opened fan. "So what was the Spartali–Stillman connection?"

According to the caption beside the portrait, Maria Spartali Stillman, who had painted the picture of the monks, had also drawn this charcoal-on-white-paper. It was a *self*-portrait.

Maria Spartali Stillman, the label said:

. . . WAS ONE OF ROSSETTI'S FAVORITE MODELS; MRS. STILLMAN, BORN IN GREECE, ALSO MODELED FOR EDWARD BURNE-JONES.

Georgiana raised an eyebrow.

Across the room, she spotted the image of a pale, long-necked woman on a dark green background. Her beautiful features were both fierce and refined.

STUDY FOR HEAD OF NIMUE FOR
THE BEGUILING OF MERLIN
by Edward Burne-Jones

The woman held an open book in her hands. Her eyes were focused off to her right: Was she looking at or away from something that the observer couldn't see? And what was the meaning of the expression in her eyes?

The model for this study of Nimue, according to the label, was Maria Zambaco.

In *Le Morte D'Arthur* by Malory, Nimue is the enchantress who seduces Merlin into teaching her how to cast spells; she then uses one of his own spells against him to imprison him in a hawthorn bush.

In real life, Zambaco was the beautiful Greek sculptress with whom Burne-Jones had a passionate and near-fatal love affair.
And Maria Zambaco was also the cousin of Maria Spartali Stillman.
Georgiana read the label a second time, and then blinked.
She made her way back through the collection, noticing on the way out a portrait she had missed on the way in.

BEATA BEATRIX
by Dante Gabriel Rossetti

The subject's eyes were closed. Her burnished copper hair was encased in an ethereal light. The expression on her face was beyond prayer. A red dove holding a poppy hovered above hands that lay open . . . supine.
The caption beside the painting stated:

After her death, Rossetti painted his wife, Elizabeth Siddal, as Dante's Beatrice. Siddal met Rossetti in 1849, married him in 1860, and took a fatal overdose of laudanum in 1862.

Georgiana stared at the paragraph. Her eyes returned to the painting of Beatrice. No. Of Elizabeth Siddal *as* Beatrice. Elizabeth Siddal. Rossetti's wife.

She, too, had a long, graceful neck. Her bone structure was both aesthetic and austere, and her eyes were tired . . . oh so tired . . . and seemed to have been brushed eternally shut by a weight no heavier than that of her own eyelashes.

Georgiana drifted away from *Beata Beatrix*.

She bumped into somebody.

A man.

A woman.

It didn't matter.

She turned.

She saw a small picture.

Holy Family
c. 1856
Watercolor-on-paper

The picture was so tiny it seemed almost reluctant to presume to exist. Depicted was a delicate but awkwardly rendered group of three. Mary, the mother, was gazing fixedly out a narrow window. In her arms, she grasped the baby Jesus. Beside her stood a haloed figure whose eyes seemed to focus on neither mother nor child.

The artist was Elizabeth Siddal. The same Elizabeth Siddal portrayed by Rossetti in his painting *Beata Beatrix*. The same Elizabeth Siddal who had been married to Dante Gabriel Rossetti. The same Rossetti who was befriended by the art critic John Ruskin. The same Ruskin whose wife Effie left him for his protégé, John Everett Millais. The same Millais, who, along with Rossetti and Edward Burne-Jones, did designs for William Morris's textile firm. The same William Morris whose wife, Jane, was the mistress of Rossetti and had posed for his painting *Mnemosyne*. The same Jane Morris whose husband had produced the wallpaper that was hung behind all of the ineffably gorgeous paintings in these rooms. The same William and Jane Morris who had been given the prototype for *The Prioress's Tale* by Edward Burne-Jones. The same Burne-Jones who'd had a passionate, all-consuming love affair with the beautiful sculptress Maria Zambaco. The same Maria Zambaco whose cousin, Maria Spartali Stillman, had posed for Burne-Jones and Rossetti. The same Maria Spartali Stillman who was an artist herself and whose works were represented in these rooms.

The mind reeled.

This is incredible, Georgiana Weeks thought.

The energy and the originality and the unparalleled beauty of these paintings.

The talent.

The passions.

The sheer, inescapable *drama* of it all.

And the connections.

Always . . . the connections.

These Pre-Raphaelites, Georgiana Weeks said to herself. They are fascinating; they are glamorous, gorgeous, and sexy. They are larger than life. They are dream people.

I have to find out more about them.

I have to find out *everything* about them.

And that was how it all began.

12

"Joy?"

A man craned his head through the opened doorway to Joy Miller's office.

"Joy? Are you in there?"

"Cam?"

The top of a dark blonde head bobbed up and down behind a small photocopy machine. "There's a darn piece of paper stuck in . . . I got it!"

She stood up, waved a crumpled page triumphantly in her hand, folded it neatly, and then tossed it in the wastebasket.

The young man gently shut the door behind him.

At the soft *click* of the lock engaging, Wegman Zigfield's secretary looked up.

The man who had come into her office was wearing an aged nine-teenth-century cloak on top of a knee-length Victorian frock coat that was shiny at the elbows and frayed at the cuffs. Under his frock coat he wore a faded burgundy vest over a crisp white shirt. The collar of the shirt pointed up at its edges like genie slippers instead of lying flat over the long swath of fabric wrapped around his neck.

Part cravat, part scarf, Camden Kimcannon's necktie was a silken black band drawn twice around his collar, and then arranged into an elaborate bow.

The rest of Camden's wardrobe consisted of polyester slacks old enough to have carried his pocket change through high school, and shoes scuffed beyond shape or style, that denoted years of hard usage.

Camden pulled a battered woolen beret out of his pocket and began to twist it nervously between his hands. His hands were long, strong, and bony . . . hands that seemed formed specifically to hold a chisel or a paintbrush. They were both masculine and beautiful at the same time.

Camden flipped his beret over tousled brown hair. Beneath a strand that hung dejectedly over his forehead, his brown eyes locked onto those of Joy Miller.

"His skin is as pale as a prisoner's or a poet's," Joy thought. "And he always looks as though he's going to burst into tears. Even when he's excitedly telling me about some new idea he's just had, or a poem, painting, or artist he has just discovered."

Joy thought that maybe it had something to do with Camden being too sensitive. She didn't quite know what she meant by sensitive, but felt that it had something to do with life making him wince.

"What's wrong, Cam? Is there something that you want me to do for you?"

Camden reached again for his beret, tore it off his head, and stuffed it back into his pocket.

"It's the Pre-Raphaelite exhibition," he said. He had a deep voice. In love with the hard-edged harmony of words.

"Oh, is that all?" Joy sat down. "Don't worry about *that*, Cam. The fire won't affect it."

"Fire! What fire?"

"Why don't you sit down."

"I can't sit down. I'm too nervous."

"You're always too nervous."

"What fire, Joy? Tell me quickly."

"In the Parlor Gallery. The Sarkin Zahedi exhibit."

"Sarkin Zahedi? That fraud? Someone set fire to his so-called paintings? Ha! Good riddance to bad rubbish."

He sat down and leaned toward Joy.

"I want to work on the Pre-Raphaelite exhibit, Joy. And I want it keenly. Desperately. Passionately."

Joy stared at him.

"I know. I know what you're going to say. That I don't have a degree in art history. That, technically, I'm not qualified to kiss the hems of the shirts of the artists who have paintings in the collection. I know, Joy. I *know*. And I know that Mr. Zigfield only allows volunteers to work in the gift shop, or to stuff envelopes for some gala function that I, personally, will never have enough money to attend. But what *you* don't know is that I *have* to work on this Pre-Raphaelite exhibition. I *have* to."

He rose to his feet. Feline. Energetic. Compelled by the impetus of his argument to stalk back and forth like a poet in a cage.

"I never told you before, Joy, but I know everything about them. About the Pre-Raphaelites. Rossetti, Millais, Burne-Jones. I live them. I sleep them. I read them. I study them. I breathe them. But you don't believe what I'm telling you, do you? I can tell that you don't. It's true, though. It's true."

"I believe you, Cam."

"Ask me something, then. Come on, Joy. Test me. I can answer any of your questions. There's nothing I don't know . . . well, that's not absolutely true. There are probably a million things I don't know. But of their essence. Of the brotherhood itself—the Pre-Raphaelite brotherhood—there's nothing that I don't know because my soul, down to its very toes, knows everything about them. Everything!"

"Cam . . . " Joy began.

But he hurried on.

"What do you want to know about the Pre-Raphaelite brotherhood? Come on. Ask me. Don't be shy."

"Cam, I'm a secretary. All I know about art is what I pick up here at the museum. After the exhibition is installed, I might be able to . . . "

"No excuses, Joy. You don't need a masters degree in art history to know that grass is green, that lips are red, that skies are blue, and that Dante Gabriel Rossetti was a genius.

"One," Camden Kimcannon enumerated, as though at the beginning of a lecture. "The purpose of the Pre-Raphaelite brotherhood is to have genuine ideas to express. Genuine ideas, Joy. Not derived ideas. Not ideas imitated or copied from the sketch books of past masters. But original ideas. New ideas. Real ideas. That is the number one purpose of the Pre-Raphaelite brotherhood.

"The second is to study nature in order to accurately recreate it. Which means that if you are going to *paint* a tree, you don't look at someone else's painting of a tree, or at a photograph of a tree, or at a sketch of a tree, but at the bark, roots, branches, leaves . . . at the tree itself. Simple. Isn't it? But brilliant. Brilliant.

"The third purpose of the brotherhood is to sympathize with what is heartfelt in previous art, excluding, however, the conventional, the self-parading, and all of the art that has been learned by rote. Accentuate the positive from the past masters. Eradicate the negative.

"And lastly . . . " Camden dropped his hands to the edge of Joy's desk, and leaned forward on them until his face was within inches of hers. ". . . lastly, Joy, and most indispensable of all, the brotherhood held as its highest purpose *to produce thoroughly good pictures.*"

Camden spun around and exclaimed, "Good pictures, by Jove! That's what it's all about, isn't it? And that's what those Pre-Raphaelites did. They produced jolly good pictures."

Then he flopped bonelessly back into the chair and asked eagerly, "So, what do you say? Do you think that she'll take me?"

Joy stared at Camden, uncomprehending. "What are you talking about, Cam? And who is *she?*"

"She's Georgiana Weeks. *Our* Dr. Weeks. The guest curator for the Pre-Raphaelite exhibition. If you introduce me to her, then you'll be able to tell her about me. Tell her how helpful I can be to her . . . how intelligent I am . . . how reliable . . . how fabulously talented. Tell her that I'm devoted to art, and . . . Oh, this all makes me so nervous. Do you think I could ask Jiri to put in a good word? I've done the layouts of a few brochures and a lot of posters for him. Or should I get a letter of recommendation from Mr. Zigfield? Would he give me one? I think he would. He likes me. Or . . . I thinks he likes me. Anyway, he knows my name, so that ought to count for something. And I could . . . "

The telephone rang.

Joy looked at Camden Kimcannon. She said, "Make yourself a cup of tea, Cam. Right now. And calm down."

She waited until Camden was on the far side of the room, and picked up the receiver.

"Joy. This is Georgiana Weeks. Part one of this call is to thank you for setting me up in this beautiful office. Part two is to ask you how you want me to lock up when I leave. Jiri explained about key control for the rest of the museum, but . . . "

Joy looked across the room at Camden Kimcannon. His back was toward her as he poured boiling water over a tea bag.

She raised her voice loud enough for him to hear. "*I* have the key to your office, Georgiana."

Cam lifted his head.

"And I also have a young man here right now who does volunteer work at the museum. His name is Camden Kimcannon, and there are a few things about the Pre-Raphaelite exhibition that he would like to discuss with you. If it would be convenient, I can send him over with the key right now."

13

When Georgiana Weeks heard a sharp rap against her open office door, she expected her visitor to be the museum volunteer with her key.

Instead, Jiri Hozda was leaning far too casually against the door frame with his arms folded across his chest. He was wearing a black dress shirt open at the collar with rolled up shirt sleeves that exposed silver hairs on thick, well-muscled forearms. His gray wool slacks were cuffed, and on his feet were black socks and black soft leather slip-on shoes that looked both expensive and European.

Georgiana looked down at his shoes and then up into his eyes.

"My mama told me never to take candy from a man who dresses too carefully, and never to trust a man who wears loafers."

Jiri raised his right eyebrow.

Georgiana nodded. "I see your point, but nobody ever accused Mama of being rational. And anyway, my mama had her reasons."

"Indeed." Jiri uncrossed his arms.

"You see, Mama figured that a man who didn't have the wherewithal to tie a pair of shoelaces wouldn't be much good when it came time to tie the knot. You know. Wife. Children."

"I am familiar with the idiom 'tie the knot.'" Jiri strode into the room. "I take it, then, that your father wore sturdy workboots with rawhide shoelaces."

"Nope. Daddy liked to wear sandals."

Jiri's left eyebrow curled up like a question mark.

"Mama," Georgiana said, "liked to take chances. Sit down and visit for a while, Jiri."

"Alas, Georgiana, although my soul cries out to obey, my conscience forbids. Fires in museums do not provide one with the leisure for casual conversation. Therefore, to overcome what I perceive as a distinct obstacle to the development of what will no doubt be a romance, a friendship, or at the very least a large scale flirtation, I come, instead, to ask if you will join me tonight for dinner."

"Impossible."

"Previous engagement?"

"Nope. I'm pooped."

"Tomorrow night?"

"Depends. Are you working tomorrow, Jiri?"

"Like a galley slave."

"Me, too. Why don't we see what condition we're both in at the end of the day, and if we're still conscious and more or less upright, we can grab a bite to eat."

"Excellent."

"What are you doing now, Jiri? I mean, about the fire?"

"Returning telephone calls to lawyers and insurance adjusters. Arranging for a messenger to take the frames from Zahedi's exhibition to the office of our esteemed fire investigator. Calling Mikos Piatigorsky to find out when he'll be back to work. Contacting the . . . "

"Who's Mikos Piatigorsky? The name is familiar."

"He is . . . "

Someone made a distinct *ahem* sound in the hallway. Jiri turned.

Georgiana Weeks stood up, and stared at the man who had suddenly appeared in her doorway. He was anachronistically dressed like a nineteenth-century artist or poet. She shook her head as though to clear it of a hallucination, and then slowly lowered herself back into her seat.

"One moment, my friend," Jiri said cheerfully to Camden, and he returned his attention to Georgiana.

"Mikos Piatigorsky is our preparator. This afternoon I received a message that he has injured his right hand in a household accident, and he is unsure when he will again have its full range of motion. Since Mikos must install your exhibition, I must determine when he will be back. And if, once back, he will need any assistance from . . . "

"Ahem," Camden Kimcannon said again. Louder.

Jiri turned to him. "Come in. Come in, my friend. As you are usually the soul of courtesy, something that you clearly perceive as urgent must be compelling you to scatter the sum and substance of my conversation to the four winds."

Camden nodded curtly. He marched up to Georgiana's desk and flung back his cape.

"My name is Camelot Kimcannon," he proclaimed.

Then, in the deep, oratorical tone he had perfected in front of his bathroom mirror, he said:

" 'I mean by a picture, a beautiful, romantic dream of something that never was, never will be, in a light better than any light that ever shone, in a land no one can define or remember—only desire.' "

Camden Kimcannon stopped speaking and stood with his eyes locked desperately onto those of Georgiana Weeks.

Georgiana, as though mesmerized by the force of each word, had again slowly risen to her feet.

Jiri Hozda stared at Georgiana. She, in turn, was staring at Camden Kimcannon.

"What did you say your name was?"

"Camelot. Camelot Kimcannon."

"Aren't you the fellow Joy Miller said she was sending over with my key?"

"Yes. I am he."

"Where's the key?"

"I forgot it."

"I'm sure that Joy Miller told me your name was Camden, as in New Jersey. Not Camelot, as in mythical kingdom."

"My name is Camelot."

"Joy thinks it's Camden."

"It used to be Camden. I changed it to Camelot."

"When?"

"On my way over here."

"Why?"

"Because I prefer myth to reality."

"What do you know about the passage you just recited?"

"I know that it came from a letter written by Edward Burne-Jones to a friend."

"Did you also know that I had planned on using exactly that quotation as the running theme of my exhibition?"

Camden lowered his head and shook it, almost guiltily.

"No," he whispered.

"Where did you read the Burne-Jones letter?"

"I have books."

"What kind of books?"

"All kinds of books."

"Name some."

"*Pre-Raphaelites and the Pre-Raphaelite Brotherhood* by William Holeman Hunt; *Recollections of Dante Gabriel Rossetti and his Circle* by Henry Treffy Dunn; *The Pre-Raphaelite Tragedy* by William Gaunt; *Memorial of Edward Burne-Jones* by Mrs. Burne-Jones; *Design and* . . . "

"Why do you know so much about the Pre-Raphaelites?"

"Because . . . "

"You're a volunteer here, aren't you?"

"Yes."

"Do you work? I mean, do you have a real job? One that people pay you money to do?"

"I did. I mean, I'm in the process of looking for. . . . Well, I'm an artist."

Georgiana smiled. "Why did I somehow suspect that? And I know I'm going to regret asking you this, but what kind of artwork do you do, Camden?"

"Camelot. My name is Camelot."

"What do you paint?"

Camden unconsciously rearranged his body so that his shoulders were thrust back, his chin was thrust up, and his chest was thrust out.

"I paint," he said, "in a style that has been said to be reminiscent of that of the Pre-Raphaelite brotherhood."

"Why am I not surprised?" Georgiana muttered, and almost succeeded in suppressing a smile as her eyes met those of Jiri Hozda. Then she snapped at Camden Kimcannon, "Pop quiz. Name the seven men who formed the Pre-Raphaelite brotherhood, and tell me what each one of them did."

"Dante Gabriel Rossetti," Camden snapped back, "painter and poet; William Holeman Hunt, painter; John Everett Millais, painter; William Michael Rossetti, art critic and essayist; Thomas Woolner, sculptor; Frederick George Stephens, art critic; and James Collinson, painter."

"When was the brotherhood formed?"

"1848."

"When did it end?"

"1853."

"What ended the Pre-Raphaelite brotherhood?"

"John Everett Millais's election to the Royal Academy."

"Why did that end it?"

"Because the others considered it an abandonment of the Pre-Raphaelite ideal."

"What did Rossetti think?"

"In a letter he wrote to his sister, Christina Rossetti. She was a poet, and . . ."

"I know what she was. Go on."

"In his letter to Christina, Rossetti quoted a line from Tennyson's *Morte d'Arthur*. He wrote, 'So now the whole Round Table is dissolved.' "

Georgiana dropped down into her chair. She picked up a pencil, and began to tap the eraser tip against the top of her desk.

"Jiri," she said slowly. "I'm considerably under budget on this exhibition. But I'm also behind schedule on a lot of little things. And we have the added dilemma of the delays that are sure to result from Mikos's injury. And then, of course, there's the fire, which will inevitably infringe on the time you and Joy have to assist me. So, what do you think of my bringing this walking encyclopedia of Pre-Raphaelite lore and letters into the museum as my paid personal assistant for the next few weeks?"

Jiri's dark eyes twinkled. He gave Camden Kimcannon a comradely slap on the back.

"I think that would be a impeccable idea!"

Georgiana turned to Camden.

"Are you clumsy?"

"No."

"Can you use a hammer without hitting your own or anyone else's thumb?"

"Yes."

"Would you consider it beneath you to run errands, make photocopies, collate, fold, put stamps on envelopes?"

"No."

"Are you too liberated to get me a cup of coffee?"

"Dr. Weeks, I'll plant the coffee bean myself and *grow* you a cup of coffee if that's what you want."

"All right then. What do you say? Do you want the job?"

Like a character in a cartoon, Camden's mouth fell open.

"Oh. And by the way, you know that letter you quoted? '. . . In a light better than any lights that ever shone—in a land no one can define or remember, only desire—.' The Burne-Jones letter. Do you know how the quotation ends?"

"I thought that *that* was how it ended."

"No, Camden. The last line of the quote is '. . . and then I wake up.' "

14

A curious combination of circumstances drove attorney Miranda Yee into the ladies' room with her cigarette that Friday. It began with her longtime and much dreaded secretary, Irma, being out with the flu. As Irma's tyrannical disposition was only exceeded by her impeccable attendance record, Miranda had not, since the hour she'd hired Irma, spent a single day in her own office *without* her secretary's irritating presence, until this recent outbreak of the flu.

"It's wonderful," Miranda said to Wylie Nolan, who occupied the office next door. "Like what it must be like *not* to have a migraine headache all the time."

Miranda could have temporarily operated her law office without the assistance of Irma the shrew (as Wylie called her), by using her part-time clerk/typist, a student named Clarence Chang, to type contracts, address envelopes, retrieve files, and make photocopies, and by just responding to her clients' alleged emergencies on a crisis-by-crisis basis. But Miranda had already promised Clarence that he could take off Wednesday, Thursday, and Friday to study for his Law School Admission Tests.

Which left Miranda Yee alone in her office with Miss Viola True.

That Miss True spoke no Chinese went without saying, the employment counsellor at Tribecca Personnel ("Temporary Workers for All Your Office Needs") explained apologetically.

"Oh, Miss Yee, we *had* the most marvelous woman for you—Sylvia Freshman . . . Friesgood . . . Froshmier, yes. That's what it was. And she spoke *fluent*, positively fluent Mandarin Chinese. And English, of course. Daughter of a missionary, I was given to understand. But, I fear that just this morning, the Dime Savings Bank gobbled her up. Ecstatic . . . positively ecstatic to land such a treasure. I *can* send over for you, however . . . "

Which is how she ended up with Miss Viola True.

Miranda sat in her office and looked through the open door into the main room of her suite. There were two secretarial desks, an all-purpose table, file cabinets, a photocopier, two typewriters, and three computer stations.

She stared, in wonder, at Miss Viola True.

It wasn't that Miranda Yee actually disliked the woman. Disliking Miss True would be a heresy akin to thinking unkind thoughts about a well-intentioned maiden aunt. In fact, Miranda liked Viola True. Even found her disarmingly pathetic in a more or less appealing way. And quaint. She was definitely quaint. Like an old-fashioned cast iron toaster that you pick up, scald your fingers on, drop on your foot, and then it breaks your toe.

She was even more or less intrigued by Miss True's dainty ways. Her mincing steps. Her delicate speech—as though she'd had to crochet each word before it could be released from the tip of her tongue.

No . . . Miranda liked Viola True well enough.

Miranda just wanted to kill her. That's all.

It started the first morning she had come to work. That would have been on Wednesday. Viola True wore a powder blue knit suit with a ruffled silk blouse. She was as thin as a ruler, and had the sweet face of a substitute teacher who can't imagine why any one of those dear children would have wanted to pour Elmer's glue into the toe of her galoshes.

Miss True's short brown hair was pinned behind her ears with two fake tortoiseshell combs. Her pink face looked freshly dusted with talc applied with a big powder puff. She appeared to be somewhere between forty and seventy years old, and when she spoke, her eyes blinked incessantly behind wire-rim eyeglasses.

The first thing she said to Miranda Yee after being shown around the office was, "I think I understand all of your requirements, dear. Shall we just roll up our sleeves and get down to work?"

By Miranda Yee's calculations, Viola True typed one hundred and fifty words per minute. What she did on the word processor defied calculation. Which wasn't the problem. The problem was that between work spurts, when she was waiting for Miranda to give her the next letter or contract or will or envelope to type, Miss True . . .

Well, she . . .

Actually, what she did was . . . fuss.

And it drove Miranda crazy.

Because Miranda Yee was, above all things, *not* a fusser. In fact, she was the antithesis of a fusser.

She was a thirty-three-year-old attorney, meticulous about her work and comfortably laissez-faire about everything else. Her parents had been born in Denver, Colorado. Her grandparents had come from a bleak hamlet in China, in which neither Miranda nor her parents nor her parents' parents had ever taken any interest, historical, ancestral, or otherwise. During the Depression, her mother had left her father a "Dear John" note on the mantelpiece, and her father had moved with his six children to Chinatown in New York City, where he'd gotten a job as an accountant.

The Yee family eked through.

Miranda got her law degree at City College, tried working for a major corporate law firm in midtown, didn't like the regimentation, and so came back to Chinatown to develop her own clientele.

She did mostly real estate law and wills; occasionally, she drew up the papers for a partnership or a corporation; and more often than she liked, she did landlord/tenant and divorce work.

Miranda had big, dark brown eyes and brown hair that was so thick and glossy, it triumphed over its blunt cut and total lack of style. She was five feet, four inches tall, didn't know she had a perfect shape, but suspected, having heard it often enough, that she had great legs.

She hadn't bought a new dress in about five years, because it just hadn't occurred to her, and she wore A-line skirts with white blouses, like someone caught in a Catholic girls school time warp.

She was pretty.

Not gorgeous. Not beautiful. But pretty.

For leisure, Miranda liked to drop in on unconventional churches, listen to bizarre sermons testifying to the end of the world, and contemplate humanity's fate. On Sunday mornings, she watched political commentary discussions on television.

And other than a curious propensity to cut her steak into small, almost perfectly symmetrical cubes before eating it, she had only one compulsion.

On days when she was not expected in court, every morning at 10:30, and then every afternoon at 1:30 and again at 3:30 and once more at 4:45, she liked to stop everything, have a cup of coffee at her desk, and smoke a cigarette.

It was a ritual.

It was a habit.

If others thought that it was an addiction, that was their problem. As far as Miranda was concerned, it was a gift of pleasure that she gave to herself.

Four cigarettes a day.

No more. No less.

If Wylie Nolan were in his office, she would occasionally pop in next door to enjoy her slim, paperwrapped cylinder of nicotine, while he enjoyed his pipeful, and they swapped stories about the fires, lawsuits, and real estate closings of the day.

If Wylie wasn't around, she did not smoke in the main room of her suite, where all of the computers and typewriters were. She smoked in her own office, in her own chair, behind that great carved wood monstrosity with the miniature gargoyle drawer "pulls" that her father had given her before he retired to Florida.

Which is how the problem started with Miss Viola True.

And her fussing.

That interminable *fussing*.

Every time Miranda Yee tapped a cigarette out of its box (she only smoked Parliament in a box), raised it to her lips, struck a match, and inhaled, Viola True would get up from wherever she was working, and without going into Miranda's office, making eye contact, or in any way suggesting that the cigarette was a catalyst to her actions, begin to spray room deodorant from a fair-sized atomizer that she carried around in her purse.

Then, as both Miranda's cigarette and her pleasure in it diminished, Miss True would whip out an all-purpose spray cleaner and dust cloth (from who knew where?) and continue to dust the keys, screens, and casings of the computers, as well as the glass surface of the photocopier, and . . .

Fuss. Fuss. Fuss.

It started and ended with the time it took for Miranda to light, smoke, and extinguish her cigarette.

Miss Viola True never said anything to Miranda about her smoking.

And Miranda never said anything to Viola True about her fussing.

It just drove Miranda crazy. That's all.

Miranda Yee was not of the school of employers who sat down and had quiet but forceful talks with her employees about their irritating habits.

Although assertive enough as a lawyer, Miranda viewed the emotional vicissitudes of her staff with utter abhorrence. And she would no more have told Irma to mind her mouth and her manners than she would have asked Clarence to use a mouthwash before he came into work. Although both needed to do both.

And so, when Miss True atomized, sprayed, and deodorized all of the pleasure out of Miranda's nicotine breaks, Miranda had to find somewhere else to smoke her cigarette.

If Wylie had been in his office she could have smoked her cigarette there.

If it had been spring, summer, or autumn, she could have smoked it out on the fire escape.

But he wasn't and it wasn't. So as of the Wednesday when Irma called in sick, Clarence stayed out to study, and Miss Viola True came in to fuss, Miranda Yee began to bring a book of matches and one Parliament filter-tip cigarette with her into the ladies' room.

One in the morning.

Three in the afternoon.

Her altered ritual started with the walk down the hall to the ladies' room; she would open the window about two inches to release the oppressive steam heat, lean against the windowsill over the radiator, look out the window, and try to make the best of a bad situation.

Miranda's approach was philosophical.

Clarence would be back on Monday, she reminded herself, and putting up with two days of incessant fussing did not a lifetime make.

At 10:15 on Friday morning, Miranda pushed open the door to the ladies' room for her first smoke of the day. First, she took the cigarette out from where she'd tucked it, like a pencil, behind her ear; Next, she removed the matchbook from her shirt pocket.

And then Miranda Yee struck a match.

15

The fire alarm began to scream at 1:40 P.M. on Friday afternoon.

At exactly that moment, Wylie Nolan was investigating the fire on the premises of the Zigfield Art Museum, and Miranda Yee was in her office, drafting a new will. The will was for Mrs. Lorretta T. Bunch, who worked behind the counter at the newsstand in the lobby of Miranda's building. Mrs. Bunch was currently in the process of divorcing Mr. Arlo J. Bunch, who had formerly worked *with* her at the newsstand, but who, as of last week, had taken up housekeeping with the blonde with the mole over her right eyebrow who worked as a cashier in the delicatessen next door.

Mrs. Bunch's will was not a complicated affair.

Even Mr. Bunch's *affair* was not a complicated affair.

Nevertheless, Miranda was annoyed.

The management of The Lispenard Building, in an effort to comply with all fire regulations even *before* (or so Miranda suspected) they had been enacted, ran periodic fire drills. There had been two fire drills last month. There was one last week. And . . .

Miranda tossed her pencil down on her desk.

"Miss True," she called out. "Don't worry. It's not a real fire. It's just another damn fire drill."

Miss Viola True, by now, had grabbed her clutch purse and was peeking out the door into the hallway.

"Oh!" she exclaimed suddenly, and then quickly slammed the door.

"What's wrong?" Miranda demanded.

"Firemen."

"What?"

"Firemen. And hoses."

"You're kidding!"

"Oh, no, Miss Yee. I'm quite serious. There are three quite large firemen out there, and one of them is pulling a hose out of the stairwell as I speak."

Miranda shooed her secretary away from the door and walked into the hall.

She went directly to the office next door.

WYLIE NOLAN
ARSON CONSULTING
FIRE ANALYSIS & PRIVATE INVESTIGATIONS

She rapped her knuckles against the door frame.

"Wylie?"

No answer.

She turned and approached one of the firemen.

"What's going on?"

"Fire in the women's bathroom."

"Is it serious?"

"Naw."

"Do we have to leave the building?"

The fireman shook his head. "Waste of time. Fire didn't go anywhere. Was out before we got here."

"What was the cause of . . . "

Another fireman hauling a flat canvas length of hose back toward the stairwell grumbled, "Out of the way, lady."

Miranda went back to her office. She told Viola True to finish her typing. Then she returned to her own desk to concentrate on the new will for the rather old (and tired) Mrs. Lorretta T. Bunch.

• • •

The second fire alarm went off that very same afternoon at approximately 3:45 p.m. This time, both Miranda Yee and Viola True left the office and walked down the six flights of stairs.

People had gathered in clusters in the lobby, and Miranda wandered from group to group, asking each if they knew what was going on, or if they'd heard any gossip.

She got no coherent answers until she saw Harold Pittman, the building manager from whom she had rented her suite of offices.

He rushed over to her. "Miranda. Thank God I found you!" He grabbed her arm. "Come with me." He hurried her through the lobby door into the delicatessen, past the blonde cashier with the mole over her right eyebrow, and to the first empty table in the back.

"Sit," he said. Then he snapped to the waitress. "Sonia, sweetheart, get us two coffees." To Miranda. "Is coffee all right with you? Because if it isn't, we can always have soda. Do you like soda? Maybe diet soda? But with a figure like that, who needs to diet? Tea, then. Maybe you'd rather have . . . "

"Coffee's fine, Harry. What's going on?"

To Sonia. "Two coffees. A cheese Danish for me." To Miranda. "You?" To the waitress. "She doesn't want one." To Miranda. "Going on? You mean you don't know?"

Miranda reached for a pickle. The deli always had a plate of pickles and pickled tomatoes on each table.

"All I know, Harry, is that we've had two fire drills in . . . "

"Not drills, Miranda. Alarms. Fire alarms."

"All right. Then we've had two fire alarms within the last two hours."

"One hour and five minutes. But who's counting? You like those pickles, Miranda?"

She bit off an end. Chewed. Thought. And answered, "They're OK."

"Not me. I like the sweet ones with the serrated edges. How about the pickled tomatoes? Do you like them?"

"Harry."

"Okay. Okay."

The coffee and cheese Danish arrived.

"Thank you, Sonia sweetheart." To Miranda. "Where was I?"

85

Miranda shrugged. "I was standing in the lobby trying to figure out why, every time I got to the line 'to my cousin Evangeline, I leave' the fire alarm went off, when you dragged me in here."

"Oh. Right. It's about this." Harry Pittman pulled a sheet of folded white paper from the inside pocket of his jacket.

Harry was thin and fortyish. He had cinnamon-colored hair, surrounding a freckled bald pate; and he always wore V-neck sweaters under a sports jacket.

As a landlord, both Miranda Yee and Wylie Nolan rated Harry Pittman a ten on a ten scale. He had the same perspective on some of his tenants. If he liked them, there was very little he wouldn't do to keep them.

"You want your office painted sunshine yellow? You're a good tenant. No problem."

"You want to go month-to-month on your lease until business picks up? Hey. You've been with me for a long time already, and you're a good tenant. No problem."

"No problem."

"No problem."

Harry Pittman's aim, if he liked you, was to please.

And he liked Miranda Yee.

Miranda had come to The Lispenard Building six years ago. Her first lease had been for a tiny, two-hundred-square-foot office on the third floor, which she occupied alone, with an artificial ficus tree. Two years later, she moved into a three-hundred-square-foot office on the fifth floor, with a part-time secretary and without the ficus tree; and for the past two years, she had occupied the nine-hundred-square-foot corner suite on the seventh floor with both a secretary and a clerk/typist.

In two months, her lease would be coming up for renewal, and there was never any doubt in Miranda's mind that the man sitting opposite her wanted her to sign another one.

The sheet of white paper that Harry Pittman held out to Miranda had small pieces of newsprint cut and pasted onto it, like a madman's fantasy of a ransom note. Each piece of newsprint contained one word, and combinations of words had been arranged on five separate lines centered on the page.

Miranda looked down at the sheet and then up at Harry. She said, "You've got to be kidding."

She took the paper out of his hand.

Harry said, "It was slipped under my door after the second fire alarm went off this afternoon."

Miranda read aloud:

MIRANDA YEE
NICOTINE FIEND
SETS FIRES
STOP HER
OR WE ALL DIE!!!

Harry whispered harshly, "*Shush*, Miranda. Not so loud." He took back the anonymous letter, refolded it, and returned it to the pocket of his sports jacket.

"I don't get it," Miranda said.

"That's because you aren't a landlord. Would you like another cup of coffee, Miranda? A bowl of soup? A bagel? A chopped liver sandwich?"

"No. No. No. And no. What's being a landlord got to do with it?"

"Landlords, Miranda, are students of human nature."

Miranda thought about that for a few seconds. She thought about her interest in obscure religions, her interest in all manner of political discussion, debate, interview, and commentary. Then she said, somberly, "I'm a student of human nature, too, Harry."

Harry reached for a pickle. "You say these really aren't bad?" He bit. He swallowed. He said, "It's different."

"The pickle?"

"No. Human nature. What you see . . . what you study . . . is mankind. Not at its best, maybe, but at least trying to unscramble the egg. What I see . . . what the landlord sees is . . . *ugh*. Don't ask."

"Harry, that letter you showed me makes me nervous. And I don't like that whoever wrote it mentions me by name. It scares me."

"So, you think it doesn't scare me?"

Miranda patted Harry's hand. It, too, had cinnamon-colored hair and freckles. "No. I don't think that, Harry. I know you love this building. But what are we going to do about it? Did you show the note to the police?"

"And get you in trouble because some lunatic sent me a note?" Harry shook his head. "I haven't shown it to anyone . . . yet."

"Yet?"

"That's where you come in, Miranda."

"What do you mean, where *I* come in. I'm already in farther than I want to be."

"Me, too. You think I want any of this hokey smokey going on? You think I want my building to burn down? Shush. Lean forward. Listen. I got a plan."

"You've got a *plan*? A plan as in what? What can we do? You're a landlord, Harry. I'm a lawyer. That doesn't exactly constitute a paramilitary organization."

"No. But we have a secret weapon."

"What?"

"Not what. Who. Wylie Nolan. You're friends with him, aren't you?"

"We're good friends."

"And he's an arson investigator, right?"

"That's right, Harry."

"Let me summarize the situation so far. What we got here is some loony tune setting fires in the women's bathroom on the seventh floor."

"Were *both* fires set in the ladies' room?"

"Absolutely. And said aforementioned loony tune also writes me a letter from Psycho Ward B saying that the person who is guilty of setting these fires is none other than one Miranda Yee. You. And—No, don't interrupt me yet. I still have to bring up two additional points. One, that *your* office is on the seventh floor, where both of the fires were set. And two, that Wylie Nolan's office is also on the seventh floor." Harry Pittman winked. "Get it, Miranda?"

Miranda shook her head. "I'm afraid not, Harry."

"*Sheesh!*" Harry said, disgusted. "For a smart lady lawyer, sometimes you act like you forgot to grease your own skids."

Miranda stared for a moment at the landlord. Then her eyes lighted up, and she said, "Oh. *Now* I get it. You want *me* to tell *Wylie* about the fires . . ."

"And the note. Don't forget the note. I'll make a few extra copies for my insurance company and for the cops, if necessary. Which I hope it won't be. And I'll give you the original."

". . . and you want me to get *Wylie* to figure out who set the fires and what's going on. Is that it?"

Harry reached for another pickle. He chewed delicately. "To wash down the taste of a cheese Danish," he said as though imparting a new philosophic dictum, "a dill pickle really isn't all that bad."

16

Wylie Nolan parked his car at a broken meter on Church Street, threw his camera bag over his shoulder, and hauled two shopping bags out of the trunk. He walked one block to Lispenard Street, turned right, and saw Max Bramble getting out of a taxi at the intersection of Lispenard and Broadway.

Wylie positioned his tongue against the roof of his mouth and blew an ear-piercing whistle.

Max yanked his briefcase out of the cab, walked half a block to The Lispenard Building, and held the door open for Wylie.

"Nice luggage," he said, pointing to the shopping bags.

Wylie put them down, grinned, and strode to the freight elevator at the back of the lobby; he pressed a black button and a bell began to reverberate loudly.

"We have to wake Abraham up," Wylie explained.

"Well, that would wake the dead."

"Abraham might *be* dead."

Max pointed to the shopping bags. "Homework?"

"Personnel files. Exhibition files. Alarm system files. Insurance files."

"Insurance files," Max slapped his forehead. "I almost forgot. Sarah got a call this afternoon from . . ."

A loud, metallic clatter of ascending gears obliterated the rest of Max's sentence.

"Good God! What are they trying to do? Raise the *Titanic*?"

Wylie sauntered back toward Max, picked up his shopping bags, and began to walk slowly toward the freight elevator again.

"That reminds me," Wylie said. "I once knew a fireman who had a plan to raise the *Titanic*."

"Sure, Wylie. Everybody knows someone who has a plan to raise the *Titanic*. I've got one myself. I'm going to get to it as soon as I come up with a practical design for the start button on my perpetual motion machine."

The freight elevator clanged louder.

"The guy's name was Chapple. Xavier Chapple. He was a quiet guy. A good fireman. His wife was a tiny little thing with doll hands and strange eyes. She was an albino. His kids were all dark, like him. He used to read all the time. *Scientific American, Popular Science* magazine, *Popular Mechanics*. And he was always coming up with ideas. Double tongs so that you could really grab onto a log and move it around in the fireplace; traction blankets to put under your car wheels in case you got stuck in the snow. The guy's mind went on forever. But nothing ever got his attention like the *Titanic*."

The screaming gears of the elevator became more frenzied. Wylie didn't seem to notice.

"Xavier's idea for raising the *Titanic* is based on the scientific fact that Ping-Pong balls float."

Max took a step backward.

"Oh, no you don't, Wylie. I can see where this is going, so don't tell me. I don't want to know."

Wylie's smile became more ingratiating. "You see, what Xavier realized is that when you try to sink a Ping-Pong ball, it pops back up. And the harder you push it down, the higher up it pops. So, he figured that he could invent this giant tube. Something like a vacuum cleaner hose, but instead of it sucking *out* dirt, it would pump *in* Ping-Pong balls. Millions and millions of Ping-Pong balls. And given their natural buoyancy, Xavier figured there'd be enough 'float' there to raise the *Titanic*."

The noise from the freight elevator reached a frenzied crescendo and stopped. Then the two giant elevator doors slid silently open and revealed a gaunt black man hunched on a stool half a foot from the control panel. He was the oldest and tiredest man that Max had ever seen.

"Max," Wylie said. "This is Abraham. Abraham. Max."

The elevator operator ignored the introduction, and addressed his comments to the floor.

"Mr. Wylie."

"What, Abe?"

"At three-thirty this afternoon, you had a delivery."

"Good. I was expecting it."

Abraham didn't move. The elevator didn't move.

"Seventh floor, Abraham. That's where my office is. Remember? It's been there for the past two years."

Abraham slowly shook his head. It was like watching molasses swirl.

"I *know* where your office is, Mr. Nolan. You don't have to talk sarcastic to me. But you don't want to go there."

"I don't?"

"No, siree."

"Twenty questions, Abraham. *Why* don't I want to go to my office?"

"Because the picture frames as was delivered this afternoon ain't *up* there."

Wylie nodded. "Makes sense to me. The frames were too big to fit in my office, Abraham. Right?"

"Not too big. Too *dirty*. You didn't want them filthy things on your nice clean carpet."

"You're absolutely right. I didn't. And not that I couldn't find them myself if I tried, because after all I am a trained investigator, but, just for the record, where *did* I want them put?"

"Storage room," Abraham said. "Down in the basement."

"Good. Let's go there now."

Abraham raised his weary head. "See, I *told* you you didn't want to go to the seventh floor."

The freight elevator doors slid noiselessly shut. The gears engaged and the wild cacophony of metal on metal resumed.

Inch by inch, the elevator descended.

For over a minute, Abraham said nothing and Wylie said nothing. Then Max Bramble broke the silence.

"So, what happened to him?" he asked.

"What happened to who?"

"To the fireman. Xavier Chapple. The guy with the Ping-Pong balls."

"What do you mean?"

"I mean what happened to the idea he had of raising the *Titanic* with Ping-Pong balls?"

Wylie dropped his shopping bags to the floor of the elevator, pulled a pipe out of his coat pocket, and looked Max Bramble dead in the eye. Then with no hint of irony, he said, "Raise the *Titanic* with Ping-Pong balls? Max, that's just about the silliest thing I ever heard."

Wylie flicked on the wall switch in the storage room. Dim lights from fluorescent fixtures bathed everything in a pale amber glow, and objects became visible as though seen through a glass of weak tea.

"There they are." Max pointed to a stack of oversize picture frames.

They had been placed in the back of the room, at the end of an improvised aisle between two rows of old desks. Someone at the museum had wrapped the frames in a dirty plastic drop cloth before sending them over.

Wylie removed the Nikon from his camera bag and snapped on the flash attachment. He took a few photographs of the five frames just as they were, wrapped and stacked against the wall. Then he handed the camera to Max.

"Photodocument what I do," he said.

First, he took a complicated steel implement out of a side pocket of his bag. Wylie slipped his fingernail into one of the tool's minuscule compartments and pulled out a sharp, pointed scissors.

"So far," he said, "the chain of custody for the frames goes like this: Parlor Gallery at the Zigfield Art Museum to messenger service. Messenger service to Abraham at The Lispenard Building. Abraham to locked storage facility. When I get to the museum tomorrow, I'll find out from Joy Miller who wrapped the frames, and I'll have her get me copies of all the signed receipts for transporting them here."

Wylie poked a hole with the scissors into the plastic wrapping at the top right-hand corner of the first frame in the stack.

Max raised the camera to his eye and clicked. For a second, the flash emitted a blinding, bright, white light; then the room faded back to the color of weak tea.

Still using the small scissors, Wylie cut a triangular flap into the plastic on the right side of the frame. Then he drew out a short, stubby knife, and carefully wedged the blade between the top frame's wooden stretcher bar (over which the canvas had been pulled taut) and the frame itself (which had been mounted around the edges of the finished picture).

Again, Max clicked the camera, and again the room was illuminated with a blinding flash of light.

"What are you doing, Wylie?" Max asked.

"I'm prying . . . wait a second. I think . . . I think . . . " Wylie twisted the blade sideways.

"Got it!" he exclaimed.

The blade was perpendicular to both stretcher bar and frame, holding them apart like the crossbar on the letter H.

Wylie left the blade, and rummaged through his camera bag until he found a pair of tweezers.

He returned to the frames with the tweezers and began to gently . . . carefully . . . extract a long, thin strip of canvas from where it had been compressed between the stretcher bar and the exterior frame.

Max took another picture.

Wylie reached into his coat pocket with his free hand and pulled out a handkerchief. He shook it open, and using fingers and teeth, arranged the handkerchief like a tablecloth over that same hand.

Then, he let the long, thin strip of canvas he'd just removed fold itself onto the handkerchief like a dirty ribbon.

He tossed the tweezers back in his bag, held the murky mess of fabric a few feet away from Max, and said "Take a picture of this."

The room again flared into light.

Wylie extended the handkerchief to Max.

"Hold this."

He removed his blade from the frame, folded it, and shoved it in his pocket. He took his camera from Max, unscrewed the flash, and tucked both parts neatly away.

"We'll have to come back later with evidence bags and take the rest of the samples," Wylie said.

"Let's go," he said.

The two men locked the storage room and retraced their steps.

Max asked, "So, what was that all about?"

Wylie said, "Hold the stuff in the handkerchief up to your nose."

Max did.

"Now inhale."

Max inhaled deeply. Then he wretched away the handkerchief with a cringe of disgust.

"Jesus! What the hell *is* it?"

"I don't know yet," Wylie answered. "But that's exactly what I intend to find out."

17

It had taken Max and Wylie forty-five minutes to obtain fabric samples from the picture frames in the basement and return to the freight elevator for the trip to the seventh floor.

When the elevator doors opened, Miranda Yee was waiting for them with an expression on her face that mingled gratitude with fear.

"I'm so glad you finally got here," she said. "This place is so crazy, I didn't want to spend another minute alone."

Wylie walked off the elevator, stopped, and sniffed the air. He said suspiciously, "What happened?"

"It wasn't a big fire, Wylie. Just a couple of little, tiny ones. This afternoon. But . . . God, you've got a good nose."

Wylie tapped it. "My six-million-dollar hydrocarbon detector."

Max stepped around Wylie and patted Miranda's hand.

"Poor kid," he said.

Miranda turned to him. "Oh, Max."

He put his arm around her shoulder. "Take it easy, kiddo."

And the arson investigator and lawyer brought their shopping bags, briefcase, camera bag, evidence sample, and Miranda Yee into the sheltering confines of Wylie Nolan's office.

· · ·

It took Miranda ten minutes to finish her narrative. Wylie scribbled a last word onto his legal pad and then looked over his notes.

"So," Wylie said. "The way I understand the sequence of events is that two days ago, on Wednesday, Irma called in sick."

"Knowing her," Max said, "it was probably rabies."

Wylie frowned and continued. "Clarence Chang . . . "

"The future Clarence Darrow is how he sees himself," Miranda interjected.

Wylie laid down his notes. He directed a scornful look, first at Max and then at Miranda. He picked up his notes again and continued. "Clarence Chang stayed away from the office because he was studying for a law school entrance exam. And so, Miranda, finding yourself without any office help, you hired a temporary secretary whose name is Violet True."

"Not Violet, Wylie. Viola. Like the stringed instrument."

Wylie said, "What the hell is a viola?"

"It's bigger than a violin," Max answered. "And the sound is deeper."

"How do you know that?" Miranda asked.

"I . . . "

"Boys. Girls," Wylie interrupted. "Can we stick to the subject?"

"Sorry, Wylie."

"Sorry, Wylie."

"So by Wednesday afternoon, the temp agency had sent over Viola, not Violet, True. What time on Wednesday did she get to your office?"

"About one-thirty p.m. Maybe two."

"And that Wednesday, two days ago, did you bring your cigarettes to the ladies' room with you then?"

"No. Not until the next morning. On Thursday. At around twenty-five minutes after ten. I took out a cigarette, and Viola True took out her room deodorant spray. She looked at me. I looked at her. I said to myself, 'The hell with this. It isn't worth it,' and I skulked off to the ladies' room."

"You skulked?" Max observed. "Funny, you've never seemed to me like the skulking type."

"I'm not usually. But Miss Viola True . . . "

Wylie said, "Stop it. Will you two please just cut it out."

Max shrugged. "I'm hungry."

Miranda said, "Me, too."

Wylie looked back at his notes.

"So, Miranda, the first time you smoked a cigarette in the ladies' room was at ten-thirty on Thursday morning."

"Right."

"Tell me exactly where you were, what you did, and how you did it before, during and after you had that cigarette."

Miranda stood up, and unconsciously mimed the actions as she described what she'd done the previous morning.

"I took my box of cigarettes out of my desk drawer."

"Is that where you always keep them?"

"Yes."

"What about at night? Don't you put them in your purse when you go home?"

"No. I don't smoke at home."

"Okay. Go on."

"I took my matches—I always carry around a book of matches—out of my purse. And I put the matches and my keys into my skirt pocket."

"Are your office keys and the ladies' room key on the same key ring?"

"Yes. Along with my house keys. I put my cigarette behind my ear, and . . ."

"No," Max said, astonished. "You don't actually tuck cigarettes behind your ear?"

Miranda shrugged. "Sometimes, I do."

Max laughed. "That's so nineteen fifties. You're not old enough to . . ."

Wylie slammed his hand against his desk.

"Sorry, Wylie," Miranda said again.

Max said unapologetically, "It's because we're hungry. Hunger pains. Digestion. Digression. It's a downhill slide from here."

Wylie asked Miranda, "Then what?"

"Then I walked down the hall and went into the ladies' room."

"Was the door to the ladies' room locked?"

"Yes. It's always locked."

"Was anyone else in there?"

"I'm not sure."

"Then what?"

"Well, it's always too hot in the ladies' room, so I unlatched the window and raised it about two inches. Then I leaned against the windowsill, struck a match, and lit up."

"What did you do with the match?"

"I shook it out. I ran cold water over it under the faucet. And I threw it in the toilet."

"Are you always so careful with matches?"

"Yes. I'm paranoid about fire."

"How long did it take you to smoke the cigarette?"

"Four or five minutes."

"Then what?"

"Then I ran the cigarette stub under the faucet the way I'd done with the match, and I threw it in the toilet."

"Then?"

"Then I flushed the toilet."

"Did anyone come in during the time when you were smoking?"

"I don't know."

"How could you not know?"

"I was *trying* not to pay attention. I was *trying* to enjoy my cigarette."

"Okay. Forget that for now. What about the rest of Thursday?"

"Same thing, Wylie. At one-thirty. At three-thirty and at four-forty-five. Those are my smoking times. It's a ritual with me. I just shifted it from my desk to the ladies' room."

"And you did the same things with the cigarettes and the matches?"

"Exactly the same. Under the faucet. Down the toilet."

"Do you remember if during any of those cigarette breaks anyone came into the ladies' room before you lit up your cigarette? Or left the ladies' room after you had started to smoke?"

"No."

"How could you not notice anything? You're not deaf and blind, Miranda."

"I'm sorry, Wylie, but at the time, I didn't know someone was going to try and frame me for setting fires. If I'd known, I would have paid more attention."

Max said, "Wylie, let's finish this later. Miranda's tired. I'm hungry. And you're cranky."

"I'm not cranky," Wylie snapped. "One more question. This morning. Did you do everything the same way?"

"Yes. Exactly."

"Did you see anyone in the hall on your way to the bathroom?"

"No. And that's two questions."

"What about the fires? What kind of damage did they do?"

Miranda frowned. "Not much, I guess. The ladies' room doesn't look any different than usual. I really don't know anything specific about the fires. But Harry does."

"Who's Harry?" Max asked.

"Harry Pittman. Our landlord. And . . . Oh," Miranda took a folded sheet of paper out of her skirt pocket. "I almost forgot to give you this. It's the anonymous note that someone pushed under Harry's door. He told me to give you the original."

Miranda unfolded it and laid it in front of Wylie on his desk.

Max looked at Miranda. She had tilted her head to one side like a cocker spaniel expecting a pat on the head or a bone.

He resisted the urge to give her either and walked around the desk instead.

First he read the note. Then he looked at Wylie Nolan.

"Not funny," Max said somberly.

Wylie frowned. His dark blue eyes grew serious and he said, "No, Max. Not funny at all."

18

After eliciting a promise from Wylie that he would look into the fires on the seventh floor, Miranda Yee left. Then Wylie and Max ordered in sandwiches, and turned their attention to the fires at the Zigfield Art Museum. They divided the material Wylie had collected into two categories.

The first was the "Read It As Soon As Possible" pile. This contained all of Joy Miller's folders, the museum schematics, the printouts of activity on the keypads, the alarm systems, and the climate-control systems.

The second was the "Read It If All Else Fails and You Can't Solve the Case" pile. This consisted of the installation manuals for the keypads, for the alarm systems and for the climate-control systems, as well as the architectural blueprints of the museum.

When they finished a preliminary look-through of both piles, Wylie stood up and announced that he was going home.

They rode down in the elevator together.

Max turned to his left outside the building.

"Where are you going?" Wylie asked.

"It's easier to get a cab on Broadway."

"What do you want a cab for?"

"To get to my car. It's parked . . . "

"Come with me," Wylie said.

Max trailed after Wylie in a direction opposite to the one in which he wanted to go.

"Why am I following you?"

"It's my habit of command."

"Where are we going?"

"To my car. I'll drive you to yours."

For a few minutes the two men said nothing. Then Wylie asked, "Are you going to the museum tomorrow?"

"Not if I can help it. Why? Do you need me?"

"No." Wylie shook his head. "Just thinking out loud. I have to visit Sarkin Zahedi's studio sometime next week. I want to look around. Ask a few embarrassing questions. Find out more about him than he'll want to tell me. But I'm not sure how to go about doing it. That's the problem with not carrying a badge anymore. Nobody *has* to talk to you."

"Maybe nobody *else* has to talk to you," Max said. "But Sarkin Zahedi *does*. At least he'd better, if he wants to collect on his insurance."

"What are you talking about?"

"I started to tell you earlier that Sarah got a call from . . . "

"Sarah? As in your paraplegic?"

Max gave Wylie a frustrated glance.

"Paralegal, Wylie. Paralegal. Anyway, Sarah got this call from the Michelangelo Fine Arts Insurance Group, and the good news is that they insure all of the Zigfield Art Museum's exhibitions."

"Why is that good news?"

"Because they are also the insurer of Sarkin Zahedi's privately owned, by him, paintings, by which I mean, including the paintings that were burned up in the fire at the museum. Where's this ephemeral car of yours, Wylie?"

"Another block."

"Short block? Long block?"

"Long block. What good is any of this to me?"

"It's your entrée. Because if Sarkin Zahedi wants to collect on his insurance claim, he not only has to talk to his insurance company's fire investigator, he also has to show said fire investigator around his art studio, if said fire investigator wants to go there."

"Go on."

"If, however, Mr. Zahedi refuses to cooperate with his insurance company's fire investigator, then that fire investigator just might become suspicious—we don't know of what yet, but we could come up with something—and subsequently advise the insurance company to deny the claim. Now do you get it?"

"Keep pushing the edge of the envelope, Max. A breakthrough is imminent. This is my car."

Wylie unlocked the door and the two men slid into the front seat. Wylie turned on the ignition.

"So," Max continued. "Since the Michelangelo Fine Arts Insurance Group insures both the Museum *and* Sarkin Zahedi, and since both claims are for the same items, both claims went to the same office and are being processed by the same claims representative. Michelangelo had already hired you to investigate the Zigfield Art Museum fire by the time Sarkin Zahedi called in *his* claim later on this morning. And Sarkin's claims rep, who is also *our* claims rep, wants you to investigate both claims, because then Michelangelo will be able to split your fee between the two files. Get it, Wylie?"

Wylie grinned. "Sure. It's like when two cars crash into each other, and they're both insured by the same company."

He pulled into traffic.

". . . and what this all amounts to," Max took up the thought, "is that Sarkin Zahedi *has* to talk to you, because if he won't, his own insurance company doesn't have to pay his claim."

"Which is, by the way, for how much?"

"Would you believe five million dollars?"

"Five million dollars! That's a million dollars a painting. What'd he do? Paint with yolk from the goose that laid the golden egg?"

"Haven't you seen any of the photographs of Sarkin Zahedi's paintings yet?"

"No. Why? Are they that good?"

"Look at the photographs, Wylie. Then *you* tell *me* how good they are."

19

Although there had been many exhibitions featuring Pre-Raphaelite paintings since the mid-1800s, Georgiana Weeks believed that there had never before been one that focused so completely on the connections among the artists and how they were inextricably intertwined with one another's lives, loves, and creative output.

And since Wegman Zigfield was the perfect sponsor for her show (all early Pre-Raphaelite patrons had been successful, self-made businessmen like Wegman Zigfield), she wondered which elements of her exhibition had evolved out of her own commitment to the artists and their artwork, and which had been inspired solely because of the inconceivably elegant space in which the Pre-Raphaelite paintings would be hung.

The gallery in question was called The Sanctuary. Not the Sanctuary Room or the Sanctuary Gallery. Just The Sanctuary.

Before Our Lady of Perpetual Frowns was turned into a museum, this was where the worshipful had come to pray.

The ceiling was over thirty feet high. If Wegman Zigfield had wanted to, he could have doubled his gallery area by bisecting it and adding a second story.

Instead, he left the space pretty much as he had found it. He did, however, bring in restoration people to repair the stained glass windows; he removed all of the religious artifacts where possible, and donated them to the Brooklyn Museum; he replaced the insignia of faith wrought into the brass or stone work with secular designs that were consistent with the original architecture.

Fortunately for the interior designers, whose task it was to turn a church into an art gallery, The Sanctuary already possessed a significant amount of wall space. Twelve-foot-high walnut wainscoting, which began on either side of the entrance doors, extended the full thirty-six-foot width of the back wall. The wainscoting continued down the sixty-foot side aisles to where it stopped just before the altar. The altar was surrounded by exquisite, gleaming ornamental brass.

The theme of high polish and gleaming brass was repeated in the deep gloss of the cherry wood flooring and the elaborate brass grillework covering radiators and registers. Recessed lights hidden behind scrollwork cast a soft glow from the tops of supporting columns, and stained glass windows rose from three feet above the wainscoting to another fifteen feet where they ended at the molded brass ceiling.

These stained glass windows, colorful, beautiful, and extremely decorative, had been designed to be the jewels in the jewelry box that had begun its architectural life as Our Lady of Perpetual Frowns.

This, Wegman Zigfield, did not want.

What Wegman Zigfield wanted was for the *paintings* to be his jewels. He wanted the *paintings* to be stars of such magnitude that in contrast to them all else paled. He wanted the *paintings* to be the purpose, the focal point, and the main attraction at the Zigfield Art Museum.

How, he pondered, within the confines of a building designed to direct one's attention towards heaven, can I instead make a visitor want to look at paintings hung on a blank wall? And how can I do it without interfering with the architectural integrity of the structure itself?

Easily, answered the interior designer.

First, you add moveable walls. Then, you design portable light fixtures.

The practicality of this proposal was demonstrated to Wegman Zigfield with a compelling three-dimensional mock-up; then it was implemented in The Sanctuary itself.

Lush, portable panels were built in varying sizes that replicated the pattern and design of the molding and wainscoting on The Sanctuary's walls—panels that could be combined and arranged in any number of ways.

Each of them was ingeniously constructed with its own internal wiring and latching systems, so that they could be moved where required and attached to mechanisms hidden in The Sanctuary floor. The invisible floor latches were tied into the museum's electrical system, and recessed lights, floodlights, or spotlights could be positioned on the portable panels to exhibit the paintings at their best advantage.

This system, thought Georgiana, is wonderful. I can arrange the walls, paintings, and captions in such a way that the viewer is drawn from dimly lighted areas to wide open spaces. I can make him turn corners, look up, look down, and increase his involvement with the Pre-Raphaelite artists and paintings until he's ready for my emotion-packed, highly theatrical, double-whammy of a denouement.

Her attitude lent credence to those who had accused Georgiana Weeks of being more showman than art curator.

But then again, as Georgiana had so often commented herself, "What good is a show, if it isn't a *show!*"

When Georgiana arrived at the Zigfield Art Museum on Saturday morning, she thought that she would be the first person in. She wasn't. According to Luis Cabrerra, who introduced himself as the security director, Jiri Hozda had beaten her in by half an hour, and Camden Kimcannon had gotten there at 7:15, forty-five minutes before that.

Camden, Luis said, was waiting for her in her office.

Georgiana climbed the two flights of stairs, and found her office door opened and Camden Kimcannon standing in the middle of the room; he was wearing the same beret, pants, shoes, and tie from the day before, but with the added distraction of a gray, paint-stained artist's smock over a faded blue shirt.

"Greetings," he said, and with a careless flick of fingers, indicated a paper bag on Georgiana's desk. "Coffee. I grew the beans myself. Also provided are spoons, milk, cream, and various other accoutrements of the caffeine libation."

He slipped his hand in the pocket of his smock, removed a key, and held it out to her.

"The forgotten key of yesterday. I briefly considered waiting for you outside the office to show respect for your privacy, but since I had the means of access and you did not, the gesture seemed hollow."

"Good morning, Camden."

"Camelot," he corrected.

Georgiana took the key, walked to her desk, and sat down.

"Cam," she compromised. "Since we're on a pretty tight schedule, the first thing we're going to do is . . . Don't just hover like that in the middle of the room. Pull over the chair and sit next to me. Yes. That chair. No. Not so close. All right. Can you see these sketches clearly? Good. Because what I want to do first is give you an overview of my Pre-Raphaelite exhibition. Start to finish. We'll go over the graphics, the text on the labels, where the paintings go, how they're going to be grouped, and so on. Here's a pad. You'll want to write down the things that will be your responsibility. Can you type?"

"Yes."

"Do you know how to use a word processor?"

Camden made a cross of his two forefingers and held them up, as though to ward off a vampire.

"Word processor," he chanted lowly. "Instrument of the devil."

Georgiana looked to see if he was serious.

He gave her an exaggerated wink.

"I take it that you and the word processor are *not* best friends. Joy can do the labels for the paintings, then, and you can help her by proof-reading the text. As far as the exhibition itself goes, what do you know about the pictures I'm including?"

"I'm only sure about one."

"Which one, Camden?"

"My name is Camelot. And I know that *The Last Sleep of Arthur in Avalon* is going to be in your show. I found out eleven months ago, which is why I started to volunteer at the museum. There was an article in *ArtNews* about how difficult it is to transport oversize paintings. It de-scribed how you had made a Herculean effort to get *Arthur in Avalon* for your Pre-Raphaelite exhibition. For *this* Pre-Raphaelite exhibit. And there was a photograph of the painting in the article. I'd never seen one before, and when I think of standing right next to it . . . of seeing the actual work of art to which Sir Edward Burne-Jones devoted the last twenty years of his life, I . . . I . . . I'm speechless. But you've seen it already, Georgiana. Haven't you?"

"Yes. Once."

"What's it like?"

Georgiana stared up at the ceiling for a moment before she spoke.

"In the center of the picture, just as in the center of all the myths about Camelot, is King Arthur. But unlike the legendary king, *this* King Arthur has no round table, and is no longer surrounded by noble knights. Excalibur is gone. Guinevere is gone, and Launcelot, whom Arthur had once thought to be the noblest knight of them all, has proven himself to be less than noble, and unworthy to call himself a knight.

"Arthur is wearing a black helmet and black armor. His legs are covered with a black blanket, and his feet rest on the lap of a princess whose fingers are clutching at her temples with grief. Arthur's head lies on the lap of another princess whose hands are clenched sorrowfully over her head. Six other princesses surround his bier. They are beautiful, motionless, and mournful. Arthur's head is turned toward us. His eyes are shut, and the expression on his face is that of weary, noble, blessed relief."

Camden Kimcannon nodded his head. "And there received him three queens with great mourning," he recited solemnly. ". . . and in one of their laps King Arthur laid his head. 'Comfort thyself,' said the king, ' . . . for I will into the vale of Avalon to heal me of my grevious wound. And if thou never hear of me more, pray for my soul.'"

"What are you quoting, Camden?"

"*Le Morte D'Arthur* by Sir Thomas Malory. Is the painting as big as they say it is?"

"It's almost half the length of a tennis court—twenty-one feet wide and a little over nine feet tall. And it's more than just big, Cam. It's static. Magnetic. Provocative. Hypnotizing. The painting seems to draw you into it, and make you feel that not only is *it* larger than life, but that when you're in its presence, you are larger than life, too. Which means," Georgiana stopped and studied Camden Kimcannon's face for a moment, "that it's probably a dangerous picture for you to see."

"Me? Why me?"

"Think about it for a minute."

Camden gave Georgiana a puzzled glance.

"Be that as it may," she went on, "everything you read in that article was true. Transporting *Arthur in Avalon* is like trying to move a small nation. It was trucked from the Museo de Arte to the shipping port in Puerto Rico. It's going up the East Coast by ship to the Port of Newark in New Jersey. And from Newark, it will be trucked here. It gets to the museum on Tuesday. In three days."

"Three days," Camden repeated reverently. "Sometimes, I stay awake at night just thinking about it. About how all of those magnificent pictures are coming together here in America, a hundred and fifty years after they were painted, like old friends. Joined, in a building they've never been in before, and in a way they've never been joined before. And me, a man who . . . "

Camden Kimcannon's eyes flicked over to Georgiana Weeks. Suddenly, he felt odd. Exposed. And he realized that Georgiana was staring at him with a baffled, but not unkind, expression on her face.

She leaned forward.

"What is it, Cam? What's all this stuff about? The way you dress. The way you talk. Your obsession with Camelot and King Arthur? Why them? Why the Pre-Raphaelites?"

Camden bit his lower lip. He whipped off his beret and began to twist it nervously between his hands. "I live on City Island," he murmured. He wouldn't look at her.

"And I live on East End Avenue," Georgiana said. "I'm subletting an apartment there. Are we comparing notes?"

Camden continued to look down at his hands. "I'm twenty-four years old, Georgiana."

"I'm a lot older than that, Cam. But I remember twenty-four well. That was my age the first time I fell in and out of love. And I had my first professional exhibition when I was twenty-four. I was at the University of Southern California, working on my Ph.D. under Dr. Selma Holo, and for the opening of my show she lent me an Egyptian necklace that had been given to her by Norton Simon for *her* first show when she worked at The Norton Simon Museum of Art.

"The necklace was an intricate collar of turquoise and gold; and as soon as I put it on, I knew my exhibition was going to be a fabulous success. It was. And I was. And when I think about being twenty-four, what I think about is being on the verge of Life with a capital L. I wonder, Cam, when you're forty-four years old, what this year will have meant to you then?"

Instead of answering, Camden shoved his beret in the pocket of his smock and continued, as though he hadn't heard a word Georgiana had said.

"I live on City Island. By express bus, it's only thirteen miles to midtown Manhattan. But the express bus doesn't run on Sundays."

Georgiana stared at Camden for a moment more, straightened her shoulders in a businesslike way, and picked up a pencil. She said, "I'm sure City Island is a wonderful place to live, but much as I'd like to continue this travelogue, we've got a ton of work to do. What I want to show you first is . . . "

"I was thinking that maybe tomorrow, Georgiana, Sunday . . . if you aren't working, that maybe you could come to my house and meet the Mater. You could join us for tea. At, say . . . would four o'clock be a good time for you?"

The expression on Camden's face was intent. Wistful. Passionate. Idealistic. And young.

Oh, so young.

"The Mater," he continued, "is an actress. Performed on the stage in London. Quite talented and all that. Gave up her career to marry Dad, but he couldn't be bothered with us once we'd returned to the States."

"Camden," Georgiana asked gently. "Were you *born* in England?"

"Well. Not exactly. But the Mater did several seasons there. Some Tennessee Williams. A short run of O'Neill, and a revival of Thorton Wilder's *The Skin of Our Teeth*. Wonderful play. Are you familiar with it?"

"Vaguely. Camden, I . . . "

"I know that you don't know your way around New York yet, so what I was thinking is that I'd invite Jiri, too. Jiri's my best friend at the museum, and for months now I've been telling him about my house and about the Mater. The house is rather nicely located. Right on the water. And the weather tomorrow is supposed to be mild, so the wind from Long Island Sound shouldn't be too bad. And Jiri has a car, so you wouldn't have to be outside for more than a moment, and if you *do* come, I can show you my collection."

"Collection of what?"

"Oh, you'll see. I don't want to ruin the surprise. So, what do you say, Georgiana? Will you come? Say yes. Won't you *please* say yes? Please. Please."

Georgiana shook her head.

"Cam, I . . ."

"Good," Camden nodded, as though the matter was settled. He reached for Georgiana's telephone, and punched in two digits.

"Jiri, this is Cam. I'm in Dr. Weeks's office. She won't come to tea at my house tomorrow unless you drive her there, so will you be my guest and join us?"

Georgiana gently but firmly took the receiver out of Camden's hand. "Jiri?"

"Yes, beautiful Georgiana."

"Camden's got a bee in his bonnet about us having tea at his house. He lives somewhere called City Island."

"So I have been told on the numerous occasions that he has invited *me* for tea."

Georgiana eyed Camden suspiciously.

"Have you gone yet, Jiri?"

"Indeed, no. But with you to protect me, I might summon up the courage to face the ordeal of meeting . . . what does he call her? Ah, yes. The Mater. What do you say? Shall we brazen it out and hold each other's hand?"

Georgiana covered the mouthpiece. "This really means a lot to you, doesn't it, Cam?"

The look in Camden's eyes said more than Georgiana wanted to hear.

She uncovered the phone. "OK, Jiri. We'll skip dinner tonight, but I'll let you take me out tomorrow night after tea, if you want to."

"I want to."

Georgiana hung up, and stated firmly, to Camden, "All right now, repeat after me: No more fooling around."

Camden parroted. "No more fooling around."

But his eyes were twinkling.

She pushed a pile of papers to a point midway between herself and Camden. "First, we'll go through the list of paintings that are going to be included in the exhibition. Then we're going to map out where they go on my schematic. Got it?"

"Got it."

"And no more misty-eyed glances. No more compliments. No more soulful quotations. No more nothing. Repeat it."

"No more nothing."

"Excellent."

And then Camden Kimcannon, alias Camelot Kimcannon, rose to his feet, and with a light in his eyes as bright as that of Excalibur glinting in the sun, sang out, "Man am I grown, a man's work must I do. Live pure, speak true, right wrong, follow the king . . . " Camden paused, shifted his eyes to Georgiana and amended, "Queen. Follow the *queen*. Else, wherefore born?"

Georgiana blinked slowly, dropped her head weakly between her arms on her desk, and whispered into her papers, "Help!"

20

To get to City Island by car, the easiest route from Georgiana's apartment in Manhattan was to take the FDR Drive north, toward Harlem to the Triborough Bridge. This would put them on Route 278, which in turn would connect up with the Bruckner Expressway in the Bronx.

Unlike Manhattan or Staten Island, or even Brooklyn and Queens, which are surrounded by water, the Bronx is firmly attached to land. The population of the South Bronx is one and a quarter million people. At one time, it had been a predominantly middle-class borough. But that was a long time ago.

The Bronx.

Of New York City's five boroughs, the Bronx is the one that has suffered the most from domestic terrorism, looting, rioting, and arson; the area of the Bronx that was hardest hit by all of this violence was the South Bronx, described by the firemen who went into burning buildings to fight fires as the only place in the city where the good guys—the ones trying to *save* the lives and properties of the residents—were shot at by the people whose lives and property they were trying to save.

The Bruckner Expressway skirts the South Bronx, and veers off to the right where it connects with Route 95 North.

Route 95 continues north through lower-income neighborhoods of featureless, graffiti-covered buildings; then abruptly and without transition, the buildings disappear, and suddenly the car has turned again, and is on a narrow, winding exit called Charles J. Crimi Shore Road.

Shore Road ambles leisurely through Pelham Bay Park, which is two-thousand-seven-hundred acres of grass, trees, beaches, and forest, smack dab in the middle of the Bronx. It is the largest park in New York City.

After driving through the park, crossing the Pelham Bridge, and then driving through Hunter's Island, the car finally arrives at the draw-bridge that connects the rest of New York City to City Island, where Camden Kimcannon lived with a woman whom he called "the Mater."

Or, to quote Chamber of Commerce literature, "Nobody just happens on City Island. In order to get here, you have to plan on going here, or you will never find it."

Politically, City Island is represented in the Bronx by Community Board 10. Its grammar school, P.S. 175, is part of the New York City School System. Its library, founded in 1911, is part of the New York City Library System. Its crime, on the rare occasions when there is any, is investigated by the New York City Police Department, and is usually committed by what the locals call "off-islanders." And its fires are extinguished and investigated by the Fire Department of the City of New York.

Such are the ties that bind City Islanders to the sixth-largest city in the world, and the largest city in the United States.

The population of City Island itself, however, is small. Only 4,050 people.

And after crossing the drawbridge that separates it from Pelham Bay Park, even though a visitor feels that he has somehow been transported to a New England fishing village, he is really just a few miles from the most dangerous area of the South Bronx.

City Island is one-and-three-tenths miles long; at no point on the island is it ever more than three blocks wide.

It was settled in the 1760s by oyster fishermen, and the the residents have always directly or indirectly made their living off the sea.

In the early 1900s, City Island boatyards built yachts for the Astors, the Morgans, and the Vanderbilts.

During World War II, City Island produced warships.

Five America's Cup yacht winners were built on City Island, the last being *Freedom*, produced by the Minneford Shipyard, and winner of the 1980 America's Cup.

And even though the last boatyard closed in 1982, City Island can still boast of two sailmakers, eight boat repair yards, twelve marinas, six yacht clubs, and more boats than there are people.

In the 1940s and 1950s, City Island, with its single-family homes and low taxes, became a refuge for cops and firemen who wanted to raise their families away from the crime-ridden neighborhoods where they worked.

As a rule, City Islanders own their own homes; most of the people who bought their houses in the 1950s, 1960s, or 1970s, however, would not be able to afford to buy them today.

According to the map, 27 Kinshaw Street was west of City Island Avenue, nestled between Hawkins and Caroll Streets.

Georgiana looked through the windshield at the cottagelike houses on either side of the road.

"Look at that little one with the blue clapboard and flower boxes, Jiri. And the garden with the wisteria branches climbing up the trellises. And over there. That white house with the wide porch and all the ivy; it's so tiny, it looks like a painting on a commemorative plate. Jiri, these houses are so cute, I can't believe I'm still in New York City."

Jiri said, looking out the passenger side window, "The odd numbers appear to be on your side of the street. That's it. Up there. The house with the cyclone fence. Are you able to distinguish the number on the gate?"

Georgiana squinted.

"Twenty-one. No. You're right. It's twenty-seven. But don't drive any closer, Jiri. Stop. Please stop the car."

Jiri pulled over to the curb.

"See how obedient I am."

"God, Jiri, I don't know what's happening to me, but I just had a terrible premonition. I feel awful. Apprehensive. This isn't like me. This isn't the kind of a person that I am. Feel my hands. They're practically frozen."

Jiri took both of her hands in his. He started to rub them between his palms to increase their circulation. Then he placed his two fingers lightly under her chin and tilted her head upward, so that she had to look him in the eyes.

"Hello, beautiful Georgiana."

"Hi, Jiri."

"Are you currently involved with anyone?"

"No."

"Nor am I. Do you sleep with the windows open or closed?"

"Open."

"So do I. Do you keep peanut butter in the cupboard or in the refrigerator."

"Neither. I don't like peanut butter."

"Nor do I. Whom do you prefer? Bach or Beethoven?"

"Gershwin. Cole Porter. Rogers and Hart. Sigmund Romberg and Irving Berlin. Definitely Irving Berlin."

Jiri whispered, "So do I," and very slowly, he leaned forward and barely brushed Georgiana's lips with his lips. Then he released her chin and said, "Mr. Irving Berlin wrote the song 'Always.' "

"I know that."

"The lyrics are very loving. Very simple. They . . . "

"I know the lyrics."

"And they end with the word . . . "

" 'Always.' "

"Very good, Georgiana. I learned the song when I lived in Prague. Before I left Czechoslovakia. I had a very good friend who smuggled movies made in Hollywood behind the iron curtain. He was murdered by the Soviets in 1968." Jiri looked out the windshield over Georgiana's head and the tone of his voice suddenly changed. "Curious," he said.

"What?"

"The things one can tell about a house without even going inside. The Kimcannon residence, for instance. Compared to the houses on either side, what differences do you detect?"

Georgiana studied the house, and then said cautiously, "The other houses have either vinyl siding, clapboard, or shingles. Cam's house is covered with . . . oh, what is it called? I always think of it as depression siding, because I associate it with the Great Depression, but it's really . . . asbestos shingles, that's what it is. Fake tar-paper siding. I hate the stuff."

"Very observant. What else?"

Georgiana glanced around.

"Well, the cyclone fence, of course. The other houses have picket fences or no fences. And then there's the jarring aspect of the paint job."

"What's jarring about it?"

"That it desperately needs one. In fact, the Mater's house desperately needs a lot of things. Like a new sidewalk. A garden. Trees. New windows."

Jiri reached for the key in the ignition.

"No," Georgiana said earnestly. "Don't shut off the engine yet. First turn the car around. Away from the ocean or beach or whatever's at the end of this street, so that it's facing City Island Avenue."

Jiri backed into a driveway, pulled out, and swung the car around.

Georgiana said, "Thank you, Jiri. Now leave it right here. Against the curb. I don't want to get any closer to Camden's house than I have to."

He lined up the wheels and turned off the engine.

Georgiana looked at her watch.

"Four o'clock on the dot." Then she tucked her arms around her waist and huddled in her seat.

Jiri got out and walked around the car to open Georgiana's door. When she didn't look up at him, he reached out his hand.

"Shall we go inside now, Georgiana?"

Georgiana took a deep breath, expelled it, and said, "I guess we have to."

21

Many things happened that Sunday afternoon that made Georgiana want to cry. Camden's undisguised elation when they finally got there was one. And his apparent oblivion to the complete disaster of the afternoon tea party was another.

But from the moment the doorbell rang until the moment she and Jiri had crossed the Triborough Bridge on their way back to Manhattan, Georgiana felt as though a gang war was being fought somewhere between her heart and lungs, and that while it was going on she had no place to hide.

"Jiri! Georgiana!" Camden greeted them ecstatically at the door.

Camden Kimcannon, self-described artist, and aficionado of an era that had preceded his birth by one-and-a-half centuries, wore a smile consisting in equal parts of anticipation, apprehension, and pride. The suit jacket he had on was too big for him, and frayed at the collar and cuffs. But it was a *contemporary* jacket, with matching pants and dress shirt; it wasn't an outfit that looked as if it had been stolen from the nineteenth-century wing of a wax museum. His necktie was a little too nar-

row to be exactly fashionable, but it was a nice tie, with a pleasant pais-
ley print. His tie pin was shaped like a sword (probably Excalibur—after
all, this *was* Camden Kimcannon), and the same old shoes he always
wore were on his feet.

Camden grabbed Jiri Hozda while he was still in the doorway, shook
his right hand vigorously, and then enveloped him in an awkward hug.

"Welcome, Jiri. Welcome to my home."

He released Jiri quickly, turned to Georgiana, grabbed both of her
hands with his own long, sculpted fingers, raised them to his lips, lightly
kissed them, and then softly released them, in a gesture she instantly recognized as the same one Jiri had used two days before when he'd visited
Joy Miller in her office.

"Come in. My friends, come in. The Mater's not quite ready to join
us yet, but . . . come right in here. I have everything set up for us in the
living room."

And all through the preparations for tea ("I don't know what's gotten into the Mater. She should have been down by now."), from the instant that Georgiana sat on the edge of the armchair, its faded chintz
splotched with coffee and food stains, and dotted with small, round
holes where cigarette cinders had fallen before they had quite gone out,
Georgiana Weeks wished that she weren't there.

"I bought five kinds of tea," Camden said excitedly, "because I wasn't
sure which you'd prefer. Herbal. Lemon. Peppermint. Ceylon—that
sounds strong, doesn't it? And my own personal favorite, English Break-
fast Tea."

Crisp, white crocheted doilies were positioned as carefully as possible to cover the worst of the damaged fabric on the arms and backs of
the sofa and two chairs. One of the doilies on the arm of Georgiana's
chair still had a small rectangular price tag stuck to it. When Camden
reached for a tea bag, Georgiana quickly removed the tag, rolled it between her thumb and forefinger, and dropped it in her purse.

"I didn't know if you liked cream and sugar with your tea, or what."
Camden's laugh was nervous, eager to please. "So this container has
cream in it. This one has milk. And here's a honey pot, sugar, and I even
cut up some lemons."

The tea pot was covered with small violets and the tiny cracks of age that give an aura of elegance to real china.

Instead of into tea cups, though, Camden poured the boiling water into three plain, ceramic mugs. A fourth mug sat on the metal serving tray. Georgiana picked up her mug and felt the gummy residue of yet another recently removed price tag.

She selected a tea bag, and Camden asked, "Shall I pour?"

Georgiana smiled brightly and said, "Thank you, Cam. Everything is just lovely."

Camden picked up the teapot, and unconsciously mimicked the countless actors of the 1930s whom he had seen in old movies who were in turn mimicking how they thought an Englishman would serve tea.

Georgiana bit her lower lip.

The mug shook in her hand.

Jiri took it from her and placed it on the coffee table in front of them.

He soundlessly formed the word *courage*.

Camden leaped to his feet.

"Oh my God! I almost forgot. This is full afternoon tea! Not exactly English high tea, I admit." Camden bowed apologetically at the waist. "Scones, Devonshire cream, and crumpets are not readily available on City Island. But tea is tea . . . and tea *isn't* tea without pastries." He smiled elegantly, first at Georgiana, and then at Jiri. "Would you excuse me for a moment while I prepare the . . . " he hesitated as though searching for the right words, and then finished brightly, kissing his bunched fingers and flinging them open as though to release a bouquet of stars, ". . . the pièce de résistance."

Camden walked through a pair of beautiful old French doors, past the foyer, and down a narrow hallway, where he disappeared on his way to what appeared to be the kitchen.

Jiri Hozda and Georgiana Weeks did not speak.

Jiri studied Georgiana.

Georgiana looked around the room, her eyes analyzing, evaluating, judging.

Other than the light that came through the windows, there were only two dim lamps on end tables at either side of the sofa. Georgiana could smell lemon furniture polish on the tables, and dust clinging to the pleated cloth shades of the table lamps.

She smelled the fresh, pungent aroma of rug deodorant in the carpet's nap, and she could see the vacuum cleaner treads where Camden had obviously run it back and forth in futile preparation for today's tea.

But there were touches, she noted, here and there, of a house that had once been cared for—long ago. Like the mottled green wall-to-wall carpeting that still hinted at a perfect match to the green in the chintz of the chairs.

Georgiana looked across the room. There was a water stain shaped like a Rorschach inkblot on the ceiling over the fireplace, but neither painting nor mirror hung on the wall over its mantel.

Television guides, though, were jumbled haphazardly from one side of the mantel to the other, and inside the fireplace itself newspapers were stacked, along with old magazines, manila envelopes (most of which appeared never to have been opened), folders, crumpled cigarette packs, and an ugly black, snakeskin handbag.

Georgiana shuddered.

On a table in front of the fireplace sat a television set. It was the biggest single object in the room, and its large, blind eye reflected the room's contents like a convex mirror.

On top of the television sat a remote control box and a large ceramic ashtray.

On each end table on either side of the sofa was a cheap, imitation crystal ashtray. They were spotlessly clean and smelled faintly of ammonia.

Jiri, sitting on the sofa at right angles to Georgiana's chair, reached out for her hand. He squeezed it briefly, and released it just as Camden reappeared.

"I have butter cookies, macaroons, chocolate brownies, gingersnaps, and cheese Danish. The Mater—I think I'd better go up and check on her. I can't figure out why she isn't here yet. Anyway, the Mater thought that cheese Danish was inappropriate for tea, but . . . "

Crash.

Camden's tea tray trembled in his hands.

Crash again, as though somewhere on the floor above a mirror or a vase had been broken.

Camden looked stricken.

He put the tray down on the coffee table.

"Excuse me," he uttered, his face etched with panic, and he ran out of the room.

The staircase to the second floor was opposite the entrance door. Camden took the steps two at a time.

Jiri and Georgiana looked at each other.

They heard more scuffling sounds. Then Camden's voice called out from above, "Nothing to worry about. The Mater just dropped a perfume bottle."

Georgiana looked significantly at Jiri. She leaned forward in her chair, feeling as though she were somehow being set up and manipulated, but still anticipating what was going to happen next.

After a few more seconds, they heard footsteps again, this time descending. Immediately after that, the Mater finally entered the room.

Jiri, ever the European, rose to his feet.

Georgiana, too, arose, but didn't know if she did so out of curiosity, courtesy, or stupefaction.

For Camden Kimcannon's mother was the exact opposite of the dowdy, fussy little middle-aged housewife that she had somehow come to expect.

Instead, the Mater made an Entrance with a capital E.

She had large, lazy eyes, high cheekbones, and a perfectly shaped mouth.

She was tall, willowy-slim, glamorously wrapped in gold lamé lounging pajamas, and absolutely gorgeous in a 1940s drawing-room comedy sort of way. As she posed just inside the threshold to the room, and it was quite obvious that she was posing, she raised a long, black onyx cigarette holder to within inches of her lips.

"Darlings," she said in a low, throaty voice with just the right hint of a British accent. "*So* glad that you could come."

She inhaled deeply on her cigarette holder, and then exhaled a straight, horizontal stream of smoke, more to punctuate her sentence than from any pure pleasure of nicotine.

Georgiana stared impolitely.

Camden stood behind his mother and a little to her right. But instead of the pride Georgiana expected to see on his face, what she saw was fear. He reached out and gently touched his mother's elbow, as if to guide her with his right hand.

"Mum?" he said cautiously.

She violently shrugged him off.

"Oh, for God's sake, Camden, don't call me that!"

She threw back her head, and her long, silvery blonde hair shifted slightly on her neck, capturing whatever light was to be got from the room's two dim lamps and imprisoning it against her head like a halo.

"Darlings," she said again, and she took one slightly unsteady step. "Do let's dispense with all of this Mater, Mother, Mum stuff. My name, both on and off the stage, is Vidalia Kimcannon."

She laughed deeply, and said "If Vidalia Kimcannon was good enough for the Old Vic Theater in London, England, darlings, well, it's good enough for me."

Then she took another deep draw on her cigarette holder, exhaled, and for the first time seemed to notice the accoutrements for tea on the coffee table.

Without losing a beat, she pointed a contemptuous finger at the honey, milk, and pastries prepared so scrupulously by her son.

"Oh, tea. Isn't that just too, too adorable."

She tottered forward another step and turned to look behind her.

"Camden, darling," she said archly, "Don't be such a lagabout, and do . . . do help your dear Mater to her chair."

Cam rushed forward, offered his mother his arm, and after a few more unsteady steps, deposited her in the chair opposite Georgiana.

Directly beneath the light of the table lamp.

Cam hovered indecisively behind his mother's chair. His eyes were like sad clown eyes, Georgiana thought, and she pictured two huge blue teardrops, painted to linger in perpetuity on his cheeks.

123

Jiri, taking command of the situation, reached for the teapot, and said in a voice meant to placate and flatter, but which somehow came out a tinge too loud, "My dear Mrs. Kimcannon . . ."

"Vidalia, darling. I really *must* insist that you call me by my name."

"Of course, madam. May I compliment you then, Vidalia, on your charming son. We feel most privileged to have one who is so young, so enthusiastic, and so knowledgeable working at our museum."

"Young," Vidalia repeated, picking out, as though it were a prime peach, the one word in Jiri's speech that meant something to her. She again threw back her head and laughed.

Georgiana noted, this time, that her hair, the beautiful, glamorous, silver-blonde hair, in places, had clumped together, as though it were not quite all so very, very clean.

Vidalia continued, her voice brittle with indignation, "Our merry lad over here is young, all right. Why I can't have been more than a girl of sixteen on the day that he was born!"

And Georgiana noticed small, deep half moons on either side of Vidalia's mouth, like scars from frantic thumbnails that had been etched into the skin above her jaw.

"But knowledgeable! Enthusiastic!" Vidalia laughed cruelly. "Surely, we aren't talking about the same boy."

Then, without transition, she glanced around the room and said angrily, her manner that of the victim of a huge and unforgivable conspiracy, "Funny, I would have thought that *somebody* here was going to pour me a cup of tea!"

Jiri reached forward. "My apologies, madam." And he poured tepid water into her cup.

"Camden, *darling*." Vidalia turned back to her son. "Are these the people you told me about from that . . . that *place* at which you work, where you are receiving absolutely no remuneration whatsoever for the hours and hours of arduous toil that you put in?"

Camden darted a mortified glance at Jiri. He took a step forward, "No, Mother. Actually . . . "

But Vidalia had already lost interest in her son, and turned her attention to the room, her eyes glancing off the chairs, the rug, the sofa.

Georgiana Weeks studied Vidalia Kimcannon.

She noticed heavy pancake makeup over cheekbones that were nowhere near as high as they had at first seemed. And she observed that the hand that had once rocked the cradle had not been able to disguise the unsteadiness with which the eyeliner had been applied, or completely hide the shallow puffiness of the skin beneath each lower lash.

Vidalia Kimcannon's eyes stopped roving the room and came to rest on the arm of Georgiana's chair. Her nostrils flared; she spun her head around and glared at Camden.

"Doilies," she spat out contemptuously. "Well, aren't *we* the pretty little man."

Cam looked as if he had been slapped.

Georgiana stood up. Her hands were shaking. Her chest was heaving with suppressed rage.

"Cam," she said briskly. "Show me your collection."

Camden didn't move. He didn't look at her. He stared at the back of his mother's head, as though it contained the solution to a life and death puzzle that he somehow just couldn't quite get.

Jiri also stood up.

"Mrs. Kimcannon," he said, his voice harsher than he had intended. "Cam has told us so many wonderful things about your experiences in the theater. Do, please, tell me more about yourself."

He walked over to Camden Kimcannon, took him by both arms and turned him around. Then he looked briefly at Georgiana and flicked his eyes toward the stairs. She nodded grimly, grabbed Camden by the hand, and said, "Camden, show me your collection. *Now.*"

And as she led him up the staircase, hoping that the collection, whatever it was, lay in that direction, she heard Vidalia Kimcannon say, "But of course, darling. Do sit right here beside me. Ah . . . where to begin, as there's so . . . so *much* to tell."

Camden Kimcannon's room, Georgiana later told Jiri Hozda as they drove away from City Island, was exactly like the room in Henry Wallis's painting *The Death of Chatterton*.

"I think," she said, "that it's one of the scariest, saddest rooms I've ever seen. Camden sleeps on a narrow, solitary cot with an old, much-too-thin blanket. Bitterly cold air hisses in between cracks in the leaded glass casement windows over his bed. There's a small wood desk on the wall diagonal to his bed, with a few art supplies piled neatly in the right-hand corner. In the center of the desk are a quill pen and an ink bottle. Camden *writes* with a quill pen, Jiri. Oh, God, and when I stood there in the room, staring at it like that, I could just see him lying on that miserable cot with that pale, white skin of his, looking exactly like the dead poet Chatterton. Chatterton committed suicide, Jiri!" Georgiana suddenly cried out, "And if that poor man doesn't get away from that woman, I wouldn't give you two nickels for his chances, because she's going to eat him alive. Isn't that what black widow spiders do? They devour their young?"

Jiri Hozda shook his head, but he did not take his eyes off the road.

"No, beautiful Georgiana. It is their husbands whom the black widows devour. I believe they have no interest whatsoever in their young."

Georgiana snorted. "Well, this one does. She thinks it's fun to humiliate him in front of his friends. And his collection, Jiri. I could have cried. Books, posters, postcards, classic comic books, for God's sake, screen treatments, stolen library books—everything, anything—more than you could conceive of on knighthood, chivalry, King Arthur, the round table. He has every book that Sir Walter Scott ever wrote, including the poems. He has three collections of the Waverly novels, five copies in all of *Ivanhoe*. He has a whole shelf of Elizabeth Barrett Browning, Robert Browning, and Tennyson. He has books on castles, moats, coats of armor, and on the unicorn tapestries. And lately, Jiri, he's been collecting reproductions and books on the Pre-Raphaelite artists. I swear, there isn't a thing he values in his room that wasn't conceived of earlier than a century ago. He lives in the past. He loves the past. He wants to go *back* to the past. And that's no way for a human being to live. Wearing clothes from another century. Patterning his speech, his manners, his goals, his dreams after something that never was . . . that never will be . . . " She stopped abruptly and covered her mouth with her wrist. "Oh my God," she said, horrified. "The Burne—Jones quotation."

"Yes." Jiri Hozda nodded somberly. "So I noticed." And he steered the car around a tight curve, hesitated until the road was clear, and then merged into the Manhattan-bound traffic on the FDR Drive.

22

Ten years ago when Eddie had been a fireman and Wylie Nolan had been a supervising fire marshal, Wylie pulled his surveillance van into Engine Company 204 on DeGraw Street in Brooklyn to make a telephone call, because his handie talkie two-way radio wouldn't transmit.

Eddie NoName, who was on house watch at the time, asked Wylie if he wanted him to fix it.

Wylie said, "Sure. Why not?" And two minutes later, the radio worked.

Wylie asked Eddie what he'd done and the fireman rattled off sentences crammed with words like diodes, cathodes, resistance coils, transistors, and megacycles, none of which meant anything to Wylie and all of which impressed him. So he asked the fireman if he wanted to leave the firehouse, move over to the Division of Fire Investigation, and take over tech services.

Eddie asked, "What does that mean?"

"It means that you'd be able to play with gadgets all the time."

"What kinds of gadgets?" Eddie asked suspiciously.

And Wylie showed the fireman the inside of his surveillance van, with its electronic control panel, Star Wars radio system, Nikon motor-driven camera, hidden periscope, videotape/camera/recorder/monitor system, pneumatic jacks, and night scope.

"These kinds of gadgets," he said.

It took Eddie less than a minute to make up his mind to leave the firehouse, but a few more months to maneuver the political obstacle course put in his path before he was able to transfer to the Division of Fire Investigation at Fire Department headquarters (Wylie was owed a favor by the brother of a deputy chief whose cousin grew up with the chief fire marshal's sister-in-law in County Cork, Ireland).

Wylie dialed the Division of Fire Investigation and asked to be connected to Eddie in Tech Services.

Eddie NoName's name, although very few people knew it, was not NoName. In fact, once when the chief fire marshal needed Eddie on an emergency basis to wire an informant with a transmitter and a receiver, his aide ran Edward *Noname* through the computer, and Eddie NoName's telephone number was nowhere to be found.

It didn't dawn on the chief until the following day that "No Name" might be two words run together instead of a proper noun. But by mid-morning he had forgotten all about it, because the crisis was over and the informant had gone home.

Eddie NoName had a theory.

Inventors always have one theory or another, and for every brilliant idea that lights up their minds, they usually have ten or twelve that would make a Rube Goldberg contraption look like an exercise in simplicity.

When Wylie Nolan first asked Eddie his last name, Eddie responded, "The way I look at it, Wylie, is this.

"Each individual human being has only a given number of brain cells accessible for his use or misuse in one lifetime, and no matter how many we have, there are never enough. So, every little bit of information we absorb, whether it's irrelevant or not, takes up the space in our heads that could have been used to find a way to turn plastic back into petroleum, or to build an antigravity machine.

"So, let's say you ask me my last name, and I tell you. And let's say that at that point in time, you only have seven available brain cells that are open to receive information, and just a second later, you get a telephone call from an informant who wants to give up the guy who set the fire at the Fantasy Island Social Club in the Bronx, and you pick up the phone, and a voice tells you, 'The name of the perpetrator is . . .', but you never find out *who* it was that set the fire, because the seventh brain cell—the one that should have been empty to receive the perpetrator's name—it's got my name in it instead."

And so on.

Geniuses are often peculiar.

Howard Hughes was deathly afraid of germs; Nikola Tesla fell in love with a pigeon; and Thomas Alva Edison believed that he could construct a device sensitive enough to pick up evidence, if any, of life after death.

Thereby insuring that Eddie NoName, being a genius, would be entitled to an occasional peculiarity of his own.

In one instance, he had been lent to the FBI to set up surveillance cameras on an arson-for-profit ring. Eddie shook his head when the FBI tech service guys showed him the room and equipment he was expected to use.

"This is all too obvious," Eddie NoName said. "These perps aren't idiots. They'll pick up where the surveillance cameras are in two minutes."

The FBI agents looked at Eddie and shook their heads with disgust.

"That's the last time we'll call in the fire department for help," one of them said contemptuously.

Another agent, less didactic but equally skeptical, said to Eddie, "All right, fire marshal. If you're so smart, what would *you* do?"

Eddie responded, "I'd hook up a pinhole camera to transmit a video image of everything that's going on in this room, through the wires of this telephone right here."

At which point all of the agents burst out laughing, because, as one of them said, "Everyone knows you can't use telephone wires to transmit video images."

And Eddie quietly led the FBI agents into the next room, and on the television monitor that he had previously set up in that room, he played back the videotape of the interchange which had just occurred.

"*Everyone* may know you can't do it," Eddie NoName said. "But since I never went to engineering school like all of the rest of you guys, nobody ever taught me what I can't do. So I just did it."

After that, it was generally agreed upon by all who knew of him in and out of the fire department, including the FBI, that Eddie NoName was a genius.

Eddie loved to tinker with gadgets.

So, to Eddie, Wylie Nolan was the greatest fire marshal who ever lived, because it was through Wylie that Eddie got to be head of the Tech Services Department, and spend every waking hour of every single day wiring, dissecting, and inventing things.

"Eddie," Wylie said after his call was put through, "I need you to help me on something."

"*Mi casa es su casa*," Eddie said.

"What does that mean?"

"I don't know, but whenever I ask my brother-in-law for a favor, that's what he says. So I figure it can't be too bad. What's up, Wylie?"

"I have to do a surveillance."

"Where?"

"In my building. You've been there."

"On Lispenard Street. Yeah. I remember."

And briefly, Wylie Nolan described the ladies' room and the incidents leading up to and including the small fires that had been set there on the seventh floor.

"And," Wylie added emphatically, "the arsonist, whoever she is, is framing a personal friend of mine."

"She," Eddie picked out. "Why do you think the person setting the fires is a 'she'?"

"Who else could get into the ladies' bathroom in the middle of the day undetected?"

"A man in disguise."

After a moment's hesitation, Wylie said gently, "Let's just pretend it's a woman. Okay, Eddie?"

"Yeah. Sure. So, what do you want me to do?"

"Be my backup. Bring along your badge and gun. If all goes well, you're going to get a good arrest out of this thing."

"*Mi casa es su casa*," Eddie said again. "I'll call you back in twenty minutes," and he hung up.

Twenty minutes later, Eddie called Wylie back.

"I figured it out," he said. "I did a schematic, located the equipment, and I can even get you good prices on what we'll need. What we'll do is put a time-lapse video recorder in the air register in the ceiling outside the ladies' room, with the lens pointed at the bathroom door. The motion detector and fire alarm receptors will be hooked into the TLR so that if the fire alarm transmitter, which is hidden behind the air freshener over the sink in the bathroom, picks up that there is a fire, or if the motion detector outside in the hall senses that someone has opened the bathroom door, then the TLR goes into real-time mode for five minutes. Otherwise, the TLR is at the twenty-four-hour mode, set to record interval events throughout an hour. If a fire alarm is activated, though, you'll have to pull out the tape yourself, Wylie, because otherwise it automatically erases everything when it records over itself. So, you have less than twenty-four . . . "

"Eddie," Wylie said.

". . . hours to do it. I figured out the cost, and . . . "

"Eddie. This is all very nice, but . . . "

". . . and we can do the whole job for under five-thousand dollars, if I . . . "

"Eddie, buddy, can I talk to you for a second?"

"Sure, Wylie."

"That's a very good surveillance plan you devised."

"Thanks, Wylie. I like it. It's foolproof. And when we've caught . . . "

"I really appreciate the time and effort you put into designing it to help me catch the bad guy."

"Girl, Wylie. You said it was a girl."

"That's right, Eddie. But there's a problem."

"You don't like it," Eddie said, crestfallen.

"No, Eddie. I like it. I like it a lot. It's just that I had something simpler in mind."

"I think it's pretty simple."

"And cheaper, Eddie."

"Oh. Cheaper. Got you. What were you thinking, Wylie?"

"What are you doing on Thursday?"

There was a pause. "What do you want me to do?"

"Well, I sort of had in mind that I'd get permission from the export office across from the ladies' room on the seventh floor."

"Yeah?"

"And that I'd get two chairs."

"Yeah?"

"Comfortable chairs."

"Yeah?"

"And that you and me would sit *behind* the door in the export office across from the ladies' room on the seventh floor."

"Yeah?"

"And we'd look through the crack in the door, and we'd *pretend* that we were two time-lapse recorders with video motion detectors and fire alarm boxes built in."

There was another long pause.

Then, Eddie's voice said brightly into the telephone, "What the hell, Wylie. *Mi casa es su casa.*"

23

At ten o'clock on Tuesday morning, Joy Miller glanced suspiciously at the three men on the far side of her office, and without removing her eyes from them, picked up the telephone on her desk and pressed in two digits.

The shorter of the three men, the one with the granny glasses and geometric necktie, had positioned himself in front of the others, as if to insure that when the band started to play, he would be picked to lead the parade. The expression on Joy's face was polite but there was distrust in her eyes.

The telephone rang four times. Five. And on the sixth ring, Wegman Zigfield picked up.

"Mr. Zigfield. Your son is here."

Fromer Zigfield was the one in the geometric tie leading the parade.

"Ask him what he wants. He doesn't have an appointment."

"He isn't alone, sir. Mr. Zahedi and another man are with him."

Sarkin Zahedi had yellowish brown skin, thick, wavy black hair like Prince Valiant with a body perm, and dark eyes that looked as though they were fixated upon a Hindu ritual occurring at the back of his head.

"Why aren't I surprised that Fromer and Zahedi are joined at the hip," Wegman Zigfield said. "But who's the third musketeer?"

"I don't know, Mr. Zigfield."

"Well, find out!"

Joy placed the receiver down on her desk. "Excuse me, Fromer . . . and Mr. Zahedi, Mr. Zigfield would like to know who this gentleman is with you." Joy transferred her gaze to the third man and said, "If I might have your business card?"

He stared at Joy expressionlessly for about five seconds. He had lashless, hooded eyes over a large, amorphous nose bracketed by deep lines. His lips looked soft. He was wearing blue jeans with a cashmere sports jacket over a silk dress shirt and no tie. Instead of shoes, he wore soft leather moccasins without socks.

He moved forward sinuously, and pulled a gold embossed business card from his pocket. As Joy took it from him, she noticed that his fingernails were coated with clear polish, and that he wore a gold Rolex watch.

Joy studied the card and picked up the receiver. "Mr. Zigfield, the third gentleman is Lars Helmersson. His card says 'Fire, Arson, and Explosive Expert. Computer-modeled Fire Reconstruction and Analysis.' "

"Very impressive, Joy. Does he also do windows?"

Joy did not allow herself to smile.

"Ask them what they want," Wegman Zigfield commanded.

"May I impose upon you gentlemen to tell me what this unexpected visit is in reference to?"

Fromer said angrily, "Cut the crap, Joy, and tell my father that I want to see him."

Joy remained impassive. "He knows that already, Fromer. He still wants to know about *what*."

"Tell him I want to introduce him to the man I hired to look at Sarkin's paintings in the Parlor Gallery last week. He's a fire specialist. Tell him that we want to talk about the fire."

Joy spoke into the telephone, "Did you hear that, Mr. Zigfield?"

"Yes, I did. Joy, tell my son that we already have a fire investigator, and that I'm very satisfied with his work; and that our insurance company already has a fire investigator, and that they are very satisfied with his work; and that even Mr. Zahedi's insurance company has a fire investigator, and that they, too, are satisfied with his work, and that since everybody is so damn happy, Fromer and his two buddies can go home."

Joy conveyed the gist of that information.

Fromer exploded, "Well, goddamn it, you tell my father that *we* aren't satisfied with his fire investigator, and *we* aren't happy with the way this serious fire, which caused the destruction of five *masterpieces*, is being handled by the museum, the insurance companies, the fire department, and the police. In fact, we don't think that my father is treating Sarkin Zahedi *or* me with appropriate deference or respect, and that's the real reason why we're here. We came out of professional courtesy to let my father know that as a result of Mr. Helmersson's investigation, we have concluded that both father and Jiri Hozda, with whom he was so fast to replace me at a job I was doing *brilliantly,* are responsible by acts of commission or acts of omission, for the fire in the Parlor Gallery. In fact, we think that Dr. Hozda is so *obsessed* with his hatred of the American Art Development Fund, which sponsored Mr. Zahedi's exhibition at my urging, that he has become a deranged arsonist. Therefore, would you also inform my esteemed parent that the *reason* we'd like to see him is to advise him that we are going to have Dr. Hozda arrested for arson, and that we're going to sue both the museum corporately, and my father personally, for the loss of the paintings, for the loss of future earnings denied to him because Sarkin Zahedi will not be able to display these vintage paintings, thus attracting commissions for new work, and for the deep and crippling emotional pain that Mr. Zahedi has suffered." The skin over Fromer's weak jaw was quivering with rage. "And *now*, Joy, will you please let me in to see my father!"

But before Joy had the chance to respond, Wegman Zigfield said, "I heard the whole tirade, Joy. Tell Fromer that you have a message for him from me."

Joy put her hand over the telephone mouthpiece.

"He has a message for you."

She removed her hand, and asked, "What shall I tell Fromer, Mr. Zigfield?"

"Tell him to go to hell."

Joy said nothing.

"Well, go on Joy. Tell him."

"Oh . . . I couldn't say *that,* Mr. Zigfield."

Wegman Zigfield shouted, "Why the hell not? What are you? A man or a mouse?"

And Joy said sadly, "A mouse. I've often regretted it myself, sir. But I'm definitely a mouse."

Wegman Zigfield sighed.

"Oh well, Joy. Rome wasn't built in a day. Put Fromer on the telephone. I guess I'll have to tell him to go to hell myself."

Diagonally across the hall, Wylie Nolan knocked on Jiri Hozda's door and poked in his head.

"Mind if I bother you for a few minutes?"

He slipped into the chair opposite Jiri's desk, took out his pipe, and looked for an ashtray.

"Technically, there is no smoking permitted in the museum, Wylie. However, given the nature of your investigation, one doesn't wish to be petty."

From the bookshelf behind his desk, Jiri removed a beautiful white bowl with a blue dragon curling a serpentine tail around the rim. He put it in front of Wylie.

"It looks like Ming Dynasty porcelain, doesn't it?" Jiri studied the shallow bowl for a moment. "Actually, it's Pearl River discount from Canal Street in Chinatown. Feel free to get it as dirty as you please."

Wylie rested his empty pipe into the bowl. "I've got a few questions to ask you."

"And indeed, so have I you," Jiri responded. "You go first."

Wylie took a small notepad from his jacket pocket, flipped it open, and read off, "Mikos Piatigorsky, Phoebe Cullen Gill, Eleanor Overheiser, and Camden Kimcannon. I've spoken to everyone at the museum except those four people."

Jiri nodded. "This morning I sent each of them a memo explaining who you are and what you do, and telling them to be available at your convenience to answer questions."

Wylie grinned. "You're good."

Jiri raised an ironic eyebrow. "I am excellent. That is true."

"New subject. What's Lars Helmersson doing here? I saw him and two other men going into Joy Miller's office."

Jiri Hozda frowned.

"When?"

"Two minutes ago."

"Who were the other two?"

"One was the guy who threw the tantrum Friday when I wouldn't let him in the Parlor Gallery. Wegman's son. And I recognized the other from the photographs Joy gave me. He's Sarkin Zahedi."

Jiri reached for the telephone.

"What was that name again?"

"Lars Helmersson. He calls himself a fire expert, and tells people that he's my nemesis because he comes up against me regularly in court. But I come up against a lot of idiots. He just stands out from the crowd because he's slicker and smarmier than most. If he's here in this building, I can guarantee you that he's up to no good."

"I appreciate your honesty," Jiri said.

"Shit, Jiri," Wylie grinned. "If I were being honest, I would have called him a whore and told you he couldn't find his tongue with his lips if his mouth were on fire." Wylie pulled his tobacco pouch out of his pocket and began to fill the bowl of his pipe. "But I'm too much of a gentleman to talk like that."

Jiri laughed and waited through a series of rings.

"Wegman," he finally said into the telephone. "We have a scoundrel in our midst. His name is Lars Helmersson, and Wylie has just advised me that he is an agent of Satan." Jiri looked at Wylie and winked. "Wegman, can you shed some light on his presence here at the museum?"

Wylie tapped down the tobacco in his pipe, flicked a small disposable lighter, and held the flame over the bowl.

"I see . . . yes," Jiri said, listening for a few more minutes before exclaiming, "They threatened to arrest *me*! Well, my, my, my. I've certainly been the recipient of more appealing nuggets of information in my lifetime . . . What do you suggest that I do?"

Wegman spoke.

Jiri shrugged philosophically. The voice in the telephone continued to advise and Jiri continued to nod. "Yes, I would find that suitable. I, too, have the utmost respect for Max Bramble . . . yes . . . absolutely . . . I'll ask him. Thank you, Wegman. Good-bye."

Jiri hung up the telephone.

Wylie said, "So Lars Helmersson is calling the Sarkin Zahedi fires arson, is he? And he's trying to pin them on you."

"I am no stranger to skulduggery," Jiri said calmly, "but I admit that this particular accusation comes as somewhat of a surprise."

"I understand Fromer Zigfield isn't your greatest fan."

"Indeed, he is not. I replaced him as associate director of this museum."

"Does Sarkin Zahedi have it in for you, too?"

"Mr. Zahedi also is not, as you say, one of my greatest fans."

"What about the American Art Development Fund? What's that got to do with what's going on?"

"To the best of my knowledge, nothing. Now, may I pose several questions for you?"

"Sure." Wylie puffed on his pipe. "Pose away."

"Have you made a determination yet as to the cause of the fire?"

"No, and I'm not going to until I'm one-hundred percent certain how the fires started."

"Have you any ideas?"

"Yes. I sent evidence samples to my forensic lab on Saturday morning. They ran the tests I asked for on Monday. I'll have them fax me the test results when I get back to my office. If they confirm my suspicions, then I'll be ninety-five percent sure how the fire started."

"Ninety-five percent? I would have thought, Wylie, that for you, ninety-five percent is not enough."

"It isn't."

"Might one ask what you intend to do next?"

"Sure. There are still two places I have to check out. I've got an appointment to meet Sarkin Zahedi at his studio on Friday morning. And I have to visit a paint store."

"A paint store?" Jiri repeated. "Curious. Have you ruled out arson?"

"Why?" Wylie grinned. "Is Lars Helmersson right? Did you set fire to Sarkin Zahedi's paintings?"

Jiri sighed. "I'm afraid that surreptitiously burning artwork, or books, or ugly little statues of fertility goddesses with six breasts, or paintings of happy socialist workers singing on the factory assembly line . . . no, Wylie. As a political solution to an aesthetic problem, arson for me has no appeal."

"That's not what Lars Helmersson says."

"True. But I have it on the best authority that Mr. Helmersson couldn't find his teeth with his lips if his tongue were on fire."

Wylie laughed.

"I got it wrong, didn't I?" Jiri asked.

"I like it better your way."

"Wylie, Wegman suggests that you, he, and I should meet with Max Bramble at some point before Friday regarding this allegation that I am an arsonist."

"Put the meeting off for a week."

"But Fromer has told his father that I am about to be arrested."

"Not true."

"Then how can he make such a statement?"

"He's trying to scare Wegman. He's trying to scare you. Zahedi probably overinsured the paintings, and he and Fromer are afraid they won't get the full cash value of the policy from the insurance company. They're threatening to sue the museum and have you arrested because they're hoping that Wegman will think it's cheaper to settle for a large sum of money out of court than to go to the time and expense of defending his case. It happens all the time. I'm sure it's a setup. And you want to know what else I'm sure of?"

"Indeed I do."

"I'm sure that even old Lars Helmersson, who doesn't know which end of a match to strike, and as rotten an investigator as he is, that even that moron knows this is a nothing fire. And I've got better news than that. Do you want to know how the fire department is calling your fire?"

"I was reluctant to ask, but yes. I very much want to know."

" 'Undetermined.' Do you know what that means?"

"I would assume it means that the fire marshals who came here to investigate have been unable to ascertain . . . "

"Exactly. It means that the best of the best, that's what the New York City fire marshals are, that the best of the best don't know how Sarkin Zahedi's paintings went poof in the night. Guaranteed that if *they* don't know, Lars Helmersson doesn't know."

"But you, Wylie," Jiri Hozda asked quietly. "You intend to find out the cause of the fire in our museum?"

"I don't intend to find out. I will find out."

"Then Wylie, my friend, if the New York City fire marshals are the best of the best . . . what does that make you?"

The interviews Wylie conducted later that morning of Mikos Piatigorsky, the preparator; Phoebe Cullen Gill, the publicist; Bill Toomis, the guard; and the two gift shop volunteers, Eleanor Overheiser and Camden Kimcannon, were, in one instance, thought-provoking, and in the other four, just Q & A's to be gotten through.

There were two things that interested Wylie about Mikos Piatigorsky, though, and both interested him greatly. The first was Mikos's injury.

When Wylie reached out to exchange a handshake on meeting, Mikos held up a heavily bandaged right hand for inspection and said, "Sorry. Household injury."

Mikos Piatigorsky was a giant of a man, over six-and-a-half-feet tall, with shoulders and a chest as broad as a tombstone.

"What happened to your hand?" Wylie asked.

Mikos leaned toward Wylie. A vein pulsated on his huge neck like a live mouse being digested by a snake.

"Why do you want to know?" His voice boomed.

Fee fi foe fum.

"I'm investigating a fire. I ask all sorts of questions."

"Ask something else."

So, Wylie asked Mikos Piatigorsky what he remembered about having installed the Sarkin Zahedi exhibition a little over a month before.

Most of what Mikos related was consistent with what Wylie had heard before: The exhibition was small. Only five paintings. It was an easy job, because the paintings were light, merely canvas stretched over a wooden support, with simple ornamental wood frames. Each picture had a small brass plaque on the frame bearing the title of the painting and the artist's name. And all five pictures were hung on the wall with D rings. There had been no graphic work done prior to the exhibition's opening, and no titles, silk screens, or descriptive labels had been ordered by Dr. Hozda or Mr. Zigfield. Nor had any special lighting been installed. Sarkin Zahedi and Fromer Zigfield had stopped by several times to bother Mikos while he was preparing the exhibit, but since the horizontal and vertical spaces in the Parlor Gallery were so limited, the paintings could only be fitted into one, two, three, four, five obvious places in the room, which left no margin for error, and no opportunity for argument.

Wylie took an instantaneous dislike to Mikos Piatigorsky for two reasons. First, he distrusted Mikos's refusal to talk about the injury to his hand. Wylie studied the elaborate bandage that resembled the windings on a boxer's fist, and wondered if what it was covering up was a burn.

And second, Mikos affected a heavy, black mustache that, on close inspection, was neither heavy nor black, but consisted of a few spiky hairs surrounded by eyebrow pencil that had been layered thickly onto Mikos's upper lip.

Fee fi foe fum.

Wylie could not take seriously a man with a painted mustache. Nor could he take his eyes off those few, spiky little hairs when they jumped this way and that, as Mikos thundered and growled.

"Child's play," Mikos Piatigorsky grumbled. "A very easy installation. The paintings were delivered. They were hung. Except for the stink, all of my exhibitions should be like that."

Wylie shifted his eyes away from Mikos's mustache to look into Mikos's eyes.

"Stink? What stink?"

"Terrible. Disgusting. Offensive . . . I uncrated the paintings, and thought, 'I am going to vomit,' " Mikos's voice boomed. "But then ten, twenty minutes later, the stink was gone."

"What was it?"

"I don't know," Mikos thundered again. "Maybe it was a dead fire investigator."

Fee fi foe fum.

Later, during Wylie's brief conversation with the museum's publicist, he discovered that Phoebe Cullen Gill was newly divorced, had always wanted to go out with a fireman, believed in sexual experimentation, had a half share in a house on Fire Island, believed in meeting new people, had no qualms about being the aggressor in a relationship, and knew absolutely nothing about what had gone on in or out of the corridors of the Zigfield Art Museum in the last four years, let alone in the last five days.

When Phoebe asked Wylie for his telephone number, he mumbled something about not taking on any new commitments this year, because his eyebrows needed plucking and that he really had to do something about the cranberry stains in the brocade on his piano stool.

And as he made his escape, Phoebe Cullen Gill stood, looking after him in her doorway, with a distinct expression on her face that seemed to be asking the question, "Wait a second now. Is it *me* who's crazy, or is it *him*?"

Bill Toomis, the full-time guard, explained to Wylie Nolan that since the Zigfield was a relatively small museum he had no fixed position, but wandered from gallery to gallery as he saw fit.

He had only been working at the museum for five months, and had taken over the position from his uncle, who'd just retired to Florida. Bill knew little of the museum gossip, loved his job, thought that to be able to spend all day surrounded by beautiful paintings was something in the nature of a benediction, and liked everyone with whom he worked.

He was middle-aged, middle height, middle size, middle every-thing—except that he was almost completely bald. As he answered Wylie's questions, he kept removing his uniform cap every few minutes to rub a hand over his head, as though to smooth back an imaginary strand of hair.

Thursday had been Bill Toomis's day off; and he hadn't come in un-til 10:00 a.m. on Friday, when the halls were a hubbub of lawyers, insur-ance company adjusters, and fire investigators. So even though he was willing to talk, he really didn't have anything provocative to say.

When Wylie asked him what he'd thought of Sarkin Zahedi's paint-ings, Bill Toomis said that he hadn't thought much of them, and that he'd rarely gone in the Parlor Gallery.

"Why?" Wylie asked.

Bill Toomis thought about the answer for a second and then shrugged. "I guess because this is a museum, and I considered it my job to guard the *real* art."

"You mean you didn't consider Sarkin Zahedi's paintings real art?"

Bill Toomis removed his hat, flattened down a few more illusory hairs, and said, "Mr. Nolan, you got to be kidding. Every one of them was just a piece of crap."

Mrs. Eleanor Overheiser, recently widowed, struck Wylie as being a nice woman. He lent her his handkerchief once, twice, and then told her just to keep it after the third time she burst into tears as she reminisced about Manny. Poor, dead Manny.

She, too, had been isolated from the activities taking place away from the area where she worked (in the gift shop), and couldn't tell Wylie anything about the events that had immediately preceded the fire.

But she was able to show Wylie pictures of her six grandchildren, and instruct him on the proper procedure for making tea ("You have to let the water come to a full boil first. Then you pour the boiling water into the teapot, swish it around, and dump it out. That's to get the pot itself really hot in preparation for the tea.")

By the time Wylie left Mrs. Overheiser, she had managed to get the address of his office ("I promise not to give it to Miss Cullen Gill, the man-hunter."), so that the following week, she could send him a sample ("You're going to love it.") of her nonfat pumpkin cheesecake ("I know that you're as thin as a rail, Mr. Nolan, but when I think of my Manny, you can never be too careful about your cholesterol.").

By the time Wylie finally got around to his last interview, which was in the conference room with Camden Kimcannon, he had already encountered a bad-tempered behemoth with a false mustache, a divorcée with nymphomaniac tendencies, a guard who thought he was an art critic, and a little old lady with a limited supply of handkerchiefs and an unlimited supply of tears.

So, when Camden stood up wearing what Wylie didn't know was called a poet's shirt (its "arty" balloon sleeves tapered to wide, oversize cuffs), he was in a frame of mind to consider that a man who wasn't sure in what century he lived, was, if not normal, at least not unacceptably abnormal.

Camden told Wylie . . .

that Sarkin Zahedi's work was indefensible,

that Fromer Zigfield was a varlet,

that Phoebe Cullen Gill was a slut,

that Joy Miller was an angel,

that his compadre, Mrs. Eleanor Overheiser, was a delightful old "yenta," but that her six grandchildren were blood-sucking money grubbers who should be boiled in oil,

that Jiri Hozda was a prince,

that Wegman Zigfield was a king . . .

And that Georgiana Weeks was the most wonderful woman who had ever walked the planet.

When Wylie said that he had no idea who Georgiana Weeks was, Camden commented adoringly, "That's right! She didn't get here until after your fire."

Which precipitated Wylie Nolan's last shot in the dark. He asked, "How do *you* think that the fire occurred?"

"If there were any justice in aesthetics," Camden answered, "Sarkin Zahedi's paintings would have committed suicide, because they were just too damn ugly to exist."

As soon as Wylie Nolan left the conference room, Camden Kimcannon ran down the hall.

Without knocking on Georgiana Weeks's office door, he burst in.

"Am I late?"

Georgiana was at her desk, pointing out a correction on one of the papers in front of her, and Joy Miller was leaning over her shoulder.

Joy looked up. Camden's eyes were feverish, and his hands were clenching and unclenching nervously.

Camden stared at Georgiana.

Joy Miller stared at Camden, her face flush.

And Georgiana looked from Joy to Camden, and said to herself, "*Hmm* . . . interesting."

Aloud, she said, "Calm down, Camden. And sit down. You aren't late. You're early. You're like Goldilock's porridge." And Joy and Camden spontaneously recited, right along with her, "*You're just right!*"

The three of them burst out laughing.

Camden flopped into a chair.

Joy tapped one pile of papers on Georgiana's desk.

"If Cam can finish proofreading this with you, I really should get back to my office. Mr. Zigfield's threatening to write a new will leaving everything to Fromer just so that he can disinherit him again later, and I'm not sure if Jiri's trying to calm him down or egg him on, because Jiri finds Mr. Zigfield very amusing when he's angry. If you can get along without me, I think I'd better return to the scene of the crime and try to restore some order."

Georgiana smiled. She glanced at Joy's limp, colorless hair and over her dowdy two-piece business suit.

"Joy," she said impulsively, "let's have lunch together sometime before the exhibition opens. My treat."

"Lunch together. *You* and *me?*" Joy responded as though an guardian angel had dropped the seeds for a magic beanstalk in her lap.

"Sure. Just the two of us. And maybe we'll do some shopping on the side. What do you say?"

"Oh, Georgiana. I'd love to."

"Good. Monday we'll set the date. You warn your boss that I'm kidnapping you for a *long* lunch, and not to have any more fires or crises until we get back. Now, get out of here. Scoot."

Joy hesitated for a moment at the door.

"Good-bye, Cam."

Camden Kimcannon looked up. He smiled at Joy. For an incalculable instant, his jittery nerves seemed to have abated.

"So long, kid," he said.

And Georgiana settled comfortably into her chair, repeated "So long, kid" to herself silently, and then thought, "Will wonders never cease?"

Proofreading the copy for the exhibition labels took much longer than Georgiana had expected, because a lot of the sentences that she'd thought were too long were actually too short, and some of the explanations she'd thought were just right had to be edited drastically.

After about three hours, she pushed her chair away from her desk and stretched.

"Camden," she said. "You're doing a great job."

"Thank you. And my name is Camelot."

Since her visit to City Island two days before, neither she nor Camden had mentioned the disaster that had been "tea." Georgiana stared across the desk at her new assistant, marveling at his ability to concentrate at the task at hand, and at his apparent talent for evading everything else.

Suddenly, without having planned to do so, she asked, "Cam, who owns your home?"

"I do."

"You do as in poetically, or you do as in legally?"

"What do you mean?"

"I mean, who's the deed made out to?"

"I don't know."

"Where did you get the house? Did you buy it yourself with your own money, or does it really belong to your mother?"

"It's my mother's house."

"Where'd she get it from? Did she save up the money she made when she was an actress to put down a deposit?"

"No. When my parents moved here, they bought the house."

"Did you father pay for the house?"

"I don't know. Probably."

"Where is your father, Cam?"

"He abandoned us when I was ten years old."

"Is he a wealthy man?"

"I lost track of him, but I don't think so."

"Then how come your mother got the house?"

"I guess he just gave it to her."

"Who pays the electric bill, Cam? The gas bill? The taxes? Do you pay all of that?"

He shook his head.

"Does your mother pay all of those bills?"

Camden Kimcannon didn't respond.

"Well, somebody must be paying them, Cam. Are you sure that your father is as bad as you say he is?"

Camden said nothing.

"What does your father do?"

"He's a sportswriter."

"For whom?"

"I don't know. Last time I looked, it was for the *Daily News*."

"Do you ever see him?"

"No. He doesn't want to have anything to do with us."

"How do you know that, Cam? Did he ever say that to you personally?"

Camden said nothing.

"Have you ever picked up the telephone and called him?"

"No."

"Would you?"

"No."

"Cam, did it ever occur to you that there are two sides to every story, and that your father may have had good reasons for leaving your mother? That he may have felt his peace of mind or that even his sanity were at stake?"

No answer.

"You know, Cam, you refer to the house in City Island as *your* house, but it really isn't, is it? It's your mother's house."

"A mere slip of the tongue. The house belongs to the Mater."

"Cam, have you ever thought of getting your own apartment?"

"No."

"Of getting on with your life? With your *own* life? Of extricating yourself from your childhood, from your fantasies, from City Island, from your dreams of someday being an artist, and really getting down to the nitty-gritty of producing art?"

Camden Kimcannon stood up and backed away from Georgiana, horrified.

"What are you saying? I *am* an artist. I'm a painter."

"I was in your room, Cam. All I saw was a sketch pad on your desk, with a few ink drawings inside."

"I have more work. I've done a lot of painting."

"Where are your paintings, then?"

"They're in the garage."

"Did you ever consider that your mother drinks, Cam? That you could be living with an active alcoholic, and that this might affect your aproach to reality, and also be the reason why your father left?"

"No. Absolutely not. That's out of the question. It is absolutely not true."

"Cam," Georgiana also stood up. "You have brains, talent, a beautiful soul. You're handsome, you're young, you have your whole life ahead of you, and you have great sensitivity. But in all my life, I have never seen anyone less aware that he is living at the bottom of a pit paved with glass. And there's no way to climb to the top of it, Cam. It has no footholds. It has no hand holds. You can never get any traction. Because that's the purpose of a pit. To keep you inside. And that's the purpose of a pit keeper. To make sure that you never realize that there's an unlocked door at the bottom of the pit, and that all you have to do to get outside is open the door. Cam, your only chance of survival is to open that door and get out of that pit while you still have a chance."

Camden Kimcannon looked at Georgiana steadily for about sixty seconds, and for all of those sixty seconds there was nothing but unmitigated hatred in his eyes. Then, suddenly, his eyes went blank.

He sat down again, picked up a pencil, and said, "If you like, I can put in a call to the loading dock, and ask them if the Pre-Raphaelite paintings have arrived."

24

Max Bramble poked his head through the open door to Wylie Nolan's office.

"Anybody here?"

From behind the bubble glass divider that separated the minuscule reception area from the secretary's desk, Max heard Miranda's voice.

"Nobody's here, Max. Go home."

Max walked into the office and pulled the door shut behind him. He looked at his watch.

"Miranda, what are you doing here so early?"

Miranda didn't answer.

He stepped around the divider.

She was hunched over like a triangle, with her fingers entwined in thick clumps of hair, and her elbows digging into the top of the desk. Instead of her usual parochial school outfit, she was wearing paint-splattered blue jeans with a black T-shirt. In the center of the T-shirt was a raven, outlined in white, and the word *Nevermore*.

Max pursed his lips as he stared down at her.

"Getting ready to audition for a cheerleading job at the morgue?" he asked.

He reached out and carefully extricated her fingers from her hair. Then he pulled her gently but firmly out of the chair, led her back to the receptionist area, and pushed her down on one of Wylie's two brown suede chairs.

He sat down opposite Miranda.

"Now, tell Uncle Max all about it."

Miranda began to twist her hands nervously in front of her.

Max reached out and held them apart by the fingertips.

"OK," he said. " 'Fess up. What's wrong?"

Miranda looked down at the floor. "I'm depressed," she said. Her voice was bell clear.

"Clinically depressed? Or just It's-Wednesday-morning-and-I-haven't-had-my-coffee-or-a-cigarette-yet depressed?"

Miranda looked up.

Max gave her a big smile.

Despite her best effort to remain dejected, the tips of her lips curved briefly upward.

Max Bramble, although not a particularly handsome man, was like the Ping-Pong balls in the *Titanic*. He was incorrigibly buoyant, and impossible to keep down.

His short brown hair was straight. His narrow eyes, tucked under low eyebrows, were friendly. And he had high, round, pinchable cheeks. He wasn't exactly tall. Nor could he be described as thin. And he certainly wasn't fat. In fact, everything about him was just unrelentingly and unspectacularly *nice*.

Some people, particularly plaintiff's lawyers, resented the stand-up predictability of Max Bramble, and tried to egg him on to companionable acts of moral turpitude with clever little viciousnesses of their own. But Wylie Nolan liked Max's dogged, even-tempered reliability; and Miranda Yee was finding his upbeat persistence hard to resist.

Nonetheless, she continued to try.

"I should never have become a lawyer," she said glumly.

Max nodded.

"I get it. Something's askew in your office. Your clients aren't paying, right? Is that it?"

Miranda shook her head. "I just hate the law. That's all."

Max released her fingers and leaned against the back of the chair.

"John Locke said that 'Wherever law ends, tyranny begins.' "

Miranda shot back, "What he should have said was that wherever the lawyer ends, the secretary begins. And *that's* where the tyranny comes from."

Max snapped his fingers.

"Now I see it. It's not the 'Accounts Receivable Blues' that you're singing. It's the 'Amanuensis Blues.' Who's driving you up the wall this time?"

Miranda said nothing.

"All right," Max continued methodically. "Let's start with Irma the shrew. Is she the cause of your present nonclinical, if I might venture to diagnose, depression?"

"No. Irma still has the flu."

"How about Clarence Darrow?"

"His name is Clarence Chang."

"Nonetheless, is he the one," Max's eyes dropped to the malevolent image of Edgar Allan Poe's raven leering from her T-shirt, "who's inspired today's cheerful fashion statement?"

Miranda shook her head. "Clarence is all right."

"Then by a process of elimination, the crux of the problem must be your temporary factotum, Miss Viola True. Or, as Shakespeare said, ' 'Tis true 'tis pity; and pity 'tis true.' What's she done this time? Rearranged all of your paper clips into size places? Cleaned your telephone dial with a Q-Tip? Polished the handles on your file cabinet drawers?"

"I don't want to talk about it."

"You're pouting."

"I want to pout."

"My mother always told me that if you pout long enough your face will get stuck in that position. But if you don't mind looking like a prune . . . " He slapped his thighs and stood up. "Time to get this show on the road. Where's Wylie?"

Miranda shrugged.

"If Wylie isn't here, how did you get into his office?"

"I have his keys. He has mine."

"Did he tell you that we have an appointment this morning?"

Miranda didn't say anything.

Max grabbed her by the hands and pulled her to her feet.

"Damn it, woman, snap out of this! Put on some lipstick, pick up an Uzzi machine gun, throw back your shoulders, march into your office, and fire the bitch."

Miranda shook off his hands.

"I'm not going back in there, Max."

"But it's your office. You know . . . computers. Typewriters. Telephones. Desks. It isn't a snake pit or a slave galley. It's just an office."

Miranda glared at Max. "You can't make me go."

Max folded his arms across his chest, nodded, and said, "I think a reality check is in order here. *You* are Miranda Yee. You are a successful lawyer. In that suite of rooms at the end of this hallway is Viola True. She's a typist. A stenographer. A skinny, spinsterish little temp. I have a pet ferret at home that weighs about thirty-two ounces. Even he could take her. If you snarled at her once, she'd probably shatter into a thousand irreparable neuroses, like Humpty Dumpty. Tell her she's fired. If you don't want to do that, call up the temp agency that sent her, and have them tell her, but don't . . . "

Max suddenly realized that Miranda's lower lip was quivering, and that tears were forming in her gorgeous, big brown eyes.

"Ah, Miranda, Miranda, Miranda," he said helplessly. "*I'll* go in there and get rid of her if you want me to."

But Miranda Yee shook her head, and in doing so dislodged two huge tears; such big tears that when they fell to the carpet, Max actually heard them go *plop*.

"It's . . . it's . . . it's . . . " Miranda stuttered tearfully.

Max took a step forward and put one arm around what he noticed for the first time was a small, soft and feminine waist. Then he encircled her with both arms. She felt frail and delicate. As if all that her beautiful, creamy skin covered was a precarious construction of hummingbird bones.

He said softly, "What is it, dear?"

Miranda gulped, sniffled, and then sobbed into his chest, "It's . . . it's . . . it's just that nobody every accused me of being an arsonist before."

25

Wylie Nolan burst into his office, announcing, "A water main broke on Second Avenue, and everything was gridlocked for forty-five minutes. I'm sorry I'm late."

Max had left Miranda alone on the brown suede chair in the reception area only long enough to get three cups of coffee from the deli in the lobby. He was back before Wylie arrived. The coffee was still hot when he handed Wylie a cup, which Wylie almost dropped when he noticed the residue of tears in Miranda Yee's red eyes.

He looked at Max.

Max shrugged, and said, "One, she's depressed. Two, she hates being a lawyer. Presumably, this, too, shall pass. Three, she hates Viola True. And four, she feels that her honor has been besmirched because some lowlife has accused her of setting fires."

Wylie nodded to Max and then shook his head at Miranda.

"This is my fault. Come into my office. Both of you."

He sat down behind his desk. Max and Miranda each took a chair opposite.

"Miranda, I owe you an apology. I've dug myself in so deep at the museum that I didn't think to stay in touch. You probably thought I forgot about you when I didn't call after we talked on Friday. Is that it?"

"Sort of," Miranda replied. But her voice was less dejected than it had been an hour earlier. And when she looked across the desk at him she didn't avoid Wylie's eyes.

"I really am sorry," Wylie said. "I hate it that you spent the whole weekend worried. Don't ever let that happen again, Miranda. If you need me, call me. Any time. Any place. That's an order."

"Me, too," Max offered, and repeated, "Any time. Any place."

Miranda turned to him. "You? Why you? What can you do?"

"Sing excerpts from operettas. Tell lawyer jokes. Send flowers."

"Do either of you remember me talking about Eddie NoName?" Wylie asked.

"I do," Miranda said. "He's the guy in the fire marshal's office. You said that he could build a stealth bomber out of tongue depressors and rubber bands."

"That's Eddie. He's an electronics genius."

"This is scaring me, Wylie. What do we need an electronics genius for?"

"Not for his brains. I just need an extra body tomorrow, because we're going to conduct a surveillance on the ladies' room. Jubar is letting us use his office."

"Jubar Haddad? That sweet old man with the import-export business?"

"Same guy."

"Won't we be in his way?"

"Not *we*. Just me and Eddie. I have other plans for you. You're my decoy. I don't know if when you were a kid you ever wanted to play at being a cop, Miranda. But if you did, tomorrow's your chance."

"I hope I don't have to dress up like a prostitute. I'm not sure I could . . . "

"You don't have to dress up like a prostitute."

"Then I'll do it, because I can't stand knowing that someone out there is focusing all of his hostility on me."

"I wish hostility were all we were up against," Wylie said sharply. "But what we've got here is a potential life and death situation."

Max and Miranda exchanged an apprehensive glance and then turned back to Wylie.

"That's right. I said 'life and death.' You see, the biggest problem with arsonists, and the smartest one of them is still a stupid son of a bitch, is that they think they can control a fire in an uncontrolled setting. That's why so many of them wind up in the burn units of hospitals after they torch their houses and cars. That's why so many of them get into boy/girl altercations, toss a match under an apartment building stair-case—'just to put a little scare in her'—and instead end up killing fifty people and burning down an entire block. That's why Smoky the Bear warns campers not to toss out lit cigarettes in the forest, and tells them to make sure their campfires are extinguished. Because one cinder from a twig or log or cigarette stub can burn down the whole state of Califor-nia, and almost has. The fact is . . . " And Wylie looked Max and Miranda in the eye, and Miranda got goose bumps, and Max realized for the first time what Wylie must have been like when, as a fire marshal, he hunted down people stupid or evil enough to set fires.

"The fact is that whoever wrote that anonymous letter and set those fires in the bathroom . . . whoever that person is, she is an immediate and direct threat to all of our lives and property, and to the lives and property of everybody in this building. Do you understand what I'm saying?"

"I do."

"So do I."

"Do you realize how serious this is?"

"Yes."

"Me, too."

"Okay. Then this is our battle plan. Miranda, since Friday was the last fire and today is Wednesday, I'm assuming that you haven't had a cig-arette this week in the ladies' room."

"I've been smoking in my office."

"Discretion is said to be the better part of valor," Max volunteered.

"Then it's time to stop being discreet, Miranda, because tomorrow I want you to repeat everything you did last week. When are your ciga-rette breaks?"

"Ten-thirty in the morning. And then three cigarettes in the after-noon. One at one-thirty; another at three-thirty; and the last one at four-forty-five."

"Take your breaks at exactly those times. Do everything you did before, with no variation: Cigarette behind ear; matchbook and keys in skirt pocket. Open the window the way you opened it last week. Lean against the windowsill the way you leaned against it last week, and so on. The only changes I want you to make in your behavior are these: First, can you rig the door to the ladies' room so that it doesn't lock when you leave?"

Miranda nodded. "If I pull it shut behind me, I can stop it just before the locking mechanism clicks in. Lots of times, I find the door stuck open that way."

"Good. Do it. And the second thing is that I want you to pay attention this time. If someone comes into the bathroom, don't make eye contact, but notice who she is, what she's carrying, whether or not she spends too much time looking at you. Do nothing different but notice everything. That's how we're going to stop this pyromaniac."

"Pyromaniac?" Max said. "Is that what she is?"

"I'm not a psychiatrist," Wylie answered, "but that's what I think we're dealing with. And even though she may have convinced herself that she's the Joan of Arc of clean air on a sacred mission to rid the world of smokers, she's really just a sicko getting her rocks off on fire. That's her real motivation. That's the motive for all pathological fire setters. Plain and simple, they get a sick kick out of setting fires."

"I don't like this, Wylie," Max said grimly. "If what you're saying is true, then we're all at risk here."

"You're not. But Miranda and I are in a building that some lunatic is trying to burn down." Wylie paused before he added, "Miranda, let's make out a suspect list. How many women work on the seventh floor?"

"I never paid attention. I just know who's in my own office. Me. Irma. And until I strangle her, Viola True. Vincent Marchand has a secretary. Her name is Gail McGrath. But Gail hasn't been in for two weeks, because Vincent is in the West Indies. I don't think Mr. Haddad has a secretary. He always goes into his office alone. And I don't know about anyone else. How about you, Wylie?"

"My list is the same as yours."

"Then why don't we ask Harold Pittman to meet us here tomorrow morning? He knows everybody in the building; he can tell us who works on the seventh floor."

"Who's Harold Pittman?" Max asked.

"He's the building owner," Wylie answered. "Or manager. Or both. Miranda, ask Harold to meet us here at eight o'clock. I'll call Eddie NoName and tell him to get here early, too."

"How about me," Max said. "What can I do?"

Wylie thumbed through his Rolodex. He pulled out a card and handed it to Max.

"Call Chem-Test Labs and ask them to fax us the test results on the samples I sent. Then after I look them over, we can roll up our sleeves and get cracking again on the fires at the Zigfield Art Museum."

26

Wylie had sent ten samples to Chem-Test Labs, with instructions that they be analyzed for the presence of a flammable liquid. He had taken one strip of canvas from each side of the five frames for comparison samples, because he wanted to determine if the flammable liquid he was looking for was everywhere on the painting, nowhere on the painting, or just somewhere on the painting.

The test results he got back were similar for all ten samples: Pigments and other additives consistent with the composition of paint were identified, as was a varnish sold as Varnigloss containing one acrylic resin. Rubber cement, turpentine, and a solvent consistent with the chemical composition of linseed oil were also found to be present in the samples; and Chem-Test found trace amounts of petroleum distillate and naphthenic salts, both of which are components of Japan Driers.

Wylie read the Chem-Test fax and handed it to Max, who perused the contents, and dropped it on Wylie's desk.

"What does it mean?"

"It means that when I go to Sarkin Zahedi's studio on Friday, I'll know what I'm looking for."

"He agreed to see you on Friday? Nice work, Wylie. How did you pull that off?"

"I didn't. I asked the insurance company to call him and set up an appointment for their fire investigator to ask a few questions and tie up some loose ends. Zahedi had no objection to talking, but he wanted me to come to his home instead of to his studio. So I told the claims representative to say that some of my questions would relate to work in progress and pre- and postfire evaluation of future earnings, and that it would be best to meet where his reference material and files were—gobbledegook and double talk, but I don't think that Zahedi caught on."

"Do you want me to come along with you, Wylie?"

"Thanks, but no thanks, Max. Lawyers scare people. Nobody trusts them. I'll go alone, ask a few questions, make a few observations, and look sincere. And when I leave, I'm not taking any prisoners."

27

Luis Cabrerra's silver hair was softly tousled, and as his eyes looked up at the clock on the wall behind his desk, they twinkled as though geniality came as easily to him as breathing.

It was two o'clock.

Wylie Nolan walked into Luis's office exactly on time and pulled the door shut behind him.

Luis was dressed in his musical comedy Ruritanian army general's uniform, which his wife had proudly designed and which Mrs. Zigfield, before the Alzheimer's disease had stolen her sense of humor, had insisted that he had the right to wear.

Mr. Zigfield's tailor, adhering to Mrs. Cabrerra's drawings, had made four identical uniforms for Luis, which he wore interchangeably. They were impeccably constructed, and consisted of so many yards of gold braid and so many brass buttons that Wegman Zigfield had often muttered irritably to his wife, "Every time I see Luis, I keep expecting him to launch into an aria from *The Student Prince*."

Luis pulled an extra chair over to his desk.

Wylie opened his briefcase, removed three stacks of computer printouts, and gave them to the security director.

"I hate to bother you with this, Luis, but I can't make head or tails of it."

Luis nodded sympathetically.

"Truly, the printouts contain many abbreviations and also, there are a great quantity of symbols and codes." He pulled three sheets of paper out of a drawer. "I have here prepared a key sheet, and we can look first at the words and the codes, and then we can make reference back to . . . "

The door to the security room jerked open.

Fromer Zigfield, peering with unfriendly eyes through his wire-rim glasses, came into the small office. "I'm going to kick you out of the room for a few minutes, Luis. I want to have a private word with my father's fire expert."

Luis stood up. He thrust back his shoulders, and the gold braid on his epaulets gleamed with more authority than did the gentle look in his eyes.

"Mr. Fromer," he said, "it is the rules of the museum that if I am not in the security office, the room cannot be occupied, and it must be locked. You are welcome to converse with Mr. Nolan if Mr. Nolan wishes to converse with you. But with sincere regrets I must advise you that if you wish to have a private conversation, you must have it outside, because I am not permitted to leave."

"Bullshit," Fromer Zigfield snapped, and he looked at Wylie. "I want to talk to you."

Wylie took out his pipe.

"There's no smoking allowed in the museum."

"Don't worry. I didn't light it," Wylie responded lazily. "Yet."

Fromer gave Luis a dismissive glance.

Wylie shook his head. "If I stay, Luis stays. And unless you're proposing marriage or you want to know my dress size, how personal can it be?"

Fromer glanced around the security office with irritation.

"I don't suppose there's any place here for me to sit down."

Luis pushed his own chair forward.

"Please make yourself comfortable, Mr. Fromer. I will occupy myself with filing at the back of the room."

Fromer sat.

"Actually, Wylie," he said, "I'm just here as a matter of courtesy, since you happen to be my father's arson detective."

"Why thank you, Fromer. And please feel free to call me Mr. Nolan." Wylie unfolded a tobacco pouch and began to fill his pipe bowl with tobacco.

"And one more thing. I don't work for your father and I don't work for the Zigfield Museum. I was hired by the insurance company to investigate fires that occurred *at* the Zigfield Museum. Now, what else do you want to talk about? Target practice?" Wylie flipped back his jacket and looked down at his holstered .38 revolver. "Bird watching? Cleansing creams?"

"You're very sarcastic, *Mr.* Nolan, but you aren't very funny. And it doesn't matter whether you work for my father or not, because either way, you're still the investigator on this case, and if you're really doing your job, you'll be obliged to me for the information that I'm going to give you."

Wylie lifted his pipe to his mouth, and took a few experimental pulls on it, pleasurably observing the disapproval in Fromer's eyes. But instead of commenting on the pipe, Fromer edged his chair closer to Wylie and whispered, almost conspiratorially, "I know who set the fire."

Wylie leaned forward and also whispered, "Who set which fire?"

"The one in the Parlor Gallery."

"That wasn't one fire, Fromer. That was five separate fires."

"See," Fromer announced in a normal voice. "I just knew that crazy Czech did it!"

Wylie tilted his chair back on its two rear legs and folded his arms behind his head.

Fromer edged even closer. He pulled out a sheaf of folded pages from the inside pocket of his jacket.

"Jiri had a motive, Wylie."

He flipped the pages open. "It's all down here in black and white."

Wylie let the front legs of his chair bang to the floor and took the handful of papers.

"What is it?"

"It's an article. See here. It's by Jiri Hozda. It was published last August in the *National Archivist*."

"Never heard of it."

"It's an obscure museum publication written by art historians and the only people who read it work in museums. The article is called 'Funded Art—What Does It Really Mean?' and once you've read it, it becomes perfectly clear why Jiri set fire to Sarkin Zahedi's paintings."

Wylie tapped down the tobacco in his pipe bowl with his finger.

"I'm listening," he said.

"I'll let Jiri tell you himself. In his own words."

Fromer flattened out the pages he was holding and began to read:

"What Americans choose not to recognize in their cheerful, public-spirited, righteously indignant defense of this politically mandated and publicly financed organization, is that it, the American Art Development Fund, is the government, and that in the very course of its designated function—that of endowing certain artists with federally funded grants and denying those same grants to artists of whom it disapproves—it is the only political body in the United States of American through which art censorship is not only permitted, but in which it is applauded."

Fromer smiled smugly at Wylie.

"See? It's perfectly clear! Jiri didn't want any exhibition in this museum to be sponsored by the American Art Development Fund, because he doesn't believe that the government should be involved with art. He's positively fanatical on the subject. Behind his back, some curators even call him an anarchist. So you see, that's his motive."

Wylie stared into Fromer Zigfield's eyes. There was no expression at all on Wylie's face.

Fromer continued reading:

"It is critical at this point for someone, and perhaps I am the appropriate gadfly because I was once a victim of Soviet censorship, to cry out loud and clear to the people of this great country, 'Beware any government interference in the arts, because all forms of subsidy are inherently exclusionary. Every dollar given to one artist is a dollar and a dream taken away from another artist. And the artist who has not come to the government for a handout is more likely to be the one with the integrity and the vision to produce a work of art that is truly worth seeing.' "

"Here it is, Wylie. In black and white. It's practically a confession that he set the fires."

Fromer threw the article down on Luis's desk, and the pages flared out like discarded tarot cards.

"See!" he said, as though the matter was settled.

"Yes," Wylie nodded. "I see. I never thought about it before, but, yep. You're right. Jiri sure as hell had a motive."

"I told you. I told you. I knew it. That crazy Czech. Setting fires in my father's museum!"

"We do have a problem, though." Wylie gathered together the scattered pages of the article.

"What problem? Everything fits. Jiri was born in Prague. He got his doctorate degrees in art history and archeology there. When Alexander Dubcek came to power, Jiri was one of his most conspicuous supporters. When the Soviets invaded Czechoslovakia and abducted Dubcek to the Soviet Union, one of Jiri's best friends was killed in the unsuccessful resistance to the invasion, and Jiri escaped to the United States. With his credentials, he could have had a brilliant career at any museum in this country. But he'll only work in privately owned museums, because he *hates* all governmental interference in the arts, and he hated that Sarkin Zahedi's exhibition was government funded. It's a crusade for him. It's a religion. An obsession."

Wylie folded Jiri's article into a compact square of pages, put them in his jacket pocket, and said, "Jiri didn't seem all that obsessed to me. In fact, he seems like a nice guy."

"Nice," Wegman Zigfield's son snorted.

"You know, Fromer," Wylie said, "you seem a whole lot more familiar with the facts about Jiri Hozda than is altogether healthy. Considering he's a man that you don't even particularly like."

"I made it my point to know everything about him."

"Well, you get an A for effort, but there's still one thing that you missed."

"And that *is*?"

"The museum's security system makes a record of who went in and out of the museum, and it records all that data on the printouts over here on Luis's desk. And what those printouts tell us is that nobody, and that includes Jiri Hozda, entered the museum after eight o'clock on Thursday night, or reentered the museum before seven o'clock on Friday morning.

So, even if Jiri Hozda were the anarchist and fanatic that you think he is, he couldn't have gotten into the Parlor Gallery during the right time parameters to have set those fires."

Fromer smiled smugly.

"But you're forgetting something."

Wylie shrugged. "I've done that before. What did I forget this time?"

"That Jiri didn't *have* to leave the museum the night before the fire. He could have locked himself in his own office and spent the night there. And right before seven o'clock on Friday morning, he could have sneaked over to the Parlor Gallery, unlocked the door, and set fire to Sarkin Zahedi's paintings. Then he could have returned to his office, locked himself in again, and waited until there was enough commotion in the halls so that no one would notice when he arrived, or where he'd come from."

Wylie turned to Luis Cabrerra.

"Is that possible, Luis?"

The security director walked slowly, sadly to his desk. He said nothing, but he nodded his head.

"How so?"

"At night," Luis explained, "I am always the last one to depart. All who leave before me say 'Good night, Luis.' But they do not have to sign anything. They do not have to lock doors or punch time cards. And they may leave from the front door or from the rear door. No one would see them go. No one would of necessity know when they had gone home."

Wylie said thoughtfully, "And the Parlor Gallery doesn't have a keypad. I remember that."

"None of the galleries have keypads," Fromer said, and behind his granny glasses, his watery eyes glinted with unbecoming glee. "Some of them don't even have locks. So you see, Wylie, Jiri not only had the motive to set fire to Sarkin's painting, he also had the opportunity."

Wylie nodded and pulled a cigarette lighter out of his shirt pocket. He flicked it once and stared into Fromer's eyes.

Then he took a deep, long, satisfying draw against his pipe stem, blew out a thick, gray stream of smoke, and said, "There. I've gone and done it, Fromer. I just lit my pipe in the museum against all of the rules and regulations. *Now* you can worry."

28

When Miranda Yee called Harry Pittman for a meeting to discuss the case on the following morning, he suggested that they hold it in his conference room on the twenty-fourth floor, where there would be more space to spread out.

"But we don't need to spread out, Harry."

"Spread out. Don't spread out. It doesn't matter. But maybe your arsonist is an early riser, and what I'm thinking is it would look funny, all of us, at eight o'clock in the morning, going into Wylie's office. Then he/she/it sees us, gets suspicious about what we're doing, and sends me another anonymous letter or maybe even a letter bomb this time, because that's a possibility, too. Who knows when you're dealing with a loony tune what they're going to do next?"

So, Wylie told Eddie NoName to come to the twenty-fourth floor on Thursday morning instead of to his office; and Eddie NoName said sure, no problem, and that he had a surprise for Wylie. Wylie asked what it was, but Eddie replied, logically, that if he told him, then it wouldn't be a surprise.

Harry Pittman, with his cinnamon-colored hair and freckles, was wearing a rusty brown shirt under an orange sweater, and looked very much like a gingerbread cookie. The wall that separated the conference room from the corridor was made out of glass, and anyone getting into or out of the elevator had a clear view of everything going on inside. From where he sat in his conference room, Harry waved to Miranda Yee as she got off the elevator.

Miranda walked in, pointed to the glass wall, and said, "Great idea, Harry. This is discreet. Nobody will every see us in here."

Harry took the cover off a box of fresh pastries, and as he arranged the contents on paper plates, said, "Not to worry. No one ever comes up to the twenty-fourth floor. Have a Danish. I bought three cheese, two raspberry, and two prune. I, personally, could never touch a prune Danish, but who am I to judge? Miranda, you look great this morning. I don't know what it is with you. I think it's the hair."

"My hair is a mess, Harry."

"Yes. No. Mess. Maybe. But it's so thick. Black. Gorgeous. Shiny. I bet if you wanted to, you could make a fortune growing wigs."

Miranda slipped into a chair at the conference table, propped her chin against her knuckles, and stared at him.

"I *think* you mean the things you say as compliments, Harry. It's just that what you say is so crazy, I'm not a hundred percent sure."

Harry looked dumbfounded. Confused. Completely at a loss.

"What'd I say, Miranda? Something awful this time, didn't I? I hurt your feelings. I feel terrible. I'm going to kill myself. Here. Have two Danish. Have a cheese and a prune. And coffee. Tell me how you like it." He stood up. "Milk? No milk? Sugar? No sugar?"

Miranda said, "I don't want to become a hair farm to grown wigs, Harry."

Harry sat down again, ran a freckled hand over his freckled bald spot, and said, "Let me tell you, men are vain. Whoever said it was women didn't know a thing, Miranda. But me? I'd give a fortune if I could grow hair. Any time. Any place. For anyone. What time is it? It's almost eight o'clock. Where are your friends?"

Harry looked past Miranda's shoulder, through the glass wall to the elevator bank across the hall.

A green light went on over the middle elevator. The doors slid open, and Eddie NoName and Wylie Nolan walked out.

. . .

Harry flipped through the eight files in front of him and pulled out four. As he read off each label, he dropped the folder back onto the table.

"Suite seven hundred. This is yours, Miranda. And Wylie. Your file is here. These other two are for Vincent Marchand and Jubar Haddad. We're all in agreement that the arsonist didn't come from any of these offices because Miranda, if your secretary was the arsonist, you would have seen her. And Wylie, you're between secretaries now, right? I heard that the kid who worked for you quit. What happened? Did somebody offer him more money?"

Wylie liked Harry Pittman. He liked that Harry treated his building like a favored daughter. Continually worrying about her welfare, but always waiting for her to break his heart. He liked Harry's nervous energy and the circuitous pattern of his thoughts, the way they flew around like pigeons over tenement roofs, not quite knowing where to land; and he liked the guileless way that Harry instinctively knew how to say the one completely inappropriate thing.

"Where is he, this miraculous secretary of yours? He didn't evaporate into thin air, did he?"

"No Harry," Wylie said. "He didn't evaporate into thin air. He's an actor. He got a job as an understudy in a Broadway musical."

"So, mazel tov," Harry said, and he read the name on the next file folder.

"Vincent P. Marchand. We can forget Vincent, because his office is closed until Monday. And as far as Jubar Haddad goes, there are no women working for him. Not unless he has some sealed up in those big boxes he keeps in his reception room."

Harry tossed the last of the first four folders onto the conference table and reached for the rest in the stack.

"That leaves four other offices on the seventh floor."

Harry inexplicably shook the file folders for the next group of tenants up against his right ear, as though they were a pair of lucky dice. Then he plopped them down in a heap on the table and asked, "Who wants another cup of coffee?"

Eddie NoName stood up and stretched.

"I do."

He looked around at the others. "Anyone else?"

Eddie was short for a fireman, no more than five feet, seven inches tall. He had a pleasant face that was slow to laugh, smile, or frown, and serious gray eyes. Sometimes when Wylie saw Eddie's eyes blink woodenly, and his mouth open and shut like the lid of a box, Wylie thought of a ventriloquist's dummy.

Eddie was wearing a red-checked flannel shirt, black denim pants with suspenders, and workboots ("My surveillance disguise."), and was about as inconspicuously dressed for Manhattan as Paul Bunyan would have been striding down Fifth Avenue carrying an ax.

As Eddie poured himself another cup of coffee, Harry evaluated the remaining tenants on his list.

"There are four females we haven't accounted for yet on the seventh floor. Would you want any of them to marry your Uncle Myron?" Harry raised his right hand and wobbled it back and forth a few times. "But who am I to say? My building. I love it. I'd carve my initials with it in a big heart on the trunk of a tree. But let's face it, this isn't a Fifth Avenue address."

Wylie slid the stack of folders across the table and lifted the first one. "Lucille Abbot," he read. "Who's she?"

"She calls herself a travel agent. She could even be one. I don't know. Very double-oh-seven, her whole office."

"You think Lucille Abbot is a spy?"

"Not her. Her boyfriend. Daniel Ling. Big guy. At least six feet tall. Chinese. Good-looking. Stocky. But there's something about him. Mean eyes. He never talks. Never smiles. They have an office suite. Two rooms and a reception area. About five-hundred square feet. I'm not saying that she never engages in the business of travel agenting. I know she does from time to time. Once, I had an emergency and needed to fly to Scottsdale, Arizona."

"Why Scottsdale?" Miranda asked.

"Uncle Myron. So I took the elevator to the seventh floor."

"And what?" Wylie asked. "She couldn't issue you a ticket?"

"No. Not that. It was her boyfriend. I never saw so much electronic equipment in my life. Miniature cameras. Microphones the size of a pin. Boxes filled with wires, cables, tiny video monitors. Things like you see in the spy movies. Ninety-nine percent of it, I couldn't identify."

"So that's the double-oh-seven part?"

Harry Pittman nodded.

"I've been a landlord ever since I was in grammar school. I rented out our living room on Cropsey Avenue to hooligans so that they could drop water balloons on the Dobrowski twins, but Daniel Ling is my first spy."

"Other than the electronic equipment, what makes you think he's a spy?"

"He wears black gloves."

"Oh. Well, that's conclusive."

"With holes in the knuckles."

Eddie NoName said, "You've convinced me. Last guy I saw who wore gloves like that worked for the Israeli Mossad."

"Aren't we supposed to be talking about the women on the seventh floor?" Miranda asked glumly.

"Lucille Abbot," Harry said. "She's Ling's girlfriend. I think he beats her. You see a lot of that. Big, tough guys. Little, frail women. Why do they put up with it? Crazy. Who knows? Once, for a week, she came in every morning wearing dark sunglasses. And she had too much pancake makeup on her face. So, that's the tenant with the office two doors away from you, Wylie."

"I've seen her in the halls. A little bit of a thing, right? But I don't re-member him."

"How could you? He's invisible. He works for the CIA."

"Describe Lucille," Wylie said.

"About five feet, two inches tall. Weighs maybe ninety-eight or a hundred pounds. Dark hair, shoulder length. Skinny legs. Pretty face. It would be beautiful, except that she's too thin. She's always perfectly groomed. Hair. Nails. But once when I got on the elevator, I almost fell over. I couldn't believe it. She reeked of booze."

Wylie said, "It's not uncommon for a heavy drinker or alcoholic to set a fire during a blackout. So Lucille Abbot is a definite 'maybe.' Who else?"

Harry tapped the next folder.

"This one is very spiritual. I think she has lengthy consultations with the water stains on the ceiling before she decides to do anything."

Wylie read off the name.

"Grayela Cunningham."

"She has the office next to you," Harry said.

"The strange smells," Wylie acknowledged. "What's she doing in there, smoking pot? There's no sign on her door."

Harry shook his head.

"Not pot. But it stinks to high heaven just the same. All of my tenants complain. When her lease expires, I'm not going to renew. She'll probably sue me. Who knows? But what the hell."

"What does Grayela Cunningham do?"

"She calls herself an herbalist. A hypnotist. She's a practitioner, get this, of alternative medicines. Claims she can help people stop biting their nails. Stop cracking their knuckles. Stop picking their nose, for all I know. Oh, and stop smoking. She's a crusader against the tobacco industry."

Miranda reached for a cigarette, realized that she didn't have one in her purse, and grumbled, "She's brewing seaweed and rotten eggs in *her* office, and she's complaining about *my* cigarettes?"

Harry raised his hands defensively. "Whoa. Slow down. I never said that she complained specifically about *your* cigarette smoke."

Miranda dropped her head, "I'm depressed again."

"Well." Harry patted her hand. "This is a depressing business."

"What's Grayela look like?" Wylie asked. "So that we can identify her?"

"When she rented her office, she told me that she's an ex-ballerina, and she looks like one. Skinny as a needle. Long, pale hair. Not blonde. More like a dirty honey color. She doesn't wear makeup. Walks like she's moving through a cloud. Beautiful posture. Too bad she's a resident of outer space. If she weren't, she could be attractive. But, like I said, loony as a cuckoo clock."

Wylie read off the third file folder, "Randall Newberry-Boisri . . . I can't pronounce this name. Who is she?"

"She's third in line from your office, Wylie."

"Tell us about her."

"Not much to tell. Randall Newberry-Boisriveaud is married. Her husband lives in Paris. Probably because he can't stand being in the same city as her. When I see her, the hair stands up on the back of my neck."

"Why? What did she ever do to you?"

"Nothing. Just, certain people give me the creeps. She's one of them."

"What does she look like?"

"Hard face. Sharp nose. High forehead. Thin lips. Kinky blonde hair. Lots of hairspray. Big gold earrings. Nose ring."

"Nose ring!" Miranda exclaimed.

"Just kidding."

"Is she stylish or dowdy?"

"Oh, stylish. Could have stepped off the cover of *Vogue* magazine. Short, tight skirts. High heels. Matching bags. Designer dresses."

"Nothing personal, Harry, but if she's so classy, what's she doing in The Lispenard Building?"

"She's one of those bleeding-heart types. You know, the more money they spend on clothes and penthouses, the guiltier they get. So they feel they can buy the right to keep spending money at Fru Fru la Touff's if they devote the time they're not at cocktail parties to tormenting some poor schmuck working stiff."

"It sounds like you've got a personal hard-on for Randall Nuisance-Boisenberry, Harry."

"Well, maybe I do. She reminds me of my ex-wife."

"What does she do?"

"My ex-wife?"

"No. Randall what's-her-name."

"Runs an employment agency. But if you ask me, she's a shill for the American Civil Liberties Union. She sends out all kinds of people to answer classified ads, as long as they're totally, one-hundred-percent wrong for the job; then she sets up the prospective employers for job discrimination lawsuits. She has fat women answer ads for receptionists at diet clinics, she sends men for jobs as matrons in ladies' rooms, and she sends eighty-year-olds with cataracts to messenger services looking to hire kids on racing bikes."

Harry flicked aside her folder.

"She's a real card. That's what she is." Then he tapped his finger against the final file folder. "And here's the last belle of the ball."

Wylie read, "Sarah Sapinsky. Okay. Let's hear about Sarah."

Harry shrugged. "Poor Sarah. What's to say about Sarah? She's a paralegal. She's been working for the same law firm on the seventh floor for twenty-five years. Every two years since I've owned the building, when it's time to renew the lease, Sarah drops off the signed copy on my desk and says the same thing. 'This year, Mr. Pittman, is the last year I'll be working for Lapitus and Goldfarb. Why should I spend my whole life slaving for other attorneys, when I have more knowledge of the law in my little finger than they have in both their empty heads. This year, I'm enrolling in law school, and you'll see. In no time, the lease I'll be signing for a law office won't be for Lapitus and Goldfarb, it will be for Sarah Sapinsky!'"

Harry Pittman shook his head.

"But she never does enroll in law school, and she never will. She's a little shlump of a woman, all shriveled up inside. Every two years, she pokes out her head and remembers that there's something she once wanted to do. But after a few minutes, she tucks her head back in again and forgets. The lease is coming due in a week or two, so any day now she should be getting ready to go back to law school."

Wylie said, "What does she look like?"

"She has brown hair parted in the middle and pulled back in a knot. She's short, wears plain blouses and flower-print skirts that look like someone's drapery; she usually has on the same pink cardigan sweater, and low-heeled shoes with straps across her arches, like old-fashioned tap shoes. And there's something dwarfy about the way she walks. Maybe because she's short waisted. Oh, and one more thing."

"What?"

"She carries a public television shopping bag. You know. The kind with a big channel number on it. I can imagine her watching one of those fund-raisers until one, two o'clock at night. Every night. Alone. And the high point of her life is getting one of those damn public television shopping bags."

Harry gathered up the eight folders.

"That's the whole lot of them. Any other questions before you go?"

Wylie said, "Harry, tell us about the fires. The first one was . . . when?"

"Just a second. Let me put these away. Tenants files. They're confidential. Everything I said this morning, I didn't say it . . . right? I could probably get sued."

Harry Pittman slipped the files in his briefcase, took out a narrow folder, and flipped it open.

"OK, Wylie. It says here that the fire department got the first alarm on Friday at one-forty P.M."

"Give me a sequence of events."

"As soon as the fire alarm went off, I checked with security to find out where it was. José told me that someone had pulled the alarm box on the seventh floor."

"I didn't know that," Miranda said.

"So, the alarm wasn't triggered by a heat or smoke detector?" Wylie asked.

"Absolutely not."

"What about the fire itself?"

"Some fire," Harry said sarcastically.

"Big fire? Small fire? What?"

"Small fire. Not a fire even. Just some crumpled up paper towels in the sink. Singed. A little brown and black around the edges. And in the middle of them, a cigarette."

"A cigarette?" Miranda said apprehensively. "Harry, don't tell me."

"I hate to say it, Miranda, but the cigarette was a Parliament. Your brand. The fireman showed it to me."

Miranda moaned. "Oh, this is so depressing. I don't think I can stand it anymore."

"Sure you can," Wylie said. Then he said to Harry, "Too bad you didn't save the actual paper towels and cigarette. I would have liked to look at them."

"I wanted to, but one of the firemen took the whole mess away with him."

Wylie shrugged. "Can't win them all. How about the alarm? Did you ever find out who pulled it?"

"No."

"Where is the alarm box?"

"Across from your office. On the wall outside Miranda's office. A couple of feet from the stairwell."

"Okay," Wylie said. "Let's move on to the second fire. When was the alarm called in?"

"At three-forty-five P.M. And like the first fire, no smoke or fire detectors went off. As a matter of fact, there aren't any in the bathrooms. But now, I guess I'll have to install them in there, too. I hate to do it, because it'll be one hell of an expense. Anyway, someone, identity unknown, pulled the same alarm box across from your office, Wylie. The second fire was bigger than the first one. This person crumpled up towels and toilet paper, put them in the wastebasket, and threw in a match. The toilet paper was pretty well incinerated, but none of the toweling caught fire. One handful of paper towels was a little bit brown along the bottom, like a baked marshmallow. And another one was singed where the lit cigarette had been thrown in."

"Parliament again?" Wylie asked.

Harry nodded.

And Miranda Yee groaned.

29

Mr. Haddad graciously welcomed Wylie Nolan into the reception area of his import-export office, which, as Harry Pittman had said, was filled, floor to ceiling, with boxes. Anonymous boxes, unlabeled, containing everything, or so Mr. Haddad said, from false teeth to blue jeans. From battery jumper cables to Navajo jewelry.

Miranda Yee had been right when she'd referred to Jubar Haddad as a sweet old man.

On the morning of the surveillance, he was wearing an aged, but impeccably pressed pin-striped suit over a crisp, white shirt. The knot in his necktie was so neat, it could have been tied with a micrometer. Mr. Haddad's eyes, when you spoke to him, moved slowly, appraising what he saw as though it were, indeed, fine to look at, but if he'd had to look at something else, that would be fine, too.

He told Wylie Nolan and Eddie NoName to move the largest boxes blocking the doorway into his inner office, where his desk was. When Wylie expressed concern that this might be too much of an imposition, Mr. Haddad nodded his head gently and told Wylie not to worry, because after he had finished his "observations of the criminal who has been causing such great discomfort in our lives," Mr. Haddad would permit Wylie and his friend to put the cartons back where they belonged.

Mr. Haddad gave Wylie and Eddie one straight-back chair each to accommodate their surveillance. Then he returned to his inner office, closed the door, and was neither heard from nor seen for the rest of the day.

Wylie had positioned himself at the door opening. Eddie's chair was next to the door's hinge. Wylie put a paperback book, edge-up, on the floor to prop the door open about an inch, and then put a point-and-shoot 35mm flash camera under his chair.

Jubar Haddad's import-export office was the perfect place from which to conduct a surveillance, because it was diagonally across from the ladies' bathroom, and provided an unobstructed view of every office on the seventh floor, as well as all four elevator doors and the entryway to the staircase.

"Don't you even want to know what the surprise is?" Eddie NoName asked.

"Sure, Eddie. Sorry. I forgot all about it."

"It's a doorbell."

Wylie squinted suspiciously.

"A what?"

"It's a contraption called a 'wireless remote.' It's been out on the market for a few years, and the one I bought only cost fifteen dollars. It runs on a nine-volt battery. The battery goes into the push-button part. That's where you press your finger to let someone know that he has to open the door. You plug the other half into an outlet. It can go into any outlet, because you don't need an electric cord. See. Look over there. That's where I plugged it in."

Eddie pointed to a white plastic rectangle plugged into an outlet between two cartons six feet away.

"What does it do?" Wylie asked.

"It goes *ding-dong*. Before the meeting this morning, I jerry-rigged the button part outside the ladies' room. It's on top of the door frame, high up where you can't see it. I adapted a pronged, rubber doorstop, so that when someone opens the bathroom door, even if only part way, the prong pushes the button, and the bell rings over here, in Mr. Haddad's office."

"You're kidding," Wylie said. "Did you really do that?"

"Sure I did."

"Does the person going into the bathroom hear the bell when it rings?"

"No. I turned the sound down very low."

"Can we hear it?"

"Sure. I tested it this morning. Mr. Haddad was here early. He let me in. We're great buddies now, him and me."

Wylie smiled.

"I'm impressed, Eddie. That was very clever of you."

"No it wasn't. My original surveillance plan was clever. This is just a piece of cake."

"True. But your original plan would have cost me five-thousand dollars. This is only costing me fifteen."

"Piker," Eddie NoName said.

And Wylie Nolan laughed.

The doorbell that Eddie NoName rigged up worked so well that after the first half hour, neither Wylie nor Eddie bothered to look down the hallway to see who was coming and going.

During the critical time periods, though, at 10:30 A.M. and 1:30 in the afternoon, when Miranda Yee was scheduled to smoke her cigarettes, Wylie stared out the door opening, attentive to every move.

Ten-thirty came and went without incident.

A few seconds after that, Sarah Sapinsky, wearing an outfit amazingly like the one Harry had described, shopping bag with big channel number on it included, followed Miranda in. About two seconds later, Lucille Abbot, looking frail and tiny, as though a strong breeze could snap her in two, entered the hall. Then Grayela Cunningham, as insubstantial as a ballerina enduring the Irish potato famine, and Randall Newberry-Boisriveaud, wearing a designer suit and an expression on her face that combined arrogance with false humility, left their offices and walked down the hall and into the ladies' room at the same time.

"What the hell is going on?" Eddie NoName asked. "A pantyhose convention?"

Miranda, first to arrive, was also the last to leave. When the door to the ladies' room closed behind her, she pretended to drop her keys. She bent to pick them up, turned toward Mr. Haddad's office, whispered, "I'm still depressed," and then returned to her office.

Things really started to perk at 1:30. After lunch. Miranda left her office. She was wearing a double strand of pearls over an ivory silk blouse, and a short blue skirt with sheer stockings and low-heeled shoes. There was a cigarette behind her ear. She looked pretty, pert, brave, and efficient; when she walked down the hall, there was even the suggestion of a military bounce in her step.

Wylie motioned for Eddie to join him at the crack in the door.

"Bravado," Wylie said. "I knew she could pull it off. She's a good kid."

"Is she really a lawyer, Wylie?"

"Yes. She is."

"She looks like she's fourteen years old."

"Add twenty years, and you'll have it right."

"I'm buying a new house. Is Miranda any good?"

Wylie laughed. "Miranda Yee hates her secretaries and she hates her clients. If you asked her this week, she'd probably tell you that she hates the law. But other than that, yes. She's a very good attorney."

"Why does she hate everything so much?"

"Poor Miranda. She's good-natured. Even-tempered. Calm. Rational. Philosophical. But everyone she works with is angry, excitable, and short-tempered. And they're always shouting."

"Do you think she'd help me and my wife with our house closing?"

"Guaranteed."

Miranda darted a look in the direction of Jubar Haddad's import-export office. Despite her confident stride, the expression on her face was one of total despair, as though she had dressed up to go to her own execution.

The bathroom door swung shut behind her.

In Mr. Haddad's office, a plastic box the size of a cigarette pack went *ding-dong*.

It was 1:30.

At 1:30 and twenty-five seconds, Lucille Abbot's office door opened. Lucille struggled with a leather briefcase that looked far too heavy for her.

She turned towards the ladies' room.

Stopped.

She turned toward the elevator bank and she pressed the down button.

Ten seconds later, the door to Grayela Cunningham's office opened. She was holding a butane cigarette lighter in her right hand. As she walked down the hall, she *flick, flick, flicked* the flint wheel on the lighter, looking intently at it instead of where she was going. She did not greet Lucille as she walked by.

Grayela passed Lucille Abbot's office, Randall Newberry-Boisriveaud's office, and the law offices where Sarah Sapinsky worked. When she reached the door of the ladies' room, she looked up as though awakening from a dream, and spun around. Just as Harry Pittman had described, she moved gracefully, like a soul lost in a cloud, back in the direction from which she'd come.

When she got to Randall Newberry-Boisriveaud's door, she knocked, waited for a few seconds, and then opened the door and went in.

In the meantime, the elevator doors slid open in front of Lucille Abbot. She shot a frightened glance back toward her office and then quickly stepped inside.

The elevator doors slammed shut.

For about two minutes, nothing happened.

Then the door to Sarah Sapinsky's law office started to creep open. An inch at a time.

One inch.

Two inches.

Three inches.

By the time it was opened eight inches, Sarah Sapinsky poked out her head. It was a narrow head, shaped something like an allergy capsule. It looked carefully to the right. It looked apprehensively but excitedly to the left. Then the shoulders followed the head. The cardigan sweater, floral skirt, and ankle-strap tap shoes came next. And the canvas public television shopping bag came last.

The door swung shut behind her and she was out in the hall.

She walked with quick, short movements of quick, short legs to the ladies' room; she unlocked the door and pushed it open.

Wylie flipped the paperback book onto its back so that the door was propped open wider. He leaned forward. Eddie squeezed behind Wylie's chair and also stared through the opening.

Wylie reached his hand under his chair. His fingers closed around the camera.

"What do you think?" Eddie NoName asked softly.

"It's her."

"That's what I think. What are we going to do?"

"Wait."

A minute went by. Two minutes. At 1:37 P.M., Miranda Yee walked out of the ladies' room. She briefly held onto the door and eased it shut so that when it closed it didn't latch. Then, without looking toward where she knew Wylie was standing, she turned left and walked rapidly down the hall.

Wylie whispered urgently to Eddie NoName, "Now!"

The two men crashed through Jubar Haddad's import-export doorway and rammed across the short hall.

Eddie NoName got to the ladies' room door first. He flung it open. Wylie Nolan, a fraction of a second later, entered with his camera raised.

Click.

Click.

Click.

The point-and-shoot's flash exploded against the white tile walls and bounced off the mirror of the ladies' room.

Click.

Click.

Click.

Sarah Sapinsky was stupefied.

She was paralyzed with fear. Stunned. Mortified. In a state of abject horror.

And yet, intermingled with those expressions there also glimmered a look of lurid satisfaction. As though *finally*, something was happening to her.

She knelt on the checkered tile floor over the metal wastebasket.

The wastebasket was completely filled with toilet tissue and paper towels. On top of all of those combustibles, Sarah Sapinsky had placed an empty box of Parliament cigarettes.

In her left hand, she held a metal container of lighter fluid. In her right hand, she held a single, small match.

A flame darted upward from the stick of the match.

Sarah looked at Wylie, looked at Eddie, and smiled. Then she dropped the flaming match into the wastebasket.

Click.

Click.

Click.

The flame extinguished as the match plunged through the air.

Wylie reached forward, grabbed Sarah Sapinsky by both hands, and pulled her to her feet.

"Gotcha!" he said.

Miranda Yee slipped quietly into the ladies' room, stared at Sarah from behind Wylie Nolan's shoulder, and said, "I'm not depressed any-more."

And Eddie NoName pulled a small, laminated card out of his pocket and began to read, "You have the right to remain silent . . . "

30

Having lived in New York his whole life, Wylie Nolan had been a casual observer of the development of SoHo as an artists' community. He'd read about the takeover of industrial lofts by painters and sculptors who'd swarmed like western land grabbers from Greenwich Village and the Upper West Side to that area south of Houston Street (ergo, SoHo), where they could inhabit vast spaces for comparatively low rent.

Therefore, when Wylie Nolan realized that Sarkin Zahedi's address was on West Broadway between Broome and Spring Streets, he assumed the studio would be housed in a former factory, like so many others that had been sectioned off into artists' lofts.

But just as it's said a hooker can identify another hooker who has left the trade, even if she's presently chairman of the Ladies Holding Their Pinky Fingers at Just the Right Angle to Drink Tea Club, as soon as he saw it, Wylie recognized Sarkin Zahedi's building as an old firehouse. The large overhead door had been bricked shut, and the walk-in entrance had been replaced by a massive steel monstrosity that resembled a morgue refrigerator door. But when Wylie looked at it, what he *saw* was a fire station, and what he *heard* was the melodious wail of a phantom fire engine's siren.

There was a doorbell, of sorts, on the right side of the door.

It was shaped like a ceramic breast. Pink. And in the center of the breast was a dark brown nipple. Erect. Taped to the door frame beneath it on a scrap of paper was the handwritten word *doorbell*.

Wylie took a pencil out of his pocket, touched the nipple with the eraser end, and pushed.

He didn't hear anything.

He waited about thirty seconds and then pressed the nipple again.

After a few more seconds, he heard a soft electronic buzz, and when he tried the handle of the morgue door, it opened. He stepped into a dimly lighted expanse which had been stripped of all fire-fighting apparatus, except for a single dull brass pole extending through a man-size hole in the ceiling. Wylie felt an uncomfortable twinge of guilt. When he'd been a fireman, an unpolished pole was akin to blasphemy.

Wylie let the door swing shut behind him. He waited for his eyes to adjust and then saw several ladders, heaped like giant pick-up sticks against the east wall. Next to the ladders were a pile of dirty, industrial-size drop cloths.

"Mr. Zahedi," Wylie called out. "My name is Wylie Nolan. I'm here for our one o'clock appointment."

Arranged along the back wall of the firehouse were a row of head-less, naked mannequins; their arms were draped around one another's waists and their legs were lifted in high kicks like a macabre chorus line.

To the left of the pole was a narrow staircase.

"Mr. Zahedi! I'm coming up now."

In the area beside the stairs, there was an array of dead animals: mounted and stuffed.

As Wylie slowly climbed the stairs, an eight-point buck observed his ascent through plastic eyeballs stuck on the tips of each antler like olives on the ends of toothpicks. He saw a wolf clenching a bloody rubber doll, the doll's chubby legs dangling indecently from between its fangs. He saw an eagle suspended from the ceiling by invisible wires with Mickey Mouse in its beak. And almost hidden beneath the staircase (Wylie had to lean over the bannister to see it), he saw a huge grizzly bear rearing up on its hind legs. Someone (doubtlessly Sarkin Zahedi) had dressed it in a mammoth, pink brassiere, with a garter belt around its belly, and white nurse's stockings over the ferocious stumps of its legs.

Wylie winced.

In some unspeakable way, it was a horrible desecration.

Wylie stopped midway up the stairs to take a small, panorama camera and some photographs out of his briefcase. Then he continued to the top, and stepped into a large, well-lighted room. He held up his camera, and immediately began what he called "doing a 360" of the room.

Brick wall on the left. No windows (*click*). Back wall. Brick, three floor-to-ceiling windows (*click*). Right wall. All brick (*click*). Move camera to right but not all the way. The left side of the next picture must slightly overlap the right side of the first picture, and the left side of the third picture must slightly overlap the right side of the second as the camera goes around (overlap), and around (overlap), and around (overlap), until Wylie had photographed a complete panorama of the room.

Wylie said again, "Mr. Zahedi?"

In front of him was a long, narrow table. On top of it were a hodgepodge of artifacts usually associated with artists: Tin cans filled with paintbrushes, some inverted with the brush end out (most of the brushes were covered with hard, dry paint), and others with the handle ends showing. Large palette knives, also crusty with paint, were strewn among pliers with T-bar noses, broken sticks of charcoal, a staple gun, and big, crumpled tubes of oil paint.

Also on the table were a paint-smeared telephone and a half-eaten sandwich, as well as a clutter of large rectangular cans labeled: linseed oil, turpentine, Japan Driers, and rubber cement. A spray can of varnish was lying on its side in the middle of what looked like a moldy slice of lemon chiffon pie.

Wylie shot the table, front and back.

Then he continued into the room, inhaling the thick, airless, claustrophobic smell of oil paint and varnish, as he looked to his left and to his right.

Dramatically positioned in the center of the room so that a diagonal shaft of light from the middle window fell on him like a spotlight, sat Sarkin Zahedi. On a prayer rug. On the floor.

His eyes were closed. He was wearing black slacks and a black suit jacket over a collarless white dress shirt, buttoned tight at the neck. His legs were folded in the Indian position, and his arms lay away from his body, palms up, in a pose that was clearly meant to suggest he was meditating.

What the hell, Wylie thought, and he snapped a picture of Sarkin Zahedi, too.

Click. Flash. And the eyelids of the man on the floor began to flutter. He turned his head.

Wylie Nolan noted, as others had before him, that Sarkin Zahedi's vision seemed to be directed inward, at something that was going on inside his head. It was a look Wylie associated equally with religious charlatans and the blind. When you looked into the eyes of either you would see that same relentless, nonreactive stare.

Sarkin Zahedi's eyebrows were like dark smudges left behind by a dirty eraser, over large, unblinking black eyes. His thick and wavy hair stood away from his head, either wildly unkempt or carefully coiffured to look that way, depending on what it had taken to achieve exactly that effect.

His face itself was striking, with a high forehead and a long, straight nose. But his features were too smooth and unindividualized to be considered handsome; and when not speaking, Sarkin Zahedi had an unattractive way of compressing his lips in a tight line that suggested he could enjoy being cruel.

He rose gracefully to his feet like a dancer.

"Ah, Mr. Nolan." He extended a hand, but not to shake. Instead, he circled it downward three times before his body in a ceremonial salaam.

Wylie said, "Uh huh," to himself, and cast his mind back over the file material he had just read.

Name: Sarkin Zahedi. Age: Forty-nine plus years. Native country: U.S.A. Third-generation American. Parents' religion: Episcopalian. Education: Poly Prep High School in Brooklyn. New York University in Manhattan. Dropped out of college after one semester. Professional history: Moved into art commune in Greenwich Village. "Discovered" by art world at age twenty-five. School of art: Varied. Some expressionist, some abstract expressionism, some assemblage. Years of greatest fame: Late 1970s. The value of the work done during that period has held up.

Newer paintings have not sold well. Newer "scenario" work, of which Wylie assumed the headless chorus line was a sample, has not sold at all. Greatest achievement: Painting on permanent exhibit at the Museum of Modern Art. Title: *Belly Button*. Size: Six feet high by eighteen feet long. Description: Completely empty flesh-toned canvas with large three-dimensional belly button suspended dead center on the canvas. Value of *Belly Button*: Said to be eight-hundred-thousand dollars. Owner of *Belly Button*: The Museum of Modern Art.

Recent exhibits of Sarkin Zahedi paintings: The Zigfield Art Museum (last week).

Previous exhibitions of Sarkin Zahedi paintings in the last seventeen years: None.

Wylie looked around the studio.

"Is there any place we can sit down?"

Zahedi smiled. It was a very slight movement, as unforthcoming as his motionless eyes. He indicated the prayer rug with a twist of his wrist and a curve of his hand.

"No thanks," Wylie said.

He took five eight-by-ten photographs out of his jacket pocket. "I appreciate your taking the time to see me, Mr. Zahedi, so if you can just answer a few questions about these paintings, I'll stop bothering you and we can both go home."

Sarkin Zahedi took the photographs from Wylie and walked toward the middle window in his studio. He held the pictures away from his body, the way farsighted people read newsprint.

Wylie continued his silent inventory of the artist's studio.

There were canvases everywhere. Large canvases six-feet high by ten-feet long leaned against the walls. Smaller canvases four or five feet square were stacked on the floor and on tabletops. And all of them looked to Wylie less like works of art (they were covered with smears and splotches of paint) than like track marks on the floor after a homicide, where the victim had been dragged over the oily cement of a filthy garage.

The room that Sarkin Zahedi had turned into a studio had once been the bunk room of the old firehouse. Its floor was gobbed thick with dried, muddy-colored paints: blacks, grays, browns, and some moldy-looking greens. Gallon-size paint cans had been stacked under tables and tossed haphazardly in all four corners of the studio. Some of the cans had the lids on. Some of them didn't have lids. Some of them contained paintbrushes the size that house painters use; one contained a small toilet bowel plunger; another what looked like a blonde wig on the end of a broom handle.

Wylie waited as Zahedi flipped through the color photographs of the five paintings that had been consumed in the Parlor Gallery fire. When Wylie held out his hand for them, Sarkin Zahedi gave the photographs back.

"What I want to do, Mr. Zahedi, is have you *walk* me through the process of making these paintings. From the first brush stroke all the way to whatever you consider the end to have been. Probably when these paintings were sold."

"They were never sold. They were stolen."

"How long ago?"

Sarkin Zahedi threw back his head and seemed to be studying the ceiling, as though the answer to Wylie's questions would be inscribed there. "One cannot ascertain such lapses in time terms we measure by a corporal habitation, yet if recollection can be trusted as a signpost, this series was painted in 1972."

"That's twenty-four years ago."

"Measured in solar ellipses, perhaps. Yet in the cosmology of celestial rotation, it is but . . . "

"Right. So it's 1972. You wake up one morning. Then what?"

"You represent the insurance company, Mr. Nolan. Is that not true?"

"No, it is *not* true. I work for the insurance company. I don't represent them. If I represented them, I would have their best interests at heart. That's not what they hire me for, though. What they want from me is the truth, and the truth isn't always in their best interest."

"Ah, yes. And your task here today is . . . ?"

"Short-term goal, to find out about the five paintings that burned. Long-term goal, to determine the origin and cause of the fires in the Parlor Gallery."

"That is indeed a commendable excursion. You are aware, no doubt, that my great friend and patron, Fromer Zigfield, is of the opinion that the fire which consumed my paintings was caused by a human agency."

"He thinks Jiri Hozda set fire to your paintings."

"Are you in agreement?"

Wylie's face was expressionless. "That's a possibility."

"And after we have terminated this conversation, Mr. Nolan, will you then recommend to the insurance company that they send me a check for the paltry fraction of the sum that my paintings were actually worth?"

"Mr. Zahedi, I understand that each one of your paintings was insured for one million dollars. Five million dollars doesn't constitute a paltry sum in anybody's book."

The artist closed his eyes momentarily, as if in great pain. "Nevertheless."

"Nevertheless," Wylie repeated. "And it's not my job to tell the insurance company to pay or not to pay a claim. I just tell them where and how I think the fire started."

"But they will do nothing until they have received your findings?"

"That's true. They won't cut a check until after I give the claims rep at the Michelangelo Fine Arts Insurance Group an oral or a verbal report."

"I see," Sarkin Zahedi said, suddenly businesslike. "Perhaps, then, we should begin. My recollections of the genesis of this series go far, far back in time. When the powerful Hindu God Vishnu . . . "

"This will go faster if *I* ask the questions."

Zahedi again waved his hand in three descending circles and Wylie took that as an assent.

"Okay, Mr. Zahedi, tell me how you put a painting together."

The artist closed his eyes. When he reopened them, he looked as though he had just come out of a trance. "Years of devotion . . . years of training . . . years of concentration evolve, revolve, and combine to . . . "

"I don't mean the *conceptual* part of putting together a work of art, Mr. Zahedi. I mean the nuts and bolts. Like where do you get the big canvases? How do you buy your paint? What layer goes over what other layer on the painting? Things like that."

Zahedi blinked again and his expression became marginally less ethereal.

"I see."

"OK. Let's start at the beginning. Where do you get your canvases?"

"They are custom made."

"Who makes them?"

"An art supplier named Thomas Hook. He has a loft near here. I have my stretcher bars built there, too."

"What are stretcher bars?"

Sarkin Zahedi pulled one of his larger canvases away from the wall and showed Wylie the wood framing on its back.

"These are made out of wood strips that are tongued and grooved on the ends. I specify how big my canvas must be, and Thomas Hook cuts them to the right size and assembles them. After they are delivered, I attach the canvas to the stretcher bars myself."

"How do you do that?"

Zahedi led Wylie back to the table he'd photographed on his way in. Zahedi picked up a large tool with a long grip and a wide, flat nose that joined the grip at a right angle.

"These are called stretcher pliers," Zahedi said. "They are used to stretch the canvas over the wooden strips. Since my paintings are so big, I use two-by-fours for my stretcher bars, and I reinforce the corners with triangles. Then I attach the canvas with a staple gun, pulling at it with these pliers as I staple, so that when I'm finished the canvas is taut and straight."

"Then what?"

"Then I seal the canvas so that nothing penetrates the linen."

"Linen? Is that what you use?"

"Yes. First I seal or size the linen with a layer of rabbit skin glue. On top of that, I put a layer of true Gesso, which is a commercial mix of chalk or plaster of Paris with glue that absorbs oil from the paint. Over that, I apply a coat of priming white, which is very thick, dries rapidly, and prepares the surface of the canvas to accept my paint."

Wylie said, "Go on."

"Then I paint."

"Twenty-four years ago, is that how you painted the five pictures that were destroyed in the fire?"

Sarkin Zahedi looked disdainful. "One is unclear about details."

"Forget twenty-four years ago. How about now?"

"Yes. This is how I work now."

Wylie pointed to the first photograph. "Tell me about this one, *Process*. How did you paint it? What's it composed of?"

"First, I applied a layer of gray paint."

"Oil paint?"

"Of course."

"How? From a bottle? From tubes? I don't know these things. Help me out."

"From gallon cans," Sarkin Zahedi said. "Since I paint on such a large scale, I have my paints mixed in quantity."

"They're in those aluminum cans?"

"Yes."

"Thomas Hook? Your art supplier again?"

"Yes."

"How do you apply the paint?"

"What do you mean?"

"Does it go straight on from the can?"

"No. That would be much too thick. One could never apply oil paint directly from the tube or can over such a large area of canvas."

"How do you apply it then?"

"I add linseed oil, as a rule."

"And what does the linseed oil do?"

"It thins the consistency of the oil paint and accelerates the drying time."

"What else?"

"Well, of course, I use finish varnish."

"What's that?"

"It's a thin, protective coating that I spray on the completed painting after the paint has dried."

"How about turpentine?"

"I use that, too."

"Tell me about this picture, Sarkin. Tell me about *Process*. What are all these clumps here? What's this stuff stuck in the canvas?"

The artist's nostrils flared. "Nothing is *stuck*, as you put it, onto my canvas. Everything that you see in my painting represents a step in the creative process of art."

"Fine. Sorry. Tell me about the steps then."

Wylie pointed to the upper right-hand corner of the photograph. "What's this?"

"Those are tissue papers representing the tears an artist sheds for his work."

"What's this?"

"A cotton ball."

"Are there more of them on the canvas?"

"Yes. They harken back to the cotton fields before the Civil War, and represent one's slave labor to his art."

"And this big clump here? And this one over here? All five paintings have clumps like this all over the place. How'd you get them to stick to the canvas?"

"Epoxy glue."

"How'd you get glue to stick to wet paint?"

"I didn't. Those clumps, as you call them, are glued directly to the dry, primed canvas. Then, I apply a thick layer of oil paint called 'impasto' over them with a palette knife."

"What are the clumps?"

"Bits and pieces of rags."

"Rags?"

"Yes. The five paintings which I exhibited at the Zigfield Art Museum were a series: *Process*, *Germination*, *Creation*, *Destruction*, and *Chaos*. They speak of the creative process in its entirety. From the original conception out of which the work evolves, through its germination, creation . . . "

"I get the picture, no pun intended. But why rags?"

"The rags incorporated into each painting are the handmaidens of my work. They dab, they polish, they . . . whatever. As opposed to the small clusters of tissue that represent the drying of the *artist's* weary tears, these rags represent the tears shed not by the artist per se, but by the almighty realm of *art!*"

Wylie nodded.

He raised the second photograph, the one of the painting entitled *Germination*.

"OK, Sarkin, only four more pictures to go."

And Wylie pointed to a conglomeration of debris in the middle of the picture, and said, "Now tell me about this."

31

"Cam, can I talk to you for a minute?" Georgiana said after her new assistant had made two telephone calls to caterers about the exhibition's reception on opening night.

Camden Kimcannon looked up.

"I've got a guilty conscience about the way I interrogated you last week," Georgiana said. "And I want to apologize. I am very, very sorry."

Camden's eyes flicked on and off Georgiana's, and then he started to nervously move pencils and pads from one side of his desk to the other.

"Do you think we should have assorted cheeses at the party or would you rather have a vegetable dip?" he asked.

"I had no right to meddle in your personal life the way I did, Cam."

"I'm a cheese man myself." He bit his upper lip, and began to unfold a large paper clip until it had straightened to a wavery wire stick. "Cheese and crackers, actually. Now, that's a jolly good combination." Then he threw the mutilated paper clip into the wastebasket.

"Cam, I'd be a whole lot happier if we could talk about this. I know you're angry, so you can scream and yell at me if you want. I just think that . . . "

"Crackers!" Camden looked up and said brightly. "I knew there was something we'd forgotten. Do you have a preference as to what kind of crackers we should order? Something simple, don't you think? But for the cheeses, I definitely recommend an assortment. Brie, Gruyere, Swiss, of course, and maybe a really sharp, extra-sharp New York State cheddar."

Georgiana sighed and leaned forward. She wanted to observe Camden Kimcannon more closely. She wanted to figure out who he was and what made him tick.

He was wearing his mid-nineteenth-century artist's uniform again. His cloak was hanging in the office closet. He'd worn his frock coat for half an hour, but as work progressed that, too, had been tossed aside. A silk tie, however, was still tied in an elaborate bow around his neck, and the vest he had on was as shabby and as velvet as the one he'd worn the first time they'd met.

Georgiana studied Camden Kimcannon's long, lean body and the preoccupied expression on his pale, thin, vulnerable face.

The clothes that he wore may have been ridiculous, but the man who was wearing them appealed to her in a way that nobody else ever had.

Camden was too old for her feelings to be maternal in nature. And he was too young and much too fragile for those feelings to have been romantic. So the only way she could explain her curious attraction to him was that Camden Kimcannon aroused in her the same feelings that others felt (but *she* never did) when a whale accidentally beached itself on Coney Island, or a little baby took a wrong turn and got stuck at the bottom of an abandoned well. As minutes and hours or days crawled by and an emotionally overwrought public waited for news of those innocent creatures' fates, so were Georgiana's feeling somehow involved with the fate of this young man who was so desperately in love with the past and who called himself an artist.

He had taken particular attention today with his comb, and his hair, nice hair, not too long and not too short, was not, for a change, flopping into his eyes.

Georgiana studied Camden's face.

There was nothing inherently weak about it.

Regular nose. A few isolated freckles. A rather long jaw. High forehead. Standard operational lips.

But the eyes . . . . Oh, God. The poor, unrelenting sensitivity of those eyes!

Without knowing that she was doing so, she said aloud to herself, "What a waste."

Camden's head jerked up; he glared at her sharply.

"What did you say?"

Georgiana hesitated only a second. "I said 'what a waste,' because if we buy too much cheese, nobody will eat it. So many people are on diets."

Camden laughed. It was an easy laugh, without apprehension or tension. Whatever, a moment before, had aroused his suspicions was already forgotten. He was happy to be preparing for what he was sure would be the greatest party on earth, and the most important day of his life.

"To hell with diets," he laughed again. "I'll tell you what, Georgiana. Why don't we forget the cheese and crackers and vegetables and dips. Forget cholesterol and blood pressure and saturated fat. Here's what I want to do. Do you need me for the rest of the morning?"

"Yes. But when a man's got a gleam in his eye like you do, I don't want to be the one who stands in his way."

"Then is it all right if I go immediately? Right now?"

"Sure. Go. But do you mind telling me first *where* you're going?"

"To the library."

"For what?"

"Picture this, Georgiana: Opening night. The Pre-Raphaelite exhibition. The Sanctuary. There's a small chamber orchestra playing Haydn string quartets. Everybody is dressed to the hilt. And then, at just the right psychological moment, the waiters enter. And what they're serving are exactly the same hors d'oeuvres that Edward Burne-Jones and Dante Gabriel Rossetti would have served at a similar gathering a hundred and fifty years ago. Victorian food for a Victorian art exhibition. It's a great idea, isn't it?"

Georgiana laughed.

"It's a wonderful idea."

"And you don't mind if I go to the library to research Victorian cookbooks?"

"Not at all. Go out and find some recipes for London Fog soup and I'll . . ."

There was a knock at Georgiana's door.

Camden rose to answer it, and as Jiri Hozda walked in, continued out the door without a nod, a hello, or a good-bye.

Jiri raised an eyebrow.

Georgiana shrugged. "He's a man with a mission."

Jiri sat, pulled a folded sheet out of his pocket, and handed it to her. She unfolded it, scanned the salutation, and looked up.

"Who's Lars Helmersson?"

"He is the arson expert hired by Fromer and Sarkin to investigate the fire; and he is, as the expression goes, 'out to get me.' "

Georgiana began to scan the contents.

"This is a memo dated today and addressed to you, to Fromer Zigfield, Sarkin Zahedi, and Lars Helmersson. It's also addressed to Joy Miller, Max Bramble, and Luis Cabrerra, with a cc to Wylie Nolan.

" 'Gentlemen and Miss Miller,' " Georgiana read aloud. " 'I have been given to understand that the disruption both to our museum and to our peace of mind that has resulted from the fire that occurred eleven days ago in the Parlor Gallery is coming to an end. This Tuesday, November twenty-ninth at one P.M., Wylie Nolan, who has been retained by the Michelangelo Fine Arts Insurance Group to determine the origin and cause of the fire, would like to meet with us to discuss his findings. For the convenience of the Zigfield Art Museum's staff, Mr. Nolan has agreed to conduct this meeting in our conference room. I have taken it upon myself to confirm the presence at the meeting of all museum staff members. As to those of you who are not in my employ, your attendance at this meeting is, of course, optional.' "

Georgiana gave the letter back to Jiri.

"Why did you say Lars Helmersson is 'out to get' you?"

"It seem that he is."

"But why?"

"He is of the opinion that the cause of the Zahedi fires was arson."

"What's that got to do with you?"

"He thinks that I am the arsonist."

"You?" Georgiana said, totally astonished.

"Yes, beautiful Georgiana. Me."

"I thought you'd stopped calling me that."

"Merely an interval of inadvertent abstraction. I've had other things on my mind."

"Like being called an arsonist. Where the hell does this guy get off . . . ?"

The telephone rang.

"Excuse me," Georgiana said, and picked up the receiver. "Yes?"

The voice was unmistakable.

Georgiana pressed a button, and Camden's mother came in loud, blowzy, and faintly British over the speaker phone.

"Georgiana . . . darling."

"Yes, Vidalia. This is Georgiana *darling*. Although some people, out of respect for my credentials, call me *Doctor* darling."

Georgiana crossed her eyes at the telephone and stuck out her tongue.

Jiri laughed silently.

"Georgiana . . . daaahrrling."

"Mrs. Kimcannon, is there something I can do for you?"

"Last night . . . "

Georgiana waited.

"Yes. Go on. What about last night?"

"Last night . . . "

Georgiana again put her hand over the receiver and whispered, "Do you have any advice on how to kick start a drunk?"

"Last night, darling, when Camden, my dear, dear boy, came home. Late, again, one might add. He . . . "

"Vidalia, why are you telling me this? Nothing that goes on in your household is really any of my business."

"Last night, darling, he told me that you think . . . you think . . . you think he is an art*ist*." She heavily emphasized the last syllable of the word. "He, being Camden, of course, my dear, dear boy."

"He *is* an artist, Mrs. Kimcannon."

"And he said he told you that all of the things he has painted . . . all

200

of his artwork . . . is stored away for safekeeping. Safely, safely stored away in the garage."

"Mrs. Kimcannon, I don't think that . . . "

"Well, let me tell you a thing or two *darling* Doctor Georgiana . . . and that's all I hear, damn you, whenever the dear lad is home, which more and more lately, is becoming so very, very *rare*. It's Georgiana this, and Georgiana that until one begins to wonder, darling. Whatever did you do? Bewitch the boy?"

"He isn't a boy, Mrs. Kimcannon. Camden is a man."

"Boy. Man. It's all the same to me, because what he is is a liar. A liar and a fool. A do-nothing fool that doesn't write, and doesn't paint, and doesn't work. All that he does is read those damn foolish fairy tales about Camelot. And he dreams. Dream, dream, dream. And so I called, darling Georgiana, to tell you that there *are* no paintings in the garage. Not five paintings. Not four. Not three. Not two. Not one. No, not one single little, itty-bitty painting stored in the garage."

Georgiana inhaled sharply. Her hand clenched the telephone receiver, and her voice was dangerously low.

"How *dare* you . . . how *dare* you try to sabotage your son's reputation with me like that!"

Vidalia Kimcannon laughed.

"My son is a fake, Georgiana. A fake and a phony and a dreamer. He lied to you about those paintings, Doctor Look-Who's-a-Hot-Shot-Now. And he lied to you about . . . "

"If Camden wants me to believe that he has a whole amphitheater of canvases, that is his prerogative. And if he's lying to me about it, that lie is something that has to be resolved between him and me and has absolutely nothing to do with you. And not only is none of this any of your damn business, but your motive in deliberately trying to create a rift between your son and his employer, which is what I am, is just about the ugliest form of . . . "

Georgiana and Jiri heard a loud *click*.

"She hung up, the miserable bitch!" Georgiana slammed down her own receiver. "Did you *hear* that?"

"Yes. In technicolor. When you are angry, Georgiana, your eyes flash.

It is like green lightning. Flash. Flash. Flash. Flash. Very dangerous. Eyes like yours have burned down barns. Perhaps whole countrysides."

Georgiana took a deep breath, held it a moment, and then exhaled.

"What are we going to do?" she finally asked.

"Must we *do* anything?"

"Well, we can't just stand around and watch that woman trample Camden's dreams as if they're so many rotten grapes."

"As you have said yourself, Georgiana, Camden is a man, and a man must take responsibility for his own dreams."

"But what about the dream snatchers?"

"There will always be dream snatchers. When I lived in Czechoslovakia, the Soviet Union snatched our dreams."

Georgiana slumped back in her chair, picked up a pencil, and began to tap the eraser nervously against the top of her desk. She looked speculatively at Jiri.

"What *did* you dream about when you were a young man?"

Jiri smiled. Both eyebrows went up at the same time and then he laughed. It was a deep belly laugh. A low, masculine rumble.

"When I was a young man, what did I dream about? I dreamed about making love to beautiful Hollywood movie stars with hair like golden chiffon and perfect white teeth. I dreamed of living in a big, art deco apartment in New York City with a white grand piano and friends from the theater so talented that for an evening's amusement, they would come to my apartment and play songs they had composed that very day. I dreamed of taking the Staten Island Ferry, and of walking across the Brooklyn Bridge. I dreamed of Broadway musicals and Chicago gangsters and cowboys riding tall in the saddle and wearing white hats."

"Jiri." Georgiana threw down her pencil. "You say that the Soviet Union snatched you dreams, but they didn't, did they? Because there they are. Sparkling. Amusing. Intact. And you can even laugh about them."

Jiri said, "Perhaps that is the secret I share with our young friend who spends so much of his time in Camelot. That we wrap our souls around our dreams, and no matter how vicious the attack or how merciless the attacker, we keep our dreams unsullied and pristine. But in the process, we, ourselves, are battered and bruised. And sometimes, even our souls become horrendously scarred in deep, quiet, invisible ways. But our dreams . . . our dreams . . . "

"What?" Georgiana demanded.

A sad smile twisted one corner of his mouth. "Our dreams shall live to see another day."

Vidalia Kimcannon had telephoned Georgiana Weeks on Tuesday, November 22nd, at 11:10 in the morning. Shortly after that, Jiri returned to his own office to do work relative to the insurance coverage and extra guards that would be necessary for the PreRaphaelite exhibition's opening night.

At 3:45 P.M. that same day, Camden Kimcannon returned from the library with a stack of books, many of which were filled with narrow paper markers.

He spread out the books on a table and alternately took notes and read aloud excerpts of recipes to Georgiana, who had decided *not* to tell Camden about his mother's telephone call.

At about 5:20 P.M., after listening to Camden recite a recipe for something named Blood Pudding which went on for about ten minutes and consisted of a whole host of unpalatable ingredients, including blood, Georgiana dialed Joy's extension, and demanded that Mr. Zigfield's secretary come into her office, *right now*, to listen to a recipe that was hysterically funny. By 5:45 P.M., Georgiana Weeks, Joy Miller, and Camden Kimcannon were all dissolved in helpless laughter. Joy, at one point, was laughing so hard that she had to be pounded on her back; and Camden was laughing so hard that the tears were streaming down his face.

Later that night, at 11:45 P.M., when Georgiana Weeks was propped up against two downy pillows in her bed, reading *The Selected Letters of William Michael Rossetti*, her bedside telephone rang.

She picked up the receiver.

"I can't stand it anymore." Camden Kimcannon's voice crackled with emotion. "I've got to get out of here."

"Camden. What's wrong?"

"If I don't get my own apartment, Georgiana, I'll kill myself. I'll kill her. I don't know what I'd be driven to do."

"Where are you now, Camden?"

"I'm at home."

"On City Island?"

"Yes."

"Can your mother hear this conversation?"

"No. She's asleep in front of the television and I turned the volume up loud."

"Okay, Cam. Tell me what happened."

"Nothing happened. I just have to get out of here. I have to get away from her. I have to get a place of my own. I have to get a life."

"What can I do to help you?"

"*Will* you help me? Is it really all right? I mean, is it really all right for me to leave?"

"Of course it's all right for you to leave. You're a grown man. You should have left a long time ago."

"But what if she needs me to . . . no. *No,* I can't think that way. That's how she wants me to think. Tonight, when I got home, Georgiana, she told me."

"She told you what, Cam?"

"That she'd called you and said I wasn't really an artist, and that there really are no paintings in the garage."

"Cam, I don't care if there are or aren't paintings in the garage. And I don't care if you told me that you'd painted the Sistine Chapel or had done a ten-foot portrait of Porky Pig."

"Georgiana."

"What?"

"I'm scared."

"Of what?"

"Of leaving. Of staying. Of being out on my own. Of never having the chance to be on my own. I have to get out of here tomorrow, Georgiana. I have to get out of here, or I'll die."

"Don't worry. I'll help you. I'll get Jiri to help you. Do you have a place to stay tonight?"

"Yes."

"Where?"

"Here."

"Is that wise?"

"Don't worry. I'll be all right for one more night. But after tonight . . . "

"Do you have a suitcase, Camden?"

"I think there's an old one in the garage."

"Pack it up with enough clothes to hold you for a few days, and bring it to the museum tomorrow morning. Will you do that, Cam?"

Georgiana heard a strange, unidentifiable sound.

"What's that?"

"My—my—" Camden Kimcannon said. "My teeth are chattering."

"Cam, why don't you come here? You can sleep on my sofa. I *want* you to sleep on my sofa."

"No. I have to stay here to—to—tonight."

"But you sound terrible. Are you sure you're going to be all right?"

Camden laughed bitterly. "Don't wo—wo—worry, Georgiana. If I lasted this long, I can ma—ma—make it through one more night."

32

Georgiana had always been fascinated by the endless games of leapfrog that seemed to be going on in her own head. How one minute she could be walking down Fifth Avenue, wondering if she'd get to her appointment for tea at the Plaza Hotel on time, and the next minute she'd be thinking about the nude painting of Mrs. Kidder behind the headboard in Mr. and Mrs. Kidder's bedroom.

What she had often wondered, did one thing have to do with the other?

And *why* was she thinking of Mrs. Kidder now (she had been Georgiana's Girl Scout leader), when she hadn't given her a thought in over twenty years?

Georgiana, when she had the time, loved to follow the hopscotch pattern of her own thoughts.

Starting point: Fifth Avenue.

Initial subject matter: Being on time for tea.

But then what?

Then she had seen that same sad, lost soul of a woman whom she saw sitting on that same park bench every single day. A pretty woman, easily seventy or seventy-five years old, with the smile of a child or an angel, wearing four layers of coats and a feather boa, surrounded by shopping bags, and usually feeding an army of dirty pigeons and cats.

And on her feet, regardless of the season or the temperature, the woman always wore glamorous, open-toe, backless, gold lamé slippers.

That was it.

Subconsciously, Georgiana had noticed the slippers, and flashed back to her old Girl Scout leader who, unlike other Girl Scout leaders, was always so glamorous and so beautifully dressed.

She had been a starlet, she'd once confided to the adolescent Georgiana. Under contract to one of the big Hollywood studios. But she gave it all up when she met Mr. Kidder ("He looked *so* good in a uniform!").

On one rainy afternoon, when Georgiana was following Mrs. Kidder around like an adoring puppy (there weren't too many people with "star quality" in a small Oklahoma town—she had to grab at her stardust where she could find it), and Mrs. Kidder was wearing her gold lamé backless open-toe slippers, she showed Georgiana the painting. It was a nude portrait that had been done of her when she was just a kid of twenty-one, by the world-famous set designer who worked at the Hollywood studio where she was under contract, and who was in love with her at the time.

That was how it went.

Fifth Avenue to shopping bag lady. Shopping bag lady to gold lamé slippers. Gold lamé slippers to Girl Scout leader. Girl Scout leader to glamour. Glamour to Hollywood. And Hollywood to a nude painting of Mrs. Kidder behind the headboard in her bedroom.

And that was exactly how, within twelve hours of hanging up the telephone after talking to Camden Kimcannon, she was able to find him an apartment.

Leapfrog and hopscotch.

Georgiana was acquainted with four people at the Zigfield Art Museum. She called all of them up within ten minutes of hanging up on Camden, and explained to each one that her new assistant was in dire need of an apartment in Manhattan. And that he needed it yesterday.

Each of the four people she called (Jiri Hozda, Joy Miller, Mikos Piatigorsky, and Luis Cabrerra) called people whom they knew, who called people whom *they* knew, and before Wednesday morning was over,

Mikos Piatigorsky's cousin Lamaar telephoned the man who rented bicycles at the foot of the Verrazano Narrows Bridge. Which had something to do with Mr. Falkenberg. Nobody knows who called Mr. Falkenberg, but it was he who called Luis at work, who called Joy to have her check it out and see if the rumor was true.

Joy, hoping against hope, found out that Amanda Falkenberg had decided to give up her apartment *that very morning* in order to marry Claude, and that since she already had a passport (wasn't *that* a piece of luck!), there was nothing to stop her from selling all of her furniture (Yes, we think Mr. Kimcannon would like to buy it; and by all means, include the bed linens and the pots and pans), and there would be no reason why she couldn't just move in with Claude until they got married and moved to France. The apartment was very inexpensive (it was small and cramped, but it was a happy, sunny little place, and the neighbors were nice, and the landlord loved artists, and even though the bathroom was down the hall, there was a sink, a hot plate, and a refrigerator in the apartment itself), but sure, if this fellow really needed a place to stay, he could come by and leave a deposit. She could have all of her stuff out by Thursday afternoon, and he could move in, toothbrush, toothpaste, and pajamas, by Thursday night.

Leapfrog.

Hopscotch.

One thought to another. One phone call to another. One proposal of marriage. One passport. One guy and one gal. A not-too-large advance against your salary for the furniture and your first month's rent. And . . . congratulations, Camden Kimcannon!

You are finally living on your own.

33

The invitation was not widely distributed.

Camden had written it out with a calligraphy pen, photocopied it three times onto handmade, one-hundred-percent cotton paper (inlayed with flowers from Charlevoix), rolled each one up like a scroll, tied them with brown ribbons, and put one each on the desks of Georgiana Weeks, Joy Miller, and Jiri Hozda:

INVITATION—TO CELEBRATE!!!
Date: Sunday, November 27th
Time: Four o'clock
"FOR A MAN'S HOUSE IS HIS CASTLE"
Please Come to a Housewarming Party
At My Castle
My tiny room may not be great
(Two chairs, a bed, a small hot plate),
But once you're there . . . what's mine is yours
(I recommend the cold hors d'oeuvres).
We'll wine, we'll dine, we'll celebrate,
We'll start at four, and stay till late.
I don't care when my party ends,
As long as I am with my friends.

After Georgiana read the scroll, she got weepy and walked into Jiri's office.

She waved the invitation in the air. "Have you seen this yet?"

"Yes. I received mine just this morning."

"It's so corny," Georgiana said. "And it's so cute. Do you know if Joy is coming?"

"No. But I doubt that she would turn down an invitation to the party of the century."

"Are you going?"

"I'll go if you go."

"Well, I'm going. May I use your telephone?"

Georgiana dialed.

After two rings, Joy Miller picked up.

"Joy," Georgiana said. "Did you get Camden's invitation?"

"Yes, I did."

"Are you going?"

"Yes, I am."

"Isn't it exciting!"

"Yes, it is."

"OK. See you there."

Georgiana hung up.

"That girl lacks vitality. There must be something I can do to juice her up."

"Maybe she does not want to be, as you say, 'juiced up.' "

"Nonsense. No woman would want to be a moth if she could be a butterfly. What are you bringing to the party?"

"Am I bringing something?"

"Well, a bottle of wine would be appropriate."

"Then I shall bring a bottle of wine."

"And, of course, you'll have to bring a present."

"I will?"

"This is a *housewarming party*. We all have to bring presents. You're about the same size as Camden. Do you have any old clothes you want to get rid of?"

"I can consult with my closet."

"And shoes. He needs shoes."

"I will look for shoes. Anything else?"

"Nothing I can think of now, but stay tuned. May I use your telephone again?"

"You may use my telephone, my credit cards, my wallet. You may read love letters I wrote when I was sixteen years old to the girl with the red hair who flew on the trapeze. You may have my stamp collection, my baseball card collection, and my second-century silver Greek coin."

Georgiana picked up the telephone.

"You don't really have a stamp collection, do you?"

"No," Jiri responded.

"And I don't quite see you collecting baseball cards."

"A keen observation."

Joy dialed again.

"Do you really have a second-century silver Greek coin?"

"No," Jiri Hozda said, smiling the smile of a man who was very sure of himself. "But I was once passionately enamored of a girl who flew on a trapeze." He reached forward and between his thumb and forefinger began to lightly caress a wild lock of Georgiana's hair. "And she *did* have red hair."

34

Georgiana Weeks was the first to arrive at Camden Kimcannon's castle.

It was located on East Eighty-fourth Street, in a five-story brownstone with a wide cement stoop.

There was a window box on the ledge outside the first floor apartment. There were no flowers in it, because it was November; but in honor of the season, someone had decorated it with an assortment of small straw pilgrims, scarecrows, Indians, and turkeys, each on its own sturdy wooden stick.

The door to the lobby was covered with colorful variety store signs wishing all comers a Happy Thanksgiving—three days gone, but apparently not forgotten. And inside the small, brightly lighted foyer, Georgiana was happy to see a polished brass doorbell, beside which was a label embossed with the name: KIMCANNON.

She rang the bell.

Two minutes later, she had climbed five flights of stairs, and Camden was standing at the door to welcome her.

"Cam!" Georgiana exclaimed. "Blue jeans and a western shirt. I can't believe it. You look fantastic."

Two minutes after that, her coat was off, the gift that she'd brought was on the kitchen floor (there was no room for it anywhere else), and she was watching Camden at his window as he described the view.

"And if I stick my head way out . . . "

"Be careful, Cam. Don't fall."

"I can see . . . I can see . . . " Camden ducked back inside. "Actually, I can't see much of anything except more brownstones and the sky. But the sky looks different when you're seeing it from your own apartment window."

Georgiana stuck out her head and looked up.

"Best sky *I've* ever seen."

Then she ducked back in.

Camden's studio apartment was small, even by New York City standards. It had one window. A twin-size sofa bed. A small rag rug with a folding card table on it that could be put beside the sofa and laden with food, which was its condition at present. There were two folding chairs. A three-drawer dresser. A small kitchen area with a doll's sink, a hot plate, and a refrigerator big enough to hold a quart of milk, a dozen eggs, and a few bowls of leftover soup. All of the walls in the small apartment were covered from floor to ceiling with bookshelves, and all of the bookshelves were filled with Camden Kimcannon's collection of books.

"Where is everybody?" Georgiana asked. "It's ten minutes after four already. They're late."

Camden sat down on a chair and indicated that Georgiana should sit on the more comfortable sofa.

"Jiri called and said he'd be here by four-thirty." Camden's voice was jittery. "Joy called and said she had to stop at Bloomingdale's on her way over." He leaped back up to his feet. "But I don't have the right to be a bad host just because my other guests are late. What can I get you, Georgiana? I have soda and I can make you instant coffee or tea. Here. Have one of these little pieces of salami. Or have some crackers and cheese. I've got some toothpicks around here, too. Or, I thought I did. Maybe I forgot to put them out. Well, try a grape, then. They're sweet for this time of the year. I wanted to make spaghetti, but . . . "

"Cam, sit down."

He sat.

"Calm down."

He fidgeted with his hands.

"What's wrong."

"Nothing's wrong. I'm just nervous."

Georgiana smiled.

"Cam, I'm just so damn proud of you."

He looked up. Astonished. A strand of hair flopped over his forehead into his eye.

"You are?" he said, incredulous.

"Darn tootin' right, I am. Proud of you. Honored to be here. Glad to be your friend." Georgiana looked around the room again. "And I love your new apartment. I see you brought all your books with you."

Cam stared at his hands and nodded.

"It must have been quite a job to get them here."

He nodded again.

"Did anybody help you?"

"Luis."

"Luis Cabrerra?"

"Uh huh. He has a van. I asked him if he would move me. I offered to pay him, too. But he wouldn't take my money. Luis brought along his grandson. His name is Luis, too. It took us all day Saturday to get the books up to my apartment. Luis had the day off from the museum. Luis's grandson wouldn't let him climb the stairs because of his heart condition, but Luis helped with everything else. I didn't invite him to my party though, because I thought he might feel that he had to accept, and . . . I don't know. I just didn't want him to have to come up all of those stairs."

Georgiana smiled and patted Camden's hand. "You're a nice man."

Camden's face contorted.

"You're hurting, aren't you? What's eating at you? You're going to have to tell someone eventually, Cam, and since I'm the only one here, it may as well be me."

He shook his head miserably. "It's just that . . . you . . . when you said that I was nice . . . "

"You *are* nice, Cam."

"But . . . the Mater."

"You mean your *mother*."

He nodded.

"Then *call* her your mother. That's what people call human females in this country after they've given birth: mother, mom, mama. But not 'the Mater.' This is American, not a rehearsal for a performance at the Old Vic Theatre in jolly old England. Welcome to the real world. Now, what did your mother do? Did she try to stop you from moving?"

"No."

"Then what?"

"She laughed at me."

"She's done that before."

"She said I wouldn't make it on my own. That I wouldn't last a week in my own apartment. That I wouldn't even make it through a single night."

"Well, you slept here on Thursday night, and you slept here on Friday night, and last night was Saturday night. That's three nights, so it looks as though she were wrong."

Camden said nothing.

"You don't look convinced."

"She . . . the Mat—my mother . . . she said I was a loser. A born loser and a failure. And that the only reason I've gotten as far in life as I have is because she's always lied to people about me and told them that I was better than I am."

"The only reason you've gotten this far in life, Cam, is because people meet you and realize in a very short time that you're one of the best people they're ever likely to meet."

"You know my sketchbook? The one I had on my desk in my bedroom."

"Yes. I looked through it. You're very good, Cam. You are very, very good."

"She . . . she tore out all of the drawings I'd done of Merlin and of King Arthur. And she set fire to them over the gas stove."

"Well, that was nice of her. That's just what the world needs. Another supportive parent. Oh, for heaven's sake, Cam, listen to yourself. What kind of a person would *do* what she did to anybody, let alone to her own son!"

Camden shrugged.

"Okay. If you don't want to talk about it, we don't have to talk about it. But you *do* have to think about it, because I can guarantee you that your mother isn't through with you yet. Cam, you have to think before you do things, and you have to think before you allow other people to do things *to* you. Now, tell me how you're doing otherwise. How are you handling living on your own?"

"It's scary."

"It's only scary until you get the hang of it, but I bet you twenty dollars that after a month you'll be an old pro. Now where's that cup of coffee you promised me?"

Camden leaped to his feet.

"Coffee . . . coffee," he muttered, as though he was trying to figure out where he had misplaced a diamond-studded key.

Georgiana also stood.

"Cam, I think what this housewarming party needs is a shop foreman."

The doorbell rang.

A second later, it rang again.

"I'll be the shop foreman, Cam . . . you're labor. *You* find that jar of instant coffee, and *I'll* boil up a pot of water. But first, hit the door buzzer. And then, Mr. Kimcannon, let the festivities begin!"

Fifteen minutes after Joy Miller and Jiri Hozda arrived at Camden's party he began to relax. Partly because he and his guests were squeezed so tightly around the table in his little apartment, they made a daisy chain of elbows and knees that continually bumped into one another, and each bump precipitated a wry comment that inevitably led to another bump, a joke, or a smile; and each smile seemed to segue into something that made one or all of them laugh.

Jiri, as he had promised, brought the wine. But instead of bringing just table wine, he brought two bottles of champagne.

Joy delivered an enormous tin of Saks Fifth Avenue chocolate lace cookies, which Wegman Zigfield had sent, along with his best wishes for Camden in his new apartment.

And everybody brought a housewarming present.

Jiri gave Camden a very large box which he said was *not* a gift, but merely contained old clothes he'd grown tired of (a cashmere sports jacket, a pair of shoes worn only once, and six Lord and Taylor dress shirts so new they'd barely lost their original crease); he also gave Camden a smaller box which he said *was* a present, and which contained a high-tech answering machine that did everything (record time, date, etc.) except take your blood pressure and make scrambled eggs.

Joy's housewarming present was sweet.

She had, indeed, stopped at Bloomingdale's department store on her way there and had bought Camden a soft, thick, luxurious, dark purple, terrycloth robe.

Why purple? Somebody asked her.

"Well, that's simple," she explained. "Because Camden invited us to his castle, and because a man is the king in his own castle, and because purple is the royal color—the color of kings."

Georgiana muttered, "I'll be damned. The moth has a hidden reservoir of butterfly."

But it was Georgiana's present that brought tears to Camden's eyes.

She gave him a wooden box. With a handle. Inside the wooden box was an assortment of brushes, a palette, twenty-six 1.25-ounce tubes of different color oil paint, a 4-ounce bottle of linseed oil, a 4-ounce bottle of retouch varnish, and an engraved invitation to attend the gala celebration on the opening night of the Pre-Raphaelite exhibition. By invitation only. Black tie.

Nobody had dinner that night.

But nobody went hungry.

Art was the major topic of conversation from five o'clock to about 7:00 P.M. After that, Jiri regaled the party with funny stories of growing up with what he called "a Hollywood complex" in Communist Czechoslovakia. Georgiana told some Oklahoma stories ("Heck, sure I can rope a calf."). And Joy Miller described her job interview with Wegman Zigfield, and how she had knocked over her coffee cup, backed into his prize cactus plant, and then couldn't stop crying.

"I think he only gave me the job because he couldn't figure out how else to get me out of his office."

They laughed.

They talked.

They ate.

And when Jiri and Georgiana left Camden's apartment at two o'clock in the morning, Joy Miller stayed behind "to help him clean up."

And after they had walked five blocks, Georgiana looked down and said to Jiri Hozda, "You seem to be holding my hand."

And Jiri looked down, too, and said, "I wonder how that could have happened."

And after they had walked another three blocks, Jiri said, "I would not have thought that it was possible, but I believe, tonight, that you actually saved his life."

And Georgiana Weeks nodded her head ever so slightly and she did not have to ask whose.

35

Seymour Fishbine was ninety-two years old.

If you met him at a party, with his carefully combed white hair (perhaps a little bit too long behind the ears), his dapper bow tie and his bushy, expressive eyebrows . . . and if you listened to the rolling cadences of his vowels and observed his exaggerated hand movements and repeated glances toward heaven as though to confirm a shared joke with God, you would think, you would *have* to think that Seymour Fishbine was just a kid of seventy-two. Seventy-three at most.

And you would know, unquestionably and without a doubt, that he had lived his life upon the stage. Most likely performing Shakespeare in the Yiddish theatre.

And you would have been wrong.

For Seymour Fishbine's life was paint.

He lived with paint. He lived for paint. He knew everything about paint.

He loved paint.

He and his wife Fanny started out, as did so many in his generation, with a pushcart on Essex Street on New York's Lower East Side.

His original merchandise had been hardware: tools, buckets, thumbtacks, scissors, scrubbrushes, nailbrushes, paintbrushes.

He and Fanny did well.

After they had expanded from one pushcart to two (his and hers), and increased their stock of merchandise to include sandpaper, sponges, window shades, and alarm clocks, a recently widowed lady named Mrs. Kelly asked Seymour one afternoon if he would leave his pushcart for a few minutes (no problem; he could push it up the street and Fanny could watch it), and help her open up a can of paint.

Mrs. Kelly wanted to rent one of the rooms in her apartment, she explained, and she thought that she would get a better class of tenant if it were covered with a nice, clean, new coat of white paint.

Seymour followed Mrs. Kelly up five flights of stairs.

She was an old lady. She was poor. She was feeble. She needed the income from renting her back bedroom.

"Here's the can, Mr. Fishbine," Mrs. Kelly said.

Seymour looked at it, looked up to heaven to see if God was perhaps perpetrating a small joke, and then looked back down again at the paint can.

"Where did you get this, Mrs. Kelly?" he asked. "When they were unloading Noah's ark?"

For the paint was very old. And the paint can was paint-encrusted and layered with cobwebs, dead flies, and dust.

Seymour Fishbine, however, brought up by his wife to be a gentleman ("Seymour always makes me feel like a queen, I'm telling you.") pried the lid off the container with a screwdriver. Then he rubbed his prominent jaw between his thumb and his forefinger, and he stared down at the solidified and parched paint inside the can.

When he turned and caught the double whammy of hope and expectation in Mrs. Kelly's eyes, he said to himself, "If Moses could make dry land in the Red Sea, I can make wet paint in the Mojave desert of this can."

It took Seymour Fishbine four hours and over a pint of turpentine to do it. He broke two stir sticks, got a splinter in his palm, and was almost asphyxiated by fumes because he forgot to open the window when he painted Mrs. Kelly's back room for her ("No, of course Seymour didn't charge her. His own mother a widow. What can I say? Seymour has a heart."), but when he was finished . . . when the dirty deed was done, he returned to his pushcart, walked over to Fanny, took her in his arms, gazed deeply into her beautiful hazel eyes (their children, Maurice and Myra, had their mother's eyes), and said just one word.

Paint.

It was the beginning of an empire.

OK. So a small empire. But from two pushcarts, a building four stories high and all filled with turpentine, shellac, varnish, paint, and paint-brushes, is an empire nonetheless.

Seymour Fishbine discovered that he had a gift.

If it was solid, he could liquify it; if it was wet, he could dry it; if it was too oily, he could take the oil out of it; if it dried too slowly, he could speed up the drying; if it peeled, he could strip it.

He could make paint adhere to anything.

He could remove paint from everything.

If you said you wanted a shade of blue to match the blue in your daughter's eyes the day she got married (the ceremony was outside and the sun was shining), he could match it. Without meeting your daughter, and without looking into her eyes.

It was a spiritual thing.

I want, you would tell Seymour, to paint my room green. But not just any shade of green. It has to be the shade of green on the hyacinth leaves just as they peek through the winter snow on a warm day of false spring.

And Seymour would look up to heaven, have a momentary color consultation with God about exactly how much yellow to mix with blue, and if, perhaps, a touch of white would be appropriate, and in no time at all, the fantasy of your hyacinth leaves would become a reality.

Seymour always knew how many gallons you would need to paint your wall, even if you didn't know square feet from square dances; and just by looking at you, he knew if you were a roller man or if your personality required brushes.

Seymour knew everything about paint and everyone who wanted to know anything about paint knew about Seymour.

On the top floor of Fishbine Paints, Seymour had created a Museum of Paint. It was his hobby. (Paint was his life. Paint, and, of course, Fanny.)

The FBI consulted with Seymour when the paint at the scene of a crime defied interpretation by their forensic chemists.

The New York City Police Department often came to ask Seymour questions if they had an obscure, paint-related piece of evidence.

And Wylie Nolan, on three separate occasions when he was a New York City fire marshal, had visited Seymour Fishbine at Fishbine Paints.

Wylie had not seen Seymour for five years.

The last case he'd consulted him on involved arson and the deaths of three firemen.

Seymour was not a sophisticated laboratory.

Seymour did not work with spectrometers, computers, or gas chromatographs.

Seymour had a nose though.

And his nose was never wrong.

And Seymour had eyes.

And his eyes could make color distinctions so subtle, that if they had been ears, they would have had perfect pitch.

Seymour Fishbine was ninety-two years old.

Wylie Nolan had already gotten his findings from Chem-Test Labs. He'd sought his answers. He'd gotten his results.

But before he went into that meeting on Tuesday afternoon, he knew that he would have to consult with the court of last resort.

The man, the alchemist, the magician.

The best laboratory in the world and the best equipment were all well and good.

But if you really wanted to know about paint, paint finishes, paint solvents, paint oils, paint mediums, paint attributes, paint properties, and paint characteristics, there was only one place in the world to go, and only one man to talk to.

Wylie picked up the telephone.

"Information," he said, "give me the number of Fishbine Paints."

36

Wylie Nolan sat at the head of the large oval table in the conference room at the Zigfield Art Museum. An assortment of small glass jars and metal containers were in front of him. Behind him was a portable easel on which were balanced a stack of poster boards. To his left sat Wegman Zigfield, compact, perfectly groomed, with eyes like miniature spy cameras, and even while sitting down (grab for pencil, jam pencil in pocket, bob head forward, jab finger at telephone), as pugnacious as ever.

Seated next to his father, with a fashionably scruffy day's growth of beard and his signature granny glasses, was Fromer Zigfield, as intent on catching his father's eye as his father was on avoiding his son's.

Sarkin Zahedi, wearing a black linen Nehru jacket over a white T-shirt, sat to Fromer's left. He seemed to have abandoned his most recent wild man of Borneo haircut for ringletlike curls; his hands were clasped together, his fingers serenely intertwined; and as always, his eyes seemed to be watching reruns of religious epiphanies taking place at the back of his head.

To Sarkin Zahedi's left sat Lars Helmersson. Lars's calfskin briefcase was opened in front of him. He was, as before, dressed in moccasins with no socks, and blue jeans with a cashmere sports jacket over a silk shirt. His lidless eyes didn't blink, and his entire body faced Wylie Nolan, motionless and confrontational at the same time.

The first chair to Wylie's right was occupied by Max Bramble. Max's eyes darted back and forth between Wylie Nolan and Wegman Zigfield like a teacher unsure if his favorite student was going to ruin a job interview by having put a whoopie cushion on the boss's seat.

Jiri Hozda sat next to Max, somber and lacking his characteristic *je ne sais quoi*. He was elegantly dressed in a perfectly cut gray business suit with a white shirt and gray tie, but by the standards that would have normally applied to Jiri Hozda, he looked as though he were on his way to a funeral.

Joy Miller sat beside Jiri, steno pad and pencil at hand. There was a sweet but slightly askew expression on her face, which was somehow prettier today than usual, and she had a redder shade of lipstick than she usually wore on her lips.

When she took her seat, Jiri leaned toward her and said softly, "You look quite lovely today, my dear," and when she blushed, her face became lovelier still.

And Luis Cabrerra sat in the last chair on the right side of the conference table, resplendent in his Ruritanian army general's uniform. He showed evidence of extra care having been taken in his grooming that morning, though, because he would be attending a meeting of such tremendous importance to the security of the museum (the brass buttons running down the front of his jacket positively gleamed, and as he walked by, Joy was certain that she caught a whiff of cologne).

At exactly nine o'clock, Wylie Nolan stood up.

"You're all familiar with the circumstances surrounding the fire that destroyed Sarkin Zahedi's paintings, so I'll just recap them briefly.

"On Friday, November eleventh, at seven o'clock in the morning, Luis Cabrerra arrived at the museum. About two minutes later, the smoke alarm in the Parlor Gallery went off. The heat alarm did not go off though. And the smoke and heat detectors in the hallway outside the Parlor Gallery and in the adjacent rooms were silent.

"A few minutes later, when Luis Cabrerra checked the doors of the Parlor Gallery, he found them locked, just as they had been the night before. When he unlocked them, he saw the remains of what appeared to have been a fire, which was already out by the time he opened the doors.

"The fire damage in the gallery was restricted to the five Sarkin Zahedi paintings on display. The Zahedi exhibition was paid for by a subsidy from the American Art Development Fund. Fromer Zigfield was associate director of the museum at the time the grant was applied for, but not at the time of the fire. The relevance of this grant becomes clearer as we go along."

Fromer Zigfield darted a malicious glance at Jiri Hozda.

"Except for the five canvases having been destroyed," Wylie went on, "the Parlor Gallery exhibited no other damage from heat or flames, which suggested to Mr. Zigfield that the paintings had been removed prior to the fire, and the fires then set to hide evidence of the theft. This particular scenario hadn't occurred to me. But, as Mr. Zigfield later explained, when a museum employee sees a frame that isn't supposed to be empty, he always thinks someone has stolen the canvas.

"Mr. Zigfield also pointed out that since the museum had been locked from the night before when Luis Cabrerra set the alarm, until Luis returned the following day, and since nobody had reentered the museum during that period, *and* since the Parlor Gallery was still locked at two minutes after seven in the morning, when the smoke alarm went off, then what we were looking at here was a classic 'locked room mystery.'

"So, we were faced not only with the problem of 'whodunit,' but also with *how* it was done. How someone or something managed to materialize inside a locked art gallery to set what's got to be one of the strangest fires I've ever seen.

"But before I explain what happened, I want to point out what was particularly unusual about this fire, from an arson investigator's point of view."

Lars Helmersson's unblinking eyes narrowed and he snorted contemptuously. He took a gold fountain pen out of his jacket pocket and conspicuously scribbled a word or two on a pad in his opened briefcase.

Wylie ignored him.

"The first unusual aspect of this fire was brought to my attention by Luis Cabrerra, who doesn't have a background in investigating fires, but who did ask a damn good question. Why, he asked me, didn't the heat detector go off when the smoke alarm was activated by the fire? Since fire generates both smoke and heat, and since heat is an inevitable by-product of flames, then why did we have the one without the other?

"Another interesting aspect of this fire was how fast it was. At two minutes after seven, smoke in the Parlor Gallery triggered an alarm. Less than five minutes later, Luis Cabrerra was *inside* the Parlor Gallery and there was nothing burning. No smoke. No heat. No fire. Only sooty walls where Sarkin Zahedi's pictures had hung, and char and ashes under the five empty picture frames.

"So, these were the facts I had to work with the day of the fire. I poked around the museum, asked a few questions, and by the time I got back to my office, I'd already come to a few preliminary conclusions.

"First, that the doors to the Parlor Gallery *were* locked at the time of the fire, as Luis had said.

"Second, that before the fire started, the structural integrity of the museum hadn't been compromised. Doors weren't jimmied; locks weren't picked; and nobody had been fooling around with the security system's computer printouts.

"Third, that the fire wasn't electrical in nature. I checked all the wall switches, light fixtures, and outlets in the Parlor Gallery, and didn't find any evidence of unusual electrical activity or short circuiting.

"Which left only one possible explanation for the fire. That a ghost set it."

Wylie paused for a long moment and then went on.

"What I had to do next was ferret out who or what that ghost was, which didn't preclude good, old-fashioned, tangible, physical evidence. So, to make sure I wasn't overlooking anything, I had the empty Zahedi picture frames sent to my office, where I . . ."

"You did *what*?" Lars Helmersson exclaimed, and banged the lid of his calfskin briefcase shut.

Wylie turned to Lars Helmersson.

He said so softly, he almost seemed to be miming the words, "You heard what I said."

"Why did you take the frames?" Lars Helmersson demanded.

But before Wylie could answer, Fromer Zigfield blundered into the showdown between the two fire investigators.

"Those frames belonged to Sarkin Zahedi. You had absolutely no right to take them!"

Wylie turned to Joy Miller and then to Luis Cabrerra.

"Joy. Luis. You were both in the Parlor Gallery after Mr. Helmersson was finished in there, but before he left the museum. Did either of you ask him if he'd need to come back to the gallery later to inspect anything else?"

Luis said, "I did."

"What did he say, Luis?"

"He said 'no.' That he was finished."

"Did he ask you to save the picture frames or to put them in storage for him?"

"No. I ask him if that is all. Does he need anything more, and he answers me that he does not. They all say 'no,' that they are finished with the Parlor Gallery."

Wylie turned to Wegman Zigfield's secretary.

"Joy? Did you say anything to Mr. Helmersson before he left that day?"

"Yes. I asked Mr. Fromer, Mr. Zahedi, *and* Mr. Helmersson if we could clean up the gallery and dispose of the debris; and all three gentlemen said yes."

Lars Helmersson's voice was an angry hiss. "I insist on an answer. What did you want with those frames?"

Wylie shrugged. "Nothing much. Just samples."

"What kind of samples?"

"This and that. A little something to send along to my lab. But we're getting away from the real subject here, because what I want to talk about is ghosts: First, if there was one; and second, who the ghost was. Because from day one, I had three likely candidates. Two of my ghosts had motives that mirrored each other; the last ghost didn't seem to have a motive, but he was injured and for me to write off the injury just wouldn't have been good investigative work.

"I'll tell you about my last ghost first. Mikos Piatigorsky. What drew

Mikos to my attention was an accident he'd had . . . an accident that he *said* kept him out of work the day of the fire. Coincidence? Maybe. Maybe not. But I had to find out what *kind* of an accident and if it had anything to do with heat or flames.

"When I interviewed Mikos Piatigorsky on Tuesday, November fifteenth, I was more suspicious, because even though the kind of bandage that was wrapped around his right hand isn't exclusive to fire injuries, it did look exactly the way a hand would look if Mikos had been treated by the Cornell Hospital's burn unit.

"And I got more suspicious when Mikos wouldn't tell me how he'd gotten hurt.

"So, one day when he was at work, I went to the apartment building where he lives. I explained to the doorman that the landlord had sent me to fix the stove in Mr. Piatigorsky's apartment, because the oven had exploded and burned the tenant's right hand.

"The doorman said to me, and I quote 'Poor dumb bastard. You'd think a guy as big as him would be more careful. Last Friday, right in front of me, I saw him slam a taxi cab door on his fingers. Now you're telling me he went and burned himself. Worse luck, too, on the same hand . . . ' and so on.

"It was clear to me now that the only reason Mikos didn't want to talk about how he'd hurt himself was because he was embarrassed about being clumsy, not because he was guilty of setting a fire.

"Which meant I only had two ghosts left. The ones with what I called the mirror motives.

"Fromer Zigfield was the first one. I was suspicious of him because . . . "

Fromer leaped to his feet. "Now, just a minute here. How dare you . . . "

"I suspected Fromer," Wylie went on unperturbed, "because he wouldn't stop hounding me about Jiri Hozda. Dr. Hozda, he insisted, was an arsonist, and Dr. Hozda set the fire in the Parlor Gallery. Over and over and over. To me, it was a clear case of 'The Gentleman Doth Protest Too Much.' "

Wylie looked at Jiri. "The flipside of that mirror though, was Jiri

Hozda himself, and regardless of what I thought personally, the accusations against him were coming in fast and furious, so I was forced to treat Dr. Hozda as a suspect."

Wegman Zigfield turned to his son and barked, "Fromer, sit down."

Fromer sat.

"On the first Wednesday after the fire," Wylie continued, "Fromer Zigfield came to see me in Luis Cabrerra's office and accused Jiri Hozda of setting fire to Sarkin Zahedi's paintings. In support of this allegation, he read aloud some excerpts from an article Jiri wrote attacking the American Art Development Fund. According to Fromer, the article proved that Dr. Hozda had a motive, and that he was everything from an anarchist to a pyromaniac, and probably more dangerous around fire than a three-year-old with a book of matches."

Jiri Hozda straightened himself in his chair and said, "Excuse me, Wylie, but might I . . . "

"No, you might not," Wylie cut him off sharply. Then he continued, "When Fromer accused Dr. Hozda, though, what he didn't realize was that he was also pointing a finger at *himself*. Why? Because if Dr. Hozda hated the American Art Development Fund so passionately that he would set a fire to stop Sarkin Zahedi's exhibit, then Fromer Zigfield's hatred of Jiri Hozda was just as passionate, and Fromer was just as likely to set a fire to *frame* the man who'd replaced him as the associate director of this museum."

Fromer Zigfield slammed his hand against the tabletop.

"This is slander! I don't have to listen to this!"

Jiri Hozda's eyes were politely fierce as he turned to Wegman Zigfield's son. "You are correct. It is most unpleasant to be accused of a crime that one has not committed. Perhaps you should consider that next time, as you are the one who has done the accusing."

"I . . . you . . . how . . . " Fromer sputtered.

"Oh, shut up, Fromer," Wegman Zigfield commanded.

"Go on, Mr. Nolan. Explain to me which of the two ghosts here set a fire in my museum."

"Neither one did," Wylie answered.

Fromer banged his fist against the table and exclaimed, "See!"

Max Bramble leaned forward. "I don't get it, Wylie. If neither of them set the fires, then . . . "

"I'll get to that, Max. After I tell you about the second accusation Fromer Zigfield made against Jiri Hozda. That Jiri could have easily compromised the museum's security system simply by staying put. He suggested that Jiri never left the museum the night before the fire. That he locked himself in his office overnight, and that a few minutes before seven o'clock on Friday morning, he crept down the hall to the Parlor Gallery, unlocked the doors, set fire to Sarkin Zahedi's paintings, re-locked the doors, and then returned to his own office to hide until there were so many people at the museum his presence would go unnoticed."

Wegman scowled at Wylie Nolan and then looked at Jiri Hozda with the first hint of doubt.

"What Fromer didn't consider, though," Wylie continued, "was that if Jiri Hozda could have done it, so could he. And by the way, I just found out that you never turned in your keys to the museum after your father fired you, Fromer, and that nobody ever changed your keypad security code; it's still in the system. That's true, isn't it, Luis?"

Luis Cabrerra suddenly looked stricken. He turned to Wegman Zigfield. "I am so sorry, Mr. Zigfield, but he is your son, and I did not like to ask him to return the keys. I . . . "

"Forget it, Luis," Wegman Zigfield snapped.

Wylie went on, "But none of Fromer's accusations really mattered anyway, because his hypothesis is flawed. What he forgot, and so did Luis, is that after hours when the museum is empty, not only are all of the security keypad systems activated, and not only do the utilities go into an off-hours mode, but the motion detectors in the hallways outside the galleries are also turned on."

Jiri Hozda smiled and saluted Wylie Nolan. "That is what I had been wanting to tell you. Thank you, my friend."

Wylie grinned and winked.

"So, no ghost," he said. "I finally had to admit to myself that not even Tinkerbell could have gotten past the motion detectors and through the locked door of the Parlor Gallery without setting off the museum's alarms."

Wegman Zigfield frowned and said in a voice that could cut dia-
monds, "Do you mean to tell me that you don't know *who* set the fire in
my art museum."

"Sorry, Wegman."

"Then what the hell am I paying you for?"

"You aren't paying me. Your insurance company is." Wylie included
Sarkin Zahedi with a glance. "And so is *yours*, Mr. Zahedi. And it's a
damn shame that insurance companies don't give their fire investigators
a bonus when we save them a lot of money, because after I submit my report, they're going to be welcoming home about five million dollars they
thought they'd already seen the taillights on as it sped down the road.

"I'll tell you what, though. Instead of confusing you with the end of
the story, why don't I start at the beginning, and just leave the police part
for later. That'll be my little surprise."

Wylie indicated the bottles and containers on the table in front of
him and said, "This is the beginning."

He picked up a small round can with a twist top.

"This is rubber cement. A container of this brand of rubber cement
was in Sarkin Zahedi's studio when I interviewed him a week after the
fire. Let me read you from the can's warning label: 'Caution—flammable
mixture. Do not use near fire or flame. Vapors may ignite explosively or
cause a flash fire. When using, extinguish all flames and pilot lights, turn
off stoves, electric motors, and heaters. Avoid sparks, static discharge,
and other sources of ignition.' "

Wylie replaced the can and picked up a small, clear glass bottle with
a white plastic bottle cap.

"This next culprit is called a Japan Drier. It's a combustible liquid,
and it's relevant to this case because of what it does when it's mixed with
paint, which is to accelerate the drying time of paint; it's also relevant because when I last saw a Japan Drier, it was in Sarkin Zahedi's studio.

"And this," Wylie said, exchanging the Japan Drier for a large, rectangular can. "This is plain old turpentine. It's used to thin paint and to
thin the Japan Drier I just showed you. Like the rubber cement, turpentine is very flammable. Let me read you from the label here. 'Warning:
Vapors may ignite explosively. Combustible!' And there's an exclamation

point after the word *combustible*. 'Keep away from heat and open flame.' "

Wylie put the can of turpentine back on the table and then he picked up two more containers, one in each hand.

"But these two are what I consider the stars of our exhibit. This one." He raised the pressurized spray can in his right hand. "This is a product called picture varnish. It was made by Daubin and Kline, which has been in the artists' materials business since 1908. Let me read you something off the label of this can. It says, 'This is a final varnish for oil painting that enriches the appearance of completed paintings. Apply when the painting is thoroughly dry (six to twelve months).' "

Wylie lowered the spray can of varnish and lifted the container he was holding in his other hand.

"And this is Boiled Linseed Oil. Linseed oil comes from flax seeds, and it's used by artists to thin the consistency of oil paint and advance or slow down the drying time of paint. What we're interested in here, though, isn't slowing down the drying time of paint, but speeding it up. Now, let me read you something off this warning label, and it's a good one, too. Makes the others I read look like nursery rhymes: 'Caution. Oil-soaked rags or other oily waste may be subject to spontaneous combustion. To avoid possible fire hazard, promptly discard in water-filled container or burn all rags, mop heads, etc., used in application.'

"This label doesn't fool around by warning you against what it considers negligible dangers like heat, sparks, or open flames. Linseed oil is a solvent. And this solvent is so combustible that it isn't even the oil itself that scares the bejesus out of the manufacturers; it's what the oil touches, and where it's used, and how it's stored, and if it's disposed of properly. Because if it isn't . . . Well, I'll get around to telling you more about that later."

Wylie paused and looked into the eyes of those sitting around the conference table. He said, "Rags. Mop heads. Etcetera. Think about it for a second. Think about rags. Think about etcetera. Think about how *much* etcetera there was in each one of Sarkin Zahedi's paintings. And then, think about spontaneous combustion."

He put down the container he had been holding in his left hand.

"Linseed oil," he said again. "*This* is our ghost."

He placed the spray can of varnish that he'd been holding in his right hand next to the linseed oil.

"And this is our ghost breaker. Now, I'm going to tell you how the fire occurred.

"We can positively date the scam that resulted in these accidental fires to sometime within the last eighteen months, because that's when Sarkin Zahedi, the gentleman sitting at the end of this table, decided to perpetrate a fraud on the art world."

The artist in question peered at Wylie Nolan, and despite his prior unbroken record of blank stares, he looked as though he hadn't missed a single syllable of what Wylie had said.

Fromer Zigfield turned to Sarkin Zahedi, "Don't worry, Sarkin. We'll sue him for libel. We'll . . . "

Wylie ignored them both and went on.

"According to Mr. Zahedi's press clippings, ten 'masterpieces' he'd painted over twenty years ago had been recently rediscovered. How he'd managed to smuggle them into that abandoned loft undetected; where they were found; who 'rediscovered' them for Sarkin Zahedi; and whether or not that person was in on the scam from the beginning, are all questions the New York City Police Department will have to answer after I've briefed them on this case.

"I was hired by the Michelangelo Fine Arts Insurance Group to find out where and how the fire started in the Parlor Gallery at the Zigfield Art Museum.

"That's exactly what I've done.

"Sometime within the past eighteen months, Sarkin Zahedi bought the materials he would need to create ten canvases. Each canvas measured six-feet wide by five-feet high. But our concern is only with five of them. The five on display in the Parlor Gallery at the time of the fire."

Wylie walked to the easel behind his chair and flipped around the poster boards so that a blowup of Sarkin Zahedi's painting *Process* was facing the conference table.

"These are enlargements of the work that was destroyed in the fire. The titles of those five paintings are: *Process, Germination, Creation, De-*

struction, and *Chaos*, and who knows? Maybe there's even a weird sort of poetic justice in how Sarkin Zahedi named them, because sure as hell, the same man who created *Creation* destroyed it. The same man who created *Destruction* destroyed it. The same man who . . . "

Sarkin Zahedi's black eyes glazed over with a velvety malevolence and he began to chant, "Liar. Liar. Liar. You are a liar. Devil. Devil. Devil. You are a devil. Hell. Hell. Hell. You will burn in a hell as you . . . "

"Give it a rest, Sarkin," Wylie said. "And when I say you destroyed your own paintings, I don't mean that you intended for them to burn, or that you stood next to them and struck a match. Far from it. In fact, *you* were far from the paintings at the time they went on fire."

Wylie's glance traveled around the table.

"You all were. Nobody here, Sarkin included, had a motive for setting fire to those paintings. But one of you had a very strong motive for fraud. Sarkin Zahedi is an artist whose new work wasn't selling, but whose old paintings were changing hands at a profit and still making money for everybody but himself. So Sarkin decided to do what art forgers have been doing ever since civilization began. It would be easy. All he had to do was create some *new* old paintings.

"Maybe he ordered custom stretcher bars, but what's more likely is that he got the wood from a lumber yard and hammered them together himself. It's my guess that Sarkin constructed and painted his canvases in the same loft where they were eventually 'rediscovered.' How he painted, compiled, or put them together, since there was so much combustible material adhering to the canvas, is the 'how' and 'why' they ultimately went up in flame."

Wylie took out a pencil and used it to point at various spots on the picture as he explained.

"Paint. Rubber cement. Japan Driers. Linseed oil-soaked rags. That's what these bunches of stuff are on all five paintings. And let's not forget impasto. Impasto is important here, because it was the impasto that kept the linseed oil from dissipating into the atmosphere. Impasto is a thick, heavy coat of paint. Impasto is paint applied with a tool called a palette knife. Or it can be layered on with a finger, a spatula, a letter opener, or even a popsicle stick. It's gobbed on and once it's on, it stays gobbed. In the case of these five paintings, what we had wasn't just an impasto, though, it was a fatal mix. The rags that Sarkin Zahedi had thought were dry were still saturated with linseed oil; and Sarkin used highly flammable rubber cement to attach these solvent-soaked rags to a primed canvas that he then layered with a thick impasto of oil paint. After the painting was finished, Sarkin sprayed this entire mumbo jumbo of combustibles with a thin coat of picture varnish.

"Linseed oil is a solvent, and like other solvents, it begins to evaporate or oxidize as soon as it's exposed to the air. The faster it dries, the faster it generates heat. But if you don't allow that heat to dissipate into the air, it's eventually going to ignite. In the case of Sarkin Zahedi's paintings, the thick impasto of oil paint that covered the linseed oil-saturated rags prevented the linseed oil from evaporating, and over a period of time there was a predictable buildup of heat.

"In fact, we have evidence the linseed oil was already 'cooking' before Sarkin Zahedi's paintings were hung, because Mikos Piatigorsky told me that a terrible stench was coming from them while they were still in the crate. This rank odor is a phenomenon often associated with spontaneous combustion.

"I don't know specifically what triggered the ignition of those five paintings on Friday morning, November eleventh. None of us will ever know, because Sarkin Zahedi put together a combination of combustibles in quantities and under circumstances that can't be artificially reproduced. But whatever the quantities and qualities of those materials were, something in the Parlor Gallery—maybe it was the sun coming in through the skylights at a particular angle—or maybe the mix of solvents and cotton balls and glues and rags was just ripe to ignite, and the time of day, or the ultra-violet rays had nothing to do with it. But whatever it was, its time had come. And because all of the paintings were so saturated with oils and so packed with flammables, they gobbled themselves up, the fire in the first painting catalyzing the fire in the second, third, fourth, and fifth paintings, creating a chain reaction that didn't stop until every single canvas was consumed."

Wylie turned to Luis Cabrerra.

"That's why the heat detectors never set off an alarm, Luis. The paintings went up so fast, it was like laying a piece of tissue paper on top of a small crate and then setting it on fire. The tissue would burn, but the box would never go on fire, because there wouldn't be enough time for a buildup of heat before the tissue was completely consumed by the flames.

"Which is also why the stretcher bars and the picture frames didn't burn. Because the fire was so fast, it went out before it could generate enough heat to ignite the wood."

"Liar. Liar. Liar." Sarkin Zahedi resumed his chant and glared at Wylie Nolan. "Liars spell the word of infamy. Evil in the liar's heart abides for . . . "

Fromer Zigfield stood up.

"You can't prove any of this, Nolan, and if you even suggest at the defamatory things you're saying in your report, and as a result the insurance company denies Sarkin's claim, not only will we sue you personally, but we'll also sue them for triple damages, which means that instead of owing Sarkin five million dollars, they'll owe him . . . "

"Fromer," Wegman Zigfield said sharply, "sit down."

Fromer opened his mouth to protest.

"Don't argue with me, I'm not in the mood." He stabbed the air with an accusatory finger in Sarkin Zahedi's direction. "And you—you are worse than a con artist, and don't have the stature to be a charlatan's apprentice. Max!"

"Yes, sir."

"If my son is arrested as an accomplice in this Sarkin Zahedi skulduggery, will you represent him?"

"I don't practice criminal law, Mr. Zigfield, but I have an associate who can help him."

"Excellent. Then we'll . . . "

Fromer stamped his foot.

"Goddamn it, Father, stop that. I don't need a lawyer. I haven't done anything wrong and Wylie Nolan hasn't proven anything he's said. All we've heard from him so far are ghost stories and unsubstantiated allegations." Fromer appealed to his own fire investigator. "You tell them, Lars. It's all double talk, isn't it? They're just trying to scare us out of . . . "

Without answering, Lars Helmersson stood up. He gave Fromer Zigfield a contemptuous glance, shut his briefcase, and started for the door. Before opening it, he turned back for a moment and said to Fromer Zigfield, "I'll send you my bill." Then he walked out and closed the door behind him.

Fromer dropped into his chair. In a voice that lacked conviction, he said to Wylie, "You can't prove any of this."

"Oh, but I *can*. I can prove all of it."

Wylie picked up the spray can of varnish.

"Daubin and Kline has been manufacturing picture varnish like this for over fifty years. During all those years, its varnish formula has contained a combination of two acrylic resins. Recently, Daubin and Kline realized that over a long period of time, Varnigloss—that's the brand name—had a tendency to turn yellow. So exactly eighteen months ago, they changed their formula and eliminated one of the two acrylic resins.

"I've already told you that when I was done at the Parlor Gallery, I asked the museum people to send me Sarkin Zahedi's five empty frames. Max Bramble helped me to remove canvas strips from between the stretcher bars and the frames of each one of them; and all of those strips of material emitted a rank smell, just as Mikos Piatigorsky said they had when he'd unpacked the same paintings a few weeks earlier. I sent those canvas samples to my forensic laboratory and instructed the lab to test them for age, composition, content, and whatever else they could find out.

"The report I got back told me that my samples contained paints, Japan Driers, turpentine, rubber cement, and linseed oil. Informative, yes. But not helpful in putting a date on the paintings, because each of those materials could have been found in a picture painted two, twenty, or a hundred years ago. So, that part of the lab report didn't convince me that Sarkin Zahedi's paintings weren't a fraud; but it didn't convince me that they were a fraud, either."

Fromer Zigfield said sullenly, "That's what I've been saying all along. You have no proof."

Wylie raised the spray can of varnish. "Sorry, Fromer. You're forgetting this. This is Daubin and Kline's finish coat picture varnish, sold as Varnigloss."

"So?" Fromer demanded.

"Liar. Liar. Liars to the devil go. Heathen thief. Liar and devil." The Sarkin Zahedi chant continued.

"Oh, shut up, Sarkin," Fromer spat out. Then he said to Wylie, "What about this Varnigloss?"

"A few paragraphs down in the report, my lab said that they'd also found traces of Daubin and Kline Varnigloss on the surface of the samples I sent them for analysis."

"Keep talking," Fromer said.

"And that the Varnigloss Sarkin Zahedi had sprayed on those canvas samples contained only one acrylic resin. Not two. And this was critical to my investigation, because up until a year and a half ago, the Varnigloss formula which *excluded* the second acrylic resin had never been manufactured, wasn't distributed, and couldn't be obtained in any store. Therefore . . . "

"Therefore, Fromer," Wegman Zigfield preempted Wylie's explanation, "your protégé's so-called 'rediscovered masterpieces' were less than eighteen months old, thus proving that Sarkin Zahedi has perpetrated a fraud upon this museum, upon his insurance company, and upon the taxpayers of the United States through the auspices of the American Art Development Fund!"

"Amen," Jiri Hozda said softly.

Joy Miller walked over to Jiri, took his hand, and squeezed it.

Fromer took a desperate step toward his father.

"Dad, I swear to you, I didn't know."

Wegman Zigfield got up and snapped, "Sit down, Fromer. Of course you didn't know. You're an idiot, you aren't a criminal."

And just as Luis Cabrerra was maneuvering out of his chair, Wylie Nolan held up both of his hands like a maestro poised to conduct.

He didn't say anything. He just held them there.

And one by one, everybody in the room stopped talking. And one by one, slowly, slowly, as Wylie lowered his hands, they lowered themselves back into their seats.

Wylie said, "I've put in a call to the Manhattan District Attorney. The evidence I'm turning over will provide the city prosecutors with more than enough grounds to charge Sarkin Zahedi with art forgery, insurance fraud, mail fraud, theft of . . ."

The door to the conference room burst open.

Wylie turned.

Georgiana Weeks, her face stark white, her hair a wild fiery mass, stood framed for an instant in the doorway. Her eyes frantically searched the room, going from one face to the next until they stopped on Wegman Zigfield. She took a quick, shallow breath and approached him.

"Mr. Zigfield!"

"Calm down, child." He awkwardly patted her shoulder.

"Mr. Zigfield, is your fire expert still here?"

"Yes, Georgiana. Wylie Nolan, may I present a somewhat overwrought Dr. Georgiana Weeks. Dr. Weeks is the guest curator for our Pre-Raphaelite exhibition."

Georgiana turned to Wylie.

"Help me," she said.

"Help you to what?"

"One of our people, Camden Kimcannon. He works for . . ."

Wylie cut her off. "Tall. Thin. Eccentric. I know who he is. What about him?"

"A neighbor of his who knows that he works at the museum . . . she called. She said that Camden's just been arrested."

"Arrested for what?"

Georgiana walked to where Joy Miller and Jiri Hozda were now standing; she took each one by the hand. Then she turned back to Wylie.

"Mr. Nolan, last night Camden was charged with setting fire to his mother's house on City Island. He's been arrested for the arson homicide of Vidalia Kimcannon."

Joy gasped.

The expression on Jiri Hozda's face hardened.

"He is innocent," Jiri said. "We will vindicate our young friend."

Georgiana bit her lower lip.

"It gets worse," she said.

"Worse!" Joy cried. "How could it possibly get any worse? There must be some explanation. Someone must have . . . "

But Georgiana shook her head. She dropped Jiri's and Joy's hands and collapsed into a chair. Then she barely whispered, "Camden confessed."

37

"Marshals' office."

"Hello, Virgil. Are you still on light duty?"

"Yes, sir. Who is this?"

"Wylie Nolan. For how long?"

"Another month. Come January first, I'm out of here."

"Retiring?"

"Hell no. I'd pay them to be a fireman. If my wife didn't tie me down every morning, I'd get to work four hours early. But don't tell the union that. They're renegotiating our contract with the city."

"Where are you out of?"

"Ladder 122 in Brooklyn."

"Are you going back there, Virgil?"

"Hell yes. But next time I get a job-related injury, I'll request Belle-vue Psychiatric instead of this zoo. You know, eliminate the middleman. You fire marshals are crazy. Who do you want to talk to, Wylie?"

"Gus Grogan. Is he there?"

"I'll ring him."

Thirty seconds later, Gus Grogan was on the line.

"Hey, Wylie. I heard you retired and went private. Congratulations. How do you like it?"

"I love it. You ought to try it yourself, Gus. How long do you have in the job?"

"Twenty years a fireman. Five years a fire marshal. Five years a supervising fire marshal. Another thirty years, and I figure I'll know everything, so I can die. Meantime, somebody's got to give these snot-nose college types a hard time. They're starting to refer to good, old-fashioned, home-spun pyromaniacs as 'serial fire-setters.' And they've already brought in two arson dogs, for God's sake. So what can I do for you, Wylie?"

"You had a fire yesterday on City Island."

"Yeah. What about it?"

"A friend of mine wants me to look into it for her."

"Her?"

"It's not like that, Gus. Her assistant, a kid named Kimcannon, lives on City Island. It was his house."

"Let me guess, Wylie. You're calling because my men arrested your friend's assistant, right?"

"Right."

"Sad case. Sad sack. Sad world. Hold on a second. Let me get the file . . . OK, Wylie, I'm back. You still there?"

"I'm here."

"The nine-one-one alarm came in at nine-oh-seven P.M. Engine Company 70 and Ladder Company 58 responded within two minutes."

"Is there a firehouse on City Island, Gus?"

"Yeah. And the apparatus that responded are the whole enchillada. It's an engine and a ladder company. One and one on Schofield Street. Captain Hamish Coats filled out the incident report. I'll give you the highlights. The fire premises was located at 27 Kinshaw Street. Single-family, unattached frame, private dwelling. Three stories with unfinished basement. Upon arrival, there was heavy black smoke issuing from front door and front windows. Engine 70 stretched inch and three-quarter line to front door. No forced entry. Front door was open on arrival. Smoke and some flames showing under living room doors. Low flames inside living room on carpet, in doorway, and in area of fireplace. Arrived seconds before the whole room would have lit up. Extinguished flames with a fog nozzle to preserve evidence of possible arson. Ladder 58 vented windows, checked for fire extension, and searched top floors and basement. Female DOA found on chair in living room. Later identified as Mrs. Vidalia Kimcannon, the owner of the residence. Captain Coates notified fire marshals of a 10–45 1 at this location. That's a DOA, Wylie."

"No kidding. I was only on the job twenty years, Gus. You want to tell me what smoke is, too?"

"Smart ass."

"What do you have on the DOA, Gus?"

"There's no medical examiner report yet, but my guys talked to the deputy chief at the morgue, and he's ninety-nine percent sure it's smoke inhalation—carbon monoxide poisoning. When they found her, she was cherry red."

"Do you have a time of death?"

"Good question. Let me tell you something, Wylie. On the q.t. I'm not satisfied with the way this job was covered. I partnered a guy right out of the firehouse with a hairbag, because I had nobody else to put him with. When the call came in, I wasn't in the office, or I never would have sent those two out."

"Who were the marshals?"

"The kid's name is Tommy Castro. I like him. Someday he'll make a good fire marshal. But he's still wet behind the ears, and thinks he should be putting fires out instead of investigating them. And the moron is Jerry Fogel."

"You mean 'do-nothing' Fogel?"

"You got it. So, when you ask me a question like do I have a time of death, with these two, I'm lucky they even found the occupancy. Tell you the truth, Wylie, if I were you, I'd talk to the captain. Hamish Coates. He was the one who baby-sat the perp until my guys got there. The kid was holding a two-gallon can of kerosene in his hand when they arrested him. And then he confessed, so Curly and Moe figured they didn't need to do a thorough investigation of the fire scene. Idiots. Just a second, and I'll get Captain Coates's telephone number for you."

"Thanks, Gus."

"OK. Write this down."

Gus Grogan read off the unlisted telephone number for the firehouse on City Island and then told Wylie, "I called the photo unit and told them to shoot the fire room eight ways to Sunday. A rush job. When they got there, the body was still on the scene. I would have gone myself, but I had an emergency at home. I still want to go."

"When can you get the photos back from the lab?"

"Three, four days."

"How about the day after tomorrow?"

"In your dreams."

"What are friends for?"

"I don't want to be your friend, Wylie. Nobody does. You're a pain in the ass. Just the other day, the deputy chief was talking about getting an unlisted number for the Bronx base, to keep you from calling all the time."

"Me? When have I ever called before?"

"How about the Zigfield Museum fire."

"You know I called on that?"

"Sure. I got your message."

"You shit. And you never called back."

"The last time I looked at my paycheck, it was signed by the City of New York and not you, Wylie."

"Tell you what . . . "

"I don't want to hear this."

"I've got a perfect deal for you, Gus. If you can have those pictures in your office by five o'clock Thursday afternoon, I'll give you two fires. Signed, sealed, and delivered. And I'll do you one better—I'll give you one of them right now. Zigfield Art Museum. Cause: Spontaneous combustion of flammable solvents imbedded on paintings in gallery where fire originated, with attempt to defraud the insurance company. Like it?"

"No shit? I kind of had a feeling it would be something like that, but that was the day the fire went down at the Harlem Social Club, so I never got back to the museum. But I like what you're saying, Wylie. Tell me more."

"Better than tell you, I'll hand-deliver my report on Thursday when

I look at your photos. You're welcome to anything in it. You can copy it. Plagiarize it. Cannibalize it. Whatever you want. Deal?"

"Deal. What's the second fire?"

"This one. I know you're still knee-deep in that Harlem fire with the six DOA's, so tomorrow I'll go to 27 Kinshaw Street and get you your origin and cause. I have permission to enter the house from the owner, and the next-door neighbor is giving me the front door key."

"So, what do you want from me?"

"I need those photographs."

"Wylie?"

"What, Gus?"

"Remember Chief Brody?"

"I remember him."

"You know what he used to say about you?"

"No, what?"

"He used to say that you were his albatross."

"No shit. And I didn't even think he liked me."

"Well, Wylie. I never thought Chief Brody got a single thing right the whole time he was the boss, but he got *that* right."

"I guess that means we're engaged."

"I guess."

38

Wylie had picked up Max Bramble outside his Wall Street law office, not far from the South Street Seaport.

"Thanks, Wylie," Max said. "Usually I don't get to see a fire scene until the building's been torn down or remodeled. So this is a first for me."

"Max, Max, Max." Wylie sped past a slow-moving station wagon, shook his head, and looked down at the attorney's feet. "I told you never to wear soft-soled shoes when we're doing a fire investigation. If you step on a nail, it'll go right through those rubber soles and stick you in the foot. Do you want to get lockjaw?"

Max smiled sheepishly.

"It's not at the top of my 'things to do' list, if that's what you mean."

"I've got an extra pair of boots in my trunk that you can use. Have you ever been to City Island before?"

"I've never even heard of it."

"One of the guys from my firehouse used to live there. He said it was a good place to raise kids, but this is my first time, too."

Wylie drove through Manhattan and the South Bronx to the drawbridge that joined Pelham Bay Park with City Island; he took a slip of paper out of his pocket and handed it to Max. "Instructions from Captain Coates. Read them to me."

Max read.

After a few minutes more, they turned onto Kinshaw Street. Wylie pulled into the narrow driveway of the three-story Kimcannon residence. The front windows on the right side of the house were covered with large sheets of plywood; and dark patterns of smoke streamed out from the front door and windows like black funnel stains that curved up and around the porch eaves and roof, and extended to the asbestos siding on the second and third floors.

Wylie slammed the car door shut and moved past a mound of debris the firemen had discarded during their overhaul operations.

"First, we walk around the perimeter of the building," he said.

Wylie headed toward the backyard.

Max followed him and asked, "Why are we doing this?"

"Because I want to get an overview of the house, yard, street, everything, to see how much fire and smoke damage there is to the exterior of the structure and to the grounds. Then I'll come up with a preliminary hypothesis of the area of origin of the fire."

Wylie led Max past two ancient, galvanized steel garbage cans next to the backdoor. He tried the doorknob. It was locked. The top half of the door was a window. Wylie peered through the dusty glass and saw no evidence of fire damage to the kitchen area inside.

"I feel like a burglar," Max said, his nose almost touching the glass. "Or a Peeping Tom. I haven't sneaked around people's houses like this since I was a kid playing kick the can. And even back then, I was always sure I'd get caught with . . . "

"Yoo hoo!"

A tinkly voice from somewhere in the backyard darted out at the lawyer and the fire investigator.

Max jumped.

"See," he said. "I told you we'd get caught."

"Yoo hoo!" The bell-like voice called out again from behind a group of tall bushes. And then a minuscule, pretty little old lady, dressed like an ornament that had escaped from a Christmas tree, tripped daintily on shiny silver high-heeled shoes to the cement slab outside the kitchen door.

"Are you Mr. Nolan?"

Wylie turned and answered, "Guilty as charged."

"I'm Betina Bintiffe. I was expecting you."

Betina Bintiffe was elderly and stylish. She had dainty aquamarine eyes that twinkled like fairy lights at a party. She wore large costume pearl earrings, had a silver chiffon scarf wrapped around her neck, and a beautiful silver fox fur coat flung over a gray silk dress.

Max thought she looked like Tinkerbell's grandmother.

She confronted Max.

"And you, young man. What is *your* name? I see that there are *two* of you, but I was only told to expect *one*."

"I'm Max Bramble, Mrs. Bintiffe. I'm sorry if my presence is disconcerting you."

"Nonsense, my boy. The more the merrier."

Betina Bintiffe touched her hair here . . . there . . . to make sure that no strands had strayed.

"And when you've both finished here, you can come over to my house and I'll brew you boys a *nice* pot of tea."

"Thank you, ma'am," Wylie said. "But I doubt that we'll have the time. If I could bother you for the key to the front door, though . . ."

"Oh. Of *course*. How *silly* of me. I have it right here. Mr. Kimcannon called me this morning and told me you were going to pick it up. *Such* a nice man. *So* tragic. And, of course, you know all about *her*."

Wylie looked at Max.

Max looked at Wylie.

They both looked at Betina Bintiffe and said, "Her?"

"Her. Her . . . *such* a dreadful mother. I know it's unkind to speak ill of the dead, but really, I can hardly *blame* him for leaving her."

Wylie put his hand out. "Mrs. Bintiffe. The key?"

She pulled it out of her pocket but ignored Wylie's hand.

"I understand that the poor boy's been *arrested*," her happy, tinkly voice went on. "As soon as I saw, I, *of course*, called his father, and then I called up the museum, because so *many*, *many* times, young Camden has told me how *much* he enjoys working there. I thought that surely *somebody* at the museum could help. I understand from Mr. Kimcannon that you're *all* cooperating for his sake, and that is such an *excellent* idea. Which reminds me to ask, are either of you two gentlemen an attorney?"

"Not me," Wylie said. "But if you'd give me the key, we'd . . . "

"*Well*," Betina Bintiffe continued, "after I find out *who* Camden's lawyer is, I'll certainly bend *his* ear with a tale or two. Fire in her house! Good gracious, what *could* they have been thinking! That woman set off smoke alarms so often, one day she just up and threw them all out! She told me so herself. But when I got into my car yesterday at a quarter to five to visit my daughter . . . really, I feel quite *penitent*. I should have *known* that it was much, much worse than usual. Why, the windows to the living room were absolutely *black*. And the smell, my dears. *Noxious*. That terrible metallic odor that sets your *teeth* on edge. *Exactly* as if she'd left an aluminum pan burning on the stove. Not that she ever would *cook* a meal for that poor boy. And *such* a nice young man. Why, I remember the time . . . "

Wylie plucked the key out of Betina Bintiffe's hand.

"Thanks, Mrs. Bintiffe," he said. "And can I ask you one more favor?"

She fluttered her hand at her silver hair again.

"Why, certainly, Mr. Nolan. I'd be *most* happy to assist you."

"I can't seem to find Mr. Kimcannon's address and phone numbers. The father's. Not the son's. So how about you write that out for me on a piece of paper, and we'll just ring your doorbell after we're through here. Then when I pick it up, we can return the key. Would you do that for me, Mrs. B.?"

Betina Bintiffe simpered at the "Mrs. B."

"Oh, of *course*, Mr. Nolan. And I'm sure you'll be very fond of Mr. Kimcannon. He's a *writer*, you know. He writes a sports column for the *Daily News*. And when my husband was alive, he found him *most* entertaining. He's not one bit like a writer in person, though. Not at *all* neurotic. Very down to earth. Of course, when he lived with *her*, he always looked *dreadfully* unhappy. And if you'd asked *me*, I would have thought that *he'd* be the one to have murdered Vidalia. In *fact,* I'm surprised they weren't just standing in *line* to see who would throw in the match first. And when I *think* of that charming young man . . . "

Wylie cupped his hand under Betina Bintiffe's bony elbow and maneuvered the doll-size woman down the driveway and over to her own front door.

Seconds later, he was back.

Alone.

"Wylie, we already have Buck Kimcannon's address and phone numbers," Max said. "Why did you ask Mrs. Bintiffe to write them down?"

"It was the only way I could think to get rid of her without hurting her feelings."

"She is a ditsy little old thing."

"Not so ditsy."

Max smiled. "All right, then. Eccentric."

"Not eccentric either, Max. She's just a plain, old-fashioned, all-American, busybody. When I was a kid, lace curtain busybodies like Betina Bintiffe held back the tide of crime and juvenile delinquency on your block. The Mrs. Bintiffes of the world ruled the world. They were the ones who told your mother when you came home late or if you were hanging out on street corners smoking cigarettes. They were our surrogate cops, town criers, and truancy officers. In fact, if you want my tencent sociological opinion, it's not the breakdown of the family unit that's demoralizing this country, Max. It's the disappearance of the neighborhood busybody."

Wylie led Max to the backyard, stepping around an armchair, one side of which had been savagely burned, to continue his inspection of the exterior of the house.

When they'd finally circled the structure and gotten back to Wylie's car, Max asked, "How many cameras did you bring with you today?"

"One."

"Can I take the pictures?"

"Sure." Wylie opened his car's trunk. "We won't need our boots, though, so you can forget my lockjaw lecture. At least for today."

Max took out the camera bag and two flashlights. Wylie hoisted out his battered black suitcase, popped the lock on it, and took out a crowbar and a hammer.

"Why only one camera?" Max asked.

Wylie slammed down the lid of his trunk.

"The fire department photo unit already documented the fire scene.

Their pictures are my backup. Anyway, I want to keep my costs down on this job."

"How come?"

"Because this one's a freebee. Whatever I spend is out of pocket."

"Aren't you charging them anything?"

The fire investigator shrugged.

Max nodded and smiled. "I know. They can't afford *me*, either."

Wylie walked to the front window of the Kimcannon house; he slipped the flat end of the crowbar under the plywood panel covering the window and he pushed. Six nails came loose. He handed Max a hammer and said, "Do the windows on the right side of the house. And don't lose any nails. We'll need them to put back the boards before we leave."

Ten minutes later, when Wylie was inserting the key in the front door lock, Max turned toward the plywood sheets and said, "I thought we took them down because, for some reason, you wanted to climb through the windows to get inside."

"No, Max. We took them down because they were blocking the light. After the fire department puts out a fire, as a safety precaution, they turn off the utilities. So by the time we get to a fire scene, it's cold, wet, and dark. If we want electricity, we have to bring our own power source, and if we want visibility, we have to provide our own light."

"Who nails up the plywood?" Max asked. "The fire department?"

"Usually what happens is that an insurance adjuster gets to the fire before it's extinguished, and if the ladder company has broken any of the windows, the adjuster calls a board-up company to protect the house from looters."

Wylie unlocked the front door.

"Max, give me a flashlight. And turn yours on. OK. Follow me in. But don't go anywhere I don't go; and don't step anywhere I don't step. It's going to be dark inside."

Wylie pushed. The door swung open.

"Got your camera, Max?"

"I'm armed and dangerous."

"Is it loaded?"

"It is if you loaded it."

Wylie stepped into the foyer and looked around.

"We're in luck, Max. You can turn off your flashlight. There's enough light coming through the dining room windows to perform brain surgery."

Max held the frame indicator of the camera up to his eye.

"Camera's loaded. We're on picture number one."

"Is the lens cap off?"

"Sure. I checked that first."

Wylie laughed. "When I first went private, half the jobs I did, I shot with the lens cap on. I thought I'd been buying film from Helen Keller."

Max looked through the viewfinder.

"What do you want in the hallway? A long shot? A shot of the stairway? The dining room? What?"

"First give me a few establishing shots, and then take some pictures of the lowest panel on this French door. I want you to take particular notice of the burn pattern. It's very low, and you can see obvious indications of smoke having seeped through that half inch or so between the bottom of the door and the wood flooring."

Wylie opened the French doors.

"And look here. On the inside. There's burning at the base of these doors and underneath them. And look at these corresponding burns on the carpet. Two things are obvious from these burn patterns, Max. One, that the doors were closed when the fire was burning; and two, that somebody poured flammable liquid on the rug just inside of them."

Max lowered his camera.

"Then the burn patterns fit the confession, Wylie. Because Camden Kimcannon was holding a can of kerosene when the fire marshals arrested him."

Wylie Nolan stepped into the living room.

Max started to ask him something, but he held up his hand for silence, and within a few seconds Wylie was completely absorbed by the paths and patterns that the fire, smoke, and char had made in the ceiling and walls, and in the debris that littered the floor of what had once been Vidalia Kimcannon's living room.

Slowly, concentrating first on one object and then on the next and first on one area and then on the next, Wylie explored the damage that the fire had done to the room.

As Max Bramble watched in silence, Wylie approached a small, up-ended table. He turned it right-side-up and then crouched down to study the carpet for indentation marks. After examining either side of the water-logged sofa twice, he placed the small table to the left of the couch. He went through the same routine for the other end table and then repeated it for the television set and the table on which the TV sat.

He returned to the sofa and stared at the coffee table in front of it. It seemed to be where it belonged. Wylie lifted one set of the coffee table's legs and checked the ruts in the carpet to see if they lined up; he did the same thing on the other side.

Somebody had left a bouquet of flowers on the coffee table. They were still wrapped in paper and they were covered with soot. Once they might have been irises and daisies. Now they were just dead. With thumb and forefinger, Wylie raised the flowers off the coffee table, examined the underside of the bouquet, and the tabletop beneath it. Then he carefully let the flowers drop back where they had been.

He located two table lamps in the sodden debris. One was half-buried in curtains the firemen had torn down. The ceramic bases of both lamps were cracked, and the lamp shades had been mangled by dirty boots. Wylie studied the tops of the two end tables and the cracked bases of the lamps. Then he placed one lamp on each end table, perfectly positioning it within the circumference of some invisible perimeter that Max could guess at, but couldn't see.

Wylie continued to sift through the debris. He picked up books, picture frames, the bases of small, broken figurines and knickknacks. He put one object here and another one there. He examined streaks on walls, burns in the flooring, and smudges on the furniture. And when he was certain that he knew where an object belonged, he put it there, as if he were fitting a new piece in a puzzle.

Max took pictures of things he thought Wylie wanted him to record, or their location in the room, aligning the viewfinder the way that Wylie had shown him in order to create panoramas.

This was the first postfire premises that Max had ever been in, and he was concerned with perceiving the cold devastation of being victimized by flame, from a fire investigator's point of view. And it was the cold itself—the cold *inside* the house—that Max was acutely aware of as his body tensed against the bitter chill.

The date was November the 30th, but New York City's weather was what meteorologists were calling "unseasonably mild." When he'd walked around the outside of the house with Wylie, Max had unbuttoned his jacket, and enjoyed the smell of the sea off Long Island Sound. The sun had been shining with that antiseptic bright, white light of winter, but no breezes had blown, and even Betina Bintiffe's fox fur coat seemed to have been worn more for show than for warmth.

Inside the house, though, the atmosphere was murderously dank and chill.

Max said, "Wylie, it's freezing in here."

Wylie Nolan, concentrating on two pieces of a small, broken bowl, didn't even hear him.

The attorney shrugged, took photographs of the living room where Wylie had finished his reconstruction, and then continued to study the fire scene.

The room where Vidalia Kimcannon died had experienced much less damage than Max Bramble would have expected. Sunlight that streamed through the three side and two front windows revealed that the room was still structurally intact.

The firemen hadn't needed to tear open the ceiling, walls, or flooring to look for hidden pockets of flame. They'd broken all the living room windows during their overhaul operations, but Max didn't have to see what they'd looked like before they'd been broken to know that they were thickly covered with soot. He ran a finger down one of the glass panes of the French doors leading to the foyer and he looked at his finger. It was covered with a jet-black, grimy residue that was almost, but not quite, viscous. Like a cross between oil and honey.

The walls, the ceiling, the carpet . . . every object in the room was covered with soot, water, and smoke stains. There was soot on every surface of every table, chair, book, lamp, light switch, and piece of fallen drapery.

Max watched Wylie pick up a small clock; he held it for a moment above the end table to the right of the sofa, frowned, and tossed it back into a heap of debris.

Then Wylie mumbled something to himself, nodded, and walked back to the open French doors. He jerked his head in the direction of the foyer and said to Max, "I know what happened here, but we still have to inspect the rest of the house. You bring the camera, and I'll tell you which elimination photographs to take."

Max advanced the camera to the next frame.

"What are 'elimination photographs'?"

"Pictures we take to show where the fire *didn't* start. Let's say you think a fire originated in the toaster in the kitchen. You take a picture of the toaster to prove where it started. Then, if you're thorough—and we are—you also take a photograph of the stove, to show that it *didn't* start on the stove. Because guaranteed, if you say toaster, somebody else is going to say stove. Where's my flashlight? Here it is. Where's yours? In your hand. Good. We'll start in the basement, and there's no light down there."

A narrow hallway behind the kitchen led to the basement door. Casting the flashlight beams to their right and left, they inched down the steep cellar stairs. On the last step, Wylie pinpointed the utility area with his flashlight and quickly found the main feed which led to the electric fuse box; he meticulously examined each fuse with his flashlight.

None of them had blown.

"I knew they wouldn't be," Wylie said. "But I had to make sure. Max, a fire investigator is like a medical examiner. If I get to a fire scene and I'm one hundred percent convinced the fire started in the living room, I still have to look at the rest of the house, in the same way that a good forensic pathologist still has to examine a body for heart disease and drug overdose, even if the guy was brought to the morgue with a bullet in his brain. And we both do it for the same reason. Because you never know what you're going to find."

Wylie told Max to photograph the fuse box.

The ceiling of the cellar underneath the living room floor was the only other area of the basement that they examined thoroughly. Wylie ran his flashlight over the subflooring. Vertically. Horizontally. Along the edges where the floor joists met the walls.

"I don't see anywhere the fire broke through," Wylie said. "Do you?"

Max scrutinized the ceiling of the basement with as great care.

"Negative," he said.

"Take a few wide-angle shots of the ceiling before we go, Max."

Max took the pictures and they went upstairs.

They started on the third floor.

Camden Kimcannon had removed all of his personal possessions from the attic bedroom before the fire. There was one interesting item left in with the furniture he hadn't taken, though.

"Here's the fuel source for our arsonist," Wylie said, and he hunkered down beside a kerosene heater. "There must have been a can of kerosene in the house before he set the fire, and that's what he used as his accelerant."

Wylie stood up and nudged the heater with the toe of his shoe.

"Did you know that these things are illegal in New York City?"

"I never thought about it," Max said.

"They've been illegal for as far back as I can remember."

"Why's that?"

"Because back in the 1950s, they were potentially dangerous to operate. But it wasn't the heaters that were the real problem. The real problem was kerosene storage. Let's say you have an eighty-family multiple dwelling and each unit has its own kerosene heater. And let's say that each family is storing a five-gallon can of kerosene. If, from whatever cause, a fire should break out in that building, everyone who lives there is sitting on a potential bomb. Flash forward to the present. So may laws have been passed and so many devices have been installed to protect the consumer, that if they're used properly, kerosene heaters aren't a fire hazard. But since nobody's solved the problem of how to *store* kerosene on a residential property, it's still illegal to use the heaters in all of New York City's five boroughs. City Island, though, where it gets colder than it does on the mainland, pretty much ignores the law, and a lot of people use them anyway. Illegal or not."

Wylie and Max continued to search the rest of the house and found very little of interest from a fire point of view until they got to the kitchen.

Wylie did a quick look around, walked over to the sink, and stared down at the sink's contents. Then he rummaged through the kitchen drawers and pulled out a pair of plastic salad tongs.

"Max, check out those cabinets and find me a platter or serving tray."

Max rooted around and took out an oval, two-handled tray.

Wylie pointed to the items inside the sink.

"First take a picture of this."

Max put down the tray beside the sink and took the picture.

Wylie then used the salad tongs to transfer a small, sooty glass from the sink to the tray. He did the same with a coffee cup and a slightly larger glass, both of which were also covered with soot.

Wylie next noticed a heavy glass ashtray on the kitchen counter.

"Photograph it," he told Max.

Then he transferred it to the metal serving tray.

A plastic trash bucket was jammed between the stove and refrigerator. Wylie lifted off the lid and looked inside.

"Ah ha!" he said, and grinned at Max.

"Some fires are easy, but this one is so easy, it's like a paint with numbers kit. Will you look at this."

All Max saw when he looked in the trash bucket were sooty cigarette butts scattered over a crumpled white plastic shopping bag. There were also a soiled pink paper towel and an empty box of cereal.

"What am I looking for?"

"Never mind," Wylie said. "Just take a picture and come with me. I want to check out something in the back."

Wylie unlocked the kitchen door and walked to a galvanized steel garbage pail. He lifted off the lid and looked inside.

"Unbelievable, Max. This is too good. Take a look. Can you beat that?"

Max saw a cardboard milk container and a crushed box of laundry detergent. Two sooty liquor bottles had been placed on top of some empty frozen food tins and a dented pizza box. The bottles were dirty, but Max could read the labels through the layers of smut. Both said Gordon's gin.

"So?" Max said to Wylie.

Wylie was staring back at the house.

"Photograph it, Max. Then give me a pencil."

"I don't have a pencil."

"What do you have?"

Max probed his jacket pocket. He pulled out a fountain pen and a ballpoint pen.

Wylie took them.

"Hey! Give those back. I got that fountain pen for my bar mitzvah."

Wylie shook his head and stuck the fountain pen into the neck of one of the Gordon's gin bottles.

"Fifteen years ago, Max, the Waterman Pen Company did a study."

Wylie took the ballpoint pen and stuck *it* into the neck of the other Gordon's gin bottle.

"They found that after ten years, not a single fountain pen was still in the possession of the boy, now a man, who'd gotten it for his bar mitzvah. What the Waterman people said was that all the boys had been careless and lost their pens."

Wylie delicately, meticulously, as though he were lifting up two sticks of dynamite, used the shafts of each pen to lift both bottles out of the garbage can.

"But my theory is that after a few years, the pens self-destruct. That keeps people like you from handing down your old fountain pens to your sons when they have their own bar mitzvahs. It forces you to buy new ones. It's an environmental thing. Old replaces new. Spring replaces winter. It's like natural selection and the nitrogen cycle."

Wylie slowly, carefully, walked in the back door, and then continued through the kitchen with the two Gordon's gin bottles balanced on the two pens and extended in front of him like the ends of a divining rod.

He said, "Bring the tray and the tongs, Max. Follow me, and don't break anything."

"I *will* follow you and I *won't* break anything. Is what you just told me about the Waterman Pen Company true?"

"Be careful at this door, Max. Don't step on the burn pattern. Of course it's not true. OK. Come here. And just watch me for a second. I want to show you something on this end table. See this?"

Max looked where Wylie was pointing.

"What about it?"

"Think like a fire investigator, Max. No, better than that; today, I want you to think like a fire *marshal*. You've been called in to investigate an arson homicide and this table is an important clue. What does it tell you?"

Max bent to within six inches of the table's smutty surface. He leaned to his left. He leaned to his right.

"OK," Wylie said. "That's long enough. What do you see?"

Max shrugged. "All I see is a table covered with soot that has a couple of circles on it where the soot isn't as thick."

"Brilliant!" Wylie exclaimed.

Max studied Wylie's face for sarcasm but there wasn't any there.

Wylie told Max to hold the serving tray steady, while he cautiously positioned the two gin bottles over the areas of the table where the circles of soot had been slightly lighter, and used the two pens to lower them into place.

It was a perfect fit.

"OK, Max. Now tell me about the coffee table."

Max studied the smoke-stained surface of the table in front of the ruined sofa. After a few minutes, he found two small circles and a rectangle that were a little bit cleaner than the areas of the coffee table surrounding them.

Wylie used the salad tongs to align the large glass, the coffee cup, and the ashtray with the two circles and rectangle outlined in soot on the tabletop. But one smudged glass still didn't corresponded to any of the faint markings on any of the tables. He pulled out a handkerchief, wrapped it around the glass, and put the glass in his pocket.

"Do you understand what's going on here, Max?"

The attorney said, "I understand zero."

"Well, then follow me. This will clear it all up."

Wylie walked to the fireplace.

"Newspapers. Magazines. Envelopes. Old television guides. The fireplace is jammed up with the stuff. Now look at these burn patterns.

This is where he poured kerosene, probably thinking that paper is combustible, so the more paper there is, the more combustible it would be. But these papers are too tightly stacked for oxygen to circulate between the pages. No air. No fire. And look at this, Max. Except for the trail of char where the kerosene was poured and a little soot on the covers of these magazines, there's hardly any burning. And none of the fire extended beyond the fireplace."

Wylie led Max to the end table on which he'd positioned the Gordon's gin bottles.

"The chair was here," Wylie said.

"Which chair?"

"Vidalia Kimcannon's. Right here, next to the table. Now, Max, look at the floor where the chair *was*, and tell me what you see."

Max looked down.

"I don't see anything. I see a dirty carpet."

"Is the carpet burned?"

"It doesn't look burned to me."

"Great work, Max. We'll make a fire investigator out of you yet. Now let's go outside. Bring the camera."

"Why are we going outside?"

"I want to look at the chair."

"We already saw it when we walked around the house."

"We saw it, but we didn't examine it. But look here. Before we go, I want to make sure you understand the burn pattern on the carpet by the double doors."

Max studied the floor area and then shrugged.

"I don't know what I'm supposed to be looking at, Wylie. All I see are a couple of spent matches."

"Exactly! And over here. And there. And there are . . . one . . . two . . . three more. Five spent matches in total. What does that tell us, Max?"

Max gave him a "beats me" look.

"From the burn patterns and from the spent matches, we can deduce that the arsonist stood in this open doorway and splashed what was left of his kerosene on the rug. Then he struck one match and threw it on the kerosene-soaked carpet."

"And it went *boom?*"

"No. It went out."

"But I thought kerosene was a flammable liquid."

"It is, Max. But it's not a volatile flammable liquid. The volatility of a liquid fuel depends on how rapidly the molecules of gas disperse into the atmosphere. The faster the dispersal, the more volatile it is. Gasoline is extremely volatile. The instant that it's thrown, the gas molecules are already up there, dancing around your nose. That's why the smell is so strong. And that's why so many arsonists become their own victims. They throw around the gasoline and then they toss a match. But by that time, they're already surrounded by molecules of gas, and since it's the vapors in the atmosphere that combust when you throw a match, not the liquid itself, they go *boom*. Kerosene's more sluggish, though. It's a heavier fuel. Not as volatile. So when our arsonist threw his first few matches, there hadn't been enough time for the vapors to disburse into the atmosphere yet. By the fifth match, though, the mixture was ripe enough for the kerosene vapors to ignite. Understand?"

"Sure. What I *don't* understand is why the room didn't blow up or become some sort of a cowering inferno, pun intended. Maybe I'm on the wrong wavelength, but except for the carpet, it looks to me like most of the damage in here is just from water and soot."

"Another brilliant observation, Max. This is what happened. The arsonist struck his matches. One, two, three, four . . . but they all went out. When he struck and threw the fifth match, the kerosene ignited. He watched the flames for a few seconds; when he was satisfied that the fire was really going, he closed the doors to the living room behind him and left. And that's where he screwed himself."

"How so?"

"When he closed the doors to the living room, he starved the fire of oxygen."

"Why did he want to do that?"

"He didn't want to. He just didn't know any better. The only thing most people know about fire is that it lights cigarettes and roasts marshmallows. When he closed the door to the living room, he was thinking that fire is like water. If you have a hole in a bucket, you seal up the hole, and the bucket fills up. If you have a hole in a room, like a door, the arsonist thought that if he sealed *it* up, the room would get filled with fire, like the bucket does with water. But the opposite happened. When he shut the door, he deprived the fire of oxygen, and slowed down the rate of burning so much that the fire department got here before it could really take off. Now, let's go outside."

Max again followed Wylie out the back door.

When they got to the armchair, Wylie said, "Photodocument what I do."

Wylie knelt down in front of a fire-gutted object that was barely recognizable as the large, comfortable, overstuffed chintz reading chair it had once been. It consisted of two loose pillows on a stationary frame. The worst fire damage had occurred to the left side of the chair. Most of the roll arm had burned off; and most of the left side of the seat cushion and part of the left side of the back cushion had been eaten away by fire. Both cushions looked as though a ravenous giant had taken a bite out of them with savage, flaming teeth.

Wylie used Max's ballpoint pen to push aside burned tufts of cotton wadding and foam rubber. He continued to do this for a few minutes before he put Max's pen in his pocket and stuck his hand between the cushions.

After a few more seconds of blind probing, he pulled out his hand.

"Got it," he said.

Max moved forward.

Lying on Wylie's open palm was a slim, graceful object about three inches long, with a circumference no wider than that of a pencil. It was hollow and circular at one end, and narrow at the other end, as if someone had pinched it with pliers; it almost looked like a stylized golf tee.

Wylie polished it on the leg of his blue jeans and then held it up to the sunlight.

It was glossy black. It gleamed.

"Beautiful, isn't it, Max?"

Max nodded. "I had a high school drama teacher who wore an ascot and a goatee, and I always thought he used a cigarette holder just like this one to keep his beard from catching on fire."

"It's made out of onyx," Wylie said admiringly. "That's why it didn't burn."

Max looked down at the cigarette holder.

Wylie clenched his fist around it, and said, "So, Max. What do you think?"

And Max said, "I think that you should give me back my pens."

39

Mrs. Betina Bintiffe was disappointed that Wylie wouldn't stay for tea when he dropped off the keys, and picked up the address and telephone numbers he didn't really need for Buckminster "Buck" Kimcannon, the man whose son had confessed to the arson homicide of Vidalia Kimcannon, Buck's ex-wife.

Wylie and Max left the fire premises and drove the five or six city blocks to the fire station on Schofield Street that housed City Island's Engine Company 70 and Ladder Company 58.

Captain Hamish Coates was waiting for them.

Hamish Coates had steady don't-fool-with-me eyes and a face like a Spanish conquistador. His skin was the color of wet cork. He was of indeterminate age, but old enough to have worked for the fire department when black firemen had to sit by themselves at meal time and eat out of their own sets of plates.

Despite the years he'd spent shadowboxing with racial prejudice, Hamish had no patience with self-pity and despised bullies of all stripes. His favorite enemies were hate-baiters—the white ones who cold-cocked you with the word *nigger*, and the black ones who slapped you around with the phrase Uncle Tom. Both had tried to manipulate Hamish's beliefs and his behavior. Neither had succeeded.

Hamish Coates was the only black fireman anyone knew who wasn't a member of the Vulcans, a group that purported to represent the special interests of black New York City firemen. When pressed to join, he had spat out contemptuously, "What's my color got to do with fighting a fire!"

He had one loyalty: to the fire department. He had one passion: fighting fires. He was a knight in shining armor. His armor was his turn-out coat. His dragon was flames. He was a firefighter. That's what he did. That's what he was. Nothing else mattered.

Reduced to its essentials, Captain Hamish Coates's philosophy was simple.

"See this circle here? That's me. Stay out of it."

And there was an implied "or else" that earned Hamish Coates a freedom of behavior that would have been denied to a man with eyes that blinked when you tried to stare him down.

Hamish Coates's men called him Cap or sometimes Cap'n Hamish, and they often joked to his face or behind his back that he was a crazy old coot like Captain Ahab, but that instead of going after a great white whale, his Moby Dick was fire. Captain Coates never minded being teased about fire by firemen, and although he did not smile when, for one Christmas, his men presented him with a wooden peg leg (it was inscribed with a brass plaque), he didn't grimace either.

For Hamish Coates loved firemen. Loved everything about them. He loved their antics, their loyalty to one another, their generosity, their bravery, and most of all, he loved their commitment to the job. After one particularly fierce fire-fighting operation, when his men were covered with grime, with black snot coming out of their nostrils as they heaved for oxygen, he looked at them proudly, and with inextinguishable love in his eyes said, "Shit, I could go queer for a fireman."

Captain Hamish Coates's employment records indicated that he was sixty-five years old; it was commonly believed, though, that about twenty years ago, he'd wooed, wined, and dined the personnel manager's not-unattractive secretary at fire department headquarters, and that as a result of the affair, both Hamish Coates and the birthdate on all of his personnel records had become ten years younger.

But nobody knew for sure, because nobody other than Hamish was old enough to remember that far back.

Officially, Hamish Coates would reach his sixty-fifth birthday come January, and fire department policy is mandatory retirement at age sixty-five.

Wylie Nolan's dark, penetrating, marble blue eyes met the dark, impenetrable brown eyes of Hamish Coates. A click of recognition. The twain met.

"Captain Coates. I'm Wylie Nolan. This is Max Bramble."

"I see you got here all right, Nolan. How can I help you?"

"Did Supervising Fire Marshal Grogan give you a call?"

"Yes, he did. He asked me to make you a copy of my incident report, which I've done. I understand that you were in the job, Nolan."

"Twenty years."

"Miss it?"

"I'd miss it if I weren't working with fire, but I still am."

"I see. I'm retiring this year."

"Hey, Cap. Congratulations."

"I'm not looking forward to it."

"You'll live. There's life after the firehouse."

"My men don't think so. Instead of giving me a retirement party, they're throwing me a funeral. You're invited."

Wylie laughed.

"Thanks, but I think I'll pass." Then Wylie said more seriously, "I don't want to take up a lot of your time, Cap, but can you give me a quick overview of what happened? Gus Grogan already read me your report, so what I'm really interested in is what you didn't write. What's in between the lines."

Captain Coates was silent for almost a minute before he said, "I was just thinking back over the incident. The alarm came in at seven minutes after nine. We responded in two minutes. As soon as the apparatus pulled up to the occupancy, I knew we had an arsonist on our hands. He was holding a kerosene can. He didn't move. He was standing in the middle of the street. He didn't respond when the fire truck almost ran him over. He seemed like a nice kid. Can't be more than twenty-four, twenty-five years old. I've seen him a lot around the neighborhood. Always has a book in his hands. I instructed my men where to stretch the line and I went directly to the living room. That's where the fire was. The doors were unlocked. We extinguished the fire in a few minutes. Small fire. When the smoke cleared, I saw the DOA. I returned to the apparatus and notified the dispatcher that we had a 10-45 1, so I knew the marshals would be getting there any minute. But . . . " Hamish Coates looked off into the distance for a few seconds. "I don't know, Nolan. I had a funny feeling about this fire. Maybe because I'd seen the kid around the neighborhood before. So I told the dispatcher to advise the marshals that they should also have a photo unit respond."

Wylie Nolan said, "What happened to the kid?"

"Thirty, thirty-five minutes after we got there, the fire was out and my men were cleaning up. I went outside. He hadn't moved. He was still holding the kerosene can. I walked up to him. I didn't want to scare him. I told him who I was, and asked him if that was his house. He looked at me. I'll give him that. Looked me right in the eye. He wasn't crying, but I've seen a lot of pain in my life, Nolan, and I know when I'm seeing it in a man's face. What I saw there was anguish. Naked anguish. But, like I said, he met my eye and he said, 'I did it, sir. I set the fire. I killed my mother.' And I felt sorry for him. I hate fire setters, Nolan, and I never felt sorry for any of the SOB's before, but I looked at this one, and I'm telling you, what I saw on his face made me want to cry. I don't know what I said to him after that, or what he said to me. I just remember thinking that I wanted to keep him calm so that there wouldn't be any trouble when the fire marshals arrived."

"When was that?"

"Not long after I went outside. Four, maybe five minutes. The photo unit arrived at the same time the marshals did."

"What did the marshals do after they got there, Cap?"

"One of them stayed with the kid. Read him his rights. Cuffed him. Pushed him into the backseat of his car. The other one went inside. Couldn't have been in there five minutes when he came out again and told me we could put the body away."

Again Captain Coates grew silent and thoughtful before he went on. "One of the marshals was obviously a greenhorn. The one who'd read the kid his rights. The other one was an asshole. You know the type. Put in their twenty, collect their pensions, and spend the rest of their lives complaining about how much they gave to 'the job.' And I know how a fire marshal is supposed to conduct an arson investigation with a DOA. I've seen enough of them. These guys didn't do shit. So after they left—they went to book the kid at the forty-fifth precinct—I asked the guy from the photo unit to stick around, because I was concerned the marshals hadn't instructed him to photograph the room properly. But he told me he'd gotten a call from their supervisor, your friend Grogan, and that Grogan had told him what to do. After that, the ladder company put the body in the body bag, and brought the chair outside and hosed it down. Then my men took up. That's about all I can tell you, Nolan. What's going to happen to the kid?"

"I don't know yet, Cap. Why do you want to know?"

Hamish Coates looked off toward the horizon for about ten seconds. When he looked back at Wylie, his eyes were somber.

"Something about this fire stinks, Nolan. When you find out what it is, tell me. You owe me one."

Wylie Nolan met the fire captain's eyes with equal solemnity and said, "It does, I will, and I do."

Wylie hadn't planned on making any more stops before he left City Island, but after he left the firehouse, he drove past a bookstore and noticed the sign for a city bus stop reflected in its large plateglass window. He screeched into a U-turn, and pulled up against the curb.

Max, his voice shaking from a near collision with a bus, said, "Jesus, Wylie. Do you have to . . . "

But when Wylie grinned back at him as though he were proud of his driving skills, Max just shook his head and shrugged.

"Never mind. I guess you do."

He followed Wylie into the bookstore.

An old-fashioned bell that was attached to the top of the door jangled as they went inside.

On first glance, there didn't seem to be anyone inside. Its clean and well-lighted interior was filled with bookcases. Each section was identified by a hand-printed sign: FICTION. BIOGRAPHY. SCIENCE. MYSTERY. TRAVEL. FIRST EDITIONS. PHOTOGRAPHY. GARDENING. And there was one large section toward the back that bore the label: ARTHURIAN LEGENDS.

Max immediately drifted to the shelf that contained the first editions, while Wylie walked toward the back of the store.

The bookcases ended abruptly after Wylie passed the POETRY and MAGIC sections, and opened into a small office area in front of a large window. Wispy ribbons of smoke wove in and out of bright sunbeams surrounding the bald head of a man seated at a battered wood desk, who looked exactly like Santa Claus. He was smoking a corncob pipe, and wearing a collarless red flannel shirt with big white buttons that ran down his chest like tiddlywinks. Wide plaid suspenders held up his ample pants, and an enormous book lay opened in front of him.

Wylie glanced down at the book; he saw etchings of pyramids.

The man looked up at him with "Who are you?" written in his eyes.

Wylie Nolan introduced himself and said, "I'd like to ask you a few questions."

The old man puffed two times on his pipe. As a stream of smoke encircled his head like a halo, he laid his pipe down in an ashtray.

"Pleasure to meet you, Wylie," he said, his voice businesslike and not the least bit grandfatherly. "My name is Simon McCorkell. You look like a pipe-smoking man to me, and I'm never wrong about anything as important as that. Get settled, take a pipeful, and we'll talk."

Wylie sat and reached into his pocket for his pipe.

"You know what Rudyard Kipling wrote," Simon McCorkell said comfortably.

Wylie frowned. "It's been a long time since school, but I think it was 'East is east, and west is west, and . . . ' "

The bookseller puffed again. "No. Not that one. 'A woman is only a woman, but a good cigar is a smoke.' That one. But he could have written 'A good pipe is a smoke' for my money. Who's paying you?"

Wylie blinked and leaned forward.

"Excuse me?"

"You said you were investigating the fire on Kinshaw Street, and I asked you who you're working for."

"Oh," Wylie nodded. "I'm working for friends of Camden Kimcannon."

"Have you been at the house yet?"

"Yes. I've already been there, looked it over, and left."

"What did you find out?"

"Not enough, Simon. Not enough."

"I see. Not talking, eh? Well, since you're doing this for Camden, I'll help you. Who told you he was a friend of mine?"

"Nobody," Wylie answered. "I didn't even know that you two knew each other."

"Then what are you doing here?"

"I'm here because of the bus stop in front of your store."

"What are you talking about?"

Wylie rose to his feet.

"Follow me."

He led Simon McCorkell to the plateglass window overlooking the street.

"When I was driving by just now and I saw your store opposite the bus stop, I thought you might have noticed something the night of the fire. And since your friend Kimcannon isn't talking, I . . . "

"Camden isn't talking?"

"Not a word since he confessed."

"He *confessed* to setting the fire?"

Wylie nodded, and added, "He confessed, but we don't have any corroborating evidence yet. We don't know what time he left Manhattan on Monday, or even if he left from there to get here. And if he did, how did he get here? Subway? Bus? Taxi? We don't know what time he got to City Island. We don't know zip."

"Well, I can tell you when he got here," Simon McCorkell said, "because I saw Camden get off the bus."

"Which bus?"

"The BX29."

"When?" Wylie pressed the book man.

"At eight o'clock."

"Are you sure?"

"I'm as sure as I'm standing here. Eight o'clock, give or take sixty seconds."

"How can you be so certain?" Max had wandered over and pushed himself into the conversation.

Simon looked inquisitively at Wylie.

"Who's the peanut gallery?"

"This is Max Bramble. Max is temporarily acting as your friend's lawyer. Max, meet Simon McCorkell."

The two men shook hands and then Wylie repeated Max's question.

"How *can* you be so sure that Camden Kimcannon got off the bus at exactly eight o'clock?"

"Give or take sixty seconds."

"Right. Give or take."

"I always close up the shop at eight. Monday night, I was getting ready to leave, looking for my key in my pocket, when I saw Camden get off the bus. I wanted him to come inside, because I'd found a copy of a book he's been looking for, *The Chronicles of King Arthur*. He collects books on the Arthurian legend. So do I. That's what we talk about. So I called out to him, but he waved me off and said, 'Later.' " Simon Mc-Corkell shook his head. "I don't suppose there's going to be a 'later' now."

Wylie asked, "How did he look?"

"What do you mean?"

"Did he look annoyed? Angry? Depressed?"

"You want to know what frame of mind he was in, right?"

"Right."

"Well, he looked great. On top of the world. Happy. He reminded me of the title of that old musical, *The Most Happy Fella*. He looked like a most happy fella. Oh, and one more thing."

"What?" Wylie asked.

"He was carrying a bouquet of flowers."

At 2:30 p.m., Max made Wylie stop work and have lunch. He wouldn't listen to any arguments.

"Look," Max said. "I know you're the bloodhound in hot pursuit and that you're smelling hydrocarbons or whatever it is that you people smell, but I'm just a lowly lawyer who can't function on 'the thrill of the chase' alone. I need food. So as a charitable act to a lesser mortal, stop the car at the first delicatessen you see."

After Georgiana Weeks had made her dramatic announcement the day before, Wylie and Max had realized that they would need much more information than she'd provided if they were going to be able to help Camden Kimcannon.

Wylie first called a fireman he knew in the records room at department headquarters. He asked who was the owner of record of the Kimcannon residence at 27 Kinshaw Street, City Island.

Buckminster Kimcannon was the answer.

Max Bramble dialed the telephone number listed, and first confirmed that Buckminster was, indeed, Camden's father. Then he identified himself as Camden's attorney, working on behalf of the museum to represent the newspaper man's son at the bail hearing later on that same day.

Buckminster Kimcannon, who'd been informed of Camden's arrest by everybody's favorite gossip, Betina Bintiffe, was unequivocal.

"I'll do anything I can to help, Mr. Bramble. But you should know that my son hasn't spoken to me in over ten years, and when I called the precinct this morning, he unconditionally refused my assistance."

"You don't need a prisoner's permission to negotiate with a bailbondsman," Max explained. "So, it doesn't matter what Camden wants or doesn't want. Would you be willing to put up the City Island house as collateral for his bail?"

"Absolutely."

Max then made two requests on Wylie Nolan's behalf. First, that Buckminster Kimcannon would grant them permission to inspect the fire premises the following day. And second, that he would agree to meet with the fire investigator for coffee on Thursday, before Wylie had to go to headquarters to look at the fire scene photographs.

Buckminster Kimcannon agreed to both requests.

After Max hung up, Wylie then asked Georgiana Weeks for the key to Camden's apartment.

"Why?" Georgiana asked.

"I want to search it."

"But what for?"

"I don't know yet. I'll know what I'm looking for when I find it."

"But I don't have the key, and I wouldn't know how to get it. Camden won't talk to me; he doesn't want to see any of us. And I'm sure I can't convince him to . . . "

At that moment, Joy Miller slipped into Georgiana's office. She said, blushing furiously, "I was eavesdropping."

Wylie said. "Good. It'll make you a better arson investigator."

"Sit down, Joy," Georgiana said. "You're involved in this, too."

But instead of sitting, Joy ran down the hall to her own office and then rushed back with her handbag clutched tightly in her hands. She sat down and fumbled through the purse's various compartments. When she pulled out her hand again, she was holding a key.

"It's to Cam's apartment," she said. "He gave it to me on Sunday as a backup in case he lost his key." She thrust it at Wylie. "Take it. Do whatever you have to do. You have my permission, for what it's worth, to search his apartment. But help him, Wylie. Please. Please, please help him."

On Tuesday afternoon, at about 4:30, with Max Bramble acting on his behalf, Judge Marilyn DeSoto released Camden Kimcannon on fifty-thousand dollars bail. Georgiana Weeks, Jiri Hozda, and Joy Miller were waiting to meet him after he signed his release papers, but Camden had obviously not wanted to be met. He left the courthouse through a back exit and disappeared into the streets of the city.

At 3:30 on Wednesday the following afternoon, after returning from City Island and consuming the mandatory sandwich Max had insisted on, Wylie drove to Camden's apartment on East Eighty-fourth Street.

Wylie did most of the complaining ("Jeez. If I wanted to spend the rest of my life climbing tenement stairs, I never would have left the fire department."), but it was Max who had to stop at every landing to grab a lungful of air.

"I don't get it, Wylie. You don't exercise, you smoke, you spent most of your adult life breathing fire and inhaling toxic gasses, and *I'm* the one who can't breathe."

Wylie knocked loudly on Camden's apartment door.

Nobody answered.

He knocked loudly again.

Max staggered up the last step.

Wylie grinned at him.

"My heart is pure, so I have the strength of ten."

Max said, "My heart is pure, too." *Huff.* "So why don't I have the strength of ten?" *Puff.*

"Bad genes."

Wylie unlocked the door to Camden's apartment. The two men walked in and looked around.

"This is the smallest apartment I've ever seen," Max said. "Gerbils should live here. What are we looking for, Wylie?"

"Appointment calendars. Address books. Recent correspondence. Memos. Notes." Wylie opened the drawer of a small desk tucked between the minuscule sink and a ceiling-high bookcase; he thumbed through some papers and shut the drawer. "If there's a closet, Max, it doesn't hurt to go through the shirt, pants, and jacket pockets." He suited his actions to his words, and then rifled through the drawers of a small bureau next to the sofa.

"Where's the bathroom?" Max asked.

Wylie pulled back a curtain. Behind it were shelves stacked with dishes, cereal boxes, pots, and pans. He dropped the curtain.

"The bathroom must be down the hall."

Wylie returned to Camden's cramped desk and pushed aside a sketch pad and two empty manilla envelopes. Under the bottom envelope, tucked between a stack of index cards and an American College Dictionary, he found what looked like a brand-new answering machine.

The machine was not on. Somebody had clicked the switch to PLAY and then turned it off. Wylie took a pencil from Camden's desk and pressed it against the ON button. Then he pressed REWIND, and when the tape stopped, used the pencil again to press PLAY.

First, a mechanical voice announced: "Monday, November twenty-eighth. Two-oh-five p.m."

Then there was a low click, followed by an affected voice with a faint British accent. "Cam, darling! Do you . . . are you . . . dear, dear boy . . . "

Wylie said to Max, "She's drunk."

"Are you sure? To me she just sounds . . . oh, I don't know. Affected . . . theatrical."

"No. Drunk."

"Cam, darling." The voice sounded less inebriated, more articulate, and more British as it picked up speed. "Do, do forgive your desolate mother, darling, for her wicked, wicked ways. I am deservedly alone. Contrite. Ashamed. Abashed. I should be hung by my thumbs and subjected to forty . . . no, make that fifty lashes. My embarrassment at my inappropriate behavior and harsh words is exceeded only by my . . . damn it all, where'd I drop the blasted . . . oh. Here it is. Camden, darling. Where was I? Ah, marvelous things, these answering machines. Aren't they? I didn't even know that you had one. But dear boy, now that you're a man of the world, out on your own as it were, there will be so very, very many things about you that I will never know, and . . . How the hell much time do I have to talk on this thing, anyway? One minute? Two? Ten? Ah, well. Rather than risk a premature curtain, I'll get to the point, Cam, darling. Dinner. Tonight. Eightish. I'll order your favorite Chinese dish to celebrate your new apartment. And you must, must come. No argument, or I'll think that you haven't forgiven me for my wicked, wicked ways."

The caller hung up and the answering machine clicked softly once, and then turned itself off.

Wylie looked at Max Bramble and jerked his head toward the hall. They locked the door to Camden Kimcannon's apartment behind them, and as they walked down the stairs, Wylie Nolan said just one more word.

"Bingo."

40

On Thursday afternoon Wylie Nolan met Buckminster Kimcannon at a small coffee shop near the *News* Building. He recognized the writer from the photograph printed beside his column, "The Buck Starts Here," in the sports section of the *News*.

Wylie slid into the seat opposite the journalist.

A waitress showed up.

"Just coffee," Wylie said.

She transferred her glance across the table, "You ready to order now, Buck?"

He shook his head. "My stomach's a little uneven, Flo. I don't suppose you have any Bromo-Seltzer?"

"It ain't on the menu, sweetie, if that's what you mean. But I think the boss has some in his office." She jabbed her pencil into a complicated bun at the back of her head. "Be back in a jiff."

Wylie Nolan took out his pipe.

The other man seemed to shrink into himself.

"This is a bit awkward," he said.

He swallowed hard. His Adam's apple made a quick up-down motion, like the latch handle on a gate, and Wylie studied him, silently comparing the father and the son.

Both Buckminster and Camden Kimcannon were tall, thin, and

wiry. Both projected an aura of shyness or inwardness that seemed to put them at odds with the world. But whereas Camden's shyness led him to a fantasy world in which he could be an aggressive, if solitary, player, Buck wore his shyness the way a farmer at a wedding would wear a boutonniere: What? Where did this come from? Do I have to put it on? Well, all right, I guess. As long as it doesn't get in the way of what I have to do.

Buckminster Kimcannon wore a rumpled khaki raincoat over a sports jacket over a V-neck sweater over a striped cotton shirt so faded it looked like mattress ticking left over from World War II.

His hair was wispy, tousled, and fair. His jaw was narrow, with a cleft in his chin. His nose was long. His forehead high. And over reticent, almost triangular blue eyes, he wore large-lensed eyeglasses that made him look like an owl about to blink.

The waitress came back with a big carafe of coffee and a small glass of Bromo-Seltzer.

She said, "Drink up, bubelehs. Make a noise if you want anything else," and disappeared.

Wylie Nolan spoke first.

"I asked you to meet me, Mr. Kimcannon, because I need you to tell me about Camden."

The sportswriter lifted the glass of Bromo-Seltzer to his lips and knocked it back as if it were a stiff drink.

"Tell you *what* about Camden? I mentioned to the lawyer on the telephone that I haven't seen him in over ten years. And that I am, I'm ashamed to say, the classic absentee parent."

"Tell me about that then. It might help me understand more about why he set the fire."

"Where do you want me to start?"

"At the beginning."

"The beginning," Buck Kimcannon repeated. "All right. The beginning would have been forty-four years ago, in Vidalia, Georgia. That's the town where Camden's mother was born; she was named after it. Parallel universe. Fifty years ago, Manchester, England. That's where I was born. Mother, a violent, uncontrollable alcoholic. Father, an absentminded professor. One day, mother, in drunken fury, beats son. Me. Father comes out of pedantic haze long enough to realize that something is wrong, divorces her, takes son to live in Columbia, Missouri, where he resumes role of absentminded professor at the university there. Son grows up, goes to journalism school at Columbia. Gets degree. Mother still in Manchester, dies prematurely of alcoholism. Son goes to England to make funeral arrangements. After funeral, in pub where he is feeling neither pain nor grief, he meets beautiful, third-rate American actress with honey-blonde hair and come-hither lips who is in Manchester with a touring company of *A Streetcar Named Desire*. Young journalist marries actress, returns to the U.S. of A. First job as family man is at *Philadelphia Inquirer*. First residence, Camden, New Jersey. First and only child, son, born twenty-four years ago *in* Camden. Hence, his name. Second job as husband and father in Big Apple. New York City. The *Daily News*. Family of three gets apartment in Manhattan. Saves money. Puts down payment on house in City Island. Camden is one year old. Family moves to City Island. Can any of this really be relevant? It's hard to see what these personal details can have to do with your investigation. Aren't you supposed to be investigating a fire?"

"It is relevant, and I am investigating the fire," Wylie said. "Do you want some coffee?"

"Yes, thank you."

Wylie waved to Flo, who returned with another cup.

Buck Kimcannon went on, "Almost from the day that Vidalia got pregnant, her theme song became who she had been, and what she could have become—Dame Thistle-Whistlestop of the British Royal Theater, or something equally ludicrous—if she hadn't given it all up for me and Camden. She had lived less than six months in England, had toured with one play, had given up her so-called 'career' at the age of eighteen, had never tried out for another play, had never read another script, and had never gone on another audition; but somehow, it was I who had been mystically transformed into Simon Legree, and she who had become the persecuted Eliza. I put up with it, with the posturing, with her nasty jabs at everything I said or did, with her incessant drinking, for ten, almost eleven years. And then, I realized that if I didn't get out of there, get out of that house, get out of that marriage . . . I was going to die."

278

"Was she a heavy drinker?"

"No. She wasn't a heavy drinker. She was a drunk. We both were. I had driven her to drink because if it hadn't been for me, she would have been knighted for her thespian talents by the queen. And she drove me to drink because I didn't have the guts or the manhood to kick her out. I'm a sportswriter. That's what I do for a living."

"I know."

"And I'd started to show up at sporting events drunk. I was writing lousy copy and turning it in late. I was drinking my lunches, abusing my coworkers, and hating myself. So eleven years ago, my boss pulled me aside and told me that either I checked into an alcohol rehab and got sober or I was fired. But I didn't want to leave Vidalia and Camden alone long enough to go to a rehab, so I went to an Alcoholics Anonymous meeting instead. I liked what I heard, so I went to another one. I went to two, sometimes three meetings a day, until that miraculous occurrence, it was on December seventh; funny, isn't it? Pearl Harbor Day. But on December seventh, after eight months of being on the wagon, I finally lost the compulsion to drink. And it's never come back. Not so far, anyway. During that whole time, I begged Vidalia to come to an Alcoholics Anonymous meeting with me. But she refused. She didn't drink. Not her. Sometimes, on rare occasions, darling . . . that's what she called me. That's what she called everybody. Sometimes, on a rare occasion, like the coming of Halley's comet, or the advent of the seventeen-year locust, she might have a social drink. Maybe even two. But Lady Thistle-Whistlestop, formerly of the stage, didn't have a drinking problem. She would have died before admitting that she was an alcoholic. Alcoholics are bums. They aren't ladies. They aren't retired actresses, God forbid . . . like *her*."

"What was Camden doing when all this was going on."

"Camden was just like me when I was his age. He was sensitive. Inclined to be dreamy. And, pity the poor soul, he had a sense of honor. He was born to be gallant. Vidalia was an expert manipulator. A genius at mind control. She knew how to play on Camden's sympathy in exactly the right way to get exactly what she wanted. It had worked on me, too. For ten long years. But I was a grown man. I had power and resources at my command, both mentally and physically, that were unavailable to Camden."

"Give me some specifics, Buck."

"All right. After I sobered up, I saw what our drinking was doing to my son. He had no friends his own age. He was nervous. Terrified of offending either me or his mother. He was starved for our approval. He was lonely. Desperate to be liked. To be loved. He was scared to death of life, but wanted like crazy not to miss any of it. He'd been a precocious child. Reading before he was three years old. Reading Mark Twain and Charles Dickens when he was seven, and Shakespeare when he was ten. At first, as I said, I tried to get Vidalia to come with me to Alcoholics Anonymous meetings, but when that didn't work, I tried to talk to Camden. To apologize to him for the kind of a father I'd been. To tell him about the dangers of alcohol addiction. To explain how it changes your personality. You know the story. I brought home books from the library. I took him to an Alateen meeting, where kids were learning how to deal with their parents' alcoholism. I explained that his mother didn't mean to do the things she did or say the things she said, and . . . "

Buck Kimcannon swallowed hard, his Adam's Apple moving up and down on his neck like a piston. Then he reached for his coffee cup, lifted it, put it down. When he began talking again, he raised his hand to his forehead, and shaded what was going on in his eyes. His voice cracked with emotion.

"And that was when Camden started to hate me. His mother, he assured me, was *not* an alcoholic. How dare I say that she was! How could I be so callous as to think that someone like her, someone so cultured and refined, would ever become an alcoholic! His mother was wonderful! His mother was beautiful! Why, if it hadn't been for her great love of him, she would be a celebrated actress, and she . . . "

Buck stopped talking and swallowed again. "I'm sorry, but reliving it is hard."

"Take your time."

"I'm all right. But you can see where I'm going with this. I told you that my son was born with a sense of honor. A sense of gallantry. Inadvertently, I had nurtured it, because I'd wanted so badly to bring something bright and colorful into his dreary childhood. After I brought home that first book about King Arthur and Camelot, though, whatever chance I might have had to extricate him from a bad situation was gone. Because knights in shining armor don't abandon damsels in distress. Varlets like his father might abandon them, but not a man sworn to uphold the principles of the round table."

Buck Kimcannon shook his head.

"What more can I say? I failed. I took Vidalia to court and tried to get custody, but I didn't have a chance in a million. *I* was the drunk and the alcoholic. Not she. She was the retired lady of the stage. Nobody had ever seen her drinking. Nobody had ever seen her drunk. Nobody, that is, except for me and Camden. And if when I looked at Vidalia I saw a woman so close to evil that I wanted to wring her neck, what Camden saw when he looked at his mother was a defenseless creature abused by an uncaring husband who had left her to fend for herself. Oh, Jesus, Mary, and Joseph, I abandoned him, that's what I did. I left my son with that creature. I packed up a bag, got on the bus to Manhattan, and never went back. And I left that dreamy, idealistic, tormented youngster . . . "

He couldn't say another word.

His face was hidden by his hand. His shoulders heaved. Flo, the waitress, approached the table. Wylie shook his head. She nodded and backed away.

Two minutes later, Buckminster Kimcannon removed his hand from his eyes.

"I called him every day for four years. Vidalia always answered the telephone. She told me that Camden refused to talk to me. Maybe it was true. Maybe it wasn't. I wrote letters to him. I sent him presents. Books, mostly." He shook his head. "But nothing. No answer. No acknowledgment. Once, when he was fourteen years old, he answered the phone. I told him how much I loved him. I begged him to forgive me for divorcing his mother. But his responses were so filled with rage that they scared me. He shouted that I should leave him and his mother alone. He said that they were better off without me, that he was glad that I'd left, and that he'd always hated me. I never called back. I stopped writing. I had nothing left to fight with. It was all gone. I'd lost. She'd won."

"But you still owned the house."

"I own the house to this day."

"Who pays the utilities?"

"I do."

"Did you all along?"

"Of course. Camden's my son. He was my responsibility."

"The taxes, too? Gas? Heat? Everything?"

"Yes."

"Did you pay for the telephone?"

"Yes. Telephone. His private school. His college."

"Does Camden know that you've been doing all that?"

Buck Kimcannon looked at Wylie helplessly. "I don't know what he knows or doesn't know. I don't know anything about him. He's my son," he said in a voice of horrified awe, "and the only thing I know for a fact is that he killed Vidalia. And somehow, I can't help but think that it was my fault he did."

Wylie leaned forward and said very quietly, very low, "How your fault, sir?"

And tears welled up in the triangles of his eyes but stayed there, as though to fall would have provided a relief he did not think he deserved, and Buck Kimcannon answered, "Because I should have killed her myself a long time ago."

41

The one-hour photo developer is the fire investigator's friend. Before meeting with Gus Grogan, Wylie dropped off the negatives of the photographs he had taken of the house on City Island.

"Two sets," he told the salesclerk.

An hour and a half later, he was asking for Gus Grogan at the Division of Fire Investigation.

"He's in his office, Wylie," one of the fire marshals said. "Second door to your left."

Wylie walked down the hall and pushed open a door.

Supervising Fire Marshal Gus Grogan looked up.

He pointed to a chair on the opposite side of the long, narrow table where he was sitting.

Gus Grogan was stocky. Where Wylie was dark, Gus Grogan was darker. Where Wylie was . . . wily, Gus Grogan was blatant, exaggerated, overt. If either were confronted with a brick wall that had to be got around, Wylie would figure out a way over, under, or around it. Gus Grogan would just walk through the bricks. But both investigators got results, and neither was popular with the bosses for the way they went about getting them.

"So," Gus said, indicating the black-and-white enlargements on the table in front of him, "tell me something I don't already know."

Wylie handed one set of the prints he'd just had developed to the fire marshal.

"I'll show you mine if you show me yours."

Half an hour later, Wylie Nolan was finishing his analysis of the fire and Gus Grogan was nodding.

"It makes sense," Gus said.

Wylie took a manila envelope out of his briefcase and removed the glass that he'd taken from the fire scene. He unfolded enough of his handkerchief for Gus to see what it was, and then handed the glass to Gus.

"There are fingerprints on it," Wylie said. "I don't know if you can get at the ones under the soot, but if you can there should be a perfect set."

Then he started to look through the fire department photographs again.

"What are you looking for, Wylie?"

"There are two shots in here. One is of the area around the chair, before the body was removed."

Gus Grogan pulled out the picture.

"The other is a living room shot. The photographer must have taken it from the windowsill because he got everything: the French doors, the fireplace, the burn patterns on the rug, and the chair with the DOA."

Gus plucked that one out of the pile, too; he gave both of them to Wylie.

The first photograph was of Vidalia Kimcannon's body in the armchair. Her face and upper torso were untouched by fire but her entire body was covered with soot. The picture was preternatural. Almost archeological. As if a volcano had erupted and she had been outlined in a fine layer of volcanic ash.

The cosmetology of death had left the face of the woman who'd considered herself to be an actress untouched. But fire had viciously attacked the left side of her body. Her left hand, which had been resting on the arm of the chair, was incinerated; all that remained were black bones that resembled the claw of a chicken.

The skin and tissue of her upper arm was so badly burned, it had melded into the chair's upholstery; it was impossible to tell where one stopped and the other began. Her left thigh, buttock, hip, and lower rib cage had also been eroded by flame; the burn patterns on the left side of Vidalia's body lined up exactly with the burn patterns on the left side of the chair.

But what Wylie was looking for in the photograph wasn't the burn patterns. It was Vidalia Kimcannon's right hand. The hand that had *not* burned, that had *not* been impinged upon by flame.

"Look here, Gus. See how her fingers are configured."

The four fingers of Vidalia's right hand were gently bent, each touching the one next to it. And her thumb was curved around an imaginary circle in juxtaposition to the fingers.

In death, Vidalia's hand was poised around a cylinder that was not there.

Wylie pointed to the handkerchief-wrapped glass he had given to Gus Grogan. Then he pointed to the empty space in Vidalia Kimcannon's right hand.

"Do you see it?" he asked.

Gus nodded.

"Now I do."

"If we have to prove that the measurements of the glass match the circumference of the circle of her hand, I have a photogrammetrist just outside Chicago who . . . "

"We won't have to."

"Good. Now take a look at this other photograph." Wylie held up the long shot that showed most of the living room, including the deceased reclining in her chair.

"Psychology one-oh-one," Wylie said. "When confronted with a potentially life-threatening situation, what is man's natural response?"

"Fight or flight," Gus answered.

"What's she doing?"

"Looks like she just dozed off."

"How about this?" Wylie pointed to a dark, irregular burn pattern that the fire had eaten into the rug. It was configured like spilled liquid. "And here." He showed Gus the shallow headway the fire had made in the debris of magazines and newspapers crammed in the fireplace. "In contrast to this." Wylie indicated the areas of the floor surrounding the chair on which Vidalia Kimcannon's body had been found.

"The floor's clean," Gus Grogan said.

"Right. No burn pattern."

"So, when our young friend poured the flammable liquid in the doorway and the fireplace," Gus continued, "he didn't go near the chair."

Wylie tossed the two pictures back on the table.

"I rest my case," he said.

"Good work, Wylie."

"Thanks. When are you going to call the district attorney?"

"I'll do it right now, and I'll make an appointment to meet him tomorrow. Can I borrow your pictures for the meeting?"

"They're yours. I made you a set. And Gus?"

"What now?"

"Can you try to see the DA before three o'clock in the afternoon?"

"Sure. Anything else you want me to do? Wax your car? Give you a pedicure? Why three o'clock?"

"I have a meeting at the museum at three. Before I leave the meeting, I'd like to be able to tell them what the district attorney said." Wylie scribbled on a piece of paper. "This is the phone number at the museum. Memorize it. Tear it into little pieces and swallow them."

"Smart ass," Gus Grogan said. "Oh. One more thing."

"What?"

"The medical examiner. I've been bugging him ever since Tuesday morning, and he says he'll give me a copy of his toxicology report by early Friday afternoon."

"Before you see the district attorney?"

"Right, Wylie. In ample time for my meeting with the DA."

42

Georgiana Weeks was uncharacteristically quiet as she and Jiri Hozda waited for Wylie Nolan in her office at the museum. Her hair was pulled behind her ears, and without the wild ornamentation of that orange-red halo, the delicate bones of her face appeared too naked, too vulnerable, like a gown from which the sequins had been removed, one by one, until all that was left was ruthlessly plain.

And instead of dazzling or flashing, Georgiana's green eyes were baleful, as though the switches on the lights behind them had been turned off.

"Poor Georgiana," Jiri said, patting her motionless hand. "Sorrow has temporarily stripped you of your immortality."

Georgiana slumped in her chair.

"It isn't sorrow. It's guilt."

"But about what could you possibly feel guilty, other than having deprived those who care about you of your natural exuberance?"

"And my natural tendency to butt into other people's lives, and when the mood strikes me, to ruin them."

"Ah, Georgiana." Jiri shook his head. "You, who are usually so wise, are now speaking nonsense."

"An old Persian saying, Jiri, tells us that there is danger for him who taketh the cub from the tiger, and danger also for whoso snatcheth a delusion from a desperate man."

287

Jiri raised his right eyebrow.

"I take it, my dear, that you are referring to our young friend."

"Yes, I am referring to our young, sweet, ineffectual, sad sack of a dreamer who never hurt a living soul in his life until I came along and snatchethed his delusion from him."

"You are being melodramatic."

"The situation is melodramatic. For once, I'm merely perceiving a situation the way it actually is."

"For once? No, Georgiana. You are always a realist."

"Oh, am I really? Well, let me tell you how the mechanism of my so-called 'realism' works. When *you* look at someone, what you see is what that person is at that moment, regardless of how he's describing himself. When *I* look, though, what I see is only what he's said he wants to be."

"*Bah!* Everybody in the arts does that to some extent."

"*Bah* yourself. And everybody in the arts doesn't do what I do. If I go to a cocktail party, and a certified public accountant tells me that his whole life all he's ever wanted to be is an airline pilot, I not only believe he means what he's said, I also believe that if he *doesn't* become an airline pilot, his soul will wander forever in a purgatory of lost wings. And, of course, since I'm not happy unless I'm poking my fingers into someone else's soul, I tell him the steps he has to take to get his pilot's license, which he probably never wanted in the first place, and has deluded himself into believing was forever safely beyond his reach. And worse than that, now I've created a lifelong enemy who will never forgive me, because I've done the inexcusable by rudely pointing out to him that what he's always fantasized about is actually attainable."

Jiri studied Georgiana. "You are an idealist," he said. "You do not only see things and people as they are. That is true. You also see the potential for what they can become."

"I'm out of control. I'm a menace. I can't leave well enough alone. When you look at Joy Miller, Jiri, what do you see?"

"I see a charming young woman barely more than a child, who appears to be indecently shy, and also of late seems to have become infatuated with our missing friend."

"Now that's what I call a reasonable assessment. That's what a normally perceptive person would see. Do you want to know what I see when I look at her, though? I see a woman with no fashion sense and drab hair who doesn't know how to apply makeup and doesn't know that she has a fabulous figure."

Jiri considered this for a few seconds.

"But, Georgiana, that is true, too. To notice such things is surely no reason to chastise yourself or to carry around such a heavy burden of guilt."

"Maybe not. If all I *did* was notice. But I go way beyond just noticing. I meddle."

"How have you meddled with Joy?"

"Without consulting with her, I made an appointment for next Wednesday to get her hair styled and highlighted, and afterward for her to have a complete makeover. Then I'd planned to take her on a shopping spree and make her buy a glamorous dress for the opening of the Pre-Raphaelite exhibition."

"But I think that is a charming idea! I would like to contribute to the expense myself."

"It's not a charming idea, Jiri. It's a terrible idea. Do you want to know why?"

"Enlighten me."

"Because if I went ahead with it, Joy would, no doubt, be enamored of her new image, and she would become vain, shallow, and self-absorbed. She would quit her job at the Zigfield Art Museum, convinced that it was now beneath her, toss off Camden like an old bathrobe, make new friends, all of whom would be beautiful, manipulative, and callow, like her new self. She'd get caught up in a jet-set world of big spenders and become the plaything of some rich, heartless, European slug. And then she'd start to use drugs recreationally, and before she even reached the age of twenty-six, she would overdose on cocaine and die."

Jiri didn't say anything for a long moment. Then observing that the bleak expression on Georgiana's face had grown even bleaker, he said, "That is quite a scenario you have painted, my friend. And it does not give Joy much credit for strength of character or personal judgment."

"How about Camden, then?" Georgiana continued. "Would it have been such a big deal for me to call that loveable goop 'Camelot,' instead of insisting he go by his given name? That's the only thing in the world he ever asked of me. He wanted to be called 'Camelot.' Big deal. It satisfied some fantastical craving he had for a lovelier and more gentle universe. Would it have been so much skin off my nose to go along with such an innocuous agenda? But no. Not me. Instead I decide that I have the right to submit an address change for Camden to God, and without his permission, move him out of dreamland. So, what do I do? I look at that sweet, gangling, patchwork quilt of fable and fantasy out of which he had constructed himself, and one by one, I snip away at the threads holding together the patches of his dreams. And after I'm through disassembling his soul for the sake of my vanity, then, just to make sure he doesn't have a single defense mechanism left, I . . . "

"Georgiana, stop."

She looked up abruptly.

"Stop," Jiri said again. "There is danger in this kind of self-pity."

Her eyes narrowed. "Self-pity?" She frowned. "Is that what I'm doing?"

"Yes. And you are playing God."

"I know I've been playing God. That's why I'm so angry with myself."

"But I don't mean you are playing God by being generous enough to see a potential for beauty in a timid young woman and in wanting to encourage it, or in seeing a potential for survival and fulfillment in an unhappy young man. I mean that you are playing God by assuming that your actions, your words, your enthusiasms or lack thereof, could be of such a monumental influence that in just the little over two weeks that you have been here, you could single-handedly, and irrevocably, ruin Camden's, or indeed anyone else's, life."

Georgiana stared at Jiri.

"But I . . . "

"But nothing. If you are so certain that you could destroy his life with just a few words, then you must be equally certain that you are potentially such a great benefactress that you could save his life with an equal number of words. And I don't believe that any of us have such devastatingly effectual oratorical prowess."

"Kind words, Jiri. But I still feel guilty."

"Perhaps the problem, my dear, is that you see yourself as being responsible for the drastic changes in Camden's lifestyle and therefore as the catalyst for the fire."

"I do and I am."

"Had you not come along, Camden never would have left home; he never would have gotten his own apartment. I do not argue that. But responsibility is not the same thing as culpability. That is what you are failing to understand. If you see a man standing in the way of a moving train and call out to him 'Run!' and he runs, it is true that your warning was responsible for having saved his life. Because if his intention had been to die, he could merely have stayed where he was. But if, after having survived a near collision with the train, he then goes out to celebrate, gets drunk, gets into his car, and on the way home crashes into a bus filled with schoolchildren, *you* are not culpable for the deaths of all of those innocent human beings."

Georgiana sulked.

"Well, it feels like I am."

Jiri continued to look at her reproachfully. Then finally Georgiana said, "So, what you're telling me is that I should get off the pity pot."

"That would be advisable."

"And I should stop playing God."

"Perhaps. But never, under any circumstances, stop playing Georgiana."

A gleam entered Georgiana's eye.

"Does that mean you want me to show you how you can get your pilot's license?"

Jiri laughed.

"And can I keep Joy's hair and makeover appointments for next week?"

"You are, my dear, incorrigible. Where *is* Joy, by the way?"

"I suggested that she stop by Camden's apartment to see if he'd turned up, so that . . . "

There was a light tap on the door to Georgiana's office.

"Come in," she called out.

And Wylie Nolan, followed by Max Bramble, walked into the room.

43

Wylie Nolan took three sheets of paper out of his briefcase and handed them to Max, Jiri, and Georgiana.

"What is this?" Jiri asked.

Wylie pulled out his pipe.

Georgiana's eyes darted around her desk and stopped at a shallow brass box filled with paper clips. She quickly dumped the paper clips in her drawer, and just as Wylie struck a match, slid the box across her desk in time for him to toss it inside.

Wylie drew deeply on his pipe, exhaled, and said, "I prepared a timeline for this meeting, and I want each of you to take a minute to look at it. The Kimcannon fire is complicated and some of the events that lead up to it seem to contradict each other. In actual fact, they aren't contradictory, but we'll get to that later."

He inhaled again on his pipe; then he put it next to the dead match in the brass box and said nothing while Max, Jiri, and Georgiana studied the brief chronology of events.

After a few minutes, he said, "Usually, after I do a fire investigation, I tell my clients how the fire started by 'explaining backward.' By that I mean that I start with the burn patterns, which are the last things that happen, and I work my way back to the first. Burn patterns are the telltale marks, shapes, or erosions in the debris of a fire that an arson investigator studies to figure out where and how the fire occurred. Next I tell my clients about the fire itself—how it burned. How hot and fast it was. Which rooms went up first. And so on. I keep going backward and talk about the sequence of events that led up to the fire. Then I tell them who I think started the fire—my suspect. And after I've talked about everything else, I finally get around to motives—what reason the suspect might have had for setting the fire in the first place. One fact at a time, I show my clients how I came to my conclusion, because that's how I arrived at the facts of the fire myself.

"But I'm not going to do it like that this time, because too many human variables are getting in the way. The fire at 27 Kinshaw Street on City Island doesn't just involve burn patterns and perpetrators; what we're dealing with here are heartbreak, tragedy, arson, conflicting witness statements, confession, guilt, *and* burn patterns and perpetrators.

"But when all is said and done, the pieces of the puzzle fit. Even the ones that seemed to have angles sticking out where curves should be. So, instead of starting with the burn patterns at the end of a fire, I'm going to start at what I consider the real beginning. Max, read the first entry aloud on my time line."

Max read, " 'Answering machine. Two-oh-five P.M.' "

"On Monday, at two-oh-five P.M.," Wylie Nolan said, "Vidalia Kimcannon called Camden at his apartment in Manhattan. From the tape of that incoming message, we know that she invited him to dinner at eight o'clock that same night. And since he was working on Monday, we also know that he didn't leave the museum until five-forty-five P.M., and that he can't have arrived at his apartment before six o'clock."

"How do we know what time he left the museum?" Max asked.

"On his way out the door, Camden asked Luis Cabrerra if he had a subway token to exchange for coins; Luis looked at his watch when Camden walked out the door. We also know that at some point when Vidalia was talking into Camden's answering machine, she dropped something and then apparently picked it up again. This might be significant; it might not. I think it indicates that her motor coordination was already impaired. And taking into consideration the mood she was in when she made the call, as well as her background and reputation, I think it's also safe to assume that she was experiencing the false self-confidence and euphoria symptomatic of the early stages of intoxication. Which brings us to the next item on our time line. Max?"

"It says 'Two-forty-five to four-forty-five P.M.—Smoldering fire.' "

Wylie nodded and continued. "We know for a fact that at two-oh-five P.M., Vidalia Kimcannon left a message on her son's answering machine. And even though we can't be sure until I get the toxicology report, I think that before Vidalia picked up the telephone to call Camden, she'd already consumed a significant amount of alcohol. Enough so that sometime after she hung up the telephone at two-oh-five P.M. and before four-forty-five P.M., she passed out. I'll tell you why four-forty-five is relevant in a few minutes.

"The facts and burn patterns also tell us that just after or before Vidalia Kimcannon lost consciousness, the cigarette holder and a lit cigarette she was smoking fell in the crack between the cushion and the arm of the chair she was sitting on, and the upholstery around that cigarette started to smolder. This conclusion is based on the burn patterns in the chair, the condition of Vidalia's body, the appearance of the living room, and witness statements. Vidalia Kimcannon, it would be fair to conclude, was habitually a careless smoker."

Georgiana said, "I saw cigarette burns all over her furniture when I went there for tea."

"That doesn't surprise me," Wylie nodded. He went on, "Since the average parameters for a smoldering fire are anywhere from half an hour to forty-five minutes, I think we can assume that the alcohol Vidalia was consuming didn't catch up to her until about forty-five minutes after she hung up the phone. Which brings us to our next entry. Max?"

Max Bramble read: " 'Four-forty-five P.M.—Betina Bintiffe goes to car.' "

"The house next door to 27 Kinshaw Street is occupied by a little old lady named Betina Bintiffe, who has eyes and a nose in the back of her head. At four-forty-five P.M., Mrs. Bintiffe left her house to visit her daughter. On her way to her car she looked over at the Kimcannon residence, which is separated from her driveway by only a few bushes, and she noticed two things. One, that all of the living room windows were black. And two, that a terrible smell was coming from that direction. To use Mrs. Bintiffe's words, it was, quote, that horrible metallic odor that sets your teeth on edge. Exactly as if Vidalia had left an aluminum pan burning on the stove, unquote."

Max said, "But we looked in the kitchen, Wylie. And nothing in there had been set on fire."

"There wouldn't have been, Max, because Mrs. Bintiffe's metallic smell wasn't coming from the kitchen. It's an odor characteristically associated with the later stages of a smoldering fire. And a smoldering fire also generates enough black, sooty smoke to coat the windows in the room where it's burning. And if the windows and doors of that room are shut tight, then after the smoldering fire has consumed all the available oxygen, it will eventually put itself out. Which is what happened here."

Georgiana Weeks looked down at the sheet of paper in her hands; she frowned, and said, "I'm getting confused, Wylie. According to what we were told before, Vidalia's fire wasn't called into the fire department until after nine o'clock at night. But on your time line, at only four-forty-five P.M., a . . . "

"At only four-forty-five P.M.," Wylie finished her sentence, "a chair in Vidalia's living room was already on fire."

"Yes. Go on."

"And four hours before the fire alarm was even turned in, Vidalia Kimcannon was already dead."

Georgiana jolted forward.

"What? But why? How?"

"Vidalia was drunk. She'd passed out. She didn't know that she was being overcome by poisonous fumes."

"But wouldn't she have smelled them? Wouldn't the horrible odor have wakened her up?"

Wylie Nolan shook his head. "In the early stages of a smoldering fire, there is no odor. Carbon monoxide asphyxiation is the single most common cause of death in all fires. After only two or three breaths, as little as one-point-three percent carbon monoxide can cause unconsciousness, and it can cause death in a few minutes.

"So, without knowing *when* it happened, we know *what* happened to Vidalia Kimcannon. She was drinking and she was smoking. She drank too much, and she passed out; her cigarette fell between the cushions of the chair she was sitting on and started to smolder. It never broke into open flames, but the smoldering upholstery produced smoke, heat, and toxic gases, and the carbon monoxide generated by the smoldering fire rapidly asphyxiated her. After smoldering for a while longer in the closed room, the fire had consumed so much oxygen that there was none left to support combustion, and it went out. But not before covering everything in the room with a thick layer of soot. Are you following me so far?"

"More or less," Georgiana said.

"OK." Wylie turned to Max. "What's next?"

" 'Five-forty-five P.M.—Camden leaves museum.' "

"We already covered that."

"Then it says: 'Six P.M. to eight P.M.—Camden in transit.' "

"Camden in transit," Wylie repeated. "I made a few telephone calls to the Transit Authority about bus and subway connections, and the assumptions I'm making here are consistent with the facts, even if I'm off by a few minutes, or by a subway station exit, because it all gets to the same place at about the same time.

"Let's say that as soon as Camden got home, at around six o'clock, he listened to the message his mother had left on his answering machine. He changed clothes and started walking to the subway on Eighty-sixth Street and Lexington Avenue about five blocks away. Along the way, he passed at least four flower shops and stopped at one of them to buy his mother flowers.

"Camden got on the IRT uptown local at seven P.M.; it took him half an hour to get to the Pelham Bay Park station in the Bronx. At about seven-thirty-five P.M., he left the subway station in the Bronx and took the BX29 express bus to City Island. At eight o'clock, Simon McCorkell saw him get off the bus on City Island Avenue. Max, I think there's a time line entry for that."

"Right. 'Eight P.M.—Bookstore. Flowers.' "

Wylie said, "Simon McCorkell's bookstore is just a few feet from where Camden Kimcannon was getting off the bus. Simon called out to

Camden, who acknowledged the greeting but didn't stop. According to Simon, Camden was carrying a bouquet of flowers. He also said that Camden seemed to be in a good mood. He was smiling and he looked happy. Keep that in mind, because it's revealing both of Camden's motives and of his state of mind. Now the next entry on my time line covers a period of a little over an hour."

Max read, " 'Eight P.M. to nine-oh-five P.M.—Camden in mother's house.' "

"Again, I may be slightly off on which events happened first, like whether Camden went into the living room before he went into the dining room or visa versa, but as far as the actual facts go, I'm as sure of them as I am that fire naturally burns up and water naturally runs down.

"Camden walked the block and a half from the bus stop to 27 Kinshaw Street. He unlocked the front door and walked in. He immediately sensed that something was wrong. Maybe he called out to his mother or maybe he looked for her in the kitchen or the backyard first. Either way, it's a sure bet that as soon as he opened the living room doors, he realized that there had been a fire.

"Since the fire had smoldered without breaking into open flames, there hadn't been enough heat buildup to damage the electrical service, so when Camden flicked a light switch the light went on. What he saw next was bad enough to give nightmares to a man who had hated his mother. That he'd loved her made what Camden was looking at much worse.

"Vidalia Kimcannon was sitting in her living room chair, completely covered with a black layer of soot, and frozen in death like a macabre sculpture carved out of coal. The left side of her body had been gnawed by the smoldering fire. She was eerie. Static. Motionless. Dead.

"I don't know how long Camden stood here. Stunned. Horrified. Staring. And we don't know if he thought about what he did next, or if he acted instinctively, without thinking. But we do know that after Camden came back to his senses, he put the flowers he'd brought down on the coffee table, and then he deliberately set about to alter the fire scene."

"Wylie," Max asked, "Does any of this explain the vague marks on the tables that you made me look at?"

"Yes. But I'll get to that later. First, you have to know what Camden did next. And if I hadn't spoken to his father, I'd never be able to figure out his motivation for doing it."

"You spoke to whom?" Georgiana asked, astonished.

"To Camden's father."

"But when?"

"Yesterday afternoon."

"I wondered about him," Georgiana said pensively. "What's he like? Is he the cruel, loveless, abandoning parent that Camden has made him out to be?"

"Not for my money. He's a nice man. Not a strong man. And not a street fighter, which is too bad, because if he'd been a little bit tougher, and a little bit less nice, he and his son might have had a better life. I'd describe him as a man who's always given a hell of a lot more to his family than he got back in return. I asked Buck Kimcannon a lot of questions about Vidalia and he told me about her drinking. About her relationship with Camden. He pretty much told me everything I had to know about the Kimcannon family to understand what I otherwise would not have understood about this fire.

"It was because Vidalia Kimcannon had such a violently negative reaction to the subject of alcohol dependency, and because she literally would rather be caught dead than admit she had a problem with booze, that Camden would confess to a fire that wasn't incendiary, and a homicide that wasn't a homicide. Camden's entire universe depended on preserving his vision of his mother, alive or dead, just as she would have wanted to be perceived, and regardless of the facts."

"That's so sad," Georgiana said softly. "I'm beginning to think that the only reason Camden Kimcannon was put on earth is to break our hearts."

Max Bramble shook his head. "You want us to believe that a young man with his whole life in front of him would risk spending it in prison, just because he didn't want to admit that his mother was a drunk? I think that's pretty far-fetched, Wylie. This is the twentieth century. Everybody knows that alcoholism is a disease."

"I had a case once on Staten Island," Wylie responded. "A cop died in his bed. Same scenario. Booze. Cigarettes. The fire marshals did the investigation. And they called the fire right. But the family wasn't having any. They hired me to second-guess what the fire marshals were doing, because they didn't want to believe their report. They wanted me to find out what *really* happened, and how their husband/son/father/brother had *really* died. I inspected the fire scene. I reviewed the photographs. I looked over the medical examiner's report. And I came up with exactly the same cause. Booze and cigarettes. So they fired me. And after me, they hired another fire investigator, and then another, and another, and another. They kept hiring fire investigator after fire investigator until they finally found one, a guy who, by reputation, should have been drummed out of the business a long time ago. He concocted a story for the family about the cop having been attacked by a motorcycle gang who tortured him, beat him unconscious, stole his wallet, drove him home, dumped him into his own bed (after first putting him in his pajamas), and then set fire to the bed, killing him. But after the family got that report from this quack fire investigator, they were happy because they liked the story he had given them better than the one they'd gotten from the fire marshals and from me."

"They liked that *better*?" Georgiana said. "They found it more emotionally consoling to believe that a man they'd loved had been tortured, robbed, and burned alive than that he had died peacefully, if not soberly, in his bed?"

"Sure," Wylie answered. "And it isn't all that unusual. Anything but admit that their Patrick or their Timothy or their Vidalia was a drunk. And in principle, the same thing happened here."

"That's a terrible story, Wylie."

"Terrible, but true. So are a lot of other stupid things that happen. But it doesn't stop them from happening. So, after Camden put down the flowers, he set about altering the fire scene. He removed the ashtray from the coffee table, and dumped the sooty cigarette butts in the trash can in the kitchen. He took the cup and glass off the same table and put them in the kitchen sink. He carefully removed the glass of gin from Vidalia's right hand. Rigor mortis had already set in. There's a photograph in the fire marshal's office of her thumb and fingers forming a perfect circle, exactly as they'd been configured before Camden had removed the glass."

"Oh, God." Georgiana's voice was shaking. "It just gets worse and worse."

"Camden also put that glass in the sink," Wylie continued. "If it's tested, it should show—everything Camden touched should show—that his fingerprints are on *top* of the soot that's covering the glasses, ashtray, and other objects. Not under them. And if nothing else confirms that Camden wasn't in his mother's house until after the fire, this should do it.

"There were also two Gordon's gin bottles on an end table next to Vidalia. He put them in the trash can outside. And then what he did next, he believed he *owed* it to his mother to do."

"Wylie," Georgiana said. "Something went on between Camden and Vidalia that you don't know about. Camden moved out of his mother's house a few days before the fire, and she had desperately not wanted him to go. After the fire, when Camden saw Vidalia in the living room like that, saw the liquor bottles, the glass, the cigarette butts . . . and he put two and two together, he probably felt that if he hadn't moved out, his mother wouldn't have been drinking, and if she hadn't been drinking, she wouldn't be dead. So he must have felt that her death was really all his fault. When Camden confessed to having killed his mother, and later refused to renege on that confession, he may have actually believed he was confessing to the truth."

"That's good," Wylie said, nodding. "I like it. It fits. That's a very plausible explanation. If you ever want a job in fire investigation, Georgiana, give me a call. Max, what do we have next?"

" 'Eight-forty-five P.M.—Kerosene can.' "

"At about a quarter to nine," Wylie said, "Camden Kimcannon went to the third floor of his mother's house and took a two-gallon kerosene can out of the attic. He carried it downstairs, uncapped it, and started to splash flammable liquid on the magazines and newspapers in the fireplace. He deliberately avoided the area around Vidalia's chair. He must have been overwhelmed by conflicting emotions by then, but the idea of disfiguring his mother's body even worse would have horrified him. He poured the rest of the kerosene on the carpet inside the French doors and he struck a few matches. After the fumes from the kerosene finally ignited, he closed the doors to the living room behind him, not realizing that by closing them he would be depriving the fire of the oxygen it needed to feed the flames. Then, still holding his kerosene container, he left the house."

Wylie reached over and took the time line out of Max's hand.

" 'Nine-oh-five P.M.,' " he read. "A neighbor across the street went outside to dump his garbage when he saw what he described as a 'flickering glow' coming from the front room of the Kimcannon residence. He also saw Camden in the middle of the street, holding what looked to him like a kerosene can in his hand. For a few minutes, the neighbor considered approaching Camden to find out if anything was wrong. Instead, at nine-oh-seven p.m., he dialed nine-one-one.

"At eleven minutes after nine, the fire apparatus arrived, and a few minutes later, Captain Hamish Coates discovered Vidalia Kimcannon's dead body on a living room chair. He called the fire department dispatcher, advising them of the DOA, and requesting that the fire marshals respond. At about nine-forty-one P.M., Camden Kimcannon confessed to Captain Coates that he had set the fire and killed his mother." Wylie returned the time line to Max Bramble. "And you know all the rest."

"I have some questions, Wylie," Max said.

"Fire away."

"What was that business about the bouquet? When you lifted it up and looked under it. And the shapes that you make me look for on the tables?"

"Those were my proof of what had happened, Max. Without them, I didn't have a case. At the time the smoldering fire killed Vidalia Kimcannon, there'd been two glasses, one cup, and an ashtray on the coffee table, and there were two gin bottles on the end table next to her chair.

"Because those objects were on those two tables, the surfaces of the tables immediately beneath them were completely protected from the soot generated by the smoldering fire. After Camden removed those objects from the living room, though, and as a result of the fire that *he* set,

301

soot was then able to accumulate in the locations that had formerly been protected from the by-products of the earlier fire.

"But the layer of soot the second fire produced was much lighter than the heavy, filmy, black layer generated by the first. This is because the second fire was of a much shorter duration. It only took nine minutes from the time the fire department was called until the fire was put out.

"So the reason I asked you to study the tables, Max, was because I wanted you to see for yourself the distinction between the surfaces that had been exposed to both fires, and the surfaces that had been exposed to only the fire that had been set by Camden.

"And as far as the bouquet goes, the patterns in the soot were the exact opposite of what they were for the glasses. There was soot both on the table under the bouquet, indicating that the flowers had *not* been there during the first fire, and on top of the bouquet, indicating that it *was* there during the second fire. Which confirms Simon McCorkell's statement that when he saw Camden get off the bus at eight P.M., he was carrying the flowers."

"Why did you make me look into both of the garbage pails?" Max asked.

"Because I wanted to show you that the only items covered with soot, like the cigarette butts and the gin bottles, had to have been put there after the first fire, because nothing else in the garbage pails was burned.

"And the reason I went to the trouble to match up the bottoms of the gin bottles with the soot patterns on the end table, and the bottoms of the glass, ashtray, and coffee cup with the patterns on the coffee table, was that a theory is only as good as the facts that confirm it, and after I matched up all the pieces, my facts were confirmed."

"I am astonished by what you have told us," Jiri Hozda said.

"Well, it's not your run-of-the-mill fire, that's for sure."

"May we assume, then, that because of your evidence, Camden will be exculpated?"

"It's not *my* evidence, Jiri. It's *the* evidence. There's a difference. And I hope that there's enough of it to clear his name, but I won't know . . . "

Georgiana's telephone rang. She picked it up and curtly, distracted, said, "Yes?" Then she handed the telephone to Wylie. "It's for you."

Wylie listened for a few minutes and nodded. He said, "Thanks, Gus. I'll give you a call in about an hour," and he hung up.

"What was that all about?" Max asked.

"That was Supervising Fire Marshal Gus Grogan. Remember the name, because you all owe him big-time. Gus Grogan's squad arrested Camden, and it was Gus just now who left the district attorney after presenting him with new evidence on this case. The same evidence I related to you a minute ago. The cause of the fire on the Division of Fire Investigation incident report was originally listed as 'arson homicide.' Gus changed it to 'smoking carelessness, alcohol contributory'; because of that change, the district attorney has agreed to drop the criminal charges against Camden Kimcannon. No arson. No homicide. No case."

"What about the second fire, Wylie? The one that Camden *did* set?"

"A bullshit fire, Max. We're all pretending that it didn't happen."

"Then Camden's off the hook?"

"He's free and clear. The arrest will be expunged from his record."

Georgiana took a deep breath and then exhaled. "Boy," she said. "I'm pooped. Wylie, you tell one hell of an excruciating story. I feel as if I've just swum fifty miles upstream in a hurricane."

"Great investigation," Max said. "I'm proud of you."

"Thanks, buddy. But before you go, there's one more thing you should know. Gus told me that this morning he got the toxicology report from the medical examiner's office, and it confirms my hypothesis about Vidalia Kimcannon's physiological condition prior to the fire. I'd asked Gus to find out what the alcohol level was in Vidalia's blood."

"What was it?" Max asked.

"It was point-three-oh percent."

"What does that mean?"

"It means that at the time when she was overcome by fumes, Vidalia Kimcannon's consciousness was already impaired. She was in a stupor, and she didn't feel a thing before she died."

"Thank heaven for small mercies," Georgiana said.

"So everything fits, Wylie?" Max asked.

"Everything fits."

"And now we can go home?"

Wylie reached over and picked up the briefcase. "Yes, Max. Now, we can all go home."

44

The gala opening night of the Pre-Raphaelite exhibition was separated into two parts. The reception in the rectory, and the exhibition in The Sanctuary. The only thread of continuity between the two areas was the music. From the rectory (which had been decorated to suggest a Victorian parlor), Mozart, Haydn, and Beethoven string quartets were being piped into The Sanctuary itself.

The reception began at 8:00 P.M. on Friday, December 9th. Attendance was by invitation only.

The Wednesday before the opening, Georgiana Weeks realized that she was unable to control her natural impulse to tamper with human potential, and, as threatened, had delivered Joy Miller into the hands of a hair stylist/beautician. After that, she'd hauled Joy up the escalator to the eveningwear department at Saks Fifth Avenue.

By Wednesday evening, the new Joy Miller had fallen madly in love with herself. As she observed the crowd, her attention alternated between the caterers, the musicians, and the guests, concerned both for the sake of the museum and for Georgiana that the evening should be a perfect success.

Joy's new pale, silvery hair curled at her shoulders as subtly as the curve of a satin ribbon. Her evening gown, a soft drape of silver, clung to her slender body. She stood motionless, looking like a cold and beautiful flame.

Wegman Zigfield, as always impeccable, was looking prouder but slightly less pugnacious than usual, as he circulated from art critics to museum members to well-wishers and society names. When he saw Joy Miller, he came to a rude halt and took an inadvertent step backward.

Wegman looked her up. He looked her down. Then he nodded and barked, "Georgiana's doing. Right?"

"Yes, Mr. Zigfield," Joy said. But instead of shrinking into herself with embarrassment, as she would have done a week earlier, she smiled softly and added. "Aren't I beautiful?"

Her voice was tinged with awe.

"Gorgeous, Joy. You're gorgeous."

"Thank you, Mr. Zigfield. Now, may I have a raise?"

Wegman Zigfield blinked. He coughed. He took another step backward. This time, though, when he stopped, he appraised not only how his secretary looked, but also how she was looking at him. Her eyes were calm, direct, and steady. And he wasn't sure, but he believed that he also saw a hint of humor lurking there.

"*Humph,*" he said.

Joy said nothing. She continued to look right at him. After a few more moments of nonverbal confrontation, Wegman Zigfield finally said, "All right already. I'll give you a raise."

Then he stepped forward, leaned toward Joy's ear, and whispered harshly, "But I liked you better when you *didn't* have a spine!"

And Joy's voice wasn't the least bit harsh when she smiled mischievously and whispered back, "No you didn't, Mr. Zigfield. No you didn't."

The rules of behavior, if you could call them that, for the opening night party were as fiercely enforced by the staff of the Zigfield Art Museum as they were implied but unspoken. Drinking, eating, smoking, modest revelry, and politicking of all kinds were permitted, but only in the reception area at the rectory. Upon leaving the rectory and entering The Sanctuary, the only thing that you were encouraged to bring with you was a love of narrative, representational, and very, very, romantic art.

The tone for the Pre-Raphaelite exhibition had been set and advertised to all comers by way of the Edward Burne-Jones quotation stenciled in Chancery-style italic script over the Sanctuary doorway:

I Mean by a Picture, a Beautiful, Romantic Dream of Something That Never Was, Never Will Be, in a Light Better Than Any Light That Ever Shone, in a Land No One Can Define or Remember—Only Desire.

One step into The Sanctuary and it was as if you had, indeed, entered dreamland. A dreamland not only of vivid colors and passionate creativity, but also of vividly colored and passionately creative relationships.

The captions beneath the portraits in The Sanctuary's entranceway revealed, in the Pre-Raphaelites' own words, with what ardor and intensity they had viewed both art and one another.

John Ruskin had cautioned them to *"Go to nature in all singleness of heart . . . believing all things to be right and good, and rejoicing always in the truth."*

Rossetti had described Burne-Jones as *"one of the nicest young fellows in Dreamland."*

And after Rossetti's death, Burne-Jones had lamented, *"He has left me more to do than I've the strength for the carrying on of his work all by myself."*

But it was Christina Rossetti, in a poem she wrote about Elizabeth Siddal, who summed up not only how the Pre-Raphaelite artists had viewed their wives/lovers/models, but also how they had viewed life itself:

"Not as she is, but was when hope shone bright;
Not as she is, but as she fills his dreams."

Immediately after he left the portrait gallery, the visitor was assaulted on every level of his intellectual and emotional being by music. The evocative strains of a string quartet, seemingly coming from everywhere and nowhere, cut him off from the metallic clatter of the city and the street.

And the immensity, the colors, the *names* of the artwork that he passed, literally led him, step-by-step, down corridors and byways, into the Pre-Raphaelite dreamworld itself. Paintings called *Love Leading the Pilgrim*, *The Sleeping Princess*, *The Rock of Doom* and *The Depths of the Sea*. Paintings with names like *The Blessed Damozel*, *The Beloved*, *My Lady Greensleeves*, *Love's Greeting*, *Queen Guinevere*, and *Reverie*. And interspersed between the paintings, and accompanied by the music, the visitor was reminded by quotation after quotation, of how each artist had been perceived, respected, revered and adored by the other artists in his circle as a talent, as a lover, or as a friend:

"To him and to your father, I owe more in life than to any other man whatever."

"Your love is not less returned by me than it is sweet to me."

"You are the noblest and dearest thing that the world has had to show me."

"By Jove! She's like a queen . . . and her hair is like dazzling copper . . . "

After serpentining through rooms created out of glossy, wood-paneled partitions and down narrow corridors that evoked ancient castle halls, the visitor finally arrived at the exhibition's denouement. Its climax. Which was, just as Georgiana Weeks had planned, the gargantuan painting by Edward Burne-Jones of King Arthur in Avalon.

Miranda Yee and Max Bramble stood side-by-side; they stared up at it.

"I never saw anything like it in my life," she said. "It's enormous; it tells such an involved story. And it's sad. Look at King Arthur, Max. It's sad enough to make you want to cry. How long did the caption say it took the artist to finish this painting?"

"He worked on it, on and off, for twenty years."

Miranda shook her head. "Twenty years! And to think of what I do for a living, and what I'll have accomplished after twenty years. I'm a lawyer, but what do I actually *do*? I shuffle papers back and forth. I console cranky clients. I don't create anything beautiful, though." Her eyes rested respectfully on the painting. "I don't do anything like *that*. I hate the law."

"And I love it, Miranda," Max said. "My law partner, Arthur M. Harris, now deceased, once wrote: 'To me, the administration of justice seems more sacred than profane. Outside of his religious worship, man in his courts of law, in the honest attempt to do justice, becomes God's minister.' "

Miranda's eyes drifted away from the painting and she studied Max.

"Do you really believe that?"

"I do."

She returned her gaze to *King Arthur in Avalon*. "Funny," she said. "How it all mixes up."

"What?"

"Well, a second ago, I was complaining that the law, what I do for a living, isn't worth a thing when you compare it to a work of art—to a painting like this. But it just dawned on me that the reason why this painting gets to you . . . why it's so tragic is because the women in Avalon are grieving because King Arthur died. And . . . " Miranda hesitated, her dark eyes growing pensive.

"Go on," Max said.

"And that the tragedy of King Arthur's death isn't just in his own dying, but in the passing of what he represented."

"Which was?"

"Justice. King Arthur's round table was established so that he could bring justice to an unjust land."

Max smiled.

"Who knows?" he said. "Maybe if Arthur were alive today, he would have become a lawyer like you and me, instead of a king."

Miranda tilted her head to one side and gave Max her cocker spaniel look. Max had a wild desire to stroke her head, tell her that she belonged to him, and take her home. Instead he said to himself, "Too soon. Slow down. Take it easy," and he said to Miranda, "So what happened to your fire setter? To . . . what was her name?"

"Sarah Sapinsky. She's out on bail, but Harry Pittman kicked her out of the building, so I don't have to run into her all the time."

"Did she ever explain why she tried to frame you for all of those fires?"

"No. But it doesn't matter why. She did what she did, and I don't forgive her."

"Why does Wylie think she set the fires?"

Miranda shrugged. "Wylie says it was a jealousy thing. That Sapinsky wanted to be a lawyer but never became one. And there I was down the hall, the female lawyer she'd always wanted to be. I'd succeeded. She'd failed. I'm young. She's old. Crazy stuff like that. Where is Wylie anyway?"

Max looked around.

"That's funny. He was just standing here a minute ago."

It was a cold, clear December night. Not bitterly cold. Not windy. But too cold for someone to have been standing outside, neither approaching nor retreating from the steps that led to the doors of the Zigfield Art Museum.

Wylie Nolan had gone outside to smoke his pipe; he recognized the other man immediately by the jut of his shoulders, his height, the shape of his head.

Wylie put his pipe back in his pocket and walked rapidly down the stairs.

Before Camden Kimcannon realized what was happening, Wylie was standing next to him. He put his hand on Camden's forearm.

"I want to talk to you," Wylie said.

Camden shrugged off Wylie's hand.

"Leave me alone."

"I'll leave you alone, but not until I've said what I have to say."

"I already know what you're going to say. You've proved I didn't get to my mother's house until after eight o'clock, and you expect me to thank you for getting me out of jail. Well, thanks. Send me a bill in the morning. Now if you don't mind, will you get the hell out of my way."

Again, Wylie clamped his hand on the younger man's arm. But this time when Camden tried to shake it off, he couldn't budge it.

"I'll get out of your way after you listen to me. Are you going to listen to me, son? Or are we going to stand around here freezing our butts off all night?"

Camden glared at him.

"All right," he said. "I'm listening."

Wylie released Camden's arm, and the younger man unconsciously rubbed it.

"This is the situation," Wylie said grimly. "Short and sweet. I investigated the fire in your mother's house. The whole story of what happened there was told in burn patterns. Burn patterns are the finger and footprints of fire. They show what the fire touched and where it went. And what the burn patterns in that house showed me was that your mother was a chronic careless smoker. I analyzed the cigarette burns . . . the little holes in the upholstery, and the cigarette scars . . . the markings left when a lit cigarette is dropped on a table; and from the amount of burns I found on all the surfaces in the house, I projected the maximum amount of time that would have gone by before a fatal fire caused by smoking carelessness would have occurred. And I can say with absolute certainty that regardless of the events leading up to the fire, unless your mother had given up smoking completely, which she showed no indication of doing, that the longest she could have lived without perishing in a fatal fire would have been another two weeks."

Camden Kimcannon stood absolutely still. He didn't say anything. He didn't blink. He didn't swallow. He didn't appear to have heard a single word that Wylie had said.

Wylie watched the young man's face.

He reached for his pipe and then changed his mind, leaving it where it was.

He looked at the moon. It was full. Colorless. Mottled.

He looked at his watch. It was almost 9:00 p.m.

He looked back at Camden Kimcannon.

Camden's face was contorted.

Tears were streaming down his cheeks.

"Really?" the young man said. "Really? Really? Then it wasn't because of me that she died?"

Wylie held up two fingers.

"Scouts honor," he said.

. . .

Half an hour later, when Wylie privately communicated to Max Bramble what he'd said to Camden, Max looked at him admiringly.

"No kidding, Wylie? You mean burn patterns can really tell you all that?"

And Wylie looked at him pityingly, and said, "Of course not."

And half an hour after that, Georgiana Weeks was standing in a quiet corner of the rectory, for the first time all evening stealing a few moments by herself, when Jiri Hozda walked up.

She looked at him and smiled.

"I like you in a tuxedo."

"Thank you, my beautiful Georgiana."

"*Hmmm*," Georgiana said. "Possessive pronoun. We progress."

Jiri took her by the arm.

"Come with me."

"To the Casbah?"

"That is very funny, Georgiana." Jiri didn't laugh. "I have a gift for you."

"What?" She tried to keep up with his long strides.

He led her down convoluted corridors and through rooms hung with Pre-Raphaelite paintings, filled with music, and electric with the presence of art. They didn't stop until they came to the vast area dominated by the Edward Burne-Jones masterpiece.

Jiri put a restraining hand on Georgiana's arm and whispered, "*Shush*."

Standing in front of *King Arthur in Avalon*, gazing up at it with his head thrown back and a reverent look on his face, was Camden Kimcannon.

Georgiana inhaled sharply.

Camden turned. His eyes darted suspiciously around the room, as though to determine from which direction the danger came.

Georgiana took a step forward.

She held out her hand.

312

"Forgive me, Camelot."

He shook his head.

"Camden," he said. "My name is Camden."

Georgiana's green eyes ignited. Her lips, her face, her eyes, her heart . . . her whole life smiled.

"Welcome to the real world," she said.

Jiri added, "It can, at times, be quite a habitable and romantic place."

And Camden Kimcannon nodded. "I know," he said firmly. "In fact, I'm going to paint it."

Author's Postscript

Although the Pre-Raphaelite exhibition in *Spent Matches* exists only in my mind, the artwork described in the Samuel and Mary R. Bancroft Collection is real, and can be found at the Delaware Art Museum in Wilmington, Delaware.

Samuel Bancroft bought his first Pre-Raphaelite painting in 1890. By the time of his death, he had acquired over one hundred paintings and drawings, as well as hundreds of early photographs and a comprehensive library of manuscripts.

Edward Burne-Jones's masterpiece, *The Last Sleep of Arthur in Avalon,* is located at the Museo de Arte in Ponce, Puerto Rico.

The Pre-Raphaelites themselves, although long gone, still literally sizzle with life through their collected letters, memoirs, and poems, and, of course, in the vibrant genius of their paintings.

To the artists themselves.

To those who collected their works.

And to the museums who preserve their paintings, and from whom, unbeknownst to them, I have borrowed so many to form my *own* Pre-Raphaelite collection . . .

I offer my profound thanks.